BA

a First Novel by Jim L.M. Miles

This novel has men who usually listen to their wives, awkward moments, computers, a coffee pot, date rape, bribes, Blackberry smartphones, Molotov cocktails, piglets, PowerPoint slides, heroin addiction, utility programming, geeks in Las Vegas, lunch with a prostitute, a car chase, parachute jumps, a drum solo, snipers, swine flu, the Boston Marathon, the American Revolution, and a satisfying post-climax final scene where a minor but significant character gets her revenge.

Morris Parker, ex-soldier, family man, and hardworking businessman, has put his nose where it does not belong. His comfortable routine of work, home life, and weekly boys night out is about to end.

Ed Smitt is ex-US Special Forces. Jacques Tremblay used to command a French Canadian Infantry Battalion. The Wednesday night beer buddies intervene in a robbery at the The Cumberland Arms pub. In self-defense, Morris kills the young gang member who is shooting at him. The police charge him with murder. Morris must rely on his business resources – and his good friends – to try and clear his name.

Morris discovers he was set up to take the fall by a dirty cop. Then he learns he is facing more than just a local gang. He is up against a vicious international criminal operation that is set on killing him and his family to stop him from finding out more.

Unable to trust the police, Morris and friends decide to take up arms and fight for information. Their investigations lead them to a remote camp in Northern Ontario, where a bio-terrorist group has found a simple method to develop a deadly new virus.

The more he learns, the more danger he encounters, and Morris and his team must ultimately choose between self-preservation and self-sacrifice. The world faces a frightening new weapon of mass destruction.

Acknowledgements

In the summer of 2009 I re-discovered reading on the back deck of our home in Orleans. One of several books I read that summer was *A Time to Kill* by John Grisham, which includes an author's note describing how he wrote the book by doing a few pages a day with the objective of simply completing it.

I undertook this novel with the same objective. Thanks to some vital early encouragement from my daughter Stephanie, I produced the first five chapters in about a month. I then realized I could probably complete the task. So I set a deadline of four months, aiming to finish before my birthday.

My Dad agreed to proofread chapters as they came out, and his encouragement and feedback served to further motivate me.

As the book neared completion, my brother-in-law Ben read almost fifty chapters in two days. He said the story made him want to keep reading, and it reads like a movie.

I missed my deadline by several days, writing THE END in mid-December, after starting in August.

This "draft edition" will go up on Createspace.com so family members and friends can get printed copies easily, read the book, and comment.

I continue to get encouragement and feedback as I prepare my attempt to self-publish. I plan to simultaneously send the manuscript out the conventional path and collect rejections from agents and publishers. Local encouragement and feedback is vital. I will use it to prepare a final edition.

Thanks to Garth, Rick, Pat and Jim for being the inspiration for the Wednesday night heroes in this story.

Thanks to Kim, Deb, Ron, Valerie, Pete, Caroline and the other family members who will participate in the coming weeks with continued interest, questions, and contributions.

Thanks to Ray, Suzanne, Wayne, Sam and Cathleen for their opinions and ideas.

And thanks especially to Thérèse, for being as patient as possible, courageous in staying with me through tough years and good ones. While I was chasing this writing dream, she had to watch the store. She is baking as I write this, giving us the best possible Christmas as we weather the recession.

I'm done, dear; we can paint the living room now.

Jim E.M. Miles
Orleans, December 2009

BACON BOXCUTTERS

Jim E.M. Miles

EIS America, Inc.
www.eisamerica.com

Bacon Boxcutters

by Jim E.M. Miles

www.BaconBoxcutters.com

EIS America, Inc.,
880 Taylor Creek Drive,
Orleans, Ontario
Canada K1C 1T1

Front cover design:
Suzanne Lukowski, We Are Multi-Media and
Jim E.M. Miles

Blackberry reader:
Ray DeBruyn, Enterprise Information Systems, Inc.

Some of the events described happened as related, others were expanded and changed. Some of the individuals portrayed are composites of more than one person and many names and identifying characteristics have been changed as well.

"This is a work of fiction. No reference to any person, living or dead, is intended or implied. Some of the author's documented personal experience in business dealings with certain individuals has been exaggerated and used as a basis to portray bad behavior on the part of the antagonists in this story."

To the soldier and his buddies:
Mutually supportive in all phases of war;

To the families awaiting their return;

And especially to the families
of soldiers who could not return.

SUPPORT THE SOLDIER

TABLE OF CONTENTS

PROLOGUE

Jaleel looked at the gauge on his air supply. It was finally empty. He had no choice but to remove his helmet and breathe the contaminated air.

He did it decisively, sucking in a lungful.

"Mohamed," he said. "I have removed my helmet."

"Your spirit pulls you upward," said Mohamed through the intercom speaker. "You are immune to the downward pull of the material world."

Jaleel did not want the others to find him in this humiliating position. He wanted to do what must be done before they returned. "I am ready."

"The camera is running," said Mohamed.

There had been no blank tapes available for weeks – all the existing tapes had been filled with testimonials and pledges of *bayt al-ridwan*, named after the garden in Paradise reserved for the prophets and the martyrs.

Now was no time for doubts. Jaleel decided not to ask Mohamed where he had found a blank tape.

Jaleel drew his pistol and disengaged the safety catch. He stood like a soldier, helmet under one arm, back straight, and placed the muzzle of the pistol against his temple.

"May Allah be with you. May Allah give you success so that you may achieve Paradise," said Jaleel.

"Wait!" Mohamed exclaimed. "Your testament, Jaleel."

Good. Now Jaleel was certain that Mohamed would not lie about having a tape in the camera at a time like this.

"This is my free decision, and I urge my friends to follow. We will meet in Paradise."

"Farewell. Your wait is over."

"*Allahu akbar.*" With a smooth, steady squeeze, Jaleel unflinchingly fired the pistol into the side of his head.

BANG.

Jaleel's lifeless body collapsed into the straw.

The loud noise startled the six small pigs, and their biosensors recorded a sudden, temporary increase in heart rate.

PART ONE – CEO IN TROUBLE

1 – BOYS BEING BOYS: A GUNFIGHT

Morris Parker arrived at the Cumberland Arms at precisely 2030 hours – also known as 8:30 PM – Wednesday. It was his usual time. He nodded to the bartender. After seven years of weekly visits, Morris still could not remember the bartender's name, because he never sat at the bar.

Morris saw that his regular table in the corner booth was already occupied, which was unusual. Morris and his army buddies occupied that space almost every Wednesday night. He decided to wait for the others to arrive, and seek consensus on selecting another table.

"Buddy, that seat's taken, eh?" stated a voice from behind as Morris was about to take a seat at the bar. Morris turned to see two broad-shouldered guys in leather jackets. They were just returning from the washroom.

Morris nodded and chose another seat farther down. A pair of tough assholes, he thought. The Arms does not normally attract the Beavis and Butthead Biker type. Beavis was arrogant and stupid looking – a real dick.

The bartender did not notice Morris waiting. Angela, a pretty, 20-something blond waitress in a short tartan skirt, had seen him come in. She had poured him a pint of Keith's Red Amber Ale, and had it ready on her tray.

"How are you tonight, good looking?" she asked, as she served him the frosted mug and a smile.

Morris could not remember the name of the bartender, but he could recall the names of several waitresses who had served him and his buddies over the years. Angela had been working Wednesdays for almost two years now, as she paid her way through nursing school.

"Cold beer!" Morris grasped the handle on the mug, feeling the cool glass in his hand. "And a warm smile. Thank-you, Angela. I am well. And you?"

"It's been a long day." Angela looked around, checking for the owner. Not seeing him anywhere, she sat down next to Morris, and put her tray on the bar. "I've been on my feet all day, doing rounds at the Ottawa Civic."

"You graduate soon," said Morris.

"Thank God for that."

"Here's to you." Morris raised his mug, then brought it to his lips and tipped it back, taking three deep pulls. "Ahhh."

Morris wiped his moustache with the back of his hand, and turned to Angela. "You look different." Morris looked at her hair.

Angela raised her eyebrows. "Go on...."

"Your hair. Did you cut it?"

She rolled her eyes. "Buzz. Wrong answer."

Morris winced.

"Are you this observant with your wife? Of course you are."

Morris took another swig of beer, suddenly feeling some pressure. "Was it a color change?"

"Maybe. Is that your final answer?"

Morris looked at her, trying to read her poker face. "Yes, I'll go with a color change."

Angela smiled and shook her bangs out of her eyes. They immediately fell back in place, partially masking a blue-eyed, steady gaze. "You are... *correct*. Now tell me what the color *used* to be."

"That's easy." Morris reached for the beer nuts. "You used to be brunette."

"Yes." Angela looked sideways to show Morris her profile, and began teasing her hair. "Now, for one million dollars, tell me when did this major motion picture change occur?"

Wow, thought Morris. She looks like a movie star. "Hmmm. Could we make this multiple choice?"

"Not this game." Angela turned her head back to face Morris, and looked at her watch. "This game is timed."

Morris started to squirm.

Angela noticed his discomfort, and batted her eyes to increase it.

Morris realized his underarm antiperspirant was about to fail.

"The pressure… the pressure!" Morris held his hands to his head and slowly said: "Head… must… not… explode…." Then he blurted out: "Last Wednesday you were brunette, now you're blonde. Final answer."

"Buzz." Angela frowned. "I changed it two months ago,"

"Ooops."

"Well, at least you noticed," she said.

"But I almost had the million dollars…"

The door swung open and Boyd MacDougall, owner of the Cumberland Arms, entered the bar. He spotted Morris and started to make his way over.

Angela stood up. "Boyd has a poker game on tonight." She picked up her tray. "He'll probably ask you to join."

"What's the buy-in?" The last time Morris played poker at the Arms was because he had to entertain a rich client from California.

"Twenty thousand."

"Last time I sat at that table in the back room I lost six thousand, to a client of mine. I only play for business reasons. Besides, I just used up all my luck playing *Wheel of Hair Color*. Wait – don't leave. He'll come and talk to me." Morris knew Boyd was interested in Morris for only one reason: money.

Angela began to wipe the bar, trying to give herself a reason to stay. "Who else is coming tonight?"

"Ed will be here. And Jacques is bringing a new guy. There may be others. Who knows for sure?"

"I'll try to get your regular table back. Those two guys in the corner have been here for a couple of hours. Only one beer each." Angela saw Boyd stepping up to Morris, and turned to get back to work.

"Morris. Now there's a good candidate." Boyd grinned. "Would you care for a seat in tonight's game?"

"It would be fun, but I don't have the buy-in."

"I would be happy to cover you with my own cash."

Oh yes, the all-cash game, Morris thought. Cash eliminated the problem of covering losses, and prevented wives from seeing large debit transactions. The players found that attractive.

The other attraction Boyd provided was sex. Morris' California client had loved that fringe benefit. Boyd had some very discrete hookers. After the game, he brought them over from his strip club – to console the losers. The regular pub staff was unaware of that activity. They all knew about the poker game, but this late-night entertainment did not arrive until long after The Arms closed for the night, and the regular staff had left for home.

"You run an honest game and provide classy entertainment," said Morris, "but tonight is just my regular pub night. The other guys will be here soon."

Boyd grinned. "OK. But I also wanted to say that your security guy – Zia – he set me up with a really great video security system. He hooked-up these cool hidden cameras, and they give the best face shots of all the systems I tried. He gave me software that zeros-in on each face, recognizes the person, and timestamps their photo and arrival time into my database."

"Face recognition? What do you need that for?"

"Just because it's cool. The players are impressed – it reminds them of Vegas security. They think I've checked out all the other players thoroughly. Besides, Zia gave me a good package price. He wants to use my place as a reference, which is OK as long as he doesn't say anything about the poker game."

Morris figured Boyd's idea of running a secure game consisted of making the players bring cash, to ensure everybody pays up, and not getting caught by the cops for running an illegal game. "I'll tell him you're satisfied."

There was a pause, as neither man could think of anything more to say.

Morris noticed Ed Smitt arrive at the main door and waved him over.

"I'll let you get on with your evening," said Boyd. "Enjoy."

Ed walked up and greeted Morris with a handshake. "Hello, Morris."

Ed and Morris had known each other for many years. Yet, at The Arms on Wednesdays, there was always a ritual handshake greeting.

"What happened to our regular table?" Ed asked.

"Those two were here when I arrived. Angela says she'll try and reclaim it for us."

Morris observed a bruise and skin abrasions on Ed's neck and cheek. "What happened to you? Lose a fight with your little sister? Lady hit you with her purse?"

"I fell off my tricycle."

The thought of Ed on a tricycle made Morris grin. Ed was six foot one and 220 pounds of muscle in a marine haircut. He was big-chested with muscular arms, and he walked like a linebacker.

Ed was formerly with the US Special Forces. He was born in Maine and married a Canadian, so he now held dual citizenship. He presently taught as a civilian instructor on contract to the Canadian Forces unit responsible for counter-terrorist operations, Joint Task Force 2, also called JTF2.

"I was teaching unarmed combat. I let a rookie put me in a chokehold so I could show him how to break it, just as a guy flipped beside us. I couldn't get out of the way in time, and my left cheek arrested his right foot. He was wearing combat boots."

"Ouch."

"You can make out the tread pattern." Ed turned down his collar.

"Yeah. Size 12. Nice."

Angela delivered Ed a Hoegaarden in a huge mug. Ed nodded and took a drink.

"What's new with you?" Ed put his mug down. "Any interesting deals? Did you get that land you wanted?"

"Almost. Our building design won the bid, and I signed agreements to purchase two of the three empty lots I need. The third owner is out of town. I think I'll be able to offer him either a good price for his land, and/or I can interest him in participating in the project. I happen to need another investor for this deal."

"How much is this deal worth?"

"The land and construction costs will run about seven million. The lease deal we just won is worth about twenty."

"Wow. How do I get into your line of business? Twenty years ago in Gagetown, you and I were lieutenants. Our idea of property ownership was renting a hotel room in Montreal. Seriously. How do you do it?"

"Seriously?" Morris said. "You have to be in the right place at the right time. I quit the army to build database systems. When that business started to take off, I took some of the revenues to buy the building we were leasing. The owner was letting it go for half of what it cost to build. Then property values in my business park skyrocketed. Demand for office space went up – I was able to rent out extra offices. It kind of grew from there."

"That sounds too hard. I think I'll just marry rich."

"What exactly would Debbie think of that, Ed?" Jacques Tremblay had arrived.

Ed looked at Jacques and offered a handshake. "You think an additional wife would be out of the question?"

"You're lucky she lets you out on Wednesday nights," said Jacques, as the two men shook firmly.

"Look who's talking, it's Mr. Mom."

"True, I am whipped. But at least Suzette doesn't leave any marks." Jacques pointed to his neck.

"A guy tumbled into me. I made him eat his ass."

Jacques shook hands with Morris. Like Ed, Jacques was another big guy. Two inches taller at six foot three, he had the build of a basketball player, with the arms and shoulders of a boxer, which he once was. His face was weather-beaten and his nose had been broken a few times. He sported a black handlebar moustache, short haircut, and had a perpetually cheerful expression.

"Guys, this is Bill," said Jacques. "He's my sister-in-law's husband. They're visiting from Halifax. Bill's a Navy pilot."

A round of handshakes followed.

"I'm Ed. I used to be airborne. Morris is ex-infantry, like Jacques. Jacques was a CO, but we still let him sit with us."

"You guys are all what, six foot four?" Bill asked, looking up at the three men.

"I'm only six-two," said Ed. "Those guys are older. That's how high they piled shit back then."

"And now, they compact it a bit." Jacques gave Ed a slap on the back. "Ed's like a brother to us. A more ugly, pain-in-the-ass, little brother."

"It's easy to miss Ed's humor," said Morris. "On one of his night insertions, the chopper dropped him on his head, we figure."

Angela appeared. She had a pint of Keith's Red for Jacques. "Are you guys going to take a table?"

"Why don't we take this one," Ed suggested, pointing to an empty table in the middle of the room.

"What can I get you?" Angela asked Bill as the four men took their seats.

"Do you have Moosehead?" asked Bill.

"Sorry. In the bottle we have Canadian, Blue, Sleeman, Bud, Coors Light, and Stella."

"What do you have on draft?"

"We carry mostly Labatt's line." Angela efficiently listed every beer The Arms carried on tap: "Tennent's, Blue, Boddingtons, Hoegaarden, Stella, Strongbow, Keith's Pale, Keith's Red and Keith's White, Bud Light, Kilkenny and, of course, Guinness."

"Go for a Keith's," suggested Ed. "Pride of Nova Scotia."

"I'm from *Torrona*," said Bill. "What do you have in the bottle, again?"

"Canadian, Blue, Sleeman, Bud, Coors Light, and Stella."

Bill popped a beer nut in his mouth. "Actually, I'll take a diet coke for now."

"Would anyone like to see a menu?" Angela asked.

"By anyone, she means you, Bill," said Ed. "We always order wings. We follow the same pattern every week. We order after the first round is done."

Bill nodded. "Could I have a plate of nachos?"

Angela smiled. "Sure." This guy must be a pilot, she thought. Bill was fitting in to the group like a fish in an anthill. She left to put in the order.

"Anyone know if Jim's going to make it tonight?" asked Ed.

"Not likely," said Jacques. "He's in Africa on a three-year posting."

"Piss poor excuse," said Ed.

Bill turned to Ed. "What did you do with the Special Forces?"

"If he told you that, he'd have to kill you," said Jacques. "By boring you to death."

"We think he killed a couple of minor terrorists," said Morris. "And Elvis."

"Elvis lives," said Ed.

"He also shot the man who killed Kennedy," added Jacques.

"Yes, I shot Lee Harvey Oswald." Ed said sarcastically. "I would have been one year old. Just a cute little baby."

"A very bloodthirsty assassin-baby," Jacques said, reaching out to pinch Ed's cheek. "Goochy-goo. Whack the nice man, baby."

The conversation level in the pub was at the usual level, with about forty people in the room. Suddenly, from the corner near the group's regular booth, a female voice shouted "HEY!"

The room went silent.

A waitress was fighting off one of two guys sitting in the booth. "Hands off, Grabbypants!"

The guy was running his hand up her thigh, so the waitress slapped him hard. The smack sounded like a shot. Bill let out an involuntary laugh.

The guy went red in the face. He turned toward Bill. "You think this is funny, asshole?" He glared at Bill.

Bill sized up the guy. He looked pretty tough. He was seated in the corner booth with another guy, an Asian. The Asian was young and skinny, with scraggly long hair. He looked like a punk who wished he were tough.

The guy got out of his booth. "*Hey!* Got anything to say, *fuckface?*"

Bill estimated the guy was over six foot and at least 250 pounds. He was beefy, with a bit of a potbelly. Bill looked at Morris, Ed and Jacques, and felt confident. "I count four of us over here, Mister, uh, *Grabbypants.*"

A couple of people laughed nervously.

Grabbypants took two steps closer. "Smart mouth? You wanna be smart with me?"

Morris leaned over closer to Bill, and spoke quietly in his ear. "Don't."

"There are only two of them and four of us," Bill whispered to Morris.

"Yeah, but those jean jackets don't make sense. It's hot and muggy tonight. The guy must have a knife or something. He's baiting you."

Grabbypants started walking toward Bill. "I think you should learn some respect." Walking slowly, maneuvering around tables, he seemed to enjoy the attention he was getting. People moved out of his way and avoided eye contact.

Morris tried to size up the situation. This guy was showing off or something, for someone. Are these gang members?

The Asian wore a New York Yankees baseball cap, dark blue. Grabbypants had left his cap on the table. It was black. These could be gang colors, Morris realized.

There had been a recent break-in at a PHL property. Morris had reviewed video of the suspect with a police officer who told him that Ottawa street gangs often wear sports team jerseys having gang colors. Dark blue was the color of the Ledbury Banff Cripps. They wore black on special missions.

These two might be part of a gang. Picking a fight in public seemed an unusual activity for a gang. Was it an initiation? Maybe this was a diversion. Could these two be working with somebody else – a pickpocket perhaps? Someone else in the bar could easily lift a purse while all eyes were on this little drama.

"These guys are up to something," Morris said to his group.

Ed leaned over to Morris and Jacques. "Should I take this guy out?"

"Hold off, and let's see what he does," said Morris. "Jacques, see if you can stall him."

Jacques stood up and moved forward to intercept Grabbypants. "Please h'excuse my friend, Monsieur." Jacques was suddenly using a thick French-Canadian accent. "My friend, 'e was laughing at some'ting I said, me."

Grabbypants stopped. The two big men stood face-to-face, looking each other in the eyes.

Grabbypants suddenly moved forward, shoving Jacques hard with both hands. "Fuck off!"

Jacques felt a surge of adrenaline as he took two steps back to recover his balance. Grabbypants waited for Jacques to react.

Jacques looked across at Morris, and rolled his eyes. "I'm terribly sorry, Monsieur! My squarehead friend was laughing at my accent. 'E was not laughing at you."

Grabbypants glared at Jacques. "Well then, why don't I just kick the crap out of *you*?"

Morris looked around the room. All eyes were on Mr. Grabbypants, except for two guys in biker jackets sitting at the bar. Other spectators were tense, but these two were not. One of the guys was ignoring the action. Instead, he was watching the short hallway leading to the back room. The other guy was leaning back, and he seemed amused, not concerned, at the disturbance being created.

This is a four-man team, thought Morris. It's warm in this room, and those heavy jackets *should* have been placed on the empty barstool between them. These guys must have weapons. Were the four of them going to rob the place?

Morris leaned over to Ed. "Check out the bikers at the bar – Beavis and Butthead."

Ed looked at the bikers while the action on the floor continued.

"But why?" Jacques asked Grabbypants. "Why should you want to fight me?"

"Here's a good reason." Grabbypants stepped forward and shoved Jacques again, forcing him back two more steps. "You're a mother-fuckin' frog!"

Ed stood up, confronting Grabbypants. Jacques took a step to the side.

Grabbypants turned his attention onto Ed. "Which one of you fucking kittens is going to stand up for yourself?"

"Meow," said Ed.

Morris realized the bikers at the bar, Beavis and Butthead, were behind Ed and Jacques. They were in a good position. From those seats, they could see everybody in the room, and had nobody behind them. They could easily back up Grabbypants. That explained why Grabbypants was so cocky.

Morris stood up suddenly. "OK, one against one. That's fair enough." It was time to get in a better position. Morris motioned to Jacques. "Let's make room. Help me move this table, Jacques. Give us a hand, Bill."

Jacques, Bill and Morris swiftly moved the table aside, clearing floor space. People who felt too close to the action vacated their seats or moved their chairs back.

Ignoring Bill, Morris motioned Jacques over to the bar. They took two seats to the left of Beavis and Butthead. There was a full Pyrex pot of coffee on the bar. Morris sat so it was within arm's reach.

Morris suddenly realized what these guys must be up to. Split four ways, there would not be enough cash in the till to make robbing the pub worthwhile. But there would be over one hundred thousand dollars in the poker game. They were creating a disturbance to draw out Boyd. Boyd was the only one with a swipe card able to access the locked, back-room area.

Grabbypants surged toward Ed. Ed stepped back and to the side, gripping Grabbypants by the lapels of his jean jacket, pulling the heavier man off balance and over his hip. Grabbypants tumbled and crashed to the floor, rolling out of control. He collided with a table. Beer, nuts and nachos went flying in all directions.

Morris noticed the Asian had his hand in his jacket. He must be holding a gun. Morris slowly reached over and firmly grasped the handle of the coffee pot.

Angela entered from the hallway. "I informed the owner," she said loudly, with authority. "He's calling the police, and he's coming out."

Beavis stood up, threatening Ed from behind.
Butthead stood up and faced the hallway leading to the
back room, waiting for Boyd MacDougall.

Beavis, closest to Morris, reached into his jacket.
Morris saw the butt of a pistol.

"GUN!" Morris yelled loudly.

Beavis looked at Morris.

Morris brought the coffee pot across his body in an
arc, striking Beavis squarely on the forehead.

Pyrex shattered on skull. Scalding coffee burst in
Beavis' face, and exploded in all directions. Blinded and
burned, Beavis released his gun and grabbed his face with
both hands, screaming. The gun clattered to the floor.
Morris scrambled after it.

Butthead, splattered with hot coffee, screamed with
rage. He pulled his gun on Morris.

Jacques charged into Butthead, knocking him up
against the wall. Butthead fired a shot wildly into the
ceiling. People screamed and ducked.

Jacques grabbed Butthead's gun arm with both hands,
and the two men began to fight for control of the weapon.

Grabbypants pulled a pistol from his jacket and
pointed it at Morris' back. Ed reacted instantly, lunging
forward to tackle Grabbypants. Slipping on the beer, Ed
skidded across the wet floor, struggling to maintain his
balance. Grabbypants aimed at Morris and squeezed the
trigger hard. The pistol did not fire.

Dropping two hands to the floor, Ed executed a
perfect low spinning sweep-kick that took Grabbypants
down from behind. The pistol went flying. Ed jumped on
Grabbypants and the two of them began to wrestle on the
floor.

The Asian stood with a gun in his hand, taking aim at
Morris.

By now, Morris had Beavis' gun in hand and he had
disengaged the safety.

With a stabbing motion, the Asian fired a shot at Morris, missing.

Morris, on the floor, spun into a sitting position and faced the Asian. Aiming quickly, he began firing.

Multiple shots blasted out from both pistols in rapid succession. BANG-BANG-BANG-BANG-BANG-BANG!

The Asian was aiming one-handed, and his pistol arm flailed with the recoil from each shot. His shots went increasingly off target.

Morris held his pistol with a firm two-hand grip, placing his left elbow on his right knee for support. Morris calmly counted each shot out loud.

"One! Two! Three! Four!" Morris counted, ignoring the bullets flying at him.

On his fourth shot, Morris struck the Asian mid-torso. The Asian dropped backwards to the floor, dropping his gun and grabbing his chest. Morris stopped firing.

"Morris!" Jacques was doing his best to control Butthead against the bar.

Butthead gripped his pistol in both hands high above his head. Jacques had a tight hold on one of Butthead's forearms, and was struggling to block Butthead from taking aim. Butthead was slowly gaining control of the pistol, and was about to align it with Jacques' head.

Morris turned to aim at Butthead. From his position on the floor, Morris could not shoot without fear of hitting Jacques.

"Jacques!" Morris yelled. "Spread your legs!"

Straining, Jacques managed to bow his right leg a bit.

Morris fired a well-aimed shot. BANG!

"Five," said Morris.

The bullet passed close to Jacques' groin and hit Butthead in the left thigh. Butthead screamed in pain, and dropped like a sack of potatoes, exposing himself for a second shot. Morris aimed for his head and fired. BANG!

"Six," said Morris.

The shot struck the side of Butthead's neck, spraying blood against the wall behind him. Butthead spun and collapsed against the wall, landing in a sitting position.

Keeping his pistol aimed at Butthead, Morris said calmly "Jacques, take his gun."

Jacques had thrown himself to one side. Jacques checked his crotch. "*Saint-ciboire, ça passé proche!*" He got up and walked over to examine Butthead.

Butthead's eyes were open. He stared vacantly at the floor in front of him, stunned. Blood spurted from the side of his neck. Jacques firmly grasped Butthead's gun arm, and carefully took the pistol.

"Got it, Morris," Jacques said, then rose to his feet. "You were trying to kill me, you piece of shit!" he said to Butthead, no more French accent. "And worse, you almost made my friend shoot my balls off. We should let you bleed out."

Morris looked around the room. Several people were lying on the floor. "Jacques, cover the Asian," he said. "Angela, how's your first aid?"

Jacques checked the safety catch was in the fire position, and then aimed his gun at the Asian lying in the far corner. Jacques could not see him fully, and he suspected the Asian might still be able to use his gun.

Morris, aware that Ed was still struggling with Grabbypants, switched aim to cover them.

Grabbypants was no longer interested in fighting Ed. He was simply trying to get away.

"You can't leave until you pay your bill." Morris said.

"I can hold him," Ed said, grunting. "If he starts to get away, though, do me a favor and just shoot him. I don't like the way you serve coffee."

Angela was looking for something to plug the spurting blood before Butthead bled to death. She found a clean bar rag and clamped it down on his wound. "Here. Hold this tight." She positioned Butthead's hand over the rag. He complied – with difficulty.

"Bill?" Morris gestured toward the Asian. "See if the guy's still alive, willya?"

Bill had been hiding under a table during the battle. He stood shakily to his feet. Then his face went white and he fainted to the floor.

"Let me do it," said Angela.

"OK Angela – just stay out of our line of fire. Walk around behind us."

Angela nodded and began walking, looking determined.

"You are always ready to go that extra mile for your customers," said Morris, trying to reassure her. "Good food. Cold beer. Checking the enemy wounded."

Angela looked down, winced, and adjusted her step to avoid a puddle of Butthead's blood, pooled with some spilled beer and still-steaming coffee.

"I expect a good tip for this," she said in a shaky voice.

Angela examined the Asian. "He's just a kid." Putting two fingers on the side of his throat, she checked his pulse. "No pulse. His shirt is soaked in blood. You must have hit his heart. He's dead."

"I could use a little help, here!" Ed said. Ed, holding Grabbypants from behind, had him in a partial strangle hold. Grabbypants was gasping for air but succeeding in slowly rising from the floor, pulling himself steadily up to the bar countertop. He was bringing Ed with him. Both Ed's feet were now off the floor.

Using his free hand, Morris reached over and gripped Grabbypants by the ear. "Put my friend down!" Morris twisted the ear sharply.

Grabbypants yelped and instantly submitted.

Ed got his feet back on the ground and quickly took control by twisting Grabbypants' arm behind his back.

"Jacques, Grabbypants' gun is somewhere around here," said Morris.

"I see it." Jacques picked up the pistol from the floor.

"He tried to shoot Morris," Ed said. "But his gun didn't go off."

Jacques looked at the guns he was holding. "These are very nice pistols – 9mm semi-automatic. Very similar to what we trained with." He put down one of the guns and examined Grabbypants' pistol with both hands. Then he walked over to where Ed was holding Grabbypants, head forced down on the bar.

Jacques looked Grabbypants in the eye. "How do you like me now, tough stupid guy? Let me show you something. Look here." Jacques held the pistol up to Grabbypants' face. "You see this little metal part, just here, above the grip?" Grabbypants looked at the small lever Jacques was indicating, going slightly cross-eyed to focus.

"Shit." Grabbypants closed his eyes, disgusted.

Using a thick French accent as he had done before, Jacques said, "I may be French, Monsieur, but I know how to use zis safety catch, *tabarnac!*"

2 – AFTERMATH

Morris heard sirens in the distance, getting gradually louder. He looked around the room. The Asian was dead. Beavis was scalded and moaning on the floor, in fetal position. Butthead had two gunshot wounds and was bleeding against the wall. Morris stood up from the floor, put the pistol on the bar, and pulled out his cellphone. He dialed 911.

"911 Emergency," said an emergency operator. "Police, Ambulance or Fire?"

"Police and Paramedics. There has been a gunfight at The Cumberland Arms in Orleans. Corner of Innes and Jeanne d'Arc. One person has been shot and another has been killed. There is also a person with burns and cuts to the face."

"Your name sir?"

"Morris Parker."

"Location, again?"

"The Arms. Corner of Innes Road and Jeanne d'Arc Boulevard in Orleans."

"Is anyone there still armed?"

"No. There were four people with guns, trying to rob the place. My friends and I have disarmed them all. Tell your people the situation is safe. I hear sirens – are they yours?"

"Yes. Several cars are responding. We received other calls." The dispatcher had called for all available resources. "Did you say one dead, and two injured?"

"Yes, one dead. One casualty has a gunshot in the leg and the neck, and the other was burned in the face with a pot of hot coffee. Oh yeah, one guy fainted. I should look at him now."

"Stay on the phone with me, please."

"I'll do that, but I'm going to put the phone down for a minute." Morris looked at Jacques. "It would probably be a good idea for us *not* to have a gun in our hand when the cops storm in here all pumped up. Let's put the pistols here on the bar. Make sure you can remember which gun came from which one of these guys."

With a puzzled look, Jacques began to retrace the events that had just occurred, trying to be sure which gun belonged to Beavis and which one belonged to Butthead.

Morris walked over and examined Bill, who had just opened his eyes. Bill was a bit confused, but unhurt.

"I'll bet you thought a Navy bar was a pretty tough place, eh?"

Bill mumbled incomprehensibly.

Morris left Bill and walked over to the bar. "Boyd? Are you there? It's safe now."

Boyd emerged from the hallway where he had retreated when the shooting started. "I'm here," he said meekly.

"It would be good it you go out and meet the police when they arrive."

Boyd nodded, and quickly headed for the front door. A couple of other patrons followed.

Morris picked up his gun off the bar. He removed the magazine, placed it on the bar, and cocked the pistol, ejecting a bullet from the chamber onto the bar. He put the empty pistol with the other two that Jacques had placed on the bar. He resisted the urge to unload the other pistols.

Ed had Grabbypants in a submission hold. Butthead looked like he was about to pass out from blood loss. Beavis was still moaning and groaning from his cuts and burns.

"Jacques," said Morris, "you keep an eye on Beavis, here, and I'll see if I can stop Butthead from bleeding to death."

Morris adjusted the rag Butthead was using to keep his neck from spurting blood everywhere. "Do you have a first aid kit, Angela?"

Angela left the room and returned a moment later with a first aid kit. She pulled out some gauze bandages and began to work on Butthead.

"It's a good thing you know how to shoot," said Ed.

"I didn't like the idea of letting someone pull a gun," said Morris.

"I figured you were going to do something," said Jacques. "When you put your hand on that coffee pot, I knew what was coming."

The three friends were silent for a moment.

"When the cops arrive," Morris began, "just tell them what happened. I didn't plan all this. Thanks for backing me up."

Jacques nodded. "You'd have done the same for us."

They looked at Ed, waiting. "What's done is done," he said, finally.

A moment later, Boyd entered the room. "Over there." Two cops followed him in, guns drawn. "This guy is Morris Parker, a regular customer. I think he saw everything."

The first cop looked at Morris. "Who has weapons?"

"Three pistols are on the bar," said Morris. "There is a fourth one over there somewhere, next to the dead body."

"Ray," the first cop said to his partner, "check for a gun over there."

"There are two injured bad guys over here." Morris pointed to Grabbypants. "And this guy pulled a gun and tried to kill me."

The first cop put his gun in his holster and pulled out his handcuffs. "You are under arrest," he said to Grabbypants. He cuffed Grabbypants, then frisked him for weapons.

"There's a gun here, and I'm calling the coroner," Ray said from the corner booth.

"Report the situation is secure."

"Roger." Ray pulled out a portable radio and began a conversation with the dispatcher.

The first cop resumed speaking to Grabbypants. "I recognize you. You are under arrest for attempted murder. Do you understand? You have the right to retain and instruct counsel without delay. We will provide you with a toll-free telephone lawyer referral service, if you do not have your own lawyer. Anything you say can be used in court as evidence. Do you understand? Would you like to speak with a lawyer?"

"Fuck you."

"I'll take that as a no." The cop turned to his partner, who was still talking on the radio. "Call for the guns and gangs unit. And where is our ambulance?"

Two more cops came in with guns drawn. One of them had sergeant stripes.

"The paramedics are right behind me, guys," said the sergeant.

The sergeant quickly took control of the scene. He ensured the remaining suspects were cuffed, searched and read their rights. He moved everyone out of the room where the shooting had taken place, and ordered a policeman to start taking names.

There was a dead body to examine, and bullets had flown, so the sergeant called for the forensic investigation team. He retrieved the fourth gun from the Asian, and established from Morris and Jacques who had been the original owner of each of the three other guns. Morris described the fight sequence to him. Ed and Jacques added details.

"We have a detective on the way," the sergeant told Morris, Ed and Jacques. "He will be taking your statements. You will be speaking with Detective Clark." He paused to glance around. "I'm not telling you this, but *good job*. This guy here," he pointed at Grabbypants, sulking in cuffs against the wall, "is a known quantity. He was involved in a drive-by shooting downtown last summer. We think he was the triggerman. They shot a guy for fun."

Colored lights were flashing through the windows. The coroner had arrived, and a couple more cop cars were now in the parking lot. Crime scene tape was being deployed. Butthead was in critical condition and was being taken out by the paramedics together with Beavis. Beavis' head was covered in bandages. He looked like a goon straight out of *The Mummy*.

"Can we call our wives?" Morris asked.

"Go ahead. This news is about to break." The sergeant observed a CJOH-TV truck arrive.

Morris dialed home on his cellphone.

Terri answered. "Hello?"

"It's me. I'm going to be a bit late."

"This better be good. You're out having a great time and I'm here doing homework."

"There's been a fight. Guns were involved. Everybody's OK, except for the guys who started the fight. I shot two of them."

There was a period of silence. "Terri?" Morris asked.

"Tell me one of them was Bruce Connor," she said finally.

"No, sorry."

"Where'd you get a gun?"

"I took it from one of the bad guys. I hit him with a pot of coffee. He dropped his gun. Then I grabbed it. His buddy started shooting at me, so I shot his buddy. Then I shot a guy who was going to kill Jacques."

"Oh, my God."

"It's OK. I killed that guy in self-defense. There were a lot of witnesses. The guy was shooting at me. The other guy I shot will probably live."

"Why'd you shoot the other guy?"

"He was going to shoot Jacques."

"Holy Crap. Just what kind of place is this? The Last Chance Saloon?"

"The Arms, our usual hangout. Two blocks from the house." Morris knew Terri was not aware of the poker game. Morris might have to tell her -- Later.

"Any other casualties?" she asked.

"Well, I scalded that guy in the face with the coffee pot."

"Crap, oh Crap. He'll probably sue us."

"What was I supposed to do? Let him pull a gun?"

"His friend also had a gun. How many guns did these guys have?"

"Four."

"You decided to fight four guys with guns. You had a coffee pot!"

"Terri, I had Ed and Jacques with me."

"If Ed and Jacques jumped off a cliff...."

"Look, I have to go. I have to give a statement. Check the CJOH News if you want to see more."

"Bye."

Ed came up to Morris. "I told the family what happened. My son thinks you're a hero."

"Terri thinks I'm an idiot."

Morris noticed a tall, dark-haired man in a well-tailored, dark suit had been speaking with the sergeant. He walked up to Morris, Ed and Jacques and introduced himself. "My name is Detective David Clark, Ottawa Guns and Gangs Unit." He held out his badge for Ed and Morris to examine. "Which one of you is Mr. Parker?"

"I am."

"Can I see some I.D. please?"

Morris pulled out his driver's license.

"I'm sending your friends to the station to give statements," said Detective Clark as he examined the license, "but I will require that you remain here and answer my questions."

"Sure," said Morris.

Two cops came in to escort Ed and Jacques away. Detective Clark led Morris to a table and offered him a seat.

The place was now buzzing with activity. A police photographer was shooting the scene. The coroner and a cop in coveralls, obviously a forensics guy, were working on the dead body in the corner. Two other crime scene investigators, one male and one female, were collecting evidence. The female was about to tag the pistols on the bar.

"Hold on, I need to use those for a minute," said Detective Clark. He went over to the bar and had a short discussion that Morris could not hear. The female crime scene investigator eventually left but was not happy about it. Detective Clark motioned for Morris to join him at the bar.

"Which gun did you use?" the detective asked Morris.

"I used this one." Morris pointed to the pistol with the action locked open. "It came from one of the two guys at the bar."

"This is the only gun that has been unloaded. Did you unload it?"

"Yes. Old habit. I'm not comfortable around a weapon until I have proved it to be safe."

"Was there a bullet in the chamber?" asked the detective.

Morris nodded and searched briefly, finding it. It had rolled off the main surface onto a small shelf, out of sight. He pointed it out. "There."

Detective Clark took a plastic bag from his pocket and rolled the bullet into it using a coaster, then placed the bag in his jacket pocket.

"Tell me how this all started," he said.

Morris described the build-up to his coffee pot attack, explaining how he deduced the suspects were armed and about to hit the poker game.

"So you suspected they were armed. Who fired the first shot?"

"The first shot came from the second guy at the bar. That shot hit the ceiling."

"How many shots did you fire, Mr. Parker?"

"Six. Three misses, three hits."

"How can you be so sure?"

"In the army, I did a lot of competitive combat shooting. I learned to keep track of my shots."

"Can you tell me about each shot?"

"Sure. The first three, I was zeroing in on the kid. I was not familiar with this particular pistol, and it took a couple of shots to realize bullets were going left. I adjusted by aiming right until I scored a hit with shot number four. Shot number five was on a new target, the guy trying to kill my friend Jacques. I had to be careful with that one not to hit Jacques. The final shot was not that good – I hit my target in the neck."

"Why don't you consider that shot good?"

"I was aiming for the head."

"That's a pretty glib answer. Look, Mr. Parker, you could be charged for what you did here."

Morris raised an eyebrow. "Then perhaps I should not be speaking with you, Mr. Detective."

"Would you like to be charged with obstruction?"

"I would like to be treated fairly."

"Look, a private citizen does not have the right, even if there is a crime in progress, to simply…."

"I am not in the habit of standing idly by in a situation where my life, and my friends, are put in danger by some obvious criminals."

"The best thing you can do for yourself is to co-operate fully with me."

"Apparently, detective, you want to control this interview. I will not lie to you. Here are the facts you need. Those guys came in armed and expecting to enjoy total dominance of the situation. They pulled out guns, but I used the element of surprise to gain the initiative. I did what I thought was best, and my friends stood by me. We did not start this fight, but we finished it."

Detective Clark looked uncertain. "What if I told you the two guys at the bar were undercover cops."

"That, I would consider bullshit." Morris glared at the detective. "They didn't act like cops. They didn't identify themselves as cops. They acted like they were going to ambush the owner as he came out of the back hallway. They behaved as if they were working with the two guys at the corner table."

The two men glared at each other.

The detective realized that Morris was not going to be intimidated. "Alright, alright." He grinned awkwardly. "Sorry, I seem to be using the wrong technique." He offered his hand to Morris. "Let's get started on the right foot, OK? You are not a suspect. Those guys are not undercover cops. We don't know who they are yet."

Morris shook hands warily. "You were testing me."

"I just need for you to tell me the truth," said Detective Clark. "I get a lot of liars in my profession."

Morris thought about that statement.

"The business world is no different. I have been lied to by the best, Detective Clark," Morris said.

3 – DETECTIVE CLARK'S INVESTIGATION

Detective Clark asked Morris to write a statement, then excused himself. Several people were already doing the same, and pub began to resemble a classroom at exam time.

The sergeant approached the detective. "The two injured suspects had no identification on them. I sent Constable Bradley and his partner with the ambulance as escorts. Their shift was just ending and they will need to be relieved. The other guy is cuffed in the back of my car. I'm going to take him to the station now for photo and prints."

"They were here to rob this place, I guess," said the sergeant, "but didn't get very far. It's harder to charge them if they didn't manage to commit their crime. At least we can charge the three survivors for carrying concealed weapons. The guy who tried to shoot Mr. Parker – we can get him for attempted murder. Did you get his ID?"

"Yes, and I know him. He was the leader in a drive-by shooting downtown last August. He's Ledbury Banff Cripps. On the street he goes by the name Big Mac."

"OK. I want to interview him at the station. I'll need a ride there. But I need a few minutes more with Mr. Parker. Wait for me."

"Yes, sir."

The detective approached Morris. "If I can interrupt your writing for a minute, I'd like you to follow me over to the bar."

Detective Clark asked Morris to describe the sequence of events again. He then made Morris walk through the steps he had taken, repeating his actions. That included getting on the floor to re-enact how he picked up the gun that had been dropped. He made Morris use his thumb and forefinger as if he was holding a gun. The detective took notes and made a floor plan sketch showing the location and direction of each shot Morris had taken.

"Your friends are at the station giving statements." Detective Clark walked Morris back to his table and motioned Morris to pick up his statement. "I would like you to go to the station, and finish your statement there. I will be there shortly. Do you need a ride?"

"No, I have my car."

"Do you know how to get to the station?"

"No."

"OK, the constable at the door will give you directions. I'll see there you in half an hour."

Morris nodded, and then went to speak with the constable.

The female crime scene investigator went over to tag the pistols on the bar. Detective Clark joined her swiftly.

Smiling warmly, he introduced himself and asked for her name. She told him it was Sandy. Sandy was plain looking, short and slightly overweight. She had huge breasts.

"I haven't seen you around before. Sandy, I admire the way you do your work," said the detective.

Sandy was not used to receiving compliments from tall, dark-haired men well above her rating. She was about a six, and the detective was about a nine-point-five.

She smiled nervously. "I just started with the crime lab about six months ago."

"No kidding. Only six months? The way you go about your job, it looks like you've been at it much longer."

Sandy blushed. Detective Clark could tell she enjoyed his attention.

"What are your procedures for handling this evidence?" Detective Clark asked, pointing to the three guns on the bar.

"Well, it depends on what needs to be done with the analysis…that is…I mean, um the objective of the analysis. In this situation, we will lift prints to try to determine the suspect who carried each gun. We do that back in the lab. Assuming the detectives need printing, of course. You do need printing, right?"

Detective Clark nodded, and Sandy resumed talking nervously, thoughts scattered.

Meanwhile outside, the sergeant stood in the parking lot, waiting. His partner was in the driver's seat of his cruiser, and Grabbypants, a.k.a. Big Mac, was handcuffed and slouching in the back seat, silent and sullen.

The sergeant watched Detective Clark and Sandy through the window. "What the hell is Clark doing now? Looks like he's trying to get a date," the sergeant said to his partner.

His partner looked amused, watching Clark nodding and smiling. "I guess he likes big boobs."

Back inside, Detective Clark looked at the guns on the bar, pointing at one. "How can you get a print off this? The trigger is very narrow and the grip is not smooth."

"The best prints are found inside – on the magazine. If we take out the clip and find a print on that smooth metal, we will be able to establish who loaded the gun."

Detective Clark smiled and turned on the charm. "Sandy, I need a bit of time to examine these weapons, but I have to interview a few more people first. Is it OK to examine this one here? This is the one that Mr. Parker used, and it fired the fatal shot that killed the Asian kid. I would like to examine it and record the serial number, if there is one. It will help me in court if I can give testimony that establishes continuity of evidence. I want to be able to prove this gun is the one I found on scene. I want a record of the serial number in my notebook."

Sandy was reluctant. "These guns have already been photographed. I was just about to tag them and bag them and lock them in our gun box out in the truck. You can examine them in the evidence room tomorrow. We should be done lifting prints by then. There will be ballistics testing in the afternoon."

"Wow." The detective sounded impressed. "Are you a ballistics expert, too?"

"No, but I hope to get that training soon. I'm not the gun expert."

"I'll just be a moment, with this, Sandy, really." Detective Clark turned up the charm. "Look, I'll handle it by the grip and I won't contaminate any print-carrying surfaces."

The detective quickly picked up the pistol before Sandy could object. He examined it, squinting. "It's pretty dark here, this being a bar." He smiled warmly. "I'll just take it over here to the light for a second. You go ahead and tag these others, I'll be right back, OK?"

"I suppose that would be all right," Sandy said meekly.

Detective Clark walked over to the hallway leading to the back room. He glanced at Sandy, and saw she was working with the other guns. He stepped into the well-lit hallway and examined the 9mm automatic pistol carefully. The action was locked in the rearward position because the magazine was empty. He saw the serial number had been ground off.

Detective Clark looked around, making certain there was nobody able to see what he was doing. He put the gun Morris had fired in his jacket pocket and drew his own 9mm automatic pistol from his shoulder holster. The model was similar. He removed his magazine, and loaded Morris' bullet into it. He then loaded his magazine into the Morris pistol, and placed it in his holster.

The detective turned and walked back to the bar. He placed his personal pistol with the other guns on the bar. It was unloaded, just like Morris had left the other pistol. The swap was complete.

Detective Clark walked over to where Sandy was working. "Thanks, Sandy." He smiled again. "Oh, one more thing. I have a full day tomorrow, and it would be much better if I could examine these guns first thing, before you get started again." He paused and looked at her breasts for a moment.

Detective Clark saw she was hesitant. He needed to get Sandy to agree to meet him.

He looked her in the eye. "And I would also like to take you out to dinner some time – I would love to hear more about how your evidence handling procedures work. You're very interesting to listen to. I love the sound of your voice."

Sandy was beaming with the warm feeling the detective had given her. "That would be wonderful."

"See you tomorrow. I start at 6 AM. Can I meet you then, at the forensic lab?"

"Sure," she nodded, smiling.

The detective winked and headed for the exit.

The sergeant saw Clark depart the pub and opened the front passenger door of his police car.

"Sorry to keep you waiting, fellas." Detective Clark declined the front seat. "You take the front, I don't mind. I'll be interviewing Big Mac back at the station. I'd like to get acquainted."

The sergeant shrugged. Both men entered the car and attached their seat belts. The driver exited the parking lot.

The front and back seats were separated by a thick, transparent acrylic shield. In the back, the detective sketched in his notebook. "You will be facing a charge of attempted murder, of Morris Parker," he said quietly to Big Mac, "and carrying a concealed weapon."

Detective Clark showed Big Mac his sketch. It showed several stick men. One had the label "Parker," another was labeled "Big Mac," and there were two stick men with integers "1" and "2" in the positions where Beavis and Butthead had been sitting at the bar.

"You attempted to shoot Mr. Parker from this position, right here." Clark pointed at the words he had just written. "And there are at least three eyewitnesses who can confirm that fact."

Big Mac looked at the detective's notebook. Clark's pen point was resting near the words SAY PARKER FIRED THE FIRST SHOT.

"That shot," said Clark, "would have been taken from here," he pointed at the Parker stick figure, "and aimed here." Clark moved his pen from the Parker stick figure to the Big Mac stick figure.

Big Mac absorbed this information. He looked at the detective. Looking at the roadway ahead, Detective Clark calmly closed his notebook and placed it carefully, together with his pen, in his breast pocket.

Big Mac relaxed. A look of satisfaction spread slowly across his face. The fix was in.

The car soon arrived at the police station. There were a few reporters and photographers at the main entrance.

"Take the main entrance," instructed the detective. "And turn on the lights. Let's give them a bit of a show."

The sergeant nodded and turned on the lights. Red and blue light beams flashed against the brick and glass of the building in a circular motion, creating a small disco ball effect. The photographers scrambled for a good position.

"Smile," the detective told Big Mac. "Time for your perp walk." The sergeant and his partner extracted Big Mac from the back seat. Big Mac stood between them in cuffs. Each policeman held him by one arm.

The detective pulled a comb from his pocket and ran it through his hair, then got out of the police car.

"I'll take this," said the detective, and he waved-off the junior policeman, who released Big Mac's arm. Then the sergeant and the detective escorted Big Mac down the sidewalk. Flash photographs were taken.

After the three men passed through the entranceway, the detective released Big Mac and headed for the interview rooms.

For the next few hours, Detective Clark shuttled between interview rooms containing Morris Parker, Ed Smitt, and Jacques Tremblay, each in a separate room alone. Detective Clark told the men they could not leave until he had reviewed their statements, and received and reviewed statements from other witnesses at the scene. The detective read statements from each man, asked questions and took notes as he compared their stories and documented the sequence of events for his report. He also made several phone calls to keep track of the progress of the crime scene investigation at the pub.

After he was fingerprinted, photographed and processed, Mr. Innes MacDick, alias Big Mac, was placed in an interview room. Detective Clark was told that Mr. MacDick had declined to have a lawyer present during questioning.

The interview rooms were individually wired for discreet video and audio recording of conversations. There was a central control room. Detective Clark entered the control room, greeting the two technicians present. He looked at four active display screens, each of which showed a live view of his subjects: Morris, Ed, Jacques and MacDick.

"Who's in charge?" asked the detective.

"I am, sir," said the first operator.

"Do you have my sessions with the three ex-military guys?"

"Yes, sir."

"I want a CD of their interviews on my desk by noon tomorrow."

"But we have a full set of Detective Scott's interviews to process. Our CD burner went down...."

"I don't give a shit if you have to work all night. Noon tomorrow, got it?"

"Yes, sir."

Without looking back, Detective Clark left the room briskly. "I'm going to do MacDick now."

The two operators sat in shocked silence for a moment.

"What did he just say?"

"I dunno. Something about doing his dick. I don't want to think about it, and I sure hope we don't get it on video. That guy's weird."

"I heard he was a jerk. He gives new meaning to the word."

Detective Clark entered the interview room where MacDick was waiting. The room contained a hidden camera and microphone. Back in the control room, Detective Clark had observed the camera angle being used. He positioned himself with his back to the camera so his face could not be seen.

The detective leaned back confidently in his chair, looking at MacDick. He reached in his pocket and pulled out a pack of gum. "Gum?" He tossed a stick without waiting for a response.

MacDick accepted cautiously. He removed the wrapper. There was writing on the inside. "YOU ARE ON HIDDEN CAMERA."

MacDick glanced around, curious, looking for a camera. He put the gum in his mouth. He looked at the detective, wondering what to do with the wrapper.

Detective Clark leaned forward and took the wrapper.

"Mr. MacDick, you are being charged with attempted murder." The detective put the wrapper in his pocket. "If convicted, under the Criminal Code you will receive a *mandatory minimum* sentence of four years."

MacDick had been thinking about the detective's message in the car: SAY PARKER FIRED THE FIRST SHOT.

"This fight was started by Mr. Morris Parker. He hit a bar patron with a pot of coffee. According to my

information, you aimed a gun at Mr. Parker, who was not
armed at the time, and you attempted to shoot him."

"He tried to shoot me first."

"Really? So far there is no evidence to support that
position."

MacDick frowned. "Well, he did."

"I have a diagram here." The detective pulled out his
notebook and flipped it open, searching for the right page.
"If he really did shoot at you, we should be able to find a
bullet and match it to the gun he was using. That would
support a claim of self-defense."

Detective Clark slid his diagram across the table.
"Where were you when he fired this shot? And where
was he? Mark this diagram." He offered MacDick a pen.

MacDick studied the diagram.

The detective leaned across the table and pointed to
the diagram. "That's the bar, that's where Parker was
seated when the shooting began. Mark the two positions
with letter 'P' for him and 'M' for you."

MacDick looked at the diagram. There was already
one 'P' and one 'M' on the diagram. He looked at the
detective.

"Mark the diagram. Put one 'P' for him. Put one 'M'
for you."

MacDick looked at the diagram, paused, then retraced
the two letters. He looked at the detective again.

Detective Clark smiled and reached for the diagram.

"Wait." MacDick realized the detective must be
planning to plant evidence to frame Parker. When
MacDick had cased The Arms job, he had looked at the
pub's security situation. There was something the
detective would need to know. "Let me double check
this."

The detective realized MacDick was about to write
something on the diagram. He stood up quickly, placing
his body between the camera and the suspect, obscuring

the suspect from the operator in the control room.
MacDick wrote something on the diagram.

"Yeah, that's about right." MacDick pushed the
notebook and pen back to the detective.

Detective Clark looked at the diagram. MacDick had
drawn the back hallway. MacDick had added a label:
SECURITY CAMERA.

The detective realized he had swapped pistols in that
hallway. The camera would have a clear view of his
evidence-tampering.

"Thank you, Mr. MacDick. That's all for now. I'll be
checking out your story."

Detective Clark left the interview room quickly and
immediately placed a call to the crime scene. He learned
investigators had found twelve bullet strikes and had
recovered four bullets, and they were about to call it a
night. Processing on the scene would resume tomorrow.
The owner wanted to lock up and leave. Detective Clark
asked to speak to him, arranging to meet with him for a
few moments before closing up. The detective
immediately arranged for a ride back to the pub. Within
minutes, Detective Clark was on his way back to the
crime scene.

"That's my car over there. Thanks for the ride." The
detective headed in to the pub.

Boyd MacDougall was waiting. There was a police
officer standing with him. They were the only two people
remaining in the pub.

"Thanks for waiting." The detective presented a
business card. "I wanted to give you this. I know you
want to go home. We have to keep this scene secure until
the forensics team has finished collecting their evidence.
There will be a policeman here on guard all night, until
the team returns in the morning. If you show me how to
lock up, you can leave."

Boyd shrugged. "Follow me." Boyd led the detective
through the back hall. "People have to leave by the back

door. All they have to do is shut the door behind them. Normally, you put in a four-digit code to activate the security system. There can't be anyone inside if you do that, they would set off the motion sensors."

"Do you have any other security systems?"

"Follow me."

On their way through the back hallway, Detective Clark searched for a camera, but saw nothing at the location MacDick had indicated.

"Any cameras?"

Boyd grinned. "That's what I'm going to show you. Look at the ceiling." He pointed at a sprinkler head. "See anything unusual?"

"I see a sprinkler head."

"Fire code for a building this small does not require sprinklers. It's a fake. It's actually a camera. I'll show you the camera monitor." Boyd was in a hurry, but the detective was taking his time.

"Very clever." The detective stood looking at the sprinkler head camera. "You keep an eye on staff with that?"

"Something like that." Boyd was getting uncomfortable with these questions. He knew his hidden cameras required a sign indicating there was a video surveillance system on his premises. The installer had told Boyd to post one, but Boyd had ignored him.

The detective examined the camera position, realizing it had a clear view of the spot he had done the pistol swap. "Do you have tapes?"

"No – we use a DVR. It's an all-digital system. Recording occurs only when motion is detected. All the clips are stored on a computer hard disk drive. The clips store both video and audio."

"Show me the monitor." Detective Clark took out his notebook. "According to my notes, the shooting started at 2149 approximately. Do you have any clips at that time?"

"I should have." Boyd led the detective into the back room.

Detective Clark observed that the poker game had been disbanded long ago. He could tell Boyd was nervous about the detective learning about the game. Boyd had no idea that Detective Clark had been aware of its existence. Boyd had no idea the detective had expected it to be robbed that night.

Boyd showed the detective a small desktop computer with a large display screen. An open window on the screen showed a list of clock times in chronological order.

Boyd searched the list and found one for 20:48:12. He played the clip.

The clip showed no motion for a couple of seconds, then Boyd was visible from behind as he headed down he hallway toward the main room. Suddenly a shot was heard and Boyd ducked, moving out-of-frame. A rapid burst of shots occurred, too quickly to count, followed by two additional shots. The clip lasted a total of 20 seconds.

"Do you have any backups of this?" Detective Clark placed his hand on the small computer and looked at Boyd.

"No. It's a new system, we don't have that yet." Boyd was embarrassed – the system had been in place for about three months, plenty of time to establish a backup routine.

"We will need this evidence. Any problem if I take this computer?"

Boyd thought about all the customers who were likely in clips on the DVR. The girls would be visible in some scenes. The machine was full of incriminating and embarrassing evidence: gamblers, hookers, and other sins. Late one night, Boyd had sex in the hallway with two girls who did not suspect he was recording them.

"Can I just make you a CD of the relevant clips?" Boyd asked.

"I need to inspect the accuracy of the computer clock and other internal workings, to establish validity of the recordings." Detective Clark emitted a smug smile. "I could just seize this unit."

Boyd dithered, unsure of what to say.

Detective Clark decided to play his trump card. "How would liquor board inspectors react to gambling in your establishment?"

"No problem, take the unit." Boyd reached over and unplugged the computer, causing the operating system to crash. "Glad to be of assistance."

"I'm afraid I don't have an official receipt."

"Don't worry about it. Just take the computer. You can use any keyboard and monitor with it. It's easier for you that way." Boyd disconnected the keyboard, mouse and monitor and offered the computer to the detective.

"Thanks for your cooperation." Detective Clark smiled.

Boyd left the pub. Detective Clark watched him get into his car, and waited until Boyd exited the parking lot.

The detective then headed out the back doorway. The door would lock automatically behind him after he went outside, so he propped it open with a nearby broom handle. He took the computer to his car and put it in the trunk. He retrieved a thick blanket from the trunk and brought it back to the pub. He re-entered the pub, removing the broom handle, and let the door lock.

Detective Clark placed the blanket out of sight and approached the policeman on guard duty. "What time does your shift end?"

"In about an hour."

"My wife is being a bitch tonight. I'm waiting for her to go to bed. Why don't you take off early? End your shift with a nice long coffee break – I'll be here until your replacement arrives."

"Sure, thanks!" The policeman left immediately.

Detective Clark entered the bar area where the shooting had taken place. He consulted his sketch, and maneuvered his body into the position from which Morris had done all his shooting. Like Morris had done, he sat on the floor. The detective looked in the direction MacDick had been standing. The detective pointed his arm and finger in a likely direction that a bullet could have flown from Morris' gun. There was a ceiling beam on the far side of the room. The heavy, dark wood beam rested on a vertical support beam running up the wall.

Detective Clark placed a chair next to the beam, climbed up, and then placed the muzzle of the loaded pistol against the inside of the 90-degree joint between the wall support beam and the ceiling beam. He glanced back to Morris' firing position to check alignment of the shot.

Detective Clark stepped down, retrieved his blanket and draped it over the pistol, taking care not to obstruct the muzzle. Multiple neat folds hung on each side of the weapon. He removed the safety catch, climbed back up on the chair and aimed the pistol at the joint between the floor and ceiling beams. He fired a shot into the soft, dark wood.

The blanket muffled the sound of the shot, and the bullet embedded itself deeply in the joint. Detective Clark checked the point of impact to be sure there was no visible gunshot residue. The dark beam should easily mask any residual powder burns, he figured, which had been mostly absorbed by the blanket anyway.

Detective Clark picked up the warm, spent cartridge casing from the floor where it had fallen. He considered leaving it at the scene, but then put it in his pocket.

After putting the chair back in place, Detective Clark checked the scene to ensure he had not forgotten anything. Then he sat down and waited for the next shift to arrive.

About 45 minutes later, a policeman arrived to replace him.

The detective entered his car and lit a cigarette. It had been a long night.

He picked up his cellphone and placed a call.

A voice answered with a thick South African accent. "Tell me what happened." It was van Praag.

"Our four friends tried to rob a poker game. They ran into trouble with some military guys. The Asian kid is dead. Your two men are in hospital under guard. MacDick will be charged with attempted murder and all three will be charged with carrying a concealed firearm."

"I need all these men back on the street as soon as possible. We have an operation underway – a very important operation, with only two remaining deliverables. There must be no delay."

"I know."

"Did you know about this job?" asked van Praag.

The detective took a long drag on his cigarette. "No," he lied.

"This was not an authorized job."

"I know. They were moonlighting. They were lucky I was on duty when it went down."

"Clean up this mess."

"I have everything under control. MacDick will get off. I have planted some evidence that will clear him and set up one of the military guys. I'll also arrange to get your two men out of the hospital. They had no ID with them, and they have not identified themselves."

"There must be no delays in the operation. We are on a tight time schedule."

"I know." Detective Clark took a final drag on his cigarette and then stubbed it out. "By the way, I will need something for this unexpected extra."

There was a long pause.

"Make this problem go away. I'll pay you twenty thousand."

"Fine."

The call ended.

Detective Clark put down his cellphone and smiled, thinking maybe he should have asked for twenty-five thousand.

4 – PARKER HOLDINGS LIMITED

The next morning, Morris was already awake when his Blackberry alarm sounded next to his head. The device played an audio clip – a laughing child. Morris had made a recording of Victoria when she was three. Usually, it woke Morris with a smile. This morning, he felt as if he was being laughed at.

Morris thought about how Detective Clark had kept him busy at the station until 2 AM. A few reporters had been waiting when Morris was finally released. There were a couple of newspaper photographers and a news cameraman, who asked Morris for an on-camera interview. Morris declined, but offered a couple of comments for the story because he felt sorry for keeping everyone so late.

The Blackberry emitted child's laughter again, and Morris picked it up to cancel the alarm. He rubbed his eyes, fumbled for his reading glasses, and put them on. He squinted and strained to focus on the small screen.

Morris saw an email from the_barbarian@parkerholdings.com. Conan Moore, an old friend and longtime employee, had sent a message a few minutes before. The subject heading was 'Fwd: Gunfight in Orleans Pub – One Killed, Two Injured by Ottawa Business Leader.' Conan had written: "Wow, I can't wait for you to tell me about this, schmuck!"

The rest of his email consisted of an article published in that day's Ottawa Citizen.

"One man is dead and two others injured after a bar fight ended in gunfire at the The Cumberland Arms in Ottawa's east end early Wednesday evening," the story began. "A 19-year old man was pronounced dead at the scene, identified by police as Kendo Kanise, a student from Carleton University. A second victim, an unidentified male, was shot in the leg and neck and remains in stable condition in hospital. A third man, also unidentified, was taken to the burn unit with undisclosed injuries.

"According to an Ottawa Police Service media release, police received numerous calls just before 9 PM Wednesday. Police recovered four guns at the scene and arrested one suspect."

The article quoted several people who gave fragmentary descriptions of the battle. Morris skipped through the text until he saw his name.

"Several witnesses observed Morris Parker, CEO of Parker Holdings, shoot Mr. Kanise dead. Mr. Parker offered little information about his involvement in the battle, saying only 'Gang members pulled guns on my friends and me. I did what I thought was the right thing to do.'"

Morris took a deep breath and sat up, rotating his feet onto the floor. "The right thing to do. Not a very good reason."

He got out of bed stiffly and went to the bathroom to relieve himself. He put on his robe and went to check on his daughters.

One bedroom door was open and the bed was empty. Morris remembered his 18-year old daughter, Victoria, was sleeping over at a friend's house in the country. Morris hoped it was a female friend.

The second bedroom door was closed and he opened it quietly. His 12-year old girl was sleeping soundly. Morris sat down carefully on the bed.

"What the hell was I thinking?" Morris thought about his willingness to take business risks that put the family in financial jeopardy. This had not been a calculated business risk.

There had been no time for a risk analysis. Morris had decided to confront several armed men with only a coffee pot. He had put his friends and himself at great risk. He had put their families at risk of losing fathers and husbands.

Morris kissed his daughter on the head, careful not to wake her. Then he headed out for his morning run. He decided to cut it short, and would run his six mile route instead of the planned ten.

While he was running, Morris reflected on his actions at The Arms. Morris did not often second-guess his decisions. He did not always make the right decision, he realized. But once the effort of reaching the best possible decision had been expended, and the decision appeared to have been made with all available information, Morris was ready to live with the consequences. There was no point in worrying.

Two hours later, Morris arrived at the headquarters of Parker Holdings Limited, PHL, and pulled into his parking spot, marked by a sign with the company logo bearing the name "Morris Parker, CEO."

He entered the building and breezed past the security station. The guard on duty nodded and they exchanged greetings. As the majority owner of the building, Morris had exempted himself from being logged-in and out at the security desk. His security staff recognized him. Any new staff member who he had not met could rely on the photo of him posted there.

Morris entered the first available elevator and placed his thumb on the fingerprint pad, unlocking access to the private floors. He then pushed the elevator button to ascend to the 22nd floor containing his penthouse office suite.

A tall, attractive, middle-aged lady entered the elevator just as the door began to close. "Morris," she said, "I've read a lot of business stories about you, but I never read anything quite like the Sun story this morning. You started the gunfight at the OK Corral."

"Good morning, Wendy." Wendy Doolittle, owner of Doolittle Media, published several specialty magazines and rented half the 15th floor from Parker Holdings.

"I heard on the radio you killed a member of a street gang."

"He was doing his best to kill me. Did they say which gang?"

"No. But they describe you as a real estate tycoon, software genius, and former owner of the Ottawa Colts baseball team."

"His gang should have no trouble finding me, then. I'm not sure this kind of publicity is going to be too good for business."

"Any publicity is good publicity. I always thought you were a straight shooter. Now you have literal proof, because they said you are an expert shot." She exited the elevator and held the door open. "If you feel inclined, we would like to do a feature on you. A heroic champion gunfighter story would sell magazines."

Morris nodded. "I'm flattered. Let me get back to you. Gotta run."

The elevator door began to close. Wendy stuck her hand in the way.

"And if I can't do an article, at least you can let me buy you a drink so you can tell me all about it." Wendy smiled at Morris for a moment, then removed her hand, letting the closing door break eye contact.

Wendy was very attractive, Morris realized, and she had never seemed interested in Morris before. He decided to get a copy of the Ottawa Sun ASAP. The elevator door opened on the 22nd floor.

"Morris!" The receptionist, Jill, a pretty brunette with a short ponytail, held up a copy of the Ottawa Sun. "Have you seen this?"

A headshot photo of Morris wearing jacket and tie, taken from the annual report of one of his publicly traded

companies, was on the cover. The headline was
BUSINESS LEADER GUNS DOWN GANGSTER."

"Mr. Latham requested to meet with you right away."
Jill was concerned. "He wants to discuss this situation."

Liam Latham, PHL In-House Counsel, had the
second-best corner office on the floor, after Morris' own
office. Morris noticed his door was closed.

"And Conan told me not to tell you he's in your
office."

"Thank-you, Jill." Morris accepted the newspaper and
looked at his watch. "Tell him I can see him in thirty
minutes."

Reading and walking slowly, Morris entered his
office and closed the door. He observed the magnificent
view of the Ottawa River, seeing his desk chair was
facing the window, opposite to its normal position.

"Conan Moore," said Morris, addressing the back of
the chair.

The chair spun around to reveal a bald, overweight
man with a bushy beard. "Nice shooting, schmuck."
Conan usually wore a plaid flannel shirt and looked like
he lived in the woods. Today, he was wearing a white tee
shirt. The word UTILITY was visible on his upper chest.

"Would you care for a seat, Mr. President?" Conan
gestured to one of the visitor chairs in front of Morris'
desk.

"If it's not too much of a bother, Mr. Utility
Programmer, sir."

"Like the shirt? Check this out." Conan stood up a
displayed huge lettering on his barrel chest: UTILITY
PROGRAMMER. He turned around and pointed with his
thumb to the Parker Holdings Limited name and logo on
the back. "I got this tee shirt made up. You remember the
shirt you gave me back when?"

"Yes, I remember offering you a job about twenty
years ago." Morris paused. "We were working in my
basement. You were joining a company of three people.

Our fourth employee had just quit because he wanted to work on database systems, but I wanted him to do integration work. He complained that all I wanted him to do was utility programming, like it was gofer work."

"And I was happy with that title," Conan grinned.

"And now your utility programs permeate this company -- like a bad smell. I made up a shirt for you back then. But it was classier than this one. It had a collar, your name and title were hand-embroidered, and the company name was spelled correctly. That shirt you are wearing says 'Parking Holdings Limited.' It's P-A-R-K-E-R, not P-A-R-K-I-N-G."

"No shit?" Conan struggled to read the writing on his back. He started to pull it off his big belly.

"Keep your shirt on, please." Morris said. "The shirt fits fine and will be good when I assign you to manage the *parking lot*. I'll give you a nametag. *My Name is Conan*, spelled S-C-H-M-U-C-K."

Conan laughed. "OK, but remember the parking lot is still within wireless networking distance of your supposedly secure systems. Secure against anyone, that is, but me! I built your network, and I know how to take it all apart."

"OK, you can keep your regular job, since you have me over a barrel."

Conan pointed excitedly to the Ottawa Sun newspaper Morris was holding. "That story said you shot a guy with his own gun. Killed him with it. Then you shot a guy he was with. You also scalded another guy with hot coffee and shot him too."

"Actually, I only shot two guys. I scalded the first guy with coffee and took his gun. I shot an Asian guy who was shooting at me, then I shot another guy who was struggling with Jacques Tremblay. Otherwise he would have shot Jacques."

"How many guys were there?"

"Four guys. Two in a corner booth, and two at the bar."

"Everyone here is going crazy with this news. Nobody knows what exactly happened. It's front page in the papers and top story on every radio station. Jill has tons of messages from press people already. All the big TV networks have called, Canadian and American. They seem to like vigilante justice."

"I guess I should read this story, then." Morris opened the paper and walked around his desk, stopping a few inches short of colliding with Conan. "See if you can utility-program me a coffee," he said without looking up from the paper.

Just then, Jill knocked and opened the office door. "I thought you might like this." She offered Morris a cup of coffee in his favorite mug with milk, no sugar.

"Good job," Morris said to Conan. "Dismissed."

Conan stood to attention and saluted.

Morris accepted the coffee from Jill. "Thanks."

Conan left with Jill. Morris could hear him, with great enthusiasm, start to tell Jill what he had just learned from Morris.

Morris closed his office door and walked over to his desk. Conan had written the word "SCHMUCK" on a notepad on his desk.

Morris read the Ottawa Sun story. It contained disjointed quotes from numerous people, and it was difficult to acquire an accurate understanding of the sequence of events. Everything happened quickly, and everyone had a different point of view. One woman was sitting near the Asian. She was terrified when the shooting started. She hid under her table and was horrified to see a person fall to the floor dead, right in front of her.

Liam Latham knocked twice and entered the office without waiting for an invitation. "I'll make this quick, Morris." He closed the door behind him.

"You may approach the bench, counselor," said Morris.

Walking briskly, Liam held up a copy of the Ottawa Citizen. Under the headline "Gunfight in Orleans Pub" was a photo of a covered dead body being wheeled out of The Cumberland Arms by an attendant with a grim look on his face. "I'm worried about this."

Morris looked at the picture with mild interest. "You worry about using expired toothpaste, Liam."

"Who fired the first shot? Tell me it *was not* you."

"It *was not* me."

"Who fired the first shot?"

"I don't know his name. Let's refer to him as Butthead."

"What was he shooting at? Why?"

"Aren't you supposed to ask questions one at a time? He shot the ceiling. Probably because Jacques tackled him as he was drawing his gun and spoiled his aim."

"What was he aiming at?"

"He was about to aim at me, probably. I had just clobbered his friend, Beavis, in the face with a pot of coffee."

Liam paused, then began pacing back and forth like he was performing in front of a jury.

"Please explain why you did that, Mr. Parker."

"I observed Mr. Beavis was about to pull out a gun with the intention of committing a crime."

"What made you think he had that intention?"

"Mr. Beavis and Mr. Butthead were in a position that they could gain rapid access to the back room. At that time, a high-stakes poker game was in progress. There was a large amount of cash available. I deduced that they were working with another pair of individuals in the room, who were creating a diversion. Their plan was to draw out the owner so they could access the back room and steal the cash."

"And you thought you had the capability to intervene and prevent that crime?"

"I was with friends. I had moved into a position beside Mr. Beavis. I saw a pot of hot coffee I could use as a weapon."

"Are you a trained police officer?"

"No."

"Are you a police detective?"

"No."

"Are you in any way associated or have you ever been associated in the past with police enforcement?"

"As a victim, yes."

Liam looked at Morris and frowned. "Do *not* say that if you face this line of questioning."

"Fine."

"So you are not a trained law enforcement official, yet you chose to initiate an attack against several armed men in a crowded public place. Are you aware of police advice in situations where an armed robbery is taking place? At a bank for instance?"

"Yes. I have a daughter who works in a bank."

"What do the police recommend in the event of a holdup, even when no weapon is visible?"

"They recommend giving over some cash."

"Mr. Parker, you acted extremely foolishly. You put the lives of innocent people, including yourself, at risk. You are a past victim of crime. Did you think you could do a better job of controlling the situation than police professionals?"

"Yes. There were no police present at the time."

Liam frowned again. "Do *not* say it that way."

"OK, how about just 'there were no police present?'"

"Better, but it's already too late. There is no way I would put you on the stand, if I was defending you."

"Defending *me*? I didn't commit the crime here! Four armed thugs are about to execute a heist. If somebody is about to point a gun at *me*, my friend, I do not just sit quietly."

"If you were on the stand and gave the answers you just gave, the Crown Prosecutor would sum you up like this: you took the law into your own hands. He would present your opportunistic business track record and past military training in such a way he could conclude you are an aggressive, authoritarian figure used to controlling every situation."

"What's wrong with that?"

"There is a lot wrong with appearing as a past crime victim with no respect for safety procedures or the rule of law. You would appear to the jury as a trigger-happy, racist, punk-hating right winger who eagerly killed a 19-year old Japanese kid."

"A kid who fired at me first."

"Can you prove it? The shooting was over before many people knew what was going on. The eyewitness statements in the newspapers are all over the map. You could be charged criminally with manslaughter. You could be sued civilly. How this story comes out in the press is certain to affect your business dealings. Right now, public sentiment could go either way."

Morris sagged. "I thought I had already heard the worst of this from Terri. I was kicking myself this morning when I got up and looked at the kids."

"Why didn't you call me when this happened?"

"I didn't need your help telling them what I did, and I didn't want to bother you. Why waste resources? Doing it myself was more efficient."

"You put too much faith in honesty and efficiency. Those are great business values, but if you screw up in a criminal matter…."

Morris paused, then continued defiantly. "All I did was tell the truth, the whole truth, and nothing but the truth."

"You act as if *that* is the only thing that matters. This is not Wonderland. You're in my world now, Alice. What we're dealing with here is our *justice system.*"

5 – DETECTIVE CLARK HAS HIS WAY

Detective Clark arrived at the forensics lab at 5:50 AM. He did not want to be late. He parked in an empty lot with a Tim Horton's coffee in his hand, sipping it occasionally. There was a second coffee cup on his dash. A wisp of vapor emitted through a pinhole in the cup cover, fogging a small section of windshield.

After he had been waiting about five minutes, Sandy's car arrived, just before 6 AM. She exited and began walking toward the main entrance. She was wearing a pale blue blouse, black mini skirt, and walked a bit awkwardly in black pumps.

Pretty good-looking legs for a short woman, Detective Clark thought as he smiled to himself. The Detective stepped out of his car, with his coffee in his left hand. He reached for the second coffee, taking it with a small Tim Horton's bag containing creamers and sugar. Both hands full, he closed the car door with his hip.

"Good Morning, Sandy," he said as he walked briskly toward her, smiling warmly.

"Hello," Sandy replied with a smile. She carried a large purse over one shoulder.

The detective approached and noticed she was wearing perfume. He offered the coffee and Tim's bag. "I brought you a coffee. Cream and sugar are in the bag. I'm not sure how you like it."

"Thanks." She adjusted her purse strap higher on her arm and accepted the coffee and bag.

They started to walk together toward the building.

"So how do you like your Tim's?" he asked.

"Oh," she said. "Double double," meaning two creams, two sugars.

"Double *trouble*? He looked at her breasts for an instant. I think I can remember that." He smiled.

Sandy blushed.

They reached the main door. Sandy had a proximity pass hanging around her neck, and she passed it by the card reader. The reader beeped and Detective Clark opened the door for her. They proceeded through the building with Sandy in the lead.

"Since we got back so late, we left the stuff locked in the truck last night." She was nervous and started talking quickly. "You want to see the guns, right? They haven't been dusted for prints yet, so you'll have to be careful. Right now, they're still in the truck in the garage. We'll be heading back to the scene in a couple of hours. I have to log the evidence items into the evidence room computer before you can sign them out. I hope you can wait a few minutes."

"What are the steps to log them?"

"I have to enter a description of the item in our database, and match each item to the photo taken last night. It won't take long."

Detective Clark realized Sandy would have to read and register the serial numbers on the weapons. His personal pistol had his police issue serial number. The Morris pistol had no serial number. He could not allow her to enter the serial numbers before he got his hands on the guns.

"If you have a bit of time, I'd like to see your cool truck. I watch CSI all the time. Can you give me a bit of a tour?"

"Sure!"

Sandy swiped her proximity pass again and they entered the garage area. In the middle of a large floor area, there was a cube van about the size of a box ambulance. It was marked CRIME SCENE UNIT in large lettering and painted in City of Ottawa Police colors.

There was nobody else in sight. They walked to the back of the truck.

There was a padlock on the door handle. Sandy placed the coffee bag and cup in the same hand. With her free hand, she reached into her purse and pulled out a set of keys. To open the padlock, Sandy would require two hands, but both her hands were full.

"Let me help you here," said Detective Clark.

Sandy held her cup hand slightly higher, expecting him to take her cup.

Instead, the detective stepped closer and grasped the padlock, twisting it so she could insert the key. Sandy inserted her key and snapped it open.

Detective Clark stood close behind Sandy. Before she could extract her key, he slid his hand down onto her hand. Then he guided her hand and they removed the padlock together.

Sandy felt a rush with the warmth of his hand on her hand. He was standing very, very close to her, and the scent of his aftershave made her want him to get closer. She had never enjoyed this kind of attention from such a good-looking man.

"I …" she began, then her voice cracked. She began to cough, and withdrew her hand from his to cover her mouth.

Detective Clark manipulated the door handle and opened the door. He placed the padlock on the floor. "After you." He motioned for her to climb the steps. He followed her into the van and closed the door behind them.

On one side of the van was a work surface with two small-backed steno chairs on wheels. There was a laptop computer in a docking station in front of each chair. The detective was unable to stand up straight – the roof was a bit too low for him. He stood slightly hunched, slightly uncomfortable.

Sandy smiled up at him. "We can sit on these." She
placed her coffee on the work surface and grabbed the
back of the chair closest to the door. She released bungee
cords holding the chairs in place to prevent them from
crashing around when the truck was in motion. The
detective sat on her left and took a sip of coffee.

Sandy opened the laptop in front of her and pressed
the power button. "We have a secure wireless network in
the building. I'll update the database from here." She
punched a code into a tall wall safe beside her, opening it.
"This is where we lock up the firearms."

Sandy reached into the safe and extracted a pistol in a
plastic zip-lock bag. She gave it to the detective. "You
can look this over while I enter the others."

"Thanks." Detective Clark put his coffee down and
accepted the pistol.

The detective examined the gun through the plastic
bag. There was a small yellow tag with the digit "2" on it.
It was not the gun Detective Clark needed. The detective
watched Sandy extract a second gun from the safe. This
pistol had the action locked rearward. This was the
detective's pistol, and he would have to swap it for the
one Morris had used, the one the detective now carried in
his holster.

Sandy waited for the laptop to finish booting,
watching the screen.

The detective pulled his chair closer to her and placed
his hand on her thigh.

Sandy didn't look at him. Blushing, she tried to
concentrate on the computer. The login prompt appeared,
but she did not react, unable to concentrate on what she
was doing.

"Come closer," he said.

Sandy turned her chair to face him. He pulled her
close and kissed her. They began necking.

The detective moved his hand up and down her outer
thigh, caressing slowly. She sighed. He got down on both

knees, pushing her legs apart. She wrapped her arms around his shoulders, pulling his face between her breasts.

A moment later, his next move was to start removing her panties.

"Wait," she said. "I'm not sure…."

"I'm clean," he said, kissing her. "And I want you." He kissed her again. "Are you using birth control?"

"Of course, but…." She drew back slightly. "We just met…."

The detective stopped, leaned back, and took a deep breath.

"Then let's get to know each other." He smiled and took her two hands in his, kissing them. "We can start with this coffee."

The detective reached for her cup and removed the lid. He opened the bag and reached in. "Two cream, two sugar. Double double. See? I'm getting to know you already."

Sandy laughed, and reached out to touch his face.

The detective peeled back the creamer cups just enough to allow liquid to escape. Then he opened the sugar bags and poured one into her cup. "Sugar will give you quick energy." He poured the other.

Making a show of it, he then picked up her coffee cup and one of the creamers. He gently squeezed the creamer container between his thumb and forefinger with multiple short pulses, causing the white liquid to shoot into the coffee in small spurts. "But certain creams," he said as he picked up the second creamer, "can have long lasting effects."

She laughed.

"You are having an effect on me, by the way. You have me in quite a state." With a boyish grin, the detective adjusted his position a bit and revealed to Sandy he had a hard-on.

Sandy looked at his bulge, then at his eyes, smiling.

"If the lady will permit me," he said. "I will take a moment to adjust this, uh, situation."

Sandy blushed again, still smiling, and turned her head away.

The detective got to his feet, turning his back to her. He reached into his pants pocket, pulling out a small plastic bottle containing a clear liquid. He still had her coffee cup in one hand. He flipped open the lid of the plastic bottle with his thumb and dumped the liquid in her coffee.

The bottle contained one carefully pre-measured dose of GHB, the date-rape drug.

Early that morning, Detective Clark had estimated her body weight when he prepared the bottle. He did not want to cause an overdose. GHB required about 15 minutes to take effect. In a drink, it had a slight salty taste. The sugar in her coffee would disguise that taste nicely.

"That's better." He returned to his seat and poured the second creamer.

He offered her the coffee. "To new friends."

They touched their paper cups together.

For the next fifteen minutes, Detective Clark was the most charming and disarming self-depreciating male on the planet. He asked her questions about her past and listened intently to her stories. He complemented Sandy on her accomplishments, her sense of humor, and her good taste in clothing. Any time she slowed the pace of drinking her coffee, he jokingly proposed a toast to something new and meaningless. She enjoyed him immensely.

Clark watched Sandy closely. He did not want her to take in more of the drug than necessary, because he needed her to be able to leave the vehicle under her own power.

When it appeared to Clark the drug had loosened Sandy up just enough, the detective tried kissing her again. This time, she reacted without inhibitions. He caressed her inner thigh and she spread herself wide. He quickly removed her panties, hoisted her skirt above her hips, embraced her from behind and fucked her doggie-style. She kept her balance by bracing both hands on the work surface.

He was quick to climax.

She wanted more, but he pulled up his pants, buckled his belt, and zipped shut.

She took a couple of deep breaths to wind down. She put her skirt back into place, and tried to straighten her hair. She could feel his seamen starting to run down her crotch.

"Why don't you freshen up?" he suggested. "I'll be here when you get back. We can make dinner plans."

She smiled weakly, feeling a bit dizzy. The drug effect was still increasing. She bent over and picked up her panties from where they lay near his feet. She put them in her purse.

"I'll wait here for you." He gave her yet another confident, warm, dazzling smile.

She stepped out of the truck.

Detective Clark closed the door. He opened the zip-lock bag that contained his personal pistol. He removed the numbered yellow tag from the trigger guard, and placed it on the Morris pistol, then swapped pistols.

Detective Clark sat and relaxed for a moment, thinking what to do next. He had a full day planned.

In the washroom, Sandy vomited. When she returned from cleaning herself, Detective Clark was gone, and she was having trouble remembering what had just happened to her.

6 – ALEX JAMES, GOVERNMENT AGENT

After his meeting with Liam, Morris spent time working on deals. He signed an Agreement of Purchase and Sale for a lot of land. He negotiated a Shareholder Agreement with two partners for a new corporation to own and develop the land. He reviewed the financial statements for a company he planned to take public, and he accepted a speaking engagement at a charity dinner.

At 10 AM, the speakerphone on his desk beeped.

"I have Mr. James for you, parked on 3."

"Thank-you, Jill."

Morris grabbed a wireless telephone headset from its cradle and put it on his head. He punched a button with the label PARKED CALL followed by the digit 3, and picked up the call.

"I hope you're not making this call on government time," said Morris.

"What's your point?" Alex James demanded.

"I expect you nearly-retired government types to push yourselves, and try to accomplish at least three or four hours of productive work *each and every day*."

"That much?" Alex James had come to expect a lot of government bashing from his old friend. "I want to assure you, Mr. Taxpayer, we are putting your tax dollars to very good use. For example, today we are planning our next reorganization. That project will likely be followed by a federal election, resulting in a change of government. Then we will experience staff cutbacks, followed by a re-reorganization, followed by a change of mission, followed by another reorganization, followed by aggressive hiring."

Morris grinned. "And your career plan is therefore: retire, collect pension, get re-hired on contract and earn double salary?"

Alex James changed to a thick and convincing Scottish accent. "Correction *laddie*: I'll be forced into retirement and *collect severance*, then collect pension, get re-hired on contract and earn double salary. Ach."

"Of course. That's why you were on French language training for the last six months, so they can release you and hire you back at greater expense into a bilingual position."

"Bien sûr. You understand government perfectly. You should run for Prime Minister."

"OK, that hurts." Morris paused. "Did you call to remind me I cannot retire like you, at age 55?"

"I see in the papers you have made new enemies. I am calling in my capacity as your security advisor."

Alex James, another ex-army buddy who ended up working in Ottawa, had self-appointed to the position of security advisor to PHL. Alex worked for the Canadian Security Intelligence Service, CSIS, for fifteen years. Morris was not sure exactly what Alex did there at the present, since his work was mostly classified.

Alex actually took his self-appointed job very seriously. "You need to increase your personal security, Morris. You killed a gang member. You have to expect they will retaliate. It's not difficult to figure out your home address."

Morris raised an eyebrow. "How?"

"As a director of PHL, your home address is listed on several corporate filings. This information is available to anybody who writes Corporations Canada to request it."

"You think a member of the Ledbury Banff Cripps is literate enough to do that? Would Corporations Canada give my personal address to a thug?"

"They would give it to a lawyer. And your new opponents have lawyers."

"I thought the Cripps were mostly young street types."

"They are. But they have new friends. The Cripps recently developed an association with the Hell's Angels Motorcycle Club."

"How do you know that?"

"I can't tell you."

"Sorry." Morris paused to think. "What *can* you tell me about them, then?"

"Hell's Angels is the biggest supplier of GHB and Ecstasy in Canada. They manage a good chunk of the prostitution in Quebec and Ontario. Over half the illegal weapons seized in the country are likely sourced by Hell's Angels. They use smart, expensive lawyers and are incorporated federally with a headquarters in Montreal."

"You think these guys will come after me?"

"Were all four of the bad guys Cripps members?"

"The cops could not identify two guys we called Beavis and Butthead. I hospitalized both of them."

"Got a pen? Write this down." Alex paused. "Get a video surveillance system for the house with perimeter intrusion sensors. I've been meaning to mention it the last few times we were over at your place. Your lot backs onto a ravine and that's a major vulnerability. Put security film on your ground floor windows. There are other things you should do, but start with these. Put in an outdoor low-light security camera system."

"OK. I'll have my security supplier give me something right away. I'll put this in TaskMan."

"What's TaskMan?"

"It's our automated task tracking and notification system."

"What kind of notification?"

"It sends reminders to people if they are responsible for overdue tasks. It notifies whoever assigned the task as well. It's not for government work. Can you imagine how much pressure it would create for a guy like you? You would get about a hundred reminders a day. A queue full of important national security tasks set by your boss: GET COFFEE FOR DIRECTOR, GET COFFEE FOR DIRECTOR...."

"Funny. Actually, I work directly for him now. He meets who I schedule him to meet, and he goes where I arrange for him to go."

"You sound like a glorified gofer. Gofer this, gofer that.... Bad dog! Sit! Heel, boy, heel."

"That reminds me, I have to shine his shoes...."

"Let's get together this weekend," Morris said. "It's your turn to bash the private sector. Why don't you and Sarah come over for steaks?"

"Did you check with Terri? If so, I'll check with my commander."

"Good point. I'll ask her first. I don't think she has plans, but if she does, this conversation never happened."

"What conversation?"

"Bye for now – get back to your government nap."

"Bye. Don't forget those security arrangements. And make sure your fire insurance is paid up!"

Morris disconnected the call, turned to his keyboard, and created a new TaskMan task. He inserted the title VIDEO SURVEILLANCE SYSTEM FOR PARKER RESIDENCE and added text describing the requirement. He assigned HIGH for severity and IMMEDIATE for urgency. Then he picked Zia's name from the ASSIGN TO list.

Morris added a sentence to the task comment history: "Zia, I need a design quote. Call me ASAP to discuss this requirement."

He was about to send the task then added to the task description: "Supply and install fire extinguishers for kitchen, garage, and back deck."

Then he clicked SEND.

7 – CLARK AND THE KANISE FAMILY

It was late in the day. Detective Clark was putting the finishing touches on his report.

He had before him a convincing statement from Mr. Innes MacDick describing how Morris Parker had fired a shot at MacDick – the first shot of the gun battle. Mr. MacDick also denied any connection to the two still unidentified men now in hospital.

The detective also had other – much more compelling – evidence against Parker. An email he had just received from the ballistics lab indicated the crime scene investigators, acting at the detective's direction, had found a bullet embedded in the ceiling beam. Using their standard procedures, the bullet had been carefully extracted and compared to a test bullet fired from the pistol Morris had used. Both bullets were proven to come from the same gun.

The statements of Mr. Ed Smitt and Mr. Jacques Tremblay supported Parker's version of events, but they could be discounted by the fact that they were his loyal friends. There were other statements from various witnesses, all of which Detective Clark ensured contained just enough contradictory information to create a good smoke screen. The most reliable evidence was the physical evidence. Detective Clark was feeling very satisfied with his day's work. He had enough to get his man MacDick out of jail.

As for the two men requiring identification, Detective Clark had managed to neglect ordering photos and prints to be taken. He could not postpone those formalities indefinitely. The sooner he could get them out of there, the better.

His report recommended the charge of attempted murder against Mr. MacDick be dropped. He knew that recommendation would be followed, now that he had an alternate person to charge. Mr. MacDick would instead face lesser charges: pointing a firearm and unauthorized possession of a firearm. If convicted, it would be Mr. MacDick's first offence. He would plead self-defense and his lawyer would tell the judge what a tough life his client led, in constant danger since childhood, because his mother did not love him and abandoned him to the street at age 16. He would likely get no jail time. Most importantly, he would immediately be eligible for bail.

The report recommended that Morris Parker be charged with three offences. First, for the coffee pot attack against unidentified suspect #1: aggravated assault. Second, for the two shots he fired into unidentified suspect #2: attempted murder while using a firearm. Detective Clark smiled. For that one, Parker had admitted to Clark he aimed at the head and missed. Clark included that information in his report. And third, for killing Kendo Kanise: manslaughter.

Detective Clark did not care if Parker eventually was convicted or not. He only cared that the heat was off MacDick until van Praag's operation was finished.

Detective Clark's phone rang. It was the front desk officer calling up to say a Mr. Masahiro Kanise and family had arrived at the station and wanted to meet with him. The detective was tired and hungry, having worked through lunch. Still, he was curious. There were four people in total. Clark told the desk officer to place the family in the large meeting room.

Clark pulled out a report on Kendo Kanise.

Kendo was 19-year old student at Carleton University. His family had been informed of the death this morning. Coincidentally, the father, mother, and grandfather were visiting their son in Canada.

The police priest had been used to inform the family at their hotel. A Japanese language interpreter was required. Normally, a 9-1-1 Communications Clerk would have informed the next of kin by telephone. This was a VIP family. The Japanese embassy had been contacted to locate next of kin, and had requested special handling due to the high profile of the family.

Detective Clark turned to his Internet browser and googled the name "Masahiro Kanise." Mr. Kanise was the subject of several business news articles. He owned a couple of textile factories and seemed to be involved in steel production and consumer electronics. One of his companies had apparently been penalized for bribery. A public official had been given a gift of golf equipment and a country club membership valued at four million yen. Detective Clark did an online conversion to learn the value: over $45,000.

Clark drummed his fingers then asked himself: "What is your expectation in dealing with the police, Mr. Kanise?" The detective googled the search words "police corruption Japan."

Detective Clark skimmed a few item headings and then found an authoritative, scholarly article on police integrity in Japan. The article summary indicated that the Japanese police system suffered from a spate of recent scandals, and those scandals might be the tip of the iceberg. In Japan, internal investigation procedures and techniques related to police misconduct were not well developed. Detective Clark learned there were three acute problems: embezzlement of money from police slush funds, endemic corruption through police control over the pachinko slot machine industry, and police tolerance of organized crime.

"Welcome to Canada, sir." He closed his browser and headed for the interview room.

The interview room had no cameras. Four people were waiting.

A well-dressed, middle-aged Japanese couple sat stoically, in two adjacent chairs, at a large conference table.

There was a thin old man with long grey hair and a long, wispy moustache and beard seated at the table resting his hands on a cane between his legs. An empty chair separated him from the couple.

There was also a young man in a business suit standing at the door. Speaking with a strong accent, he said, "You must be Detective Clark?"

"Yes. David Clark." The Detective offered a handshake.

"I am Chikara Sato, interpreter." The young man bowed, eyes down, to about a 15 degree angle, slightly to the left so as to avoid colliding with the detective. Then he quickly straightened and accepted the handshake.

"You look tired, Mr. Sato."

"I just arrived from Japan."

He was called all the way from Japan for this meeting, thought the detective. The embassy's interpreter was not good enough, apparently. Clark had met her, and she spoke English much better than this young man. Perhaps she was not trusted enough.

"Detective, may I present Mr. Masahiro Kanise and his wife," said Mr. Sato.

Mr. Masahiro bowed slightly to the detective, and Detective Clark responded with an equivalent bow. Masahiro did not seem overly impressed.

Then the detective considered the situation. Mr. Masahiro was a senior executive, and Detective Clark was a lowly public servant. Japanese etiquette required proper recognition of rank.

The detective bowed deeply and slowly, looking down to the floor. "Express my condolences to your employer and his family, and my sincere apologies for our police service being inadequate to protect your son."

Detective Clark remained bent down, forehead at tabletop level. Mr. Sato spoke to the couple in Japanese. When he finished, the detective slowly straightened himself and re-established eye contact with Mr. Kanise.

Masahiro Kanise was impressed with this apology, and he bowed about 15 degrees, eyes down, then spoke a few words, then straightened.

Mr Sato said "Mr. Kanise accepts your gracious sentiments."

The detective bowed again, slightly.

Mr. Kanise nodded.

The detective took a seat at the table. The interpreter remained standing.

"How can I help Mr. Kanise?" said the detective.

"Mr. Kanise asks what was being done to prosecute his son's killer," said Sato. "He is concerned that Mr. Parker is not in jail."

"There would need to be evidence to allow us to apprehend Mr. Parker," the detective stated.

Mr. Sato translated, and Mr. Kanise responded.

"Mr. Kanise expresses the strongest and most urgent desire possible that such evidence be found as quickly as possible."

Detective Clark liked the way this was going. "I have limited resources available to me. I am but a humble public servant."

Mr. Sato translated.

Mr. Kanise responded with a nod, eyes down. It was a mini-bow, the detective realized. Then Mr. Kanise said a few words to the old man. The interpreter did not translate.

The old man began to speak in Japanese. His voice was slow and surprisingly deep for someone of his age. He looked down at the tabletop while he spoke. The interpreter waited patiently for him to finish, trying to remember everything being said.

"*Ojiisan* is grandfather of Kendo and father of Mr. Masahiro Kanise," said Mr. Sato.

The detective nodded toward the old man. "How do you do, Mr. Ojiisan."

"I speak wrongly." The interpreter bowed apologetically to the detective. "*Ojiisan* is Japanese language for grandfather. The mister's name is Kendo Kanise, Senior. He is *samurai*. He is grandfather of Kendo Kanise Junior, victim of Morris Parker."

"How do you do, Mr. Kanise." The detective understood the significance of the *samurai* to be the honorable warrior class, highest stature in Japanese society in ancient times.

The old man nodded in reply.

"In Japan, his grandson was *bosozoku*, member of motorcycle gang. He was sent to study in Canada to break that connection. He was a good grandson."

"I understand." The detective turned his attention to Mr. Sato.

"Mr. Parker has murdered the only son and heir to the family of Kanise. The honor of the family must be recovered. Mr. Kanise seeks your approval for *katakiuchi*."

"I'm sorry, what?"

The interpreter struggled for better words. "The *Ojiisan* does not know the rules in your country. He believes in the ancient customs of Japan. In ancient times, if a family member was murdered, the family could seek *katakiuchi* – revenge."

"Go on."

"Private retribution was allowed if the criminal had not been apprehended by the state. The avenger must apply for permission from the authorities. The town magistrate must register the samurai's name on the list of official avengers and provide a copy to the potential avenger, giving him permission to attack his enemy wherever the culprit might be found."

"The Ojiisan wants me to give him and his family permission to go after Morris Parker."

"The Ojiisan is wise, and he knows these rules may not be legal in Canada." Sato turned to the grandfather and they appeared to discuss what to do next. Sato made a suggestion, and the grandfather nodded slightly.

The interpreter looked at the detective. "Can you help us?"

The detective looked at the old man. "Cut the bullshit." He raised his hand toward Mr. Sato. "Don't translate that."

"I can help in some ways," Clark said cautiously.

Mr. Sato turned to the grandfather and told him in Japanese *it appears he will accept a bribe.* The old man smiled.

The old man spoke two words, and Mr. and Mrs. Kanise stood immediately.

"We look forward to seeing you again, Detective Clark," said the interpreter.

Clark stood and watched them leave. The interpreter closed the door, leaving the detective and the old man alone.

The old man reached into his jacket and pulled out fat a business envelope, and placed it on the table.

The old man slid the envelope across the table. "A wedding gift," he said, in perfect English.

Detective Clark picked up the envelope. The flap was not sealed, so he opened it. Inside was a stack of US $100 dollar bills. The detective estimated the envelope contained $10,000. He closed the flap and placed it on the table, looking at the old man.

"I have a friend who also wishes to marry," the detective said.

With a small smile, the old man pulled a second identical envelope from his pocket and slid it across the table.

The detective stood up, gathered the envelopes, smiled, and bowed.

The old man nodded.

Detective Clark left the room with his unexpected bonus creating a visible bulge in his jacket.

8 – MORRIS, ZIA, CONAN AND TASKMAN

Morris had been working on a business proposal for five hours without a break. Terri had expected him home by 6 PM. At 6:15, he had called to say he would be another 30 minutes. At 7:00 PM, the family started dinner without him. It was now 7:30 PM. Morris was still working.

An email from Zia arrived. The subject was FWD: URGENT TASK TMID12524 VIDEO SURVEILLANCE SYSTEM FOR PARKER RESIDENCE.

Morris opened the message. Zia had forwarded a TaskMan reminder email, adding text to ask about the fire extinguishers.

The text of the reminder consisted of the statement DO NOT REPLY TO THIS EMAIL. DO NOT FORWARD THIS EMAIL. CLICK ON THE LINK BELOW TO READ YOUR REMINDER.

Zia had mishandled the message. Zia had clicked the link, Morris could see, because otherwise he would not have seen anything about fire extinguishers. All Zia was supposed to do was type his question into the TaskMan screen, not send email. The system would do that for him by notifying Morris as soon as Zia had added his question to the TaskMan database. Morris sighed.

Because Morris had marked the task urgent, TaskMan would continue sending hastener emails until Zia recorded a response in the system.

Morris clicked the reply button. "Follow instructions," he typed. "You must click the link in the reminder message. Put your response into the web page that comes up. That way TaskMan knows you have responded. Otherwise, it will keep reminding you by email. Eventually, it will escalate by sending an audio message to your cellphone. Call me at the office."

Morris clicked send and resumed working on his proposal. A few moments later, his desk phone rang.

Morris put on his headset and checked the name on his call display. "Zia, this is Morris."

"In my country, they do not harass you with reminder emails or audio messages to your cellphone. In Iran, the hardliners just send someone to kill you." Zia said E-RON, not like most North Americans would say: I-RAN.

"Which is why you left your country, right, Persian?"

"No." Zia spoke with no discernable accent. "I love to do outdoor camera installations at 30-below zero, like I did last winter." He had been living in Canada since age five.

Zia's family departed Iran after the fall of the Shaw. His father worked as a house painter to put his two sons through university. Now they all worked in a family business selling security solutions that integrated cameras, sensors, computer controllers and sophisticated software. Their systems outperformed more expensive systems from very large companies. They called their enterprise Iron Integrity Security.

"I have been advised to implement a home security system ASAP," said Morris.

"I have read the newspapers. I can see why."

"Do you understand the requirements I sent you?"

"Yes. You need all-around exterior coverage of your residence with cameras and/or sensors, perimeter intruder detection, and offsite video monitoring. I'll have to devise an illumination plan. I will also need to meter your exterior night lighting. I hope you have a site survey for your lot. Do you have streetlights nearby? Can you meet me there tonight, after dark?"

"Sure. Let's meet at 9 PM. I'll have a site plan for you."

"Good. I'll have a look at your landscaping then, and start coming up with camera positions. For your perimeter intruder detection…what kind of alerts do you want?"

"A loudhailer challenge system. You know, 'Intruder Alert!' and maybe a klaxon to scare them off."

"OK. I can also set up an automatic notification to your cellphone. You have a Blackberry with a color display, right? The system will send you a photograph from whatever camera detects the intruder. Camera location and timestamp will show on the screen. There is just one drawback – there will be false alarms, especially at first, until we tune the cameras and sensors. Birds, cats, raindrops on the lens, for example."

"It would not be good to have a lot of loud false alarms – the neighbors will complain."

"We will disable the loudhailer during the tuning phase."

"OK. For arming and disarming – what do you suggest?"

"We could give everyone a swipe card or they could enter an alarm code on a keypad, but we have a new face recognition solution that you might prefer."

"Boyd MacDougall at The Cumberland Arms says you talked him into something that did that. He was very satisfied, by the way."

"Good. The software is still a bit crude, but it's getting better. Basically, each image is analyzed to identify the shape and size of a human. A running cat would be too small. A tree moving in the wind would be too big. If the system thinks it's looking at a human, the software parses out the head area, looking for facial features. If it finds what registers as a face, it frames the face and sends a cropped face shot to the hard drive. If it has seen the face before, it stores the image in the same folder each time. The more face shots, the better it can recognize a repeating face. We can put that snapshot in the image we send to your Blackberry."

"Interesting. Can you make it send only the new faces to my Blackberry? I don't want it to send an alert for each family member or friend."

"We have the source code, but I don't have a programmer available at the moment," said Zia.

"I have one." Morris checked his watch. It was now almost 8:00 PM. Conan could very well still be at his desk. "Let me get my favorite Utility Programmer on the line."

Morris dialed Conan's four-digit office extension.

"I'm sorry," Conan answered, "I'm not at my desk right now."

"Where are you?" Morris asked.

"I'm whitewater paddling."

"I have Zia on the line. We are discussing a new security system for my house. I need to keep out whitewater paddlers. Hold on, I'm going to conference us together."

Morris linked the two calls together.

"Zia, I have Conan," said Morris.

"Yo, dude," said Zia.

"What'sup," said Conan.

"Zia has a camera system that will analyze an image of a potential intruder in my back yard," Morris began. "It zeroes in on the face and crops it out, writing just the face image on the hard drive. It recognizes repeat faces. What I need is to trigger an alarm and send a snapshot of each new face it sees to my Blackberry. Right now it will send every face it sees."

"How does it organize the snapshots on the hard drive?" Conan asked.

"It writes each similar face in the same folder," Zia said. "One folder for each person, basically."

"So each new face will go in a new folder?"

"Yes."

"Sounds easy," said Conan. "I just have to monitor for creation of a new folder, then trigger the alarm and send whatever snapshot appears to Morris' Blackberry."

"Cool," said Zia.

"What happens," Conan asked, "if I drop my drawers and moon your camera?"

"It will snapshot your ass and file it with your face, because they are similar in appearance," said Zia.

"Zing!" said Morris.

"Cool," said Conan. "Ass recognition. But, you know, there is a more reliable system than this."

"What's that?" Zia asked.

"Morris could buy a big dog," said Conan.

"Yes, but in my country, owning a dog is seen by the hardliners as a corrupting influence of decadent Western culture."

"Why do you keep calling it your country?" asked Conan.

"I want to remind you how good you have it here. I decadently own a big Newfoundland Dog. Here in Canada, he can drink from the cleanest toilet water in the world."

"Guys," Morris interjected, "I'm still trying to get past the image of Conan dropping his drawers. Zia, I need you to send source code to Conan. *Do not* send a regular email. Attach it to the TaskMan task, and then submit the task to Conan.

"You don't want me to send it to you?" asked Zia.

"No. You are responsible to return the task to me when, and only when, it is complete. You have to get Conan to contribute. He gets your software, modifies it, and then sends it back to you. Then you install and test it. Then the task is complete. Then you can send it back to me, the task originator."

"You have to be nice to me now, Zia," said Conan.

"I'll send you a nice goat for Christmas," said Zia.

"Any questions?" Morris asked.

"I still think a dog would be better," said Conan.

"OK, lets keep things simple for Conan. Make sure the loudhailer alert has a barking dog option, Zia." Morris reached for the call disconnect button on his headset. "Oh, yes. Make sure you both respond through the TaskMan system. Do not simply forward as email, because it is not secure. TaskMan will encrypt all text comments and attachments."

"Conan! Pay attention. I see you nodding off," said Zia. "You remember from Utility Programming School? *Encrypt* means jumble up the words so they have to be decoded by a person with the right password, get it?"

"Enough," said Morris. "See you at 9 PM, Zia. Thanks for your time, gentlemen."

"9 PM, yes. Iron Integrity Security thanks you for your business. See you in cyberspace, Conan." said Zia.

"Woof," said Conan.

9 – CLARK FAMILY FINANCES

At 9:00 PM, Detective Clark returned from the washroom to find a large envelope on his desk, next to the remaining slice of now-cold pizza he had ordered for his late supper. He opened the envelope. It was from the Crown Attorney's office. It contained a warrant for the arrest of Morris Parker.

He smiled and felt a rush. His pistol swap had worked perfectly.

The envelope also contained a handwritten note. "Attempted murder charge dropped, MacDick released from custody. The Arms wants their computer back. Complaining you did not provide receipt."

Detective Clark had figured out how the software worked and had deleted the video clip of his pistol exchange, so he no longer needed the computer.

The detective's desk was located in an open cubicle next to several others on the floor. Room lighting had gone to a low level because the floor was not normally occupied at this time of day. Detective Clark unlocked and opened his second desk drawer and observed it contained a DVD case. It was there because *someone wanted to be paid*.

The DVD was a well-worn copy of *The Bourne Identity*, his favorite film, still in its cardboard sleeve. He removed the sleeve and snapped the plastic case open. On the side opposite the DVD there was a concealed flap.

Detective Clark looked around to make sure he was not being watched, and counted out $2,000 in $100 bills. He placed them carefully under the flap. Anyone opening the DVD case not knowing about the flap would not see the money. He replaced the case and locked the drawer.

In the morning the case would be gone, until the next payday.

His cellphone rang.

Detective Clark flipped the phone open. "Yes, dear."

"What am I supposed to eat for supper? And when are you coming home?" she demanded.

"I'm working late on a case. I won't be much longer."

"When are you getting paid again?" She was not speaking about his police salary. That came on a regular schedule. She wanted to know when to expect the next irregular amount.

"I told you about the deal I made last night. I'll be getting ten grand in a couple of weeks."

"A couple of weeks? Tell them you want it sooner."

"They don't like to be rushed, sweetie."

"Fucking arrest them, then."

"Look, I got an unexpected little bonus from somebody new. I have four thousand. On me."

"Well, that's more like it. Now I'm really looking forward to seeing you."

"Let's have a party. Just you and me, and Mary J. I'll pick some up on the way home."

"Don't spend it all. We also have bills to pay. The neighbor wants his money. He says you owe him for your share of the fence repair."

"He wants $500. Fuck him. I don't like the color of the stain."

"He says it's the color you agreed. Anyway, you deal with him. What about the other bills? We have the house payment and my surgeon," she paused, thinking. "And other smaller ones."

"We'll pay the mortgage – and for your new tits – but screw the other bills. Your sister – does she still want that loan repaid?"

"She seems to have given up. She stopped calling."

"OK. Anything else?"

"Pick up cigarettes – I'm all out. See you later."

"Bye." He closed his cellphone.

Detective Clark picked up the arrest warrant and headed for the Communications Center on the first floor. He approached the shift supervisor.

"Dispatch a patrol to arrest this suspect." He pointed to Morris' name on the warrant. "His home and office addresses are on the warrant."

10 – DEATH THREAT

Thursday night at 9:00 PM, Morris sat having a late supper while his wife Terri watched him eat and discussed the events of the previous 24 hours. Because Morris was well known in the Ottawa area, the bar shootings had generated intense local media interest. Terri had received numerous phone calls from reporters that day, and their 18-year old daughter Victoria had received comments and questions from classmates. Victoria had programmed the family PVR to record the national news later that night.

Morris had hoped to finish eating before his 9:00 PM meeting with Zia. He had paused to help his 12-year old daughter Catherine with questions on her math homework. He was halfway through his plate of re-heated spaghetti when the doorbell rang.

Catherine answered the door. It was Zia. She invited him in.

"We can reheat this one more time," Terri said to Morris as she quickly put the rest of his meal in the fridge.

Morris regretted seeing his meal disappear. "Come on in," Morris said to Zia. "This is Catherine."

"Hello, Catherine," said Zia.

"Hello," she replied shyly.

"Catherine, it's your turn to dry the dishes," said Terri.

Morris spread the site survey plan for his residence on the kitchen table and the two men got to work immediately, discussing camera and sensor locations. Using a flashlight, Morris led Zia around the outside of the house to confirm the camera locations and viewing angles. Zia took light meter readings and identified additional illumination requirements. They went into the basement to identify a location for the computer controller and digital video recorder – DVR.

The Parker girls had migrated to the basement to watch *America's Next Top Model*. All three Parker daughters were sitting on the sofa and Terri was on a chair. Catherine pushed PAUSE on the remote control as Morris and Zia entered the family room.

A large German Shepherd stood up and began alertly watching Zia.

"Rimshot, sit." Morris pointed to the ground.

The dog obeyed immediately.

"Good dog," said Susan.

"How do you get him to be so calm?" asked Zia.

"He gets constant attention from these three," said Morris. "They take him everywhere – in crowds downtown, swimming at the beach, for a sidewalk run on busy streets – he's used to stimulation."

"As a pup, we dressed him up like a Barbie doll," said Catherine.

"He's seven years old, and completely socialized," said Susan.

"Susan is his favorite. He follows her everywhere," said Morris.

"He listens to all of us," said Victoria. "Even Dad."

"He's the only one who listens to me. I'm at the low end of the pecking order," said Morris. "Rimshot gets way more attention than me."

"That's because he's here all the time, Dad," said Susan. "Not like you."

"Ouch." Morris looked at the television screen. "I thought this show was on Wednesday nights."

"We're watching it on the PVR. Victoria missed it last night," said Terri.

Morris introduced the girls. "Zia, you already met Catherine. This is Susan. She's 22. This one is Victoria, she's 18, and today she's a blond. Yesterday, she was a redhead."

Zia looked at the three beautiful young girls, impressed. "Very nice to meet you, ladies."

"Dad calls this show *America's Next Top Bey-otch*," said Victoria.

"That's because the models are always stabbing each other in the back," said Susan.

"And that makes the show interesting, not like your hair, Victoria," said Catherine.

"Your face is interesting," Victoria said to Catherine. "It's a more ugly version of your butt."

Catherine swatted Victoria on the arm with the remote. "Shut up, Vicky."

"Don't hit me, you little slug," said Victoria. "Do something, Dad!" She glared at Morris.

"They look best in a still photograph," Morris said to Zia. "They were born over a span of ten years. For a while, we had the full spectrum, from diapers to tampons."

"Dad!" exclaimed the three girls, annoyed.

"Come on girls," said Terri. "Let Dad and Zia work. We can watch this later."

"No, please stay. Go on with your show. We won't be long," said Zia.

Morris opened a small closet door beneath the basement stairway. "How about putting the DVR here?"

"Looks good." Zia put his head in the closet to look around. "We should be able to run all the wiring to here – there seems to be quite a few wires here already. I see there are three electrical outlets." Zia pulled out a poster-size white cardboard with a child's drawing on it. "What's this?"

"I did that when I was six," said Victoria. "It's Dad's office when he used to run the business from the basement."

The drawing showed a child's representation of the basement stairway with several stick figures scattered around it. There was a clock on the wall, and three office desks with computer monitors. Each stick figure had a label with a gigantic arrow leading to it. The labels read MOM, CONAN, MARTIN, and DADE.

"I know who Conan is," Zia smiled at the picture.

"Which one is you?" he asked Morris.

"I'm D-A-D-E. Daddy." Morris looked at Victoria. "She even signed it *love Victoria*. Good job."

"That was twelve years ago," Susan said. "Back in those days, Mom used to serve soup to the employees for lunch."

"That closet used to be the computer server room," Terri said. "The wires were for telephones and computers. This whole floor looked like a small cubicle farm. We grew to four employees then we had to move. The business drove me crazy. I'm glad to have the basement back."

The phone rang, and Susan got up to answer it.

"Do any of your daughters work in the family business?" Zia asked Morris.

"From time to time. Susan got her first job as a cleaner with PHL." Morris sighed. "That was back when we had our first office building."

"She had to clean toilets," said Victoria. "I had to help her, and we had to clean the urinals too. One time, we didn't realize that Conan was in one of the stalls, and we were talking really loud about how gross this one urinal was because no one ever flushed it. Then Conan farted, and we were totally embarrassed and ran out of there. It was so funny!"

"I'm so proud of my little princesses," said Terri dryly.

Susan came back in the room. "Dad...." Her voice was breaking. Trembling, she held out the phone to

Morris. She had tears in her eyes. "This man just said he is going to kill you!"

Morris took the phone. "Whoever you are, you son of a bitch…." The line went dead.

Morris took a deep breath and stared up at the ceiling for a moment. All eyes in the room were on him. Catherine sobbed, and Victoria put her arms around her little sister.

"Everything," Morris felt a sudden surge of anger and he choked up. "Everything will be *all right*. Zia will be installing a new video security system and he will be installing security film on our windows to make them shatterproof."

"I have some equipment in my truck." Zia said gently. "I'll start right now." Zia headed up the stairs to get his tools from the truck.

Terri's expression was pure shock. "Who would want to kill you?"

"It's a cheap threat. The Asian kid belonged to a gang of punks. They are obviously pissed and want to scare us."

"What if they go after the kids?" Terri asked.

Morris looked at the girls and didn't know what to say.

"Dad, I know you can protect us." Susan put her arms around her father.

"I will. I promise." Morris embraced Susan. "I will not let any harm come to this family."

The doorbell rang just as Zia was about to step out the front entrance. He opened the door. Two uniformed police officers were standing on the step. Three patrol cars were in front of the house, and a CJOH-TV truck was unloading a reporter and cameraman across the street.

"We have a warrant for the arrest of Morris Parker," said one of the police officers. He nodded to his partner, and the two policemen entered the home.

11 – BEAVIS AND BUTTHEAD IN HOSPITAL

It was Friday morning at the Ottawa Civic Hospital.

"If only you could see this," Daniel Dejeu said to John Paxson, who was lying in the bed next to him.

"If only I could see *anything*..." John replied. His face and head were wrapped in gauze except for his ears, nose and mouth.

"Shh! Listen," Daniel said.

Daniel had been listening with headphones. He removed the plug and the sound became audible.

"...last night. Morris Parker was arrested and taken from his home at approximately 10 PM. The local business icon has been charged with manslaughter in the death of Kendo Kanise, a 19-year old student of Carleton University. Numerous witnesses to the shootout in the East end at The Cumberland Arms on Wednesday described an intense gun battle between Parker and Kanise, with Kanise eventually taking a single bullet to the heart which killed him instantly. Two other unidentified bar patrons were also hurt. More news after this."

A commercial started to play. Daniel replaced the headphone jack and killed the audio.

"I wish I could see the damn screen." said John.

"It was Parker in cuffs. He went from his house into a police car."

"Could you tell where he lives?"

"No, but we'll find out."

"It's payback time. Any family members in the picture?"

"No." Daniel took a sip of coffee and swallowed with a grimace. His neck wound made it painful to swallow. His left leg ached like hell. He had not slept well.

John's cuts and burns had not bothered him much –
John had snored like a sawmill. It was lucky for John that
Daniel could barely move, otherwise Daniel would have
gone over to John's bed at some point during the long
night and strangled him.

"Care for some coffee, John?" said Daniel.

"I never want to see another pot of coffee!"

Daniel laughed, and then grimaced again.

"I would love a nice donut, though. I think that
fuckin' cop at the door probably has some of your
favorite – Boston creams, right? Too bad you can't eat
solid food."

The door opened and Detective Clark entered the
hospital room. He placed a large briefcase on the floor.

"Which one is stupider – Beavis or Butthead? I told
you fucking idiots not to bring ID when you went in,"
said the detective. "MacDick had his driver's license on
him."

"I told him that," said Daniel.

"Did you tell him to pick a fight with somebody
easy?" Clark folded his arms, waiting. "Or did you tell
him…."

"How the fuck were we supposed to know three
fucking ninjas were going to jump us?" Daniel
interrupted.

"Is he alone?" asked John, adjusting his bandages,
wishing he could see.

"No," Daniel said sarcastically. "The Tonight Show
with David Letterman is here too. Of course he's alone."

"Letterman does *Late Night*, not the *Tonight Show*,
idiot," said Detective Clark as he pulled a chair between
the two beds and sat down. "This was supposed to be a
simple side job. Now van Praag is pissed. The whole
operation is in trouble if I can't get you two back on the
street."

"You were OK with this idea. It was some extra cash." Daniel said bitterly. "We're the ones in hospital. You were getting a cut for doing nothing."

"Nothing!" The detective stood up. "I was in the Communication Center listening for the The Arms 9-1-1 to come in, you ass. I was your goddam guardian angel. If it hadn't been for me, Martin would have been caught too. He was waiting out back. He'd still be waiting if I hadn't sent him a text message to take off. You guys fucked up beyond…."

"What's done is done," John yelled. "Fuckit, who the hell expected three middle-aged washed-up army guys to put up such a fight? The plan would have worked if not for them."

Detective Clark gritted his teeth. "Couldn't one of you at least have shown MacDick how to use a *safety catch*?"

"Don't you think we've thought about that a few times by now? Forget about it," said John. "We fucked up. We can fix it. And some day we'll have payback."

The three men stayed silent for a moment.

"How many more people do we need to ship?" asked Detective Clark.

"Two. Two fucking bums to go," said John. "We're lucky there are two subjects in Winnipeg. That took the pressure off us for two weeks. Mohamed found a couple of natives who won't be missed."

"Have you identified our two subjects?" asked the detective.

"Yes," said John. "But we'll need to choose a new escort. And I need to get these fucking bandages off."

"When does van Praag want the next subject?" asked the detective.

"He booked a flight for two weeks from now." John paused to think. "We have two Air Canada tickets, Ottawa to Winnipeg. We'll have to change Kendo's ticket."

"Can you send Daniel as escort?" Detective Clark asked John.

"I was playing the social worker," said Daniel. "I told the first subject there would be another street person with him, as usual."

"It wouldn't work to use Daniel. We'd have to change our story too much. Fuck, this bandage is annoying." John scratched his head through the bandage. "The subject would think something was fishy. He probably wouldn't get on the plane."

"Send me," said the detective. "I'll play the street person. I can win the guy's confidence. Put me on the flight."

"Yeah, we can send David," said Daniel.

"Yeah, OK." John's mood improved. "You'll have to do this one in two weeks, and the final one will be the week after. The last subject will be used to confirm the final results. After that, they close the camp."

"How much did you pay the kid for each trip?" asked the detective.

"Two grand," John said.

"I'll need triple," the detective said.

"That comes out of our cut!" said Daniel.

"I don't think we have much choice," said John.

"Right. You don't." Detective Clark put his briefcase on Daniel's bed, bumping Daniel's leg, causing another grimace of pain. "You guys are scheduled for one more day of hospital time, then you're being transferred to the jail. I'm coming back here tonight to deliver a transfer order. You're going to be moved at 8 AM tomorrow. The night shift here starts at midnight, and there is only one cop on guard duty between midnight and 6 AM. I'm going to buy him a coffee. It will be spiked with a sedative. He should be asleep within about an hour – that will be about 1 AM."

The detective opened the briefcase and pulled out two sets of street clothing. "Keep these hidden until then. And don't get caught in my town again."

12 – MORRIS IN JAIL

It was early Friday morning. Liam entered the visiting room of the City of Ottawa Police Station's Temporary Custody and Detention area with his briefcase in one hand and two morning papers in the other. Both papers were running front-page photos of Morris in handcuffs being arrested in front of his home.

"Terri will not be happy." Morris sat on his bunk, looking over the pages. "Her geraniums don't look too good."

"Are you serious?" Liam was incredulous.

Morris looked at the worried look on Liam's face. "Would you prefer I get all worked up in a knot about this situation?"

"I would prefer you understand the seriousness of your position."

"I see the seriousness. I also have you working on it. Until I get new information to process, there are no decisions I can make and nothing else I have to figure out. Worrying won't help a thing. Humor is better."

"So you think the geraniums are important."

"They're the most important new information I have available. She works hard on that garden. We both want our house to look good. It's not exactly a palace, but it's our part of the neighborhood. I think one of the bloody cameramen must have stepped on the flowers. Let's sue."

"OK, OK. What say we go for $20? Maybe we could get $30 for pain and suffering."

"Now you're getting the idea. Humor." Morris looked up from the paper at his lawyer friend. "It's important to keep cool, and especially important to appear cool. Nobody likes a boss who panics. It spreads. It's bloody bad for group morale. Humor is better than panic."

Liam pulled a notepad from his briefcase. He consulted his scribbled text. "The Crown Attorney has informally shared the key evidence against you. He has a bullet extracted from a ceiling beam. From your documented shooting position, the angle of the bullet hole proves you took a shot at Mr. Innes MacDick. Mr. MacDick claims that was the first shot fired."

"Impossible. I counted my shots." Morris closed his eyes. "I had my back to that guy. He tried to shoot me first, according to Ed."

"That would be Ed's word against his."

"I remember the sight picture for each of my targets."

"How can you do that?"

"I trained so many years in the army. I was a small arms champion shot with the pistol, assault rifle and sniper rifle. During one particular match I accidentally loaded two rounds too few in my magazine. I lost out on a championship. Ever since then, I counted my shots. Even though I have not fired a small arm for years, it comes to me as a reflex. It's the same with sight picture. I know where I placed the foresight for each shot. During a rapid fire shoot with a short range weapon like the pistol, I'm always looking for the effect of each shot, meaning where did the bullet strike versus where the sight has to be pointed to get a hit. When I was shooting at the kid, I was watching the splinters fly from behind him. The sights were off to the left. I had to compensate by aiming to the right to get a hit. I remember that sight picture."

"Very impressive, but a jury would think you are lying to protect yourself."

"What about the other witnesses?"

"Jacques and Ed made statements that corroborate your version of events, but they are your friends and they participated in the fight. The Crown Attorney will discredit them. Not only that, he has three witnesses that say you fired the first shot."

"MacDick and two guys who have not been identified, right?" Morris thought for a moment. "Somebody must have planted that bullet."

"Physical evidence like that is hard to discredit. We only need to establish reasonable doubt, but you realize we have an uphill battle to do that in this case?"

"Why?"

"A ballistic test is as reliable as a fingerprint. The bullet came from the gun you used. I would have to discredit the police evidence-handling procedures. I would have to show how the scene could have been compromised and someone deliberately planted that bullet. They will put a lineup of professional crime scene investigators who will swear to the integrity of the evidence from collection in the field through each step of analysis in their lab. They would establish a paper trail that would be very hard to discredit."

"How about some good news?" Morris stood up. "Got any?"

"No." Liam flipped to another page in his notepad. "As a result of the publicity, your potential partners in the property purchase have bowed out. Without them, or somebody like them, that deal is dead. The press is having a field day and your reputation is suffering. PHL stock fell 20% this morning. And that charity event you were supposed to speak at, well the coordinator called Jill and cancelled."

"It's time to worry for a bit." Morris began to pace.

After a few moments, Morris stopped. "I'll make a public statement."

"I would recommend against it. We should simply state you are not guilty. The less said the better."

"Every fucking crook on the planet goes *no comment*. I'll be judged guilty by the market."

"Better the market than the courts. The market won't put you in jail for 20 years."

"No, it could put me out of business *forever*. Tell me about your legal strategy."

"We get their detailed evidence. We judge the jury situation. If we go for a jury trial and there is a reasonable amount of public sympathy for you, or if the public forgets about you, we may be in a good position to plea-bargain."

"Plea-bargain? We go through months of bureaucratic legalistic crap, suffering business damage each and every goddam day, and then I accept a guilty plea? That's not much of a bargain."

"Something might go our way during the process."

"If we bargain, we do it from a position of strength. I do not intend to sit quietly while some bureaucratic weasel takes potshots at me from the safety of his hole."

"You talk as if this is just an administrative process...."

"It's a human process. The Crown Attorney is doing a public servant job and gets his paycheck whether he performs competently or not. You know that's not the way things work for us. If we have to fight, I'm going to fight my way. Our best defense is a good offence. I'm going to put those assholes to shame in public."

"I would have to advise against that approach."

"I appreciate that you are trying to protect me. You could be right – I might end up in jail. But I would rather go down fighting than take myself down."

"Alright. Give your version of events in public. Let's put something together now...."

"Not just that. I intend to go after the Crown Attorney. He has accepted fabricated evidence. That's the truth. He made a mistake. He's made others. Get me a list of his missed prosecutions and I'll start with that. He's wasting tax dollars because he's going after the wrong man."

"I know him. We went to the same school. He gave me this early stuff as a favor."

Morris stopped his pacing and turned to face Liam. "I need you to burn that bridge. If he never does you another favor, what would be the impact?"

"No significant impact."

"This guy took a swing at me. I don't want this fight but I intend to take a few swings and put him back on his heels. We can't just take this lying down."

"All right. We do it your way. Just let me suggest some of the timing. I'll try to get you in front of a justice of the peace today; otherwise you'll be in here for the weekend. I expect he will set your cash bail pretty high, and you will have to surrender your passport. The court will also give you some restrictions."

"What kind of restrictions?"

"Where you can live, how often and where you have to report. You will also be prohibited from touching any firearms."

"Any restriction against shooting off my mouth?"

"Nobody has ever restricted your ability to do that, Morris. If we get bail, I think you should make a public statement on the front steps, right here. I'll call a couple of reporters, and you do all the talking."

"OK, let's do it."

"There's just one more thing," Liam reached into his briefcase and pulled out Statement of Claim. "The Kanise Family hired an Ottawa litigator. You are being sued for wrongful death in the amount of ten million dollars."

PART TWO – ON THE DEFENSIVE

13 – PORK ROAST

The Northern Ontario black flies could not get at him, thanks to his equipment, but Mohamed Ziad wished he could wipe the sweat from his forehead that made his eyes sting. He could not reach inside the protective hood of his bio-suit.

Mohamed had a lot of work to do, and limited time in which to do it. The air supply on his back would last only 20 minutes.

Mohamed was wearing a Level "A" vapor-tight HAZMAT suit, which provided him the highest level of protection against direct and airborne chemical and biological contact. The air tank on his back maintained an overpressure in the suit to keep out intruding liquids or gasses. The suit had a multilayer design that was great for protection, but not good for flexibility or mobility. It also made the wearer very hot and uncomfortable, especially on a warm summer afternoon such as this.

Mohamed trusted none of his underlings with this task. The consequence of error was too high. He had trained one of his men, Jaleel, on proper suit use and safe carcass disposal procedures, but the man had mishandled the air lock procedure and had contaminated the clean zone between the doors. The mistake had cost him his life.

Before putting on the suit, Mohamed made sure the camp's 45-kilowatt heavy-duty propane generator was running smoothly. It provided electric power to the camp's operational facilities, including the isolation cabins, the laboratory, the barn, the 'ice cream truck,' and the furnace hut.

The isolation cabins consisted of two specially modified sea containers. Mohamed double-checked his air supply gauge, and then he opened the outer door to

Isolation Cabin Number One and entered the air lock. He closed the outer door behind him. Then he activated the compressor, and heard a short hiss and felt his ears pop. Now he was able to open the inner door.

Improper inner door operation was the misstep that had cost Jaleel his life. Jaleel had opened the door without first ensuring the airlock pressure was higher than the inner chamber pressure. He had forced the door open against the higher inner chamber pressure, and contaminated air moved from the chamber into the airlock rather than clean air moving in the opposite direction. Then Jaleel had been unable to disinfect the airlock and his HAZMAT suit because the decontamination sprayer had malfunctioned – he had forgotten to check it first. Mohamed had no choice but to leave Jaleel locked in the chamber while the sprayer was repaired as quickly as possible, but Jaleel ran out of air.

Rather than breathe the infected air, and then die slowly from the disease, Jaleel shot himself. Trained as a suicide bomber, Jaleel had proven he was a true believer. He told Mohamed they would meet again in Paradise.

Mohamed carefully checked that refrigeration mode had been set, and that the chamber had been sufficiently chilled to be safe. The animal chamber had been chilled to just above freezing in order to immobilize the germ. Mohamed took a cautious breath and entered the chamber space.

In the dimly lit chamber, there were six individual animal stalls. Mohamed could see one live pig lying huddled in its straw, shivering. It was very sick – barely alive. Now was the time to seal it up, before it died. Dead, it would release infected bodily fluids into the chamber, making Mohamed's cleanup job even more difficult.

The pig was a young adolescent, weighing about 50 pounds. The pigs were brought to the camp as piglets of about 30 pounds, and grew fast. The average weight gain was a pound per day, but that growth occurred before

each pig was infected. After infection, there was no
appetite, for either pig or human subjects. The average
post-infection life expectancy, for both species, was four
days.

Mohamed pulled a bag that had been soaked in
germicide from a pouch in his HAZMAT suit. It was a
body bag designed for a human child. The bag would
keep the fluids inside. He disconnected the pig's
biosensor rig, and maneuvered the helpless animal into
the body bag and zipped it shut. The animal would now
die of suffocation, rather than from the germ. Death from
the germ was extremely messy, because the final stages
of the disease caused the skin to fall off in chunks, and
blood flowed freely.

Mohamed carried the pig in the body bag into the air
lock, carefully following the proper procedure. Once
sealed inside, he activated the decontamination sprayers,
and his HAZMAT suit, the pig in the body bag, and the
inner chamber were sprayed with a coating of germicide
disinfectant.

He exited the airlock and brought the pig to the ice
cream truck, and placed it on the floor inside, across from
about a dozen stacked frozen pig carcasses, varying in
weight from 40-50 pounds. The ice cream truck, as they
called it, needed a lot of electric power to maintain
temperatures well below freezing, and to run the one
piece of equipment it held: a six-foot high electric
butcher's band saw. Keeping power running reliably to
this truck worried Mohamed above all else. If the
carcasses thawed, the germ could escape easily.

The frozen pigs were ready for the next step. The
latest pig would take a couple of hours to freeze up, so it
would have to wait until the next batch. It was not safe to
place a warm pig in the furnace. The furnace was not
pressurized or isolated. Only when a carcass was fully
frozen was it safe to expose the infected flesh to the
outside air. The germ must go from frozen state to high

temperature vaporization or combustion in a single step, otherwise accidental release of the live germ into the atmosphere could occur.

Mohamed loaded four frozen pigs in body bags onto a cart. "Time for a pork roast," he said to himself. It took him three trips to transport the pigs to the furnace hut.

The hut measured about the size of a single-car garage, at double the ceiling height. Inside, the industrial propane box furnace was mounted waist-high off a concrete floor. It had a venting chimney leading to the roof. The furnace interior was box-shaped, with dimensions of forty inches on each side. On one side, it had an electric door that opened vertically like a guillotine blade. The door was currently closed, because the furnace was hot, holding steady at a temperature of 1500 degrees Fahrenheit.

Mohamed checked his air supply. Only four minutes of air remained. He quickly opened the furnace door, feeling a blast of heat. Blinking sweat from his eyes and breathing hard, Mohamed stacked the eleven carcasses in the furnace chamber, hearing pig flesh searing as it came in contact with the hot metal of the furnace floor. He closed the door and checked that the chamber was venting properly. Fluids were boiling off quickly and vapors needed to escape. Intense heat killed the germ, so the small steam cloud pouring into the night sky was now harmless.

Mohamed closed the furnace hut door and then removed his HAZMAT helmet and gloves. He could now smell the scent of barbequed pork. He was finally able to wipe the sweat from his brow.

Satisfied, Mohamed thought about the purging effect of the fire. The scent of the cooking meat was appealing, but only to a non-believer, he had been taught. Pigs are carrier of diseases to man, making them unfit for human consumption. Pigs will eat everything, even human excreta.

Then Mohamed thought about his mission. For all this effort, for all his time spent living in the western world, putting up with the arrogance and greed of its people, Mohamed knew he would be rewarded. When he returned home, he would be a conquering hero. He would live a long, rich life, treated like a king.

He thought of Jaleel. The man had been an outraged young Muslim. His mother and brother had been killed as the collateral damage of an Israeli targeted assassination, and he had been easily recruited into a martyrdom cell. He had showed dedication and determination – and intelligence – so he was picked for this operation and given, at great expense, the identity papers and training to travel into Canada without detection.

Jaleel's early martyrdom as a result of the contamination accident had been costly to Mohamed. A replacement had finally been imported only recently, and it had been forbidden to use any of the other young men awaiting martyrdom for any similar risky tasks. That meant Mohamed had to clean the isolation chambers himself.

Mohamed had no pressing desire to become a martyr himself. He could wait until he had lived a full life before achieving paradise. His 72 virgins could wait; twenty earthly wives would be satisfactory.

Looking upward at the starry night, he though of Mohamed Atta, pilot of the first plane to hit the World Trade Center on September 11th. Atta had not been part of a plan to kill infidels while keeping himself alive. Mohamed Ziad had such a plan.

Still, Atta had been presented the opportunity to become an historic figure, and had taken it. Mohamed Atta, with one deed, made history far surpassing the level of significance attainable by most men. That would not be such a bad fate, should the Ziad plan require it, Mohamed thought.

Some day they would meet in Paradise, and Atta
would say his own efforts in killing a few thousand
infidels was a humble contribution in comparison to the
billions of people that Mohamed Ziad killed with his
germ.

Mohamed looked at the complex isolation chamber
and thought about the equipment and procedures they
were using to develop the germ. Using pigs and human
subjects, there was no difficulty in developing a deadly
new germ at all. Each time the infection passed from
human to pig back to human, it mutated into a more
deadly strain. The hard part was in making sure the germ
was not too deadly, as van Praag wanted.

Van Praag wanted to kill no more than a few hundred
million people worldwide. He was motivated by profit.

Without the need to continually test and manage the
strain, the only equipment needed was HAZMAT
protection to ensure the developers did not kill
themselves. The specially configured isolation chambers,
biosensor arrays, and complex computers were not
needed. A large barn in a desert area would suffice. The
air in the barn could be kept humid with simple
equipment. The germ could not live in an arid climate, so
it could not escape by accident.

The germ could have been developed back home,
Mohamed thought, much more easily than here in
Northern Ontario.

Mohamed's favorite part of the attack on the World
Trade Center was the fact that lowly knives and box
cutters had been the only weapons needed.

Mohamed opened the top of his HAZMAT suit, then
went down on one knee, and pulled out a large, sharp,
shiny knife from a sheath under his shirt. He looked up,
thinking about words Atta had written in his will. He held
his knife up to the heavens, and spoke slowly. "You must
make your knife sharp and you must not discomfort your
animal during the slaughter."

14 – BBQ AND FIREBOMBING

It was warm and sunny Saturday afternoon. Morris had been released from detention late Friday, and Liam had organized a press scrum on the steps of the police station as planned. After that, Morris went directly home without bothering to check his messages. He and Terri drank a bottle of wine and made love.

Morris had caught up with his messages that morning, and now Morris flipped steaks on the back deck BBQ and chatted with his friend Alex.

"So why are we in Afghanistan, again, Mr. James?" Morris was in the mood for a bit of a debate.

"Because it's the right thing for Canada to do. We are helping build schools and roads. We are fighting the Taliban and helping women's rights. The Taliban don't even want to let young girls have any education."

"And these objectives can be achieved at the pointy end of a gun, of course."

"Damn right. Anybody over there with a gun should be shot. Except for our guys, of course."

"The true blue conservative view." Morris pulled out his Blackberry. "I came across this article a few weeks ago and I've been meaning to show it to you. Here it is…"

Morris read from his Blackberry display. "There is a new draft law on the personal status of Shiite women, which was recently approved by both chambers of the Afghan Parliament. It places severe restrictions on women's freedom of movement, denying them the right to leave their homes except for a 'legitimate purpose.' It requires women to submit to the sexual desires of their husbands, thus legitimizing *marital rape*."

"The Afghan Parliament wants that law?"

"Yes. The Western World is officially appalled. I guess we should send soldiers into those Afghan parliamentary chambers, eh? Democracy Enforcement Squads – vote for things that don't offend us or we will shoot you."

"I assume you have a better solution?"

"No, but Terri does."

Alex noticed a steak was starting to flare. "Don't burn that steak."

"Terri thinks we should fly the women out of there." Morris moved the meat away from the flare-up. "Leave the abusive men without the ability to reproduce. It might work."

"Ha! That's thinking outside the box. Time for another beer." Alex reached into the cooler and pulled out two bottles of Budweiser. He removed the twist tops and gave a bottle to Morris.

"Support our troops," said Alex as he raised his bottle.

"Here's to the Canadian Soldier," said Morris. "I support the Canadian Soldier. I'm no longer in favor of having our army in Afghanistan."

"Why not?" asked Alex.

"They taught me one of the first principles of war is to select and maintain the aim. The aim over there has been changed more often than a poopy diaper. Enough of this Afghan misadventure. The Canadian soldier doesn't have to prove a fuckin' thing to anyone. We did that at Vimy."

"What about the war on terror?" asked Alex.

"Take our soldiers out of there and you take away the 'repel the invading infidels' motivator."

"Hold on – back the tank up! Where would you rather fight these people – over there, or over here?"

Morris smiled. "I'll be happy to answer that. First, tell me what weapons we need to fight them over here."

"The last time they used nineteen suicidal maniacs to pilot commercial airliners full of explosive jet fuel into occupied buildings! What would you like to fight that with?"

"Those suicidal maniacs didn't have an arsenal of commercial airliners. They had much simpler weapons. They had knives and box cutters."

"Box cutters, plus nineteen men with a fucked belief system, plus flight training, plus financing…."

"All of which could have been defeated with a lock on the control cabin."

"OK, the control cabins are locked now. But there are other men with the same fucked belief system still out there."

"So we better figure out where to put the next lock. And we are not in the process of doing that by putting soldiers over *there*. We have to do that by spending our money on more police and intelligence folks over *here*."

"Hmm. That might mean extra hiring and promotion opportunities," said Alex. "But there is one serious flaw with that position."

"What's that?" Morris asked.

"You are almost out of beer."

At that moment, Terri came out on the deck. "Morris, the radio is reporting those two guys you put in hospital have escaped!"

Morris and Alex looked at each other.

"That's good, and that's bad," Morris said.

"How is that good?" Terri demanded.

"Good because the Crown Attorney loses two witnesses that were up against us." Morris took a swig of beer. "And bad because there are two more guys out there with the motivation to kill me."

"We need police protection!"

"I don't think I'll get it, dear, I'm charged with manslaughter."

"Well, at least you should get whatever information the cops have on these guys," Terri said.

"I can try asking, but I don't expect much
cooperation. I launched a bit of a counter-attack against
the Crown Attorney's office yesterday in a media scrum
on my way out of jail. I basically called him
incompetent."

"Morris!" Terri scolded. "Why do you always have to
do things that way?"

"This guy is a bureaucrat, Terri," Morris said. "I'm
meeting him head on. I have no time for bureaucrats."

"Funny you should choose to live in Ottawa..." Sarah
James stuck her head out of the house. "How much longer
for the steaks? Things are ready in here."

Conversation and debate continued during dinner and
beyond, until well after dark. After the meal, the group
gathered in the basement to watch the news events that
had been recorded on the PVR.

There was a report from Friday morning showing the
Kanise parents and grandfather making a statement
through Mr. Sato, their interpreter. They were standing in
front of their son's apartment. A photo of their son,
dressed in a high-school graduation outfit, was displayed.
Detective Clark was visible in the background. The
Kanise message was their son had died and they expected
justice to be served. The report replayed the scene of
Morris being arrested Thursday night at home.

Then came the scene of Morris leaving the jail.
Morris was taking questions from a crowd of reporters.

"I have been advised by my lawyer I should be
making no comment," Morris was saying. "So I want you
all to know that Liam Latham is a very good lawyer and
if I go to jail for anything I tell you folks here, it's not his
fault."

That line got a laugh.

"I am innocent of this charge. This charge should not
have been laid against me. This charge is based on bad
evidence, and it is the result of a bad decision by the
Crown Attorney, Mr. Clive Adam. I would like to remind

you Mr. Adam was responsible for charging the Mayor of Ottawa with influence peddling last year. That decision was also based on faulty evidence and led to a costly and pointless trial, which resulted in a complete exoneration of the mayor."

"Are you saying that you are being wrongly prosecuted?" a reporter interrupted.

"That's exactly what I am saying," said Morris.

"Do you believe Mr. Adam has something against you personally?" asked the reporter.

"Mr. Adam and I have never crossed paths before."

"Why do you believe you are being prosecuted?" asked another reporter.

"I believe Mr. Adam, for reasons known to him, has made a mistake. It is interesting to note that it is in the public record that Mr. Adam, two years ago, got into a protracted small claims battle against his neighbor over a property issue. That issue was finally settled for a sum of less than two hundred dollars."

"Where did you get that information?" the reporter asked.

"From the court records. The file is about this thick." Morris held his thumb and forefinger about six inches apart.

At that moment, Liam stepped in. "I'm sorry, but we have an engagement. We have to go now."

The report ended and the station went to commercial. Morris stopped the PVR playback.

"Wow." Alex was impressed. "You went right for that guy's throat."

"Yeah, Liam dug up some pretty good stuff for me. I was a bit unfair, but tough shit. The property file was thick because the neighbor had flooded it with statements from every family member, mortgage documents, bank statements, cancelled checks and everything but the phone book in an attempt to cloud the issue."

"But Mr. Adam is unlikely to get a chance to straighten out that perception now that it's in public," said Alex, sounding impressed. "The way the story comes across is the Crown Attorney is willing to waste public resources and court time, and he is lousy at his job. You outmaneuvered him with a frontal assault."

"For now." Morris felt his Blackberry vibrate, so he drew it quickly from his holster to check for a message. One of Zia's new security cameras had caught an image of an intruder in the back yard.

"Alex, there is somebody in the back yard!" Morris started quickly up the stairs.

Alex followed Morris up the stairs, followed closely by Rimshot.

A second image arrived as Morris headed for the back door. "He's got a bottle in his hand. Shit! Everybody out of the basement! NOW! Somebody bring a fire extinguisher!"

The second image showed the intruder igniting a Molotov cocktail. Morris flung the patio door open, shouting as he dashed through the doorway "HEY! YOU!"

At that instant came the sound of the breaking bottle, followed by a whoosh as fire from the gasoline it had held ignited the outside of the kitchen picture window. Thankfully, the window had not shattered, so no flames were in the kitchen, but they were spreading onto the wooden deck below.

Rimshot burst through the open door, snarling and barking.

Morris had startled the intruder mid-throw, spoiling his aim. The intruder turned and ran toward the back fence, which was overgrown with a hedge, Rimshot right behind him. In the dark, the intruder had forgotten where the gate was located, and headed in the wrong direction. He was scrambling for an escape route.

Morris grabbed the BBQ fire extinguisher and pulled the pin. Then he tossed the extinguisher to Alex just as he came through the doorway. "You do this!"

Morris jumped off the deck and dashed after the intruder, who was now heading toward the locked gate. Rimshot slammed into him from behind, almost bringing him down. The intruder jumped on the six-foot high chain-link fence and threw himself over just as Morris grabbed him by the collar.

It felt to Morris like his arm would be jerked out of its socket. The weight of the intruder dragged Morris against the top bar, slamming his armpit painfully. The intruder struggled to escape, but Morris had a tight grip on the collar.

The intruder was wearing a balaclava to hide his face. Morris reached over with his other arm and yanked it off. Morris still could not get a good look at the intruder. The intruder was looking away from Morris, desperate to hide his face. It was dark, but Morris saw he had long shaggy hair.

Rimshot's ferocious and frenzied barking was inches from the man's face. Dog spittle was hitting his face through the fence.

"Scared, punk?!" As Morris felt his grip loosen, he reached over the fence and grabbed a handful of hair. Morris released the collar and yanked the hair. The punk's head smashed against the fence bar and a large, bloody clump of hair came free. The punk screamed in pain, fell, got up, and ran down the pedestrian path that led into the ravine.

Morris looked back at the house. Flames lit the yard. Alex was blasting them with the CO2 extinguisher. Terri joined with another extinguisher, and they put the fire out in seconds.

Morris looked at the bloody scalp in his hand. A feeling of intense rage overcame him.

Meanwhile, down the path, the punk caught up with his driver, who had been waiting in the woods. As they ran, they heard a chilling, animal sound that made them run even faster.

Back at the house, Morris let out a long, loud, lion-like roar. He held the punk's bloody scalp above his head, like a victorious apache warrior. Eyes bulging with fury, Morris screamed into the night: "NEXT TIME, I – WILL – *KILL – YOU!*"

Moments later, the punks reached their car on the other side of the ravine. They scrambled in quickly.

"What happened – your head is all bloody!" asked the driver as he fumbled for his keys.

The intruder was gasping for air. "That guy is a maniac!"

The car started and sped away from the curb, tires squealing.

"Man," said the driver. "You stink like shit."

The intruder sniffed and looked down. He had crapped his pants.

15 – MOHAMED AND QAMAR

It took Mohamed two hours to clean the animal side of Isolation Cabin One. He had to replenish his backpack air supply four times during that period, taking a five-minute rest at each tank change. With his first tank, he had bagged the straw and leftover food, then spread silica gel litter into the pig shit to dry it up. He also disassembled the feed trough so it would fit in the furnace. With his second tank, he shoveled the dried shit into burn bags and then blasted the interior chamber surfaces with a high-power electric pressure washer. With his third tank, he sprayed germicide through an applicator wand onto the feed trough, interior surfaces, and all the burn bags. He used his final tank to carry the bagged straw, food, and shit to the furnace where he burned it.

The rest of his work could be done without the HAZMAT suit. Before removing it, Mohamed sprayed it with germicide, and then rinsed under the outdoor shower.

Back in the freshly-cleaned isolation cabin, he placed fresh straw on the floor and fresh grain in a new feed trough. Isolation Cabin One was now ready for new animals. Two days later, according to the schedule, six live young pigs would be placed inside.

Mohamed brought his HAZMAT suit to the storage room in the laboratory trailer, a specially fitted 24-foot construction trailer, then he headed toward the pig barn.

The second 24-foot trailer on the campsite was a living space. It provided sleeping Accommodation for a total of six men, including Mohamed. During the daytime, its primary purpose was to hold prayer meetings and discussions. Mohamed did not often attend those sessions. His purpose was to run the camp, not train the young men. That was the job of Qamar, the cell leader.

"Mohamed," Qamar called out as he crossed the dark compound to catch up with Mohamed.

"Yes Qamar." Mohamed stopped to speak.

"I have a favor to ask. We need more video tapes."

"Why?"

"The ones we have are wearing out."

"I am not inclined to give you more tapes."

"We need additional copies of the video testaments of the martyrs from past operations. There are scenes of family celebrations after their missions, sermons in mosques, and graffiti on the walls in the martyr's neighborhoods in praise of their heroism."

"These tapes will be viewed here at the camp only?"

"Yes. We have only a single tape that will eventually be copied for distribution – after the operation has been successfully completed. I know you are tense about security, should a testament of one of our living martyrs get out. But Hesam was not serious when he expressed the desire to mail an advance tape to his mother…."

"If I relax my vigilance and we are detected, years of work will be lost and we will be killed or jailed for the rest of our lives."

"I am vigilant also. I agree with your rule to prohibit beards, and I have argued your case for security. But the men need to maintain their motivation."

"The poster is not enough?" Mohamed said dryly, referring to a drawing hung on the wall of the sleeping accommodation: green birds flying in a purple sky, a symbol of the Palestinian suicide bombers.

"Please."

"My mission is to run this camp. There must be no compromise of security. Hesam was asleep at his post the other night."

"I have spoken with him. He has apologized for his sin. I have made him perform additional recitations and pray all night."

Mohamed turned and resumed walking. "Give me your old tapes and I will replace them with new blanks."

"Thank-you." Qamar kept beside him. "There is one other thing. May I ask you about Jaleel?"

"What do you need to ask?"

"The men want to know more about your final conversation with him."

"I told you enough. He died with a smile. His final words were Allah is great, all praise to Him."

"But there was a debate before that. You had to convince him to shoot himself."

"There was no debate. There was only a discussion. I did not have to convince him. He made the choice himself."

"The men have it in their heads that Jaleel was fearful. They think you were asking him to commit suicide, which is forbidden in Islam!"

Mohamed stopped and faced Qamar. "I had to interpret his situation for him. I did not describe it as suicide."

"Tell me the whole story. None of us were present. You are the only witness, and you have not told us everything."

"Fine. I told him he would have to remove his helmet so as not to damage it. I said upon his first breath of the infected air, it was like the first drop of blood shed by a martyr during jihad. His sins are washed away instantaneously – so Allah would forgive Jaleel shooting himself in the head. He had two choices: die now by his own hand, or die later of the infection. He could not exit and spread the infection, and if he stayed in the pig chamber, he would contaminate the experiment. This was true."

"Jaleel had not made his will or his testament. He would have asked to do that. You have not told us of that discussion."

"No, I have not." Mohamed paused. "You are correct, he did ask for the opportunity to make his testament, but there was little time because he wanted to complete his martyrdom before you or your men returned. I found the video camera and told him to speak his testament. I could not see him inside the sea container, but I could record his voice through the intercom."

"Then why have we not heard his testament?"

"Because there was no tape in the camera."

"You made Jaleel believe he was being taped."

"Yes. I did it for his comfort. I deceived him. I am not proud of that. I hope to be forgiven for that sin one day."

"I understand. You should know something, then. Jaleel's fear was not about death. He did not lack the confidence to press the trigger. You saw him do that without hesitation. He did it with awe and joy. His anxiety came from his heart's wish to accomplish his task in the correct way and be propelled into the presence of Allah."

Mohamed listened intently. "He had not been prepared to die."

"Not at that moment, not in that exact way. It was an accident of the risk we are taking in our work."

"It was my fault. I am responsible for the camp and its security."

"This event has been bothering you. It was in Allah's hands. Jaleel needed reassurance that his death would have significance. Our germ is more complex than a sacred explosion. He needed to see that his death was meaningful and correctly placed on the path of helping to release our germ as an effective weapon."

Mohamed looked at the ground, picturing Jaleel's face as he struggled with the consequences of his error.

He did not want his death to be meaningless, but he had
not said that to Mohamed.

"Because the accident happened quickly, Jaleel was
denied the opportunity to prepare himself. You did the
right thing. You helped him prepare. Once he understood
the purpose of his death, as my men do, he would have
been properly in awe of the situation."

Mohamed choked up. "Thank you for telling me this."

Qatar embraced him. "I would have done the same
thing, my brother. Remember, the outcome is always in
the hands of Allah. All we can do is make the sacrifice."

16 – SUNDAY MORNING COFFEE

At 6:00 AM Sunday morning, Morris woke with a start, breaking out of a disturbing dream. The poster Victoria had drawn when she was six was burning. The stick men were moving, trying to escape the flames.

Morris walked into the bathroom and relieved himself. He washed his hands, and looked in the mirror at the huge bruise under his right arm.

Morris and Terri had gone to bed about midnight, but lay sleepless until around 2 AM. As soon as the fire was out, Morris had called 9-1-1. He described the attack, and said the suspect had left his property on foot, heading south through the ravine. Morris described the punk as about 5 foot 10, 160 pounds, with dark, long curly hair, and a big chunk of missing scalp.

Then Morris called Zia, asking him to come to the house to examine the video. The system was new, and Morris did not know how the playback worked. Zia came over immediately and they examined the images together. The clip showed the suspect had climbed over the gate, and an accomplice handed him the Molotov cocktail. He walked to the middle of the lawn area and lit the rag, and as he was preparing to toss the burning bottle, he was startled by a yell from Morris. The suspect's aim was spoiled and the throw fell short. Had it hit the roof, the breaking bottle would have spread a much more destructive fire.

Alex and Terri had extinguished the fire completely, so the fire department had not been called. The police response had been disappointing. It took thirty minutes for a single constable to show up.

Terri had packaged the punk's scalp into a Ziploc sandwich bag and presented it to the constable as soon as he arrived. This item initially confused him. Terri explained it contained ample DNA to identify the suspect, if they caught up with him at some point.

The constable was young and relatively inexperienced, but seemed capable of collecting information for a report, at least. Zia burnt a CD of the video images for him. The constable had been quite surprised to find such a sophisticated surveillance system in a suburban residence.

As Morris navigated the stairway down to the kitchen, he considered whether the police response had been dismal thanks to his remarks attacking the reputation of the Crown Attorney. It was not likely, Morris concluded, that the Crown Attorney would leave instructions for the 9-1-1 operator to give a low priority to any calls from the Parker residence.

Morris checked the video surveillance monitor. There were a couple of short clips showing action in the back yard. At about 1:22 AM a cat had crossed the deck, triggering an immediate transmission of a camera image to Morris' Blackberry. Morris had grabbed the device from his bedside and was heading for the bedroom door by the time he figured out what the image showed. There had been a second alarm ten minutes later – this time it was a moth flying in front of the camera lens.

False alarms like these were the reason the loudhailer had been turned off the previous evening. It was still off, until the cameras and sensor intruder detection thresholds could be set.

Morris made coffee and then went out on the deck to inspect the damage. It was just after dawn, and there was a clear blue sky above. The sun had not yet risen high enough to clear the neighboring houses, and the air in the long shadows was cool.

He noticed several planks of decking needed replacing – the burns were too deep to remove by sanding. The picture window was smashed, but still in

place. The security film Zia had installed the day before
had performed as designed. Although the glass shattered
like a spider web, the broken pieces remained in place
and prevented flames from entering the kitchen.

Morris sipped his coffee and started to make a list.
The siding was scorched and would need to be cleaned.
Some of it would have to be replaced due to heat warp.
He needed white paint for the window frames. He would
have to order a replacement window. Morris measured
the window dimensions and wrote them on his list. He
measured the planks that would need to be replaced.

By then it was about 7:30, and Terri came down from
the bedroom. She poured herself a coffee. "We need to
talk."

With those words, Morris realized he was in shit.
"Just a minute, dear." He sat cross-legged on the deck,
counting the various lengths of deck planking he would
require. He folded his list and placed it in his shirt pocket.
"OK, lets talk."

Terri gave him a second coffee and sat down with
him. The sun was warming the deck now.

"We have been through a lot of financial risks, but
there has never been a situation like now," she began.
"What do you intend to do about it?"

Right to the point, Morris thought. "Well, things are
not going exactly the way I expected. To be honest, I'm
winging it right now. I don't like this feeling."

"Who thought of the home security improvements?"

"Alex James."

"Good thing." Terri looked at the charred walls and
deck. "We could have lost the whole house."

Morris looked down at the deck in front of him.

"Nothing you have ever done before resulted in an
attack against the family." Terri said in a somber tone.

"Are you trying to say I should not have intervened in
the pub?"

Terri looked at him. "I am looking at a middle-aged, responsible, family man. A lot of people depend on this man. I'm not looking at a 25-year old soldier who can throw his life away on some questionable battlefield adventures."

Morris cringed. She was right. He had been looking for an explanation of his behavior at the pub ever since the fight happened.

"Well, when I was 25, I jumped out of airplanes and got that out of my system." Morris put his head in his hands. "But there was something else that happened back then. Something I never told you."

Terri sipped her coffee, listening intently.

He looked up at her. "I was in Gagetown on a training exercise. I was a lieutenant leading a 10-man night patrol through enemy positions of over 100 men. The scenario was a rescue mission. We were supposed to escort a pilot and his VIP passenger out from behind enemy lines, where their helicopter had gone down. An enemy observation post spotted us with night vision equipment and we started taking a lot of fire. They eventually chased us into an abandoned building. We were shooting it out – with blanks, of course – and the umpire was gradually declaring more of my men dead."

Terri had never seen Morris talk this way. He always spoke with confidence, as if invincible – this time he seemed a bit lost.

Morris cleared his throat. "It was obvious that we were going to lose the battle. The situation was hopeless and my mission was a failure. I reported the situation on the radio and called for assistance. I had been going without sleep for three days. The firing subsided and the enemy offered surrender terms – put down our weapons and give up our VIP. I asked HQ what to do, and they said to give up." Morris looked blankly at his coffee.

It seemed to Terri as if Morris was re-living the experience. "Then what happened?"

"My men complied with my order to stop fighting. The enemy took our weapons, then lined us up against the wall and shot us all, including our pilot and VIP."

"But it was just an exercise…."

"I forgot to ask for authentication when I received the surrender order. I had a code sheet. I was supposed to use it to confirm the identity of the person I was talking to. It was not a genuine order. Help arrived ten minutes later. We would have had a fighting chance. The exercise scenario was that we were up against a bunch of fanatics capable of anything. I should not have trusted them to honor our surrender."

"That was a long time ago, Morris." Terri had a tear in her eye. "You should forget it."

"Seven years later, a group of ten Belgian paratroopers were killed in Rwanda. Their mission had been to protect the Rwandan president. Their lieutenant had received orders to comply with enemy demands to turn over their weapons. They received a legitimate order and complied. Then they were murdered – hacked to death by machetes."

Morris took a sip of coffee. "The enemy had deliberately targeted the Belgian forces in order to get them to leave the country. After the ten paratroopers were murdered, Belgium withdrew their forces. Other United Nations forces soon followed. The country was left to the extremists, who murdered hundreds of thousands of civilians in tribal genocide."

"None of this is your responsibility!"

"I know. But things happen to you when you go for days without sleep. I learned a lesson that night in Gagetown that I can never forget. I lived the feeling of being executed, of being humiliated. When I heard about the Belgian paratroopers years later, I re-lived the experience."

Morris looked at Terri briefly, then looked down. "Then, after September 11th, I heard the story of the passengers of flight 93."

They were both silent for a moment.

"They fought the hijackers, right?" Terri asked.

"They did. They went up against them, against their knives with bare hands. And they went down fighting. And they inspired millions because of their damned determination."

Morris looked up and into Terri's eyes.

"I learned never to give in. I learned it's better to go down fighting. Win or lose. I want to protect you and the kids. I care what you guys will think about me after I'm gone. It's not that I'm reckless, I don't plan to leave any time soon!" Morris took a deep breath. "It's hard to explain, but… I will never willingly put us in a position where somebody else gets to decide our fate. Never."

There was a long pause. Terri looked away into the woods.

"So tell me your plan."

"I think you and the kids should go to the cottage until summer is over. I'm going to need all my time to fight these charges and get back at whoever is after me. I need to focus on a plan of attack, not on how to defend you guys. I need you in a safe place, OK?"

Terri nodded silently.

Morris smiled. "I'm going to offer jobs to Ed and Jacques. I'll use them to improve company security and track down the bad guys. I have a couple of ideas about where to look. The police obviously don't have the resources – or the motivation – to solve this problem for us. We're better off relying on ourselves."

Terri looked at Morris and thought about what he had just said. "You listen to Ed and Jacques. And you rely on what Alex says, too."

"I will."

She turned to look at him, and pointed with her finger. "You get control of this situation. You make us safe again."

"I will."

"I will not stand for our girls being afraid like this."

"I feel the same way."

"And one more thing…" Terri struck her empty coffee mug on the deck, making a sharp whack that echoed into the woods of the ravine.

"What?"

She looked at the smashed kitchen window, burnt decking, and soot-covered siding. "You find these people, and kick their ass."

17 – WORKOUT WITH ED AND JACQUES

Jacques looked at his Blackberry screen. "I just got a text message from Morris." Sweating, he looked at Ed beside him. The two men were running on side-by-side treadmills.

Ed felt his holster vibrate on his hip. Without missing a step, he un-holstered his Blackberry and checked the screen. "Me too."

"Job offer?" asked Jacques.

"Yeah." Ed clipped his device back into his holster. "Sixty seconds to go. I'll race you to the finish."

The two men increased their pace and the two machines started to emit a higher pitch as the belt speed increased.

"30 seconds," said Ed, breathing hard.

"15…" he said. "10…9…9…." He was grinning.

Just then a beautiful woman, a sculpted blonde in spandex, crossed Ed's field of vision. He lost his footing and crashed. The treadmill immediately ejected him to the rear.

"Abort!" said Jacques, slowing his pace. "Man down!"

Jacques dismounted from the treadmill and looked back at Ed seated cross-legged on the floor. One knee was skinned and bleeding. The spandex blonde was now standing beside him.

"Are you OK?" she asked.

Ed looked up from his knee, taking his time to enjoy the view on the way up. She had perfect legs, outstanding breasts, and was looking at him with concern.

"I got a boo-boo," Ed said, pointing to his knee.

The woman smiled and knelt beside him, exposing her knockout cleavage. "Let Mommy see."

She put her hand on Ed's knee and turned his leg gently, checking the damage.

"I think we can save this leg," she said.

Ed was struck silent. This woman's scent was incredible, and her eyes were turning him to jell-o. He held up his elbow in order to get more attention. He pointed out a minor scrape.

"Two boo-boo's," she said. "I'll be right back with a bit of gauze." She stood up and headed for the door to look for some first aid.

Ed and Jacques watched her walk away, slack-jawed.

"Great wheels," Ed said.

"That's my girlfriend," said an unfriendly voice from behind. Ed and Jacques turned to see a huge bodybuilder in a muscle shirt. Two of his bulky bodybuilding buddies stood behind him. "I don't like the way you look at her."

"She came over to me, buddy," said Ed.

"I don't give a crap." The bodybuilder positioned himself directly in front of Ed.

Still sitting on the floor, Ed turned his head and looked up at the sweaty, hulking gorilla. "How Mongo take his steroids? Mixed with banana, or straight up?"

"I think you should leave, before she gets back."

Ed looked over at Jacques. "We're being picked on, *again*. That's twice this week. If these guys *also* have guns…"

Jacques approached Ed to offer a hand up. The bodybuilder shifted his body to block.

"Are you gonna leave?" the bodybuilder asked Ed.

"Not just because you want me to," Ed said in a steady tone.

"Let me help him up," said Jacques, reaching for his friend. The bodybuilder shifted again and their arms collided. Jacques swatted the bodybuilder's arm aside. The bodybuilder turned to face him, grabbing Jacques' shirt with one hand.

As the bodybuilder looked away, Ed quickly rolled backwards onto his feet.

At the same instant, Jacques broke the bodybuilder's grip on his shirt with a sharp upward stroke, then swiftly pulled the bodybuilder off balance by hauling his upper arm across Jacques' chest. Jacques then tripped him from behind and they both fell to the floor, Jacques in control. It was a perfectly executed arm bar takedown, just as he had practiced with Ed many times.

Ed now faced the two other bodybuilders, and guarded Jacques' back. "Which one of you girls wants a new hairstyle?"

Surprised by the speed of Ed and Jacques' teamwork, the two big men backed off a step.

"I recognize you!" one of the men exclaimed. "You guys were part of the shootings at The Arms!"

"That's right. Don't mess with us." Ed turned his attention to the bodybuilder.

The bodybuilder looked up at Ed, face distorted because Jacques was pressing him against the floor.

"If you behave yourself, your girl will not see you with your head shoved up your ass," Ed said.

The bodybuilder nodded. Jacques released him.

Ed walked over and offered him a hand up. The bodybuilder took it reluctantly, and Ed pulled the larger man to his feet.

At that moment, the bodybuilder's girlfriend returned.

Ed saw her coming and changed his grip into a handshake. "Pleased to meetcha," he said to the bodybuilder, who looked at his girlfriend as Ed pumped his arm heartily.

"I see you two have met," she said. She seemed a bit disappointed that she wasn't going to have Ed all to herself.

"We were just talking about you," Ed said. Ed noticed the name 'Hank' written on the bodybuilders'

142 Jim E.M. Miles

weightlifting belt. "Henry here came over to ask if I was OK, and we got to chatting."

"Oh really?" The woman did not sound convinced.

Everyone looked at Ed with anticipation.

"Henry said he was a bit insecure about the fact that you were helping me. I kinda was watching you from behind when you went to get the first aid stuff – sorry about that – I'm actually married. Anyways, we also talked about how taking more than fifteen steroids in the program can mess up your aggression a bit."

"My God, I was trying to tell him the same thing. I was watching Oprah the other day…"

"Yeah, he told me you had that discussion. He's sorry he didn't listen better, and he thinks maybe he can cut back a bit."

The woman's lower lip quivered, and she started to tear up. "Is that right, Hank?"

Hank stood completely dumbfounded, looking at her blankly.

"I'm so worried about you, Hankie-poo. You don't have to impress me with your muscles. And the other night when little hank couldn't play…."

Hank's bodybuilding buddies turned away in embarrassment.

There was sudden panic on Hank's face. "OK, yes, I'll cut back!"

The woman dropped the first aid items she was holding, and stepped quickly to embrace Hank.

"I'm sorry I was flirting, honey, I love you. I'll stop showing off to other men. I'll make this all up to you. I'm so hot for you now…" she whispered in his ear.

Cautiously, Hank gave her a hug.

Jacques and Ed turned away from the sappy scene and left the cardio room.

The little tussle had happened so quickly that nobody else had noticed.

Ed and Jacques showered and dressed, then headed for the parking lot. Their two cars were parked beside each other.

"If that had happened to me last week, I would have just left." Ed reached for his keys. "I would have simply backed down. What the hell has got into us?"

"I suppose it was from watching Morris in action at The Arms."

"I suppose that's the Die Hard effect. You come out of the movie wanting to beat up terrorists." Ed suddenly remembered the text message they had both received from Morris. "Hey, what about that job offer?"

The two men pulled out their Blackberry cellphones.

Jacques read the message aloud. "Subject: Job Offer. Minimum two-month contract, security and investigations work. I need your help, both of you. Meet me at PHL office downtown Monday 10:00 AM if interested."

"I have the same message," said Ed.

"I'm supposed to teach two one-day seminars in government security procedures next week, but I can reschedule them or let someone else do it." Jacques pocketed his cellphone. "This sounds interesting."

"I just finished a contract with JTF2. I was going to take a couple of weeks off before looking for something else," said Ed.

"Let's do it then. Saddle up. Time for some adventure."

"I'm up for it," said Ed. "All for one, and one for all."

18 – THE HELPING HAND OF ALEX JAMES

"We've come to help you clean up," Sarah James said to Terri Parker as she and her husband Alex stepped out of their car.

"Wow, thanks guys. Morris went to get some supplies. Here he comes now."

Morris backed his pickup truck into the driveway then stepped out. "Did you guys come over to borrow coffee or something?"

"We don't need any coffee," said Alex. "We have enough adrenaline left over from last night's bonfire to stimulate a horse."

"Is that what happened last night?" asked Sarah, looking at her husband with mock admiration. "You were stimulated?"

"Did you two do *it* last night?" Morris grinned as he approached the group. "If a horse was involved in any way, I will have to report you both to the SPCA."

"No horse," said Sarah, "just a horny cowboy."

Morris looked at Sarah. "I hope you rode him hard, Ma'am," then he looked at Alex, "and put him in the barn wet."

"Ewww!" said Terri.

"Very funny, hamster dick," Alex said dryly.

"So," Terri said to Morris, "Heading for a new subject, did you get everything you need to fix the house?"

"Everything on my list, except a new window." Morris pulled out his list and showed it to the group. "That will have to be ordered. I'll do it Monday."

"Did you get deck stain?" Terri asked.

"Ooops. Forgot to put that on my list."

"White paint for the window frames? How about fabric cleaner? Did you notice the smoke damage on the awning?" she asked.

"Nope, no paint or fabric cleaner. Didn't think of those things," Morris admitted.

"How about new curtains on the inside," Sarah suggested.

"Great idea," Terri said. "Let's shop. I'll grab my purse and we'll leave these two cowboys to tend to their chores." She looked at Morris. "Don't forget to feed breakfast to the young'uns, Tex."

Terri went to get her purse and the ladies left as Morris and Alex unloaded the truck. Morris set up his bench and cutoff saw and they began to work. While Alex used a cordless impact driver to remove decking screws from the burnt planks, Morris measured and cut replacement planks to the correct length. The sounds of power tools echoed in the air.

"Considering we're just a couple of white collar guys," said Morris, "we sound pretty manly with these tools."

"I was wondering," said Alex, "your home insurance policy must cover this kind of damage."

"I suppose so. I just don't want the hassle of going for quotes. It's not that big a job anyway. Mostly, I just want to fix this scar without delay."

"Right," Alex nodded, "No need to give the pricks who did this any satisfaction from seeing the damage done."

"Deny the enemy their battle damage assessment." Morris pointed at the charred siding. "They did this, to try and scare us. Therefore, screw them."

Alex surveyed the back yard. "You have a nice little family place here, but you and Terri could afford a palace. Why do you guys still live in a regular, middle-class house?"

"Hah," Morris said. "Because we're not as rich as we look. The last three years have been pretty good, but before that we had ups and downs. This house is only 25% ours. The rest is still leveraged to invest in our first office building. Then we leveraged that building to invest in others. I work with 'high net worth' individuals – otherwise known as rich people – as partners in each of these properties. I'm in control of the projects because that's the way I set up the deals. I find or develop the properties, and I do all the work, but I'm not the guy making the largest profits on any one deal."

Morris walked over to the small pile of new cedar planks, and brought one back to his saw. "Business is risky. I started with about two years of salary saved up when I quit the army. I didn't have millions of dollars to play with. There have been times when I could not pay Terri or myself a salary. We had to live off our savings for two years during a market downturn. Our employees got regular salaries – and sometimes we had to use credit card cash advances to meet payroll. Our rents and other expenses had to be paid. The owner gets paid last."

"The Kanise family is suing you for ten million," said Alex.

"That would wipe us out. But they won't get that much, because we don't have it."

Alex removed a plank and tossed it on a pile of charred planks. "How do you feel about the manslaughter charge?"

"Liam, my lawyer, feels it's a weak charge. It's even weaker now with two fewer witnesses since the two guys escaped from hospital."

"I was thinking about the evidence they have against you." said Alex.

"Me too. I think somebody related to the Cripps gang got into the pub that night and planted the bullet in the beam. They set me up to take the fall so they could get the heat off their own guy." Morris unclipped a tape measure from his belt. "The cops arrested this guy MacDick for picking the fight and attempting to shoot me. The Cripps or Hell's Angels must want him free."

Alex watched Morris measure a new cedar plank, thinking how confident Morris always sounded. Morris wasn't always right, but he was always confident.

"I agree," Alex said, "that somebody, somehow, planted a bullet in the beam late Wednesday night – sometime between the time the forensics team left for the night Wednesday and the time they resumed Thursday morning."

"How did you get that information?"

"I phoned Ed Smitt and asked him to go back to The Arms on Friday, while you were taking the day off in jail. He spoke with your waitress, Angela. She showed him where they extracted the incriminating bullet. He said there's no way one of the shots fired during the fighting hit that particular spot. Ed sent me an email yesterday about it."

"Thanks for looking into it."

"I think something fishy is going on." Alex paused, looking at Morris. "In the Ottawa Police Department."

"Why?"

"The pub was guarded by the cops all night, until the forensics team had finished on Thursday. There was continuous police presence from their first man on the scene until all the bullets were retrieved."

Morris, with a skeptical expression, looked at Alex. "Come on. I can understand the cops making wrong deductions based on conflicting witness statements. But you're talking about a conspiracy. Why would they be part of a setup against me?"

"You are just collateral damage. The heat is on you because someone wants the heat off someone else. The heat's off MacDick. It's also off the two guys who got away from the hospital."

"If you say so." Morris positioned a plank to cut it.

"I'm the trained spy. I find it too suspicious that those
two guys were under guard by the Ottawa Police, the
same force responsible for the crime scene."

"So you think one of the Ottawa cops let somebody in
to plant the bullet?" asked Morris.

"Yes. And the bullet in the beam had to come from
the same gun you used." Alex aimed his impact driver
like a pistol. "Not a similar gun: your gun. During the
entire period when the bullet in the beam could have been
fired, that gun was under the control of the Ottawa
Police."

Alex went on, "The forensics team must have done a
ballistics analysis on Thursday and found a match. Every
gun barrel manufactured leaves a distinct set of scratches
on bullets fired through it, like fingerprints. The forensics
investigators would have fired a test bullet from your gun.
The grooves in the lead of the test bullet must have
matched the bullets they found on the scene. Your
statement did not explain the presence of the bullet in the
beam, so they charged you."

Morris pressed the trigger and the saw motor started
with a loud kick, then the plank screamed as he cut it.
"Liam says it will be hard to discredit the forensics team,"
Morris said loudly over the sound of the saw winding
down.

"Sounds like Liam's worked firearms cases before.
That kind of physical evidence has to be cross-examined
by attacking the expertise of the ballistics team members,
and that is a tough job. Whoever planted the bullet needed
two things: access to the scene, and access to the gun you
used. The evidence team will make it difficult for you to
raise either possibility as a reasonable doubt.

"I do remember a female investigator tagging the
pistols," said Morris.

Alex nodded his head. "They are trained to be very
thorough. They are trained to appear credible and

confident in court. I'm sure the guns were the first things
they secured."

"Still, they have to prove the bullet in the beam was
fired first. I could claim it might have been a ricochet. I
could also claim it was the second shot fired, or the third.
It will be my word against MacDick."

Morris gave Alex the plank he had just cut.

"You each have a reason to lie. When do you get to
see exactly what evidence they have on you?" asked
Alex.

"It could be several weeks, according to Liam."
Morris suddenly realized there was a way to get a better
idea of what he would be up against – he could ask Alex.
Alex must have access to police databases, he thought. "It
would be nice if I could find out what is in the police
reports against me."

Morris looked at his friend and waited.

Alex sighed. "I'm supposed to be on the side of law
and order. I'm not supposed to help manslaughter
suspects." Alex squatted, fiddled with the plank, trying to
fit it in. It was a bit too short. "You need to lengthen this
one about an inch."

Morris accepted the plank back, glaring at it. "How
did I fuck this up?"

"Look, any time I access a confidential, need-to-know
information system, I leave tracks. These systems make
an audit record of each and every user who reads any
police report. I would need a reason to access your file,
and I would be in big trouble if I got caught. I could be
charged myself."

"I understand that." Morris turned to get another
plank. "How could I find out the name of the cops
guarding the pub Wednesday night or Thursday morning?
One of them must be in on the frame-up."

Alex pondered. "I don't know. Maybe other cops are
named in the online report. Or if the cops on guard filed
reports of their own, which I doubt."

"We could subpoena the roster. We can investigate and question these cops. We could call them as witnesses."

"Only during the trial. Whenever that is. That could be a year or two from now."

The two men were silent while Morris measured twice and cut another plank. "So you suspect somebody on the good guy side is protecting a bad guy." Morris pointed to himself. "I'm one of the good guys. I'm innocent, and you know it. Who am I supposed to turn to?" Morris handed the plank back to Alex. "There. I added an inch."

"Hold on." Alex stood up, accepting the plank. Alex considered the risk if he helped his friend. If caught, he would certainly face internal discipline. He had never heard of anyone facing a criminal charge for improperly accessing information. He decided it was worth the risk to help his friend.

"I know a guy who would have a reason to access gang-related files." Alex positioned the plank and pulled a screw out of his pocket and drove it in smoothly. "This guy owes me a favor. I'll ask him to print me a copy of the reports. He's the type of guy who knows things sometimes need to get done by *looking the other way*. He won't ask questions. He works in Toronto now. He may not have heard of your case. He certainly doesn't know that you and I are friends."

19 – ED AND JACQUES' FIRST DAY

It was Monday morning at 10:00 AM.

"Thanks for coming in, guys," Morris said to Ed and Jacques, as he greeted them at his office. "Have a seat and I'll give you the briefing."

Morris activated a six-foot wide computer display mounted on the wall beside his desk. It showed an Organization Chart for Parker Holdings Limited. The top of the chart contained a box with the label 'Morris Parker, CEO' in it. Below the CEO box was a pyramid of department names and position titles with names of position holders. Immediately to the right was a box labeled 'Security and Investigations.'

Ed and Jacques looked wide-eyed at the massive chart.

"Holy shit, Jim, I'm a doctor, not a bricklayer," said Ed.

"You'll get to know this organization and the people in it as we go along. This is where you guys fit in." Morris pointed to the Security and Investigations box. "You are the Security and Investigations Department. You have a direct line to me, CEO of PHL, and the freedom to work with any other person, anywhere in the organization. I will inform my VP's that I expect them and their people to give you full cooperation. The VP's will have no right to know what you may be discussing with their people. But as a courtesy, you must inform them the name of anyone in their department you need to deal with. They will facilitate your meetings, and they will give you any resources you require."

"I'm a simple soldier," said Ed. "I think Jacques should be in charge of our team."

"That's pretty much what I had in mind," said Morris. "Jacques, you were in command of an infantry battalion and can handle the administration and logistics demands of an organization this size. Your title is Director of Security and Investigations."

Jacques nodded.

"Ed, you will be his operations officer. You will plan and execute investigations and missions."

"Missions?" Ed and Jacques said simultaneously, with some surprise.

"I have a couple of intelligence-gathering activities in mind. We know that the Cripps are linked to the Hell's Angels. I expect our investigations may get a little rough."

Ed and Jacques looked at each other. Ed grinned. Jacques winked.

"As you indicated to us on the phone, boss," said Jacques.

"I need you both to know what you are signing up for. I'm not some rock star, and you're not here to be my bodyguards. We seem to have an enemy, and I do not intend to underestimate him. I do *not* want to go into battle light. You both will have all the resources of PHL to face whatever challenge may present itself. I intend to be able to finish whatever we start."

"What is the overall aim of our department?" asked Jacques.

"A good question. In my book, the primary principle of war is to *select and maintain the aim*. I therefore want to be clear that the mandate of your department is *to identify and eliminate all criminal threats against PHL, myself and my family*." Morris looked at Ed and Jacques in turn, then re-stated the mandate for emphasis. "To identify and eliminate all criminal threats against Parker Holdings, myself and my family."

"Do you expect all our activities to be within the boundaries of the law?" asked Ed.

"Another good question. Especially if you look at what I've managed to involve you in so far." Morris paused.

"Our first approach will be to provide information and evidence to the legal authorities. I hope to find those legal authorities capable of using that information and evidence to satisfy your aim. If they do not, your aim still applies."

Morris let that answer sink in for a moment. "You both saw me smash a bad guy in the face. That, depending upon the outcome of a trial, may turn out to be an illegal act. I do not anticipate asking you to commit any illegal acts, but as you can see, the definition of an illegal act can come long after the decision to commit the act has been made."

"Made by armchair quarterbacks," said Jacques.

Ed spoke up. "I read in the paper a couple of days ago these two guys chased down a speeding drunk who had just sexually assaulted a woman. They found the woman on the side of the road, hysterical. She pointed out her attacker and they jumped in their Porsche and chased the guy down. They kept in contact with a 9-1-1 operator the whole time. They reached speeds of over 100 miles an hour. The 9-1-1 operator did not ask them to call off the chase at any point. They never got charged for speeding."

"Did they catch the guy?" asked Morris.

"Yes they did," said Ed. "The cops headed him off. The chase ended safely."

"Good example," said Jacques. "Count me in. I accept our aim."

"Me too," said Ed.

"Right. Welcome aboard." Morris offered a handshake and the three friends shook hands. "Your department's first priority is to identify who we are up against."

Morris walked over to the computer display. "This is a touch-screen display." He began to manipulate the objects on display, closing the window containing the organization chart to reveal a list of names in his personal telephone directory. He double-tapped a name, and the computer speakers on the wall next to the display activated and telephone dialing tones were audible. "I'm calling our security systems specialist."

"I want a phone like that," said Ed.

"This phone is a computer program. You should both have one in your office by the time we finish this meeting. You each get a new Mac computer as well, like mine, integrated with the phone software."

"With a six foot display?" asked Ed, as the sound of a telephone ring emitted from the speakers.

"If you guys need a six foot display, then that's what you'll get." Morris said. "You just have to convince your Director, Jacques. Here's his budget." Morris opened a spreadsheet window showing a budget breakdown by category with a six-figure grand total. "I spoke with my various partners, and funds have been allocated to your department as a high priority. This is just the operations and maintenance part. Salaries, special projects and capital equipment acquisitions are separate."

Ed's eyes bulged and Jacques started to laugh.

At that moment, Zia's voice sounded through the speakers as he answered his phone.

"Iron Integrity Security, this is Zia Kubra."

"Zia, you are on speakerphone and I'm here with the new Director of Security and Investigations, Jacques Tremblay and his Operations Officer, Ed Smitt."

"How do you do, sirs."

"We are well," said Jacques.

"Zia, I sent you login credentials to take over my desktop. I would like you to log in and show us the clips from my residence on Saturday. Our objective is to try to identify who we are up against. The people in this clip are most probably associated with Innes MacDick and the Ledbury Banff Cripps, and possibly the Hell's Angels."

"Morris, before you go any further, is this a public telephone line you are using?" asked Jacques.

"No. Zia and I are using Voice Over IP technology. This conversation is going over our high-speed fiber-optic link to the Internet, and it is encrypted. Zia insisted on installing the software here for me on the weekend."

"Each of you will have the same setup," Zia said.

Morris walked over and sat on the sofa next to the visitor chairs where Ed and Jacques were seated. "Zia and his firm provide surveillance and security systems on most of our properties, including my residence where the firebomb attack took place on Saturday."

The computer seemed as if it had been taken over by a ghost. The display showed mouse movement and then a new window popped up, showing Zia's face, live.

"I can't see you folks, but here I am." Zia waved at his camera. "And here is the Parker residence."

Another window popped open. This one showed four scenes, various views of the Parker back yard. There were two men in coveralls working to replace the shattered kitchen window.

"I see my new window has arrived," said Morris.

"This is the live view," said Zia. "I'll cue up the clips from Saturday…."

"Wait just a second." Morris watched as one of the workers took a cigarette out of his pocket.

"No smoking at the Parker residence," said Ed.

"I'll remind him," said Zia.

Zia manipulated the mouse and clicked a button on screen. The button had a microphone icon on it.

"You in the baseball cap! No smoking!" Zia said with authority.

The window installer jumped and dropped his cigarette.

"Pick it up!" Zia commanded.

The installer bent over quickly and struck his head on the windowsill.

"As you can see, the loudhailer is active now," said
Zia. "Watch as I zoom in with this camera."

The scene changed from four-scene to a single-scene
view, and the camera began to zoom in on the window
installer. He was rubbing his forehead, but then suddenly
started to swat at his left breast pocket like a madman.

"I think he must have put the lit cigarette in his
pocket," said Jacques.

The unfortunate man doubled over, trying desperately
to move the burning tobacco away from his skin.
Suddenly his chest burst into flame.

"Jump in the pool!" Zia ordered.

The installer took three steps and plunged into the
water. He came up sputtering.

"How the hell did that happen?" asked Ed.

"I think I know," said Zia. "Watch this."

Zia started playing the scene back from the moment
the installer struck his head on the deck. Zia zoomed in
and it was now possible to see the cigarette as the installer
placed it hurriedly in his pocket. The end was lit.

Then Zia froze the image. "See that rag in his breast
pocket? Now look at this."

Zia panned the camera view across the scene toward a
small cylindrical can on the deck. He zoomed in. The
label was visible. It said PAINT SOLVENT.

"They were removing old paint!" said Jacques. "He
put the solvent-soaked rag in his breast pocket."

"And then he lit a cigarette," said Ed. "What an idiot."

"As you can see," Morris said, "Zia's cameras can do
quite a bit."

For the next several minutes, the group examined
video clips of the firebomb intruder. Even though the
cameras were working in the dark, the images were clear
and sharp. The scenes were lit with infrared light visible
to the camera, but invisible to the human eye.

Morris had seen the first view before: it showed
Morris chase the intruder until they disappeared behind

the hedge. Then Zia showed a second scene that Morris had not seen on Sunday. This view showed Morris from behind as he chased the intruder over the gate. The scene was almost as bright as daylight.

"I worked on this clip a bit," said Zia. "Using this angle, I was able to compare the height of the intruder with the height of your fence. I estimate him to be five foot ten and about one hundred and sixty pounds."

"Where did that view come from?" asked Morris. "We didn't have anything from that camera, I thought."

"There was nothing on the disk at your house," said Zia. "Because that particular camera had not been set to trigger a recording on your DVR when it sensed motion. But I happened to be recording all cameras at all times from our monitoring facility. I searched for the appropriate time on the gate camera and found this scene."

The overall results were disappointing, however. Since the intruder had worn a balaclava until Morris had removed it out of camera view, there were no facial features visible.

"Is that all you have?" asked Morris.

"This time, yes." Zia activated another multi-camera window on the computer display. "Next time, however, we have a close-up camera at the gate. Not only will this camera show a better view of a person at the gate, it has the face-recognition software configured."

"What does that mean?" Ed asked.

"Let me show you. It's been running for a while today."

Zia manipulated the application software and a window appeared containing a series of faces. One of the faces was the unfortunate window installer. Zia clicked on his face.

"Each time the software sees a new face, it creates a folder, and puts the image there. Every time it sees the same face after that, it places the image in the same folder. Each image has a timestamp. We can therefore see what times Smokey the Installer entered via the back gate today."

There were three shots of the installer. The shots had occurred over about a 90-minute interval. In two of the shots, the installer had a short cigarette in his mouth.

"This guy takes a smoke break every 30 minutes," said Ed.

"You'll have to remember that when you see the labor bill for this installation," Jacques said to Morris.

"Oy!" Morris said from the sofa.

"Oy?" said Ed.

"Zia," Morris said, "Boyd MacDougall said you set up a face recognition system like this for him."

"That's right," said Zia.

"Does that system capture customers, or just staff?"

"It catches both. I showed him how he could count the number of customers with it. He said he was going to use the data for marketing purposes."

"He was also using it to impress the poker players. He runs an illegal game in the back room."

"No shit," said Zia.

"Can you log in to his system and review the customer faces?" asked Morris.

"Yes. I logged in yesterday."

"How many different faces are there?"

"He's been running that system for about three months. There must be about 5,000 unique faces by now."

"Task," Morris said to Jacques.

"Looks like we have some images to look at." Jacques stood up to leave. "Ed and I will see if we can spot Beavis and Butthead."

"We'll meet here again tomorrow, same time." Morris thought about Alex James and the police reports. "I should have more information for you before then. Remember, we're looking for evidence to connect

MacDick to Beavis and Butthead. If you find their
pictures, it will help us to identify who they really are."

20 – MOHAMED AND DR. TRAGAR-MIERDA, Ph.D

It was almost sunset on Monday. Mohamed had been working steadily since 5:00 AM. His chores that day included changing oil in the camp electric generator, pumping lake water into the camp's 500-gallon water tower, preparing a list of food, fuel and other essential supplies, cleaning the barn floor, and repairing a leak in the roof of the living quarters. He had taken one 15-minute meal break at lunchtime.

Mohamed was awaiting the arrival, by seaplane, of Dr. Graciano Tragar-Mierda, Ph.D. He was late, as usual.

The "emperor's suite" had been cleaned for his arrival. This particular living space had been established upon the first visit of Dr. Tragar to the camp. The planned sleeping arrangements had not been suitable, in the opinion of the doctor, because he had to share space with everyone else equally.

After a painful discussion between Dr. Tragar and Mohamed, during which none of Mohamed's objections seemed to be heard, the doctor made a firm and final pronouncement in the interests of his personal privacy and comfort. Dr. Tragar insisted on having the 24-foot accommodation trailer all to himself.

To please Tragar, Mohamed had to convert the entire trailer into a private bedroom for the sole use of Dr. Graciano Tragar-Mierda, Ph.D., Chief Scientist, CEO, and Chairman of the Board. Mohamed and the men would sleep outside in tents.

Thankfully, Dr. Tragar visited seldom. After numerous discussions between Mohamed and Dr. Tragar over various matters, Mohamed could no longer stand to be in the same space as the doctor, and the doctor could no longer stand to be with Mohamed.

Dr. Tragar was CEO and Chairman of his own organization, which he had grandly named the Institute for the Discovery, Innovation and Optimization of Bio-Technologies. This name had the acronym IDIOB, just one letter away from IDIOT, Mohamed noted.

Not only was Dr. Tragar the organization's chief idiot, Mohamed had discovered, he was the organization's sole employee. One night while cleaning the lab floor, Mohamed had spotted ten years of corporate tax returns on the desk of Dr. Tragar. He had not filed any of them yet, and was being threatened with penalties and interest on unpaid taxes. Looking through the documents, Mohamed estimated the average gross income of the IDIOB organization had been less than twenty thousand dollars per year. The financial statements showed income from one-time speaking engagements and short consulting contracts for companies mostly in Italy.

The documents also included the doctor's personal tax returns for the past ten years, as well as those of his ex-wife. Tragar's primary source of income had been his ex-wife. She was a highly paid scientist for the World Health Organization. She had divorced him about two years ago.

After finding the tax returns, Mohamed did some Internet research on Dr. Tragar and IDIOB. He found that the doctor had begun his career in biotechnology in brilliant fashion, with a discovery that led to a patent for a blood test that detected anal cancer at a very early stage. Investors poured money at the doctor's feet and he seemed to be on his way to fame and glory. But the company ceased operations mysteriously after five years without getting the blood test to the market.

Several years later, newspaper stories regarding Dr. Tragar and the same patent emerged. The doctor claimed his first company had failed because the investors had

given him too little control. In fact, he had managed his
first company very badly.

Several years after the company went under, Dr.
Tragar formed a new partnership with the objective of
exploiting his patent. This time, his partner had very little
money to invest, but was able to disentangle the legal
mess left behind by the first company and make a viable
business plan for the new venture.

New investors had become interested in the patent,
but the doctor had imposed so many unreasonable terms
and conditions that the second company was unable to
acquire financing. The partner sued Dr. Tragar, and
proved the doctor had taken the partner's money in bad
faith. The patent was released into the public domain for
nonpayment of annual maintenance fees. The partner won
a $100,000 settlement but was unable to collect because
the doctor went bankrupt.

Then the doctor lost his home and his second wife.

Shortly after that, a large pharmaceutical company
announced a blood test based on the Tragar discovery,
and began to make hundreds of millions of dollars from
it. Not a penny went to Tragar.

Mohamed realized that the doctor had been both a
personal and professional failure, until recently. His latest
tax return showed an income of over $400,000. With this
latest return, there was a photocopy of a check made out
to IDIOB for that amount, from Concourse
Pharmaceuticals. The signature was that of Joris van
Praag.

That signature was no surprise to Mohamed, because
both he and Dr. Tragar were currently receiving funding
from Joris van Praag.

Joris van Praag had also authorized payments to the
various contractors and suppliers that had built the camp.
He also funded the ongoing bills for supplies. But these
payments did not come from Concourse Pharmaceuticals
directly. It was vital that Concourse Pharmaceuticals not

be connected to Mohamed, the camp, or the germ in any way. And here was a document from the brilliant doctor that would incriminate all of them.

As Mohamed reflected on the events to come, the muscular sound of a double engine propeller aircraft became audible in the distance. The sun had set, and it would soon be dusk. Had the doctor delayed the takeoff any longer, the pilot would have refused to make the flight. There was just enough time remaining to make a landing on the lake before it was too dark.

Mohamed decided to ask the doctor about the delay. He predicted there would be no good reason, and the doctor would not admit a mistake or offer any apology. The doctor would probably try to deflect the question with some other criticism of Mohamed.

The plane landed and taxied to the dock. The pilot stopped the engine and Mohamed tied up.

"Good evening, Dr. Tragar." Mohamed noticed the pilot looked quite irritated. "I was expecting you two hours ago."

"I hope you do not expect me to maintain a schedule at a pace that is inconsistent with my duties and responsibilities as Chief Scientist!" Dr. Tragar struggled to pull a small suitcase from the plane. "I require a comprehensive and integrated platform of harnessing technologies to ensure mutually beneficial outcomes for our converging efforts!"

What? Mohamed recognized the *word salad* defense. "Dr. Tragar, the pilot...."

"I have a serious problem with your schedule, as I have told you before. You are ignoring my demands!"

Mohamed recognized the *interrupting* defense. He raised his voice, and both men began to speak at the same time. "The pilot has a contract that states at what time you must be ready to depart!" Mohamed had learned the doctor was able to hear and understand him even though Tragar was simultaneously forming words and speaking.

As Tragar continued to babble about his dissatisfaction with the schedule, Mohamed continued even louder. "You have a contract also, and it states exactly what times you are supposed to be here! If you had missed this flight, you would have been late for tomorrow's work!"

The doctor changed tactic. "You have delayed our activities here by refusing to negotiate with Concourse Pharmaceuticals!"

At last, Mohamed identified the *criticism* defense.

While the arguing went on, the pilot untied his airplane and was restarting the engine.

"As Chief Scientist, I have to attain consolidation and integration norms that…."

Finally the airplane engine drowned out the doctor's verbal diarrhea. Mohamed turned his back on Tragar and stomped back to the camp.

There would be a long, fruitless discussion ahead. For over a month now, Tragar had been trying to force Mohamed to compress the schedule for his biweekly visits. Instead of every 14 days, the doctor wanted to visit every ten days, in an attempt to end the work sooner. This pattern would wreck havoc with every other activity at the camp. Not only that, Mohamed needed some point during the busy week when he could rest.

Tragar, in attempting to get his way, was being stubbornly uncooperative in every way possible. He was making ridiculous demands at every opportunity. He wanted the all-terrain vehicles to be parked on the other side of the camp. He wanted programmable thermostats for the pig barn, rather than the standard model. And he wanted the 20,000-gallon propane tank moved from the center of the camp to the perimeter, despite the fact that extensive excavation and rerouting of underground piping would be required.

There was only a few weeks of operation left, thought Mohamed. Thankfully, he would not have to put up with these antics any longer than that.

The doctor did not say why he wanted to rush the schedule. Mohamed guessed that it was so he could finish the assignment and get paid quicker. If only the doctor knew what would happen when his assignment was finished.

Van Praag had been very clear that when the doctor was no longer needed, Mohamed was to ensure that Tragar could never provide information about the operation to anyone, ever.

Mohamed looked forward to the moment when he could forever silence the great Dr. Graciano Tragar-Mierda, Ph.D., Chief Scientist, CEO, and Chairman of the Board.

21 – JACQUES' BRIEFING

It was Tuesday Morning, 10:00 AM. Jacques waited at the podium in the boardroom while Zia fiddled with the computer display. Seated at the boardroom table, Ed Smitt sipped a coffee and Liam Latham sat writing notes.

"Can you get cartoons on that thing?" Ed asked Zia.

"We can get YouTube," said Zia.

"That's not much."

"Not much?" Zia looked at Ed with mock surprise. "It is a privilege to get YouTube. In my country, the authorities block YouTube, Twitter, and web sites associated with the leader of the opposition."

"Have you seen our official opposition leader? I would love to see him blocked," said Liam.

"Can they block teenage texting?" asked Ed. "My teenage daughter…." Just then, Ed saw Morris enter the room. "ROOM!" he exclaimed.

Morris saw Ed had snapped to attention with a big grin on his face.

"Carry on," said Morris.

"What was that about?" asked Zia.

"In the military," Jacques explained, "when the Commanding Officer enters the room, the first person to spot him arrive calls the room to attention."

"These guys are just poking fun at that tradition," said Morris. "At one point, each of us got fed up with being a career military man."

"So you are actually mocking this tradition," said Zia.

"Yes," said Jacques.

"It's either that or Ed just had another flashback," said Morris.

"I love the smell of napalm in the morning," said Ed, developing a glazed look.

Zia observed Ed's change of expression and started to
shake his head. "So none of you take military authority
seriously,"

"Not any more," said Jacques.

Morris noticed that Liam was writing on a copy of
Detective Clark's investigation report, quietly acquired on
Monday by Alex James via his Toronto contact. Alex had
provided it with the strict instructions to minimize its
distribution and not to reveal its source.

"But we do use some military techniques and
experiences," said Morris, "when it suits the situation.
Are you ready to start, Jacques?"

"Oui, Mon Capitaine," said Jacques, giving Morris a
nod.

Morris took a seat at the end of the boardroom table.
"Please begin your briefing."

Jacques nodded to Zia, who illuminated the computer
display showing a Power Point slide with the title PHL
INTELLIGENCE AND SECURITY BRIEFING,
followed by Jacques name and title 'Director, Security
and Investigations.'

"Gentlemen," said Jacques, "this will be an informal
briefing and I expect you to interrupt me if you have
questions."

Jacques cleared his throat. "Since yesterday, we have
accumulated quite a bit of new information. First I would
like to summarize the situation. Morris was arrested and
charged on Thursday night after what seems to have been
a very sloppy police investigation."

Jacques nodded his head at Zia, and a slide appeared
showing the title THREAT ASSESSMENT with two sub-
headings: PUBLIC RELATIONS and CRIMINAL
CHARGES.

Jacques went on. "I got this information from the VP
of Sales and Marketing. When the news hit the media the
next day, public opinion quickly turned against us. Online
comments on the newspaper websites, radio talk show

callers, columnists and commentators universally condemned what they perceived as vigilante-type action. Whatever reputation and popularity Morris had before the incident seemed to be working against him, in the opinion of the vocal minority. People seem to enjoy when a celebrity falls from grace."

"I'm just a minor celebrity, I assure you," said Morris.

"What was the effect of the comments Morris made against the Crown Attorney?" asked Liam.

"Morris claimed that he was being wrongly prosecuted, and I think that message got out. He also painted the Crown Attorney as incompetent, and that message also got out."

"On what information do you base these conclusions?" Liam asked.

"I asked VP Marketing to hire a public relations firm and yesterday evening they did a telephone survey. Two hundred Ottawa-area homes were called."

Liam's raised his eyebrows, surprised and impressed.

Jacques looked directly at Liam. "I considered the public relations area as part of my threat assessment. Morris is dealing with a criminal charge, and it affects him personally and also impacts PHL's reputation and ability to do business."

"I agree," said Liam. "I think the feedback I got in the past 24 hours bears out your assessment of the PR situation. I have spoken with several customers, partners and business associates who tell me that confidence in doing business with us has held up. It seems to have been a better angle than the typical 'no comment' approach." Liam nodded at Morris.

"As for the criminal charges," Jacques resumed, "I expect the PR battle will have no bearing on any future court case, right?" Jacques looked at Liam.

"Theoretically, a competent judge would not be affected by public opinion," said Liam. "Yeah, right." Liam shrugged. "Impossible to predict."

Jacques went on. "The PR situation seems to have motivated the wheels of justice at this point. They are in a rush, and the evidence against us is scattered and incomplete. Ed and I have read Detective Clark's investigation report and we have identified several flaws. It refers to written statements from witnesses. Hardly anybody saw who produced the gun Morris used, it happened so fast. Three witnesses who saw Morris pick up the gun from the floor believe he brought it to the scene with him. Ed has looked into that situation. Ed...."

Ed remained seated. "Yesterday afternoon, I took the names of those witnesses to The Arms. Working with Angela, using the receipts from Wednesday night, we were able to identify who *else* was there that night with the witnesses. There were other people who should have seen the action. I contacted most of them by phone, and learned a very interesting fact. There was a group of four people who had not been asked to give written statements. All of them said the gun came from the guy Morris served coffee to."

"In my country, such poor police work is a sure sign of corruption. Next, you will be beaten until you confess." Zia looked at Morris.

"Not only that," Ed continued, "two of these people would have said MacDick tried to shoot Morris first, and that Morris *did not* fire the first shot. The first guy I spoke with said the Asian kid fired first, the second guy said it was the guy Jacques was wrestling with. That second guy sounded like he would be very reliable as a witness. He had the presence of mind to call 9-1-1 even before the shooting started. He was actually on the phone describing the shooting as it was happening!"

"Why didn't they each give a statement?" asked Morris.

"They were sent to the station. When they got there, they were told enough statements had already been collected. They were to be contacted if additional statements were needed."

"Tell us what you got from the owner of The Arms," said Jacques.

"Right. While I was there, I spoke with Boyd MacDougall about the Asian kid. Turns out his father played in the poker game at the pub about a year ago. Boyd recognized the father from the TV news."

"So that's how these guys knew about the poker game," said Morris. "Dad told son about it. When in Canada, go here for a good time."

"Seems likely," said Ed.

"The Crown's case is looking pretty weak," Jacques said, "especially with the disappearance of the two unidentified guys from the hospital."

"Still no ID on Beavis and Butthead?" asked Morris.

"The cops have no photos, not even a sketch. But wait for it," said Jacques. "Zia…"

Zia had been waiting for this moment. "Jacques, Ed and I went through 4,800 different face shots. We were up most of the night. And we came up with this."

Three faces appeared on the screen. The first and third faces were clearly Beavis and Butthead. The timestamps showed a date about two weeks before the Wednesday night shootings.

"These images came from a hidden camera I put in to count customers for Boyd MacDougall. The face in the centre is not visible because the subject was looking down and wearing a baseball cap. But we matched the clothing in that shot to another one taken six minutes later, when the guy went for a leak."

On the screen appeared a profile view of a person with the same clothing. This time he was looking up, and his face was fully visible. It was Innes MacDick.

"Good work," said Morris. "They must have been checking out the pub in preparation for their heist."

"Ah, but there's more," said Zia. "There are two unidentified individuals who were with Beavis, Butthead and MacDick at the stakeout. They did not come in to the pub on the night of the heist, but I'll bet they are part of the same gang." Zia showed two more timestamped photos. "And on the night of the heist, there was an outside camera on the back driveway."

Two shots of a black minivan appeared on the screen. The license plate was not possible to read in either shot.

"From the timestamps on these images," said Jacques, "this van was parked at the back entrance from the time MacDick started his antics in the bar until about five minutes after the shooting ended. Then it took off quickly. It was waiting there, with the driver at the wheel, for 14 minutes."

"A getaway car?" asked Morris.

"Probably," said Jacques. "And if it is, most likely a stolen car."

"Why can't we see the plates?" asked Liam.

"The camera resolution is not good enough," said Zia.

"Still, if the cops look for a report of a stolen black minivan for that time period..." said Morris.

"As we can see, Ed's investigation and Zia's videos give a whole new interpretation to the situation," said Jacques. "We now have evidence linking MacDick and the two guys at the bar. We have a motive with the poker game, and we have a getaway driver. Do we have enough to have the charges dropped?" Jacques looked at Liam.

"The Crown has to prove Morris committed manslaughter, beyond a reasonable doubt. In light of all this evidence, they would be reckless to put him on trial, except for one thing. If Morris were charged only with possession of a firearm, I would make a motion to have the charges dismissed on the basis that the Crown had no reasonable chance of conviction. However, even if there was a crime in progress, a citizen cannot use deadly force to stop it."

Liam looked at his marked-up copy of the police report. "They have a bullet fired from the gun Morris used. It's their so-called first shot. The statement Morris gave does not account for that bullet."

"We both saw who fired the first shot. It was not Morris," said Ed.

"And we both gave statements at the time to back that up," said Jacques.

"And you are not only both life-long friends of his," Liam said, "you are both now working for him. The Crown will use your relationship with Morris to undermine your credibility."

"Physical evidence trumps all," said Morris. "Ed, did you say you met with a guy who was on the phone to the 9-1-1 dispatcher when the shooting started?"

"Yes."

"Zia, is there a video clip around that time?"

"Yes, we can see Boyd on his way to the bar area. He ducks when the shooting starts. But we cannot see who's doing the shooting."

"I know, the camera location is wrong. But can you hear the shots on the audio track?"

"Yes."

"Did you count them?"

"No."

"OK, here's what we need to do. First, count the shots. We might find the count on the clip does not match the count of bullet strikes in the room," said Morris.

"They could say two shots happened at the same instant, so only one sound would be on the recording," said Liam.

Morris nodded. "Right, that's why we also need to get the audio recording of the 9-1-1 call. The shots should be audible. Two microphones: stereo sound. If we combine the recordings, it should be possible to analyze the waveforms and get the approximate location of each shot."

Liam thought for a moment. "OK, that sounds good. To make this evidence as reliable as possible, we will need to be able to show that we have not tampered with it."

"That's easy," said Zia. "We'll work on my copy. I won't touch the copy on the system at The Arms."

"How is it that you have a copy?" asked Morris.

Zia smiled. "Our monitoring station received each video clip from The Arm's computer as soon as the clip was recorded. We have a copy of everything."

"But you have the ability to log in and use the computer at The Arms. That's where you got the face data, right?" asked Liam.

"Yes, but I have read-only access to that computer. I cannot add or erase clips."

The room was silent for a moment.

"Smells like victory," said Ed.

"Jacques," said Morris, "I'd like you and Liam to package this up, and pay Detective Clark a visit. Give him everything we have."

Jacques and Liam nodded.

Morris thought about the suspicions of Alex James. "One final thing – keep your eyes and ears open. We have reason to suspect someone with the Ottawa Police may be involved in trying to cover up something."

22 – DETECTIVE CLARK UNDER PRESSURE

Detective Clark was at a loss for words. "How embarrassing," he finally said.

Seated in front of him, Liam and Jacques were pleased with their presentation. They had just finished describing a number of items.

The Detective looked at those items on his desk.

The first item was a list of names and contact information for four additional witnesses. Jacques claimed they would state that Morris had not fired the first shot; in fact he was shooting back in self-defense.

The second item was a set of time-stamped photographs of MacDick, Beavis, and Butthead, and two other unidentified men, showing them together at the pub two weeks before the incident. They were obviously there to case the joint.

The third item was the only one that troubled him. Detective Clark saw time-stamped photos of the getaway van. The source of the images was a video clip he had not seen before. "Where did you get these photos of this van? I saw the security videos, and there was no camera angle like this."

"I have an affidavit here from Mr. Zia Kubra." Liam reached in his briefcase. "He is the installer of the video system at The Cumberland Arms. These images came from an outside camera that was being recorded at his central monitoring facility."

"Monitoring Facility?" Detective Clark was poker faced. "What else does he monitor?"

"Video signals from his various security systems customers. He has a duplicate record of all the video action at The Arms on the night of the shooting." Liam flipped to the back page of the document. "Since the defense has collected this evidence, I need to ensure it can withstand scrutiny by the prosecution. So I asked him to prepare an inventory of the various video feeds that he was tracking that night. I will be able to demonstrate the validity of these videos by comparing them to the original source – the security system at The Cumberland Arms."

"May I see that?" Detective Clark reached for the document.

"Mr. Kubra has not signed this document yet, so I would prefer not," said Liam.

"I have already seen the videos, Mr. Latham." Clark was still reaching out. "If you at least show me the list, I should be able to tell you if you are on the right track or not."

At that moment, the phone on Detective Clark's desk rang.

"Excuse me." The detective withdrew his hand and picked up the telephone receiver. "Detective Clark."

"You need to know something," said a familiar voice.

"Yes, go ahead," said the detective.

"The Parker lawyer just dropped off a demand for a copy of the 9-1-1 recording. Not the transcript. He wants the audio – he says the shots can be heard on the audio track."

"OK, thanks."

"One more thing. Mr. Bourne only had $2,000 for me on payday. I need more for this."

"OK, sure."

"You're doing some risky stuff and you need somebody to watch out for you."

"Right."

"Show Jason how much you appreciate him. I'll check with him tonight."

"OK." Clark hung up the phone. "Gentlemen, unless you have anything else?" Clark stood up.

"That's all we have for now," said Liam.

Detective Clark motioned the two guests toward his office door. "I'll walk you to the front door."

The three men made their way through the hallways in silence, Clark in the lead. They reached the main door.

"If what you have given me looks good to the Crown Attorney, I will recommend the manslaughter charge be dropped. Would I be able to reach Mr. Parker tomorrow to give him good news?"

"He won't be in the office," said Jacques. "He's taking the day off. He'll be at the cottage with his family. You can reach him on his cellphone."

"I hope I will have something that will put his mind at peace." Detective Clark offered Jacques a handshake.

Jacques and Liam shook hands in turn, said their goodbyes, and stepped out of the building into the busy downtown Ottawa street.

They headed down the sidewalk together. After a few steps, they stopped to wait for a walk signal before entering a crosswalk.

"Did he seem very eager to get that document, then change his mind after that phone call?" asked Jacques.

"Yes, I noticed that."

"That call came from inside the cop shop. I saw his call display. It was a four-digit internal extension."

"Write it down. I have a bad feeling about that guy."

After Detective Clark said goodbye to his guests, he returned to his desk. He unlocked his second desk drawer and found the Jason Bourne DVD exactly where he expected it to be. He looked around to make sure he was not being observed, and then opened the DVD case. The $2,000 was gone. He reached into his jacket pocket and quickly counted out another $2,000 and placed it in the case, then locked the case back in the second desk drawer.

Detective Clark signed out for the day and got in his car. He picked up his cellphone and placed a call.

"What?" said the South African voice of van Praag.

"Trouble. Parker is going to discover I tampered with the evidence."

"We can't have that."

"Can I use your men?"

"They're pretty banged up."

"This will be an easy job. Parker is going to be at his cottage tomorrow with his family. It will be like shooting fish in a barrel."

Pause. "You will be delivering the final two subjects to the camp?" asked the South African.

"Yes."

"You have the address of this cottage?"

"Yes."

"Send it to me by confidential text message. I will send them tomorrow. Parker caused my men a lot of pain. I'm sure they would enjoy a small fishing trip. They will leave no witnesses."

23 – KILLERS AT THE COTTAGE

"Do we have any cold beer down there?" asked Morris, looking down into the small galley of *Tacotime*, the Parker family's 28-foot Bayliner Cruiser.

"You had us on shore power, right? Your beer should be cold," said Terri from below deck.

"I know the fridge is cold, I just want to know if Susan and her friends drank all my beer again."

"Catherine, would you take a look and see if Daddy has any beer left. I'm making the bed."

Morris was busy on deck arranging the fishing equipment for their early morning cruise. It was 5:35 AM – first light.

"Dad, there are four beer bottles here," said Catherine. "Rimshot!"

"What happened, munchkin?"

"Rimshot tried to stick his nose in the fridge. There's some ham here, Dad."

"He's been on board with us all night, Morris," said Terri. "You better take your dog for a walk before we push off."

"OK, Rimshot – c'mon boy." Morris took the ten-foot leash from where it was regularly stowed.

Wishing he had time for a good hot shower, Morris picked up Rimshot and placed him on the dock. Rimshot was still cautious when moving between the dock and the boat, ever since he had fallen in the lake as a pup.

Morris had arrived at the cottage from Ottawa the night before, just in time for supper. Catherine had wanted the whole family to sleep on the boat that night to make it easier to head out for an early morning fishing trip. Susan and Victoria had opted-out of the early morning plan, and had stayed up late watching horror movies in the cottage. Mom and Dad had slept on the boat with youngest daughter 12-year old Catherine.

Morris followed Rimshot as he headed along the shore. The water was calm, and the sky was slowly brightening.

Mid-yawn, Morris noticed Rimshot react to something in the woods. The dog tensed and emitted a low growl, looking into the dimly lit clearing around the house.

Probably a raccoon, Morris thought. He walked over to the dog and grabbed hold of the collar. "Easy, Rimbo."

Rimshot was extremely tense, and Morris could feel the hair on the back of the dog's neck was up. Rimshot began to pull hard, straining to investigate something.

Morris kept a grip on the collar. "Don't wake the neighborhood, fella. Sshhh… sshhh." Morris tried to keep the dog calm as they approached the house. A dense forest surrounded the cottage. Rimshot seemed to have detected something in the treeline at the perimeter of the clearing.

Morris clipped on the leash and then let the dog move ahead through the trees. As they reached the clearing, Morris saw a crouching figure emerge from the forest. The man moved cautiously toward the house carrying a shotgun.

Rimshot snarled and erupted with loud, angry barks. Morris strained to keep the dog from breaking free. The man stopped and looked. Morris and the dog were still concealed by the trees.

Susan and Victoria were still in the house, Morris thought. This guy thinks we're all in there. He's probably not alone. This guy is covering the back door, cutting off our escape route. There must be a front door man. Maybe more than one. Was the cottage locked? Morris always locked up when the family went to bed. But not last night – Morris had not left the boat after the girls did. How to warn the girls?

Then Morris thought about the girls' cellphones. They kept them bedside. Morris had left his phone in the boat. He would have to get back to the boat and warn the girls.

Morris quickly tied the leash to a thick birch tree trunk. Rimshot, barking up a storm, strained to break free.

The armed man decided the dog must be tied up, and resumed his approach to the house.

Morris turned and ran in a crouch position back to the boat. He did not want the man or men to know Terri and Catherine were on the boat.

Terri and Catherine saw Morris on the run. He raised his finger to his lips and signaled them to stay silent as he climbed aboard.

"Turn off the lights," Morris whispered. "I need my cellphone. There's somebody on the property with a shotgun."

Terri covered her mouth with her hands, drawing a sharp breath. "Oh my God!"

Morris looked at Terri. "I'm going to call the girls in the house. Call 9-1-1. Tell them we have an armed intruder."

Terri immediately ushered Catherine to go below deck. "Find my cellphone, honey, and turn off the lights, quick!"

Morris dialed Susan's phone number. It started ringing.

Rimshot was still barking up a storm. Maybe that would wake the girls. But what if one of them came outside to calm him....

Susan answered her phone. "Dad, what's all the barking?" She sounded wide-awake.

"Susan, there is a man with a gun sneaking up to the house. Lock the doors! Wake up Victoria, and find a place for you both to hide! Mom is calling the cops!"

"I locked up last night! Victoria's in her room, I don't know if she's awake!"

"Where are you?"

"I'm in your room!"

"Hide under the bed!"

A heavy thud came from the house. Then another thud, followed by the sound of splintering wood.

"Dad! Somebody's trying to break down the front door!"

Morris did not like the situation. There were at least two men at the house. The family was split in two locations, and had nothing to fight with. These men were not burglars. From their tactics, they were either kidnappers, or killers.

Maybe he could draw them away from the house. He could lure them down to the boat, then move the boat out of shotgun range. Morris cast off the line.

"What are you doing?" Terri was back on deck.

"I'm going to try to get them to come down here. Get ready to start the engine! We'll take off when they get close. We have to give the girls a chance to escape!"

Morris cupped his hands to his mouth, and shouted toward the cottage: "HEY! What's going on up there?"

Morris raised his phone to his ear just as a shotgun blast came from the cottage.

"Susan!"

"Dad, I'm scared!" Susan was about to panic.

"Sshh! Don't let them hear you. Stay under the bed, keep listening to the phone, and don't say anything!"

A girl screamed hysterically from the house. It was Victoria's voice.

"Victoria!" Morris shouted at the cottage. He felt a huge surge of adrenaline. "Victoria!" He leaped onto the dock.

"Come back here!" Terri shouted. "Don't leave us!"

He looked back at her. "Start the engine!"

Their eyes met.

Terri had tears in her eyes. "Don't leave us!"

Morris looked at the house. "They're going to kill the girls!"

Terri's expression changed. She glared at her
husband, teeth clenched, eyes wide. "Look at me! If they
kill the girls," she paused, "they will kill you too. Don't
leave your wife and youngest child."

Morris did not know what to say.

A second shotgun blast came from inside the house.
They both flinched.

Terri looked at the house, agonizing. She looked back
at Morris. "Get in the boat," she said. "Now."

Morris could not make his legs move. He wanted to
fight, not surrender.

"Take us out of range," Terri said firmly, "and stick to
the plan. Try to lure them down here, and give the girls a
chance to escape! The cops are on their way. Ten
minutes, they said."

The dog barking continued. Morris felt his heart
beating in his chest like a bass drum. He felt sick to his
stomach.

"Daddy," Catherine said. "Stay with us."

Morris put his cellphone in his breast pocket and
jumped back into the boat. He started the engine. It roared
to life and he gunned it, churning away from the dock. At
about 150 yards from the shore, he turned sharply and
throttled back to idle speed. Then he killed the engine.

He looked at Terri and Catherine. They were holding
each other, looking back at the shore. Morris switched his
gaze back to the cottage. What were they doing to the
girls?

Morris suddenly remembered his marine loudhailer,
mounted on the front of the boat. He switched the
amplifier on and picked up the microphone.

"Attention: people in my house!" His amplified voice
was loud, clear and authoritative. "The police are on the
way. Get the hell away from there!"

Terri's cell rang. She looked at the call display. "It's
Victoria's phone!"

"Answer it."

"Hello," she said tentatively.

"Put Parker on the phone," said a menacing male voice.

Terri held out her cellphone.

Morris took the phone. "Fuck you."

"We have your daughter. Look here."

Back at the house, Victoria stepped out of the back door followed by a man wearing a ski mask. The morning light was now bright enough to see she was wearing her teddy bear pajamas. The man pointed a shotgun at her back and walked slowly, with a limp.

Morris grabbed his high-power binoculars. He took a close look at Victoria, looking terrified, followed by the limping man.

Rimshot's barking grew more intense. A second gunman emerged, also wearing a ski mask. Morris took a careful look at his face. One eye was visible, the other was obscured by fabric. He was wearing an eye patch, Morris thought. One's a limper, and the other is partially blind. These guys could be Beavis and Butthead, worse for the wear because of the fighting at The Arms.

The second gunman began talking on Victoria's cellphone.

"It's you we want, Parker," the gunman said over the phone. "Come back here, and we'll let your daughter live. Otherwise, my friend here will shoot her dead."

Morris saw Victoria was barefoot. She held her arms tight to her chest, shivering, walking on eggshells.

Morris put down his binoculars and picked up his phone. "How do I know you won't kill us all?"

"We intend to take you hostage. All we want is money," the man replied.

Morris watched the limping man move jerkily. "Tell the gimp to stop pointing that gun at my daughter! I don't want her to be shot by accident."

The gunman with the phone said a few words to his partner, and he pointed his shotgun away.

"It's you we want, Parker. Get over here or we shoot."

"I'm already aware of that part of the deal. Now here's a non-negotiable: you let my daughter move away, I move in closer, a little at a time. Got it?"

"All right, the closer you get, the farther we will let your daughter go."

Stall, stall, stall, thought Morris. "Here I come." He started the engine, and throttled up cautiously. "Let her start to move out of gunshot range, and I'll keep coming."

The gunman with the phone said something to Victoria, and she started walking slowly back toward the house.

Morris throttled back. "Let her go in the other direction, so I can see her at all times. How do I know you don't have somebody else in the house? Let her go toward the shoreline. She can take the path to the neighbor's place."

The gunman with the phone spoke to Victoria again and she changed direction, heading toward the shore.

Morris throttled up a bit. As Rimshot barked frantically, Morris tried to analyze the situation. The police were on their way, but the boat would be at the shore before they arrived. How could Morris get himself close enough to draw them away from Victoria, and still escape? If he landed the boat, would they take Terri and Catherine too? What if they kill everyone to leave no witnesses?

Morris looked below deck. Terri and Catherine were huddled on the galley floor. He looked at the small carpet next to them. His mind cleared and he came up with an idea.

"Find the duct tape!" he said to Terri. "Catherine, steer the boat. Go slow. Head for the shore. Keep your head down low."

Catherine headed up to the main deck and Morris went below.

Morris placed Terri's cellphone on the deck and removed his shirt quickly. He scrambled over to the small carpet and pushed it aside.

Terri had a roll of duct tape in her hand. "What are you doing?"

On the floor in front of Morris was a steel hatch about the size of a cookie sheet. It concealed the bilge pump. Morris reached into the two hand holes, one at each end of the rectangular shape, and removed the hatch cover. It was made of solid steel plate.

"Tape this to my chest!" he said, holding it against himself.

Terri looked at him, incredulous.

"I'm going to draw their fire away from our daughter." He turned his back to her. "Reach around and tape it solid. Hurry."

Terri peeled some tape free and started to wrap her husband with it. Morris turned his body, and she let the tape pay out like she was wrapping a mummy.

"This is crazy," she said.

"If he shoots me, I'll survive. My vital organs are protected."

"You don't consider your head a vital organ?" she asked.

"He will aim for the center of mass. He will aim for the steel plate."

She helped him replace the shirt.

"Dad," said Catherine in a shaky voice. "We're getting close."

"Stop the engine." Morris picked up the cellphone and spoke into it. "I'm coming up."

As he emerged from below deck, Morris saw that Victoria was at the shore to the right, about a bus-length away from the nearest gunman. Morris himself was about two bus-lengths away from the same gunman. Victoria was now down on her knees. She must have been ordered to stop.

Morris climbed onto the side of the boat, heading for the bow. "Let her get up and go. I'm coming."

Terri took over the controls, and slipped into neutral. Now the boat was drifting slowly toward the shore.

Morris put his hand over the mouthpiece of his cellphone. "Put it in reverse," Morris said to Terri. "When Victoria runs, gun it, and get us away from them."

Morris spoke into his cellphone. "I don't see my daughter moving yet. Either she moves away from your partner, or we back away."

The gunman closest to Victoria was aiming at her back. The other gunman was not aiming at anything because he had the cellphone in his hand.

Morris reached the bow of the boat. He remained crouched. At this distance, from the gunman's point of view, he was a smaller target than his daughter. Morris saw that Victoria was now walking away again.

Now for the tricky part, Morris thought. Surviving the next step.

Morris stood up, making himself a bigger target. The gunman turned his head, noticing, but kept his shotgun pointed at Victoria as she walked.

Rimshot's barking increased as Victoria approached him.

Morris raised his hands to his mouth. "Hey gimpy!" he shouted at the gunman. "Now's your chance to pay me back!"

Back at the house, Susan started the engine of the Parker's pickup truck. Because of the loud barking, nobody heard it. She put the truck in gear and started approaching the gunmen from behind.

Morris saw Susan in the truck.

Victoria, still walking away in the sights of the gunman, was now beside Rimshot. His barking reached a fierce crescendo of fury.

"I'M OVER HERE!" yelled Morris. He was now a single bus length away from the nearest gunman.

Both gunmen were totally focused on Morris. Finally, the closest gunman changed his aim from Victoria onto Morris.

"RUN VICTORIA!" Morris spread his arms and legs into the shape of an X. "TAKE YOUR BEST SHOT, ASSHOLE!"

"Shoot him!"

BLAM!

The impact of the shotgun pellets striking the steel plate knocked Morris flat backwards. He lost consciousness immediately. Blood started to flow from his side.

Terri gunned the engine and the boat churned away from the shore. The gunman pumped his shotgun for a second shot.

Too late, the gunman with the phone turned and saw Susan as she clobbered him with the center of the front bumper. The gunman flew into the air, shotgun and phone flying in separate directions.

Susan spun the steering wheel hard to the right, changing direction toward the gunman who had just shot her father. He saw her coming. He changed his aim from the boat to the speeding truck.

Susan saw the muzzle of the shotgun pointed at her. She bent down quickly toward the passenger side.

BLAM. The windshield shattered and glass flew all over the front seat. Susan sat up quickly, untouched except by glass fragments.

The gunman had no time to reload. He dropped his shotgun and dove to the left, trying to avoid being run over.

Susan steered left and felt the front shocks react as the wheels passed over the gunman. She slammed on the brakes, jerking the truck to a halt, and stalling the engine. She looked back, searching for the first gunman. Susan saw him crawling to get to his shotgun. It looked like he had a broken arm.

Susan cranked the ignition, with no effect. The truck did not start.

The gunman picked up his shotgun. He stood up, left arm hanging uselessly by his side. He started to walk toward Susan.

Susan cranked the ignition. The gunman was approaching quickly. Susan cranked the ignition again and again. Not a sound. The truck refused to start.

Using his one good arm, the gunman stopped and aimed his shotgun at Susan's head. Susan cringed, waiting for the shot.

Running at full speed, Rimshot clobbered the gunman with a vicious snarl. The man tumbled and hit the ground beneath 120 pounds of furious German Shepherd. Victoria had let him off his leash.

Rimshot ripped into the man, going for the throat. Blood started to flow as the gunman desperately tried to fend off the angry dog with his unbroken arm.

Susan realized why the truck would not start. It was in drive. She quickly shifted to park and cranked the ignition.

The engine started instantly. A moment later, she heard a shotgun blast coming from under the truck. Rimshot let out a sharp yelp.

The other gunman had been caught beneath the frame of the truck. His partner's shotgun had fallen within his reach. He had managed to retrieve it, aim it, and shoot Rimshot.

Susan threw the shifter into reverse gear. She pushed the gas pedal hard, the rear wheels spun in the soil, and Susan dragged the gunman along as the truck accelerated. Susan saw the shotgun tumble into her field of view from underneath the front end, and she realized the gunman was stuck. She shifted into forward gear and steered toward the shoreline. She slammed on the brakes just as the truck reached the water's edge.

Terri, still driving the boat, had seen everything. As she shifted into forward gear, she watched the first gunman struggled to his feet. Rimshot lay motionless, unable to continue his attack.

The gunman was no longer carrying his shotgun. He was trying to leave the property as quickly as possible.

Terri stopped the engine. "Catherine, tie us off." Terri climbed toward the bow to check her husband, who lay motionless and bleeding.

A faint police siren wailed.

Terri checked the growing stain of blood on Morris' side. A pellet or two must have missed the steel plate and passed through his torso. She checked his pulse. She saw he was not breathing.

"Is he alive?" Victoria was at the dock.

Ignoring the question, Terri immediately started artificial respiration on Morris. Terri had found a weak pulse. She assumed Morris had the wind knocked out of him.

After Terri administered several breaths, Morris took a deep breath on his own, and started to cough and sputter.

"Keep an eye on him," Terri said to Victoria. "Call me if he stops breathing again." Terri jumped to the dock.

Back at the pickup truck, Susan was examining the vehicle. The gunman was trapped under the truck frame, conscious, laying on his back, looking skyward. His left arm, shoulder and head stuck out from underneath.

Susan looked up from the man as her mother approached.

Terri crouched down and yanked off the man's ski mask. She grabbed the man by his hair, lifting his head. He grimaced in pain.

"You shot my husband! YOU SHOT MY DOG!" she screamed.

Susan looked up. "Oh, no."

Rimshot lay motionless where he had been shot. She ran over to him.

Rimshot's eyes were open. He saw Susan approach, and reacted with a small whine. Susan saw fur covered in blood. He had been hit from close range, and his chest had been blasted open. Susan could see internal organs. She realized she could see the heart beating.

"He's hurt real bad, Mom," she said.

The police siren was growing louder. "Susan," Terri looked at her daughter. "Call 9-1-1. We need an ambulance for your father."

Terri looked down at the gunman. "If you want to live, tell me why you did this."

"I can't." The man struggled to speak. "He'll kill me."

"Who will kill you? Who sent you?"

The man remained silent.

"Take your choice. He kills you, or else I do," said Terri.

The man smirked.

"You're one of the losers from The Cumberland Arms. My husband showed me a picture of you. You and two of your stupid buddies. You were caught on camera when you cased the joint two weeks before my husband beat the hell out of you."

The man's smirk disappeared.

"My husband is alive. You missed."

"I hit him dead center…" the man was having trouble getting enough air to speak due to the pressure of the truck on his chest.

"He's the man of steel." Terri looked at the front left tire. It had run up a large, sloped rock.

Catherine had approached the truck and was watching her mother and the injured gunman.

"I need you to turn your back, Catherine," Terri released the gunman's hair. "Look away, and plug your ears."

Catherine did as her mother instructed.

"My husband does not need your information," she said to the gunman. "You will never hurt my family again, Butthead!"

Terri reached into the truck cab and released the brake. The front wheel rolled backward down the rock, lowering the chassis and crushing the gunman's chest, ending his ability to breathe. He began to convulse violently.

"My husband was wearing a steel plate under his shirt." Terri spoke calmly and clearly. "You made a good shot. Thanks for hitting it directly."

Terri stood over the man, looking into his eyes. Her face was expressionless. The man was terrified. He slammed his head into the mud a few times, and then stopped moving. His face finally relaxed. The pressure on his chest had caused his heart to stop beating. His eyes stared blankly upwards, and the color of his skin changed swiftly from pink to blue.

Terri looked up to see an Ontario Provincial Police cruiser arrive, lights flashing.

24 – MORRIS IN HOSPITAL

"I vaguely remember taping a steel plate to my chest," said Morris.

"Do you remember why?" Jacques asked Morris from beside his hospital bed.

"I hope I had a good reason," said Morris. "I somehow ended up here because of it."

For over two days, Morris had been drifting in and out of consciousness with a head injury. Terri had stayed with him for most of that time, until she finally went home exhausted a few hours ago, letting Jacques take over. Then Morris regained consciousness. He was able to communicate for the first time, and he recognized people.

"You drew shotgun fire. The gunman would otherwise have shot Victoria. She got away while he was shooting at you. Susan ran over one of them with your pickup truck, the other escaped.

"What happened to the guy she ran over?"

"He died very painfully. Terri was questioning him when he expired."

Morris blinked. "For that guy, hell started early. She probably interrogated him to death. Did she get anything out of him?"

"She didn't tell me everything about that discussion. She wanted to speak with you first. But she said this incident was more than just a revenge attack."

"It was Beavis and Butthead, right?"

"Yes."

"How is everyone?"

"Terri and your three daughters were not harmed, but one of the gunmen killed Rimshot. I'm sorry. Your dog saved Susan's life. He prevented her from being shot."

Morris was silent for a moment. "We've had that dog a long time. He was a very good dog. How are the kids taking it?"

"They've said nothing to Terri about Rimshot because they're very worried about you. They were not allowed to visit you until just this morning, and you were out of it the whole time."

"They saw me lying here, helpless, in the middle of all this?" Morris looked at the medical apparatus that surrounded him.

"They insisted on seeing you," Jacques had a sympathetic expression. "I called Terri five minutes ago, when you regained consciousness and started to make sense. The family is on the way. They should be here in about ten minutes."

Morris looked around the room. "I need a chair. I don't want them to see me in this bed again."

"I'll get one for you." Jacques turned to leave.

"Wait. How did I get a head injury?"

"The shotgun blast knocked you flat on you back, and you hit your head on a hatch cover." Jacques walked over to the bed and pressed the call button. "You have a severe concussion. They gave you a CT scan while you were unconscious."

A female nurse entered the room.

"Holy cow, that was quick," said Morris.

"I was coming to check up on you," she said.

"Mr. Parker would like a chair, please," said Jacques. "His family is coming to visit."

The nurse looked at Morris. "You're supposed to remain in bed, Mr. Parker."

"I feel strong enough. Perhaps I should stand." Morris tried to sit up. The pain in his abdomen felt like he had just been stabbed. He swore, and his head started to throb.

"I'll elevate the bed." She manipulated the electric control and then adjusted his pillows.

Morris looked at her with gratitude. "Thanks. Sorry about that. I'm humble now."

The nurse smiled politely, and left the room.

"Terri recognized the guy Susan ran over from The Arms security photos," said Jacques. "It was Butthead. The other gunman was probably Beavis, but no way to know for sure. He wore a balaclava."

"I remember that part. Did the cops ID Butthead?"

"His name is Daniel Dejeu. You put two bullet holes in him at the pub – that helped identification. The other guy now has a broken arm, thanks to Susan."

"What do we know about Dejeu?"

"Dejeu was a Hell's Angel from Montreal. The Mounties are involved now. Their mandate is major organized crime, putting your case into RCMP jurisdiction."

"That should complicate things nicely. Now we have three layers of police. When did the Ontario Provincial Police get to the cottage?"

"After all the fun was over. The OPP responded with a single cop. He screwed around at the scene a bit trying to sort out what had happened before he finally took off to try and chase the gunman who got away."

"Is Susan charged with anything?"

"No. The guy blasted out her windshield with his shotgun, just missing her. It was kill or be killed."

Morris stared blankly, remembering something new. "I heard two shots fired in the cottage. I was afraid they might have already shot Susan."

"The first shot was fired at the front door mechanism. The second shot hit Victoria's bedroom ceiling. They forced Victoria out onto the lawn as hostage. They didn't find Susan because she was hiding under your bed. You were talking with her on your cellphone, and the line stayed open for quite a while. She could hear what you and Terri were doing on the boat. Susan timed her attack perfectly and surprised them from behind."

"Wow."

Jacques paused for a moment. "Before your family gets here, I want to apologize for something."

Morris looked at Jacques with a puzzled expression. "What could you possibly have to apologize for?"

"The gunmen located you because I told Detective Clark where you would be that day. After Liam and I gave him the evidence we had gathered, Clark asked me where he could contact you. I told him you would be at the cottage."

"Did you give him the address?"

"No."

"Then how did he get it?"

"Four years ago you reported a break-in at your cottage to the OPP. There was a police report on file. Clark accessed it."

"Now we know he's a bad cop." Morris looked puzzled. "How do you know he accessed it?"

"Alex James gave me a call when he heard what had happened to you. I told him I suspected Clark. He did a bit of investigating and called me back. Alex told me he gave you Clarks' report on the pub shootings."

"Now you know who is helping us."

"Yes, helping at great risk to his own job. He thinks there is more than one dirty cop on the Ottawa force." Jacques walked over to the window and looked out to see the Parker family in the parking lot, heading toward the hospital main entrance. "Here comes your family. We need to finish up."

Jacques went on. "Alex was able to get an audit trail report on computer users who had accessed police reports concerning Morris Parker. The report on your cottage break-in was accessed and printed by Clark last week. Alex thinks this is more than just a Cripps or Hell's Angels' revenge. So do I. Somebody is out to get you, for some reason."

"Why me?"

"Dejeu told Terri he would be killed if he revealed who sent him. Somebody big is trying to hide."

Morris paused to consider the implications of that information.

"Help me with some deductive reasoning here. If Beavis and Butthead had succeeded in their mission, I would be dead now."

"So what?"

"If I was dead, I would stop doing what I'm doing."

"What are you doing?"

"I'm looking for information to clear my name."

"And if you clear your name?"

"Somebody else's name gets dirty."

"Clark?"

"Yes, and whoever Clark is on the take with. That somebody is into something so dirty he's willing to kill a whole family for it."

"So what?"

"So I keep doing whatever is pissing him off – faster and harder! I get to him before he has another go at me. These bad guys are bigger than what we have seen so far," said Morris. "What about the good guys? The Ottawa Police force cannot be trusted. Can we report them to the OPP? The RCMP?"

"Not without getting Alex in a lot of trouble. I already told the RCMP Clark was the only one who knew you would be at the cottage. We can't reveal the audit report."

Morris folded his arms on his chest. "What are the Mounties doing about it?"

"They say they will investigate. They aren't telling us much."

Morris paused, thinking. "It takes years for them to investigate this kind of stuff. Can you imagine the coordination issues? There are three different police forces involved now. Do you have any recommendations?"

"I recommend we don't give any more information to Clark or anyone in the Ottawa Police. I don't think we can count on the RCMP to do very much for us. I suggest we increase our information gathering activities."

"Where do we start?"

"I sent Ed to the Asian kid's apartment. He was able to find it from a newscast on your PVR because the Kanise family made a public statement in front of the building. Ed found the name 'K. Kanise' on the building directory. The apartment is empty at the moment. Ed has been watching it for about 36 hours."

Morris looked at Jacques. "You want to go into that apartment?"

"I think we have to. We have to look for clues to connect Kanise somewhere."

"So, to summarize, somebody is out to get me for something we have, or will have. We don't realize what it is, yet." Morris closed his eyes and put his hands to his temples. His head was starting to throb a bit. "You gave evidence to Clark, and then he puts the hit on me. Something you told him put him on edge."

"At our meeting, Clark was very interested in our video evidence."

Morris dropped his hands to his sides and looked at Jacques. "How does a minor Ottawa detective have the connections to put a hit out on me?"

"Clark must be connected to something bigger," said Jacques. "Something else is going on. He told Mr. Big, whoever that is, that we're on to them."

"It's in the video evidence," said Morris. "Or it's in something the video will lead us to."

"We need to find it quick. Obviously, the hit stays out on you until we find out who ordered it." Jacques pulled out a notepad. "What do you want to do, boss?"

Morris thought for a moment. "Look at the videos again. Look at everything in the recording. Let's figure out what Clark already knows is there."

Jacques started to write.

Morris went on. "You know breaking in to a private apartment is illegal and you could go to jail, right?"

"You gave us a mission." Jacques shrugged. "We are dealing with murderers and crooked cops. If we have to stick to the rules, we are going to lose this game."

Morris nodded. "OK, just don't get caught. Wait. Bring Conan Moore – he's a computer hacking expert. He'll help you out. Look for computer evidence. The Asian kid probably had a laptop or desktop computer."

Morris waited while Jacques made a few final notes.

Terri entered the room. "So, Iron Man is finally awake." She smiled at Jacques. "Two days I wait for him, and he decides to wake up for his beer buddy, not me." Terri turned to look at her husband.

Morris thought she looked exhausted.

"I didn't take time to do my hair or makeup," she said. "This is all you get."

"You look great to me," said Morris.

"Let me give you two some time alone," said Jacques.

"The kids are just down the hall," said Terri. "I said I wanted a word with their father first."

"I'll wait with them. I'll let them know Dad is back in charge of the situation."

"If I decide to let him be in charge," she said, smiling. "Thanks, Jacques."

Jacques left the room.

Terri approached her husband. "I'm having a hard time holding it together for the kids," she said calmly. "Those men came to kill us."

"Detective Clark is a dirty cop. Alex discovered he pulled the address for our cottage out of an old police report."

Terri's eyes got wide.

"We are going to track down the people responsible. We'll get Clark too. He went after me because we obviously are on to something that he doesn't want us to know about."

Terri stayed silent.

"We're going to dig for more information. We're also going to take another look at the stuff we already have. The bad guys obviously think we can get to them."

Terry walked over to the window.

"Say something," said Morris.

"I killed the man who shot you," she said, finally. She turned to look at Morris. "He refused to talk, saying he'd be killed if he did. So I released the emergency brake and crushed the life out of the bastard."

Wow, thought Morris. "You did the right thing," he said. Morris looked at her steadily. "You did what I would have done."

Terri looked down.

"You don't have to tell anyone else, ever. Not the kids – nobody."

Terri reached out and took Morris by the hand. "OK." She looked at the IV needle stuck there. "You were ready to give your life to try to save Victoria."

"I would do the same for any of you."

They looked at each other for a long moment.

"None of us have cried yet." Terri put down his hand. "All we have been doing is worrying about you." She stood up from the bed. "I'm going to get the kids now."

Morris watched Terri leave the room. His head was pounding now, and he was tired. He was starting to feel overwhelmed and confused.

He looked around the room. There were flowers and cards everywhere. They must have been sent from the office people, from his associates, and from his friends. He spotted a familiar picture on a table. Morris decided to get on his feet.

This time, instead of trying to sit up, Morris rolled onto his stomach at the edge of the bed. Slowly and painfully, he pivoted his body until his feet touched the ground, and carefully pushed himself into a standing position. He grabbed his IV stand and walked it with him. He picked up the picture frame to get a closer look at the photograph.

The photo showed the four Parker girls, seated on the basement carpet, smiling, surrounding a German Shepherd puppy. The photo was six years old. Catherine, age six – beaming with pride – was holding the dog. Rimshot was licking her face. Victoria, age twelve, was stroking him. Susan, age 16, posed with a goofy grin, giving a thumbs up. Terri was showing a smile and a shrug. It had taken time to convince her to accept a dog in the family.

Rimshot had been the only other male in the family. Morris suddenly filled with emotion, and his vision clouded as his eyes filled with tears. He stood shakily, one hand holding the photo, the other hand on his IV stand. He looked up. The family had arrived.

Morris struggled to find his voice. "His barking saved us all," he said slowly, voice breaking.

Catherine walked over and hugged her father, and started to cry. Victoria and Susan quickly joined her, sobbing. Terri's eyes filled with tears, and she covered her face, weeping softly.

Jacques looked at the group, and felt a tear run down his face. He made eye contact with Morris. Neither man felt shame in the moment.

Jacques stepped out of the hospital room, and stood guard at the door.

PART THREE – THE RECONNAISANCE

25 – CONAN THE HACKER

It was 02:24 AM Sunday morning. Conan was not surprised to find zero car traffic in downtown Ottawa.

Conan checked the TaskMan printout showing the address of the Delta Hotel: 361 Queen Street. Seeing that the traffic light had turned green, he engaged his turn signal, double-checked for cross traffic, and executed a left turn onto Queen. He signaled a lane change, did a right shoulder check, and then moved from the center lane into the curb lane. He parked his rusting, 10-year old Jeep on the street within about 20 steps of the main entrance to the hotel, retrieved his laptop from the passenger seat, and took his enormous coffee mug from the cup holder. Hands full, he put his cup and laptop bag on the sidewalk, closed and carefully locked the vehicle.

Conan entered the hotel. He nodded to the clerk as he passed the reception desk heading toward the elevators. He spotted a large coffee thermos and a nice looking basket of red delicious apples set out for the hotel guests. He walked past the elevators and stopped in front of the coffee, putting his laptop case down.

Conan removed the cover from his plastic mug, and topped-up his coffee. He glanced over at the reception desk, checking for the desk clerk. The clerk was no longer in sight. Conan surveyed the rest of the lobby cautiously, then quickly pocketed four apples.

Whistling, Conan picked up his laptop and coffee mug and walked over to the elevator doors. He placed his laptop case on the floor and pushed the elevator button, and one of the doors opened immediately. Conan picked up his laptop and entered the elevator. He placed his laptop case on the elevator floor, pushed the fourth floor button, and took a sip of coffee.

Checking his watch, he realized he was right on schedule for a 2:30 AM arrival at room 412. Conan whistled all the way to the room. He stopped in front of the door, placed his laptop down again, and then re-checked his watch. The time was exactly 2:30 AM. He knocked on the door.

Ed opened the door and looked at the man he had communicated with as the_barbarian@parkerholdings.com. "You must be Conan."

"You look like shit!" Conan pulled an apple out of his pocket. "Apple?"

Ed had been awake for almost 48 hours. His last meal had been breakfast. He grabbed the apple. "God yes."

Ed bit into the apple and waved Conan into the room, letting the door close behind him.

Zia was seated at the desk in the room, intently studying the screen of a large laptop. Jacques was seated looking out the window with a pair of binoculars. There were several empty coffee cups and an empty donut box cluttering the room.

Conan placed his laptop on the bed. It had not been slept-in that night. The hotel was being used as a stakeout room, not a bedroom.

Conan approached Zia, seeing twelve rectangular video images displayed on Zia's screen like a patchwork quilt.

"Apple?" Conan offered one to Zia. "It's better than donuts."

"Sure, thanks." Zia accepted the apple and placed it on the desk beside his laptop.

"What's all this?" Conan stared at the images.

"I have twelve wireless cameras in the apartment building. I have every angle covered to protect you and Ed when you go in."

"Huh."

Conan walked over to the window, noticing Jacques was wearing a small earpiece.

"Apple?" Conan offered Jacques the third apple, and Jacques removed his earpiece and accepted it.

"Thanks. Nice apple." Jacques began to polish it on his sleeve. "We planted a couple of listening devices over there." Jacques looked at Zia. "Zia has quite a collection of gadgets for you. Show Conan what you have for this mission, Zia."

Zia nodded and picked up a large suitcase, putting it on the bed. "Just call me 'Q,' Mr. Bond." Zia opened the suitcase and pulled out a pair of night-vision goggles.

"We have two sets of these, so you don't have to turn on the lights."

"Where do you get this stuff?" asked Conan.

Zia tossed him the goggles. "You can find it on eBay."

Conan began to fiddle with the goggles.

Zia took a cordless drill from the suitcase. "You'll need this to get into the main door. I already figured out the type of lock Ed is going to have to work through, and this drill has the right bit for the job."

Zia took two cellphones and two Bluetooth one-ear headsets from the suitcase. "You'll use these to keep in contact while you're inside. These babies use encryption, so your conversations cannot be intercepted."

"While you're inside, you can prevent anyone else from entering with this." Zia pulled out an aluminum tube about the size of a roll of Christmas wrap. "This end fits under the door knob," he pointed to a u-shaped bracket on one end of the tube. "And this end goes on the floor, propping the door closed like the old 'chair under the doorknob trick' you see in cartoons."

"How are we supposed to carry all that stuff without being noticed?" asked Conan, putting down the goggles.

Zia looked at Jacques.

"We have a tool chest for you," Jacques pointed to a large, boxy tool carrier on the second bed. "It's part of your disguise as electricians." Jacques pointed to a pair of coveralls lying beside the tool carrier.

"What is this, *Mission Impossible?*" Conan marched over to the bed and sat himself against the headboard, adjusting the pillows for comfort. He swiftly unzipped his laptop case and opened the screen.

"We don't want you two getting caught," said Jacques. "This is against the law."

"I can appreciate that," said Conan as he watched his laptop boot up. "How are we supposed to fix the lock after we drilled it?" Conan took the last apple out of his pocket and bit into it heartily. "The residents are going to know somebody's been inside," he said with his mouth full.

"Good point," said Jacques.

"I can get a replacement cylinder for the lock," said Zia.

"How will you key it to match the owner's key? You need his key for that." Conan began to type in bursts. He typed a command, watched the response, gave another command, got another response.

"What if we try going in through a window?" asked Ed.

"On the third floor? Maybe you should bribe the landlord," Zia suggested to Jacques.

"What's this guy's name?" asked Conan.

"The landlord?" asked Zia.

"God, no. The Asian kid."

"Kendo Kanise," Jacques said to Conan, then looked at the others. "Sorry fellas, I'm not criminal-minded enough for this. I need help. Any suggestions?"

"Where can we hire a burglar?" asked Ed.

"In my country…" Zia began.

"Hold your horses. I'm on my way in," said Conan. The others looked at him, not sure what to say.

"There are thirteen unsecured wireless networks within range of my laptop," said Conan. "That apartment building has a lot of computer users in proximity to each other. One of these networks is called KENDOSWORLD." Conan typed a few more commands. "I have run a few network analysis tools, and there appears to be only one computer running on that network. Since it's using a wireless network card, it is likely a laptop. What kind of work did Kendo do?"

"He was an engineering student at Carleton University," said Ed.

"Engineering students use Windows laptops. He most likely leaves his computer online all the time so he doesn't have to wait for it to boot each time he uses it, and so it can do nightly updates by itself to keep it secure."

Conan looked at the group like he was teaching a small hacking class. "The problem with Windows is, you're damned if you do, damned if you don't. He leaves his computer on all the time to download nightly updates. But that means it will regularly try to add new software which can have it's own set of new problems, like the one I'm going to feed to his computer in about twenty-two minutes, if he has automatic updates turned on."

"You're going to feed it new software?" asked Zia.

"Some automatic updates require the computer to reboot after it is installed. Tonight, Microsoft is releasing an update that will reboot his computer. When it does, his wireless network card will configure itself automatically. That's where we find our 'vulnerability.' This hack only works because I'm inside his local network. He neglected to secure it."

Conan looked at his wide-eyed students with a big grin.

"His computer boots, his wireless card accepts my software and causes it to be executed, and *voila*, we have, as they say, *complete control of the affected system*. Not quite true, of course, since nobody truly has complete control of any Windows system – too many bugs."

"Are you going to need *us* for anything?" asked Zia.

"Yeah," said Ed. "Can we go home?"

"If he doesn't have Windows Update turned on, we will have to try things your way. I hope one of those coveralls will fit me."

"How do you know how to do all this crap?" asked Ed.

"I don't hack, usually, I am just a humble Utility Programmer. But I'm good at researching new tasks. I found out how to do this after lunch. I just had to ask the right friend."

"What kind of friends do you have?" asked Ed.

"I've been jumping from site to site doing all kinds of general purpose installing and troubleshooting for my whole career. I like to keep track of good people and what they know."

The room went silent for the next twenty minutes as the group waited patiently.

Conan was watching his laptop screen. "I've lost contact with his computer. It's rebooting." Conan looked at his watch. "His system clock must be fast."

"What are you going to do when you get control of his system?" asked Zia.

"All I do is one small thing. I wrote a program that uploads everything on his computer up to a server system at the PHL computer room. After that completes, the program reboots his computer as if an ordinary update has completed. It leaves no trace of itself."

"Why send it to PHL? Why not pick it up onto your laptop?" asked Ed.

"Because the speed of the connection from his laptop to Parker Systems is a lot faster than the speed from his laptop to mine. And we can examine the stuff at our leisure. I can even examine it from here if I want."

The group watched a line of text appeared on Conan's screen:

> time to go paddling
>

"I'm in," said Conan.

Conan typed a single command, hit the *Enter* key, and saw another line of text appear below his command:

> goforit
> time estimate 245 minutes, uploading to SCHMUCK CENTRAL...
>

"What's that schmuck stuff?" asked Ed.

"I wrote these programs in honor of Morris," said Conan. "Now we just have to wait until this upload is complete. It says it will take about four hours."

Conan reached over and picked up the night vision goggles. He grinned and put them on his head. "Anything good on TV?"

26 – MOHAMED PICKS UP VAN PRAAG

"We were not supposed to meet at this point," said Joris van Praag from the driver's seat of his rental car. "Unfortunately, unexpected events caused me to arrange for this visit."

The two vehicles, van Praag's rental car and Mohamed's SUV, were side-by-side with driver's doors aligned. The two men were speaking with each other through their open driver's windows. The conversation was subdued and secretive, taking place in the dark parking lot of an auto service shop somewhere in Kenora, Ontario.

"Your car has Manitoba plates. Did you rent this car?" asked Mohamed Ziad.

"It was rented at the Winnipeg airport by a colleague. I am not listed as a driver on this car. My colleague is with a different company, so this car cannot be traced to my company or to me. I must return this car to him by 8:00 AM. He thinks I have picked up a woman."

Mohamed nodded, satisfied, and looked at his watch. "It will take you at least two hours to return to Winnipeg, and the camp is one hour from here. We will have about four hours together. One hour to drive to the camp, and one hour to return here. That will leave us two hours at the camp."

"That should be sufficient."

"Park over there, next to the other cars." Mohamed pointed. "This service facility opens at 7:00 AM. The car must be gone by then. To anyone driving by, your car will look like it is here for service like the others."

Van Praag nodded, drove the short distance to the parking spot, and stepped out of the vehicle, taking a small athletic bag with him. He locked the car and got in to the passenger seat of Mohamed's SUV, placing his bag on the floor behind his feet.

"Do you have a cellphone?" Mohamed asked.

"Yes, and it is turned off as you requested. I turned it off before I left Winnipeg tonight."

"Good." Mohamed offered his hand and the two men shook. "I am not certain if the authorities have the habit of tracking wherever every cellphone may roam, but it is certainly a technical possibility."

"I am confident that the authorities are not suspicious of any of our activities at the moment." Van Praag was smug. "We have done none of the foolish things that have resulted in early detection of terrorist groups. We have not communicated in plain text over the Internet or telephone about bombs, bomb-making techniques, and ingredients of bombs, jihad, or radical fundamentalist Islam. None of us have traveled to suspicious countries such as Iran, Afghanistan or Pakistan."

"Our approach is new. It will be unexpected. But it is you who will suffer for any traces that remain after our attack." Mohamed smiled. "I will be long gone from this country, enjoying the hero's welcome of a victorious returning general. I am being extra cautious, so that you will not be linked after our attack, and so our share of the cash will come in as expected."

"I will certainly be investigated, because the authorities will have to satisfy themselves that my company had no advance knowledge of the new virus. It must appear to them that we happen to be lucky to be in the right place at the right time. They must find no connections whatsoever between the camp and my company."

"I have taken every precaution." Mohamed put the SUV in drive and exited the parking lot. "Let me tell you about these precautions."

"I would appreciate that."

Jim E.M. Miles

"I have paid every bill by cash or bank draft. The bank drafts were purchased from local banks, and no draft was for an amount greater than $5,000."

"How did you conceal the large amounts of US cash I gave you for your operations? You have expended over $500,000 since the early spring when you received it in small bills."

"I told the tellers the cash came from American and European tourists. Sport fishermen and hunters spend a lot of money in this area. I also registered three small companies with fictitious directors, and I used the false US Company you incorporated for me in Minnesota. I kept the money moving in small amounts between the companies. I made transactions each week at five different banks using three different stolen identities. The clerks know me under three different names. They have no reason to suspect what is really going on is not tourism."

"You went to these banks in person? Your image will be recorded on the bank security cameras."

"Yes, but I always wore a baseball cap and dark glasses."

Van Praag nodded. "You paid all suppliers? None of them has reason to pay extra attention to us?"

"I purchased this truck in Saskatoon, used, for cash, in a private sale. I also paid cash in Dryden for the All-Terrain-Vehicle I use at the camp. I acquired the refrigerator truck in Calgary and had it fitted-up there. That vehicle is registered in Alberta and we should dump it there when we are done."

"How do you intend to dispose of the other major assets?"

"The Lab and Living Quarters are leased ATCO trailers. They were leased in Thunder Bay, a four-hour drive east of the camp. The leasing agent believes they are being used in Kapuskasing, which is another four-hour drive east of the Thunder Bay. They will be

sanitized and returned intact to Thunder Bay. There will
be no connection to this vicinity."

Mohamed looked at van Praag to ensure he was
paying attention. "The generator will be returned to
Winnipeg. I will disassemble the furnace and haul it with
this truck into a location deeper into the forested area.
There is a lake with deep water near shore. I will dump
the furnace in that lake. It will not be found, and if it ever
is, it will not be connected to our camp."

"Where did you get that furnace?"

"eBay. Paid by PayPal, using one of the company
bank accounts."

"How will you remove the furnace hut?"

"I will burn it. I will also burn the barn. The fires will
attract no attention if done at night, when no smoke will
be visible. These buildings have concrete foundations that
will survive the fire. But it will not be possible, from the
foundation alone, to discern the purpose of the buildings
or when they were last used."

"What about the sea containers?"

"I will get them to Thunder Bay for you to ship them
wherever you want."

"How did you get them in?"

"I had them hauled by truck."

"The driver saw the camp?"

"If you are worried about the driver being able to
recall that shipment, I assure you, he will remember
hauling them in." Mohamed glanced at van Praag,
looking for a reaction. "I intend to use the same driver to
haul them out. He has assured me he will be available."

Van Praag was puzzled. "Hauling a sea container into
a remote campsite beside a lake is certainly memorable.
After our attack, there will be unending media coverage.
If your driver approaches the police, he could lead them
to the campsite."

"There is no need to kill this driver," Mohamed kept
his attention on his driving. "You can save my fee. I hired

a *distraction* that prevented the driver from knowing the location of the camp. I did the driving."

Van Praag thought for a moment. "This distraction – what was her name?"

"Valerie? Vonda, perhaps? I cannot recall. MacDick made the arrangement. She kept the driver occupied in the sleeping compartment of his Freightliner. He was not interested in observing the route to the camp. The focus of his entire attention was sex, drugs, and country music."

"The driver was comfortable with you in the front, driving?" van Praag looked amused.

"I told him I was a former trucker. I also said I was gay. I told him the girl was going to entertain some special guests at a hunting lodge after the trip, and he was welcome to indulge for free."

Van Praag laughed. "Very clever. Did the driver see the camp?"

"Yes, I needed his skill to maneuver the sea containers into position. Once they were in place, he detached his rig and I drove the return trip."

"What did he see at the camp?"

"Nothing unusual, at the time only the propane tank was installed."

"Did he seem curious about it?"

"He asked what it was for. I told him it was a tank of rocket fuel, and that we were launching experimental aircraft from the lake. He seemed to believe me. He wanted to get back to the girl as soon as possible."

"Who besides your men has seen the camp?" van Praag asked.

"Only your men Dejeu, Paxson, and my friend Kendo. They were my construction crew."

"Dejeu is now dead, by the way."

"What did he die of – stupidity?"

"Almost. He was run over while attempting to kill someone who had discovered compromising information

on our activities. That mission did not go well. I will tell
you what you need to know later."

Mohamed looked at van Praag, wondering about the
competency of van Praag's end of the operation.

Van Praag avoided eye contact. "Kendo will be
replaced by a new man for the last two deliveries. I will
give you more details later." Van Praag did not want to
tell Mohamed that his friend was dead.

The two men were silent for a few moments.

Mohamed was looking forward to seeing Kendo.
They had hit it off during camp construction and become
good friends, despite their age and cultural differences.
Mohamed realized it was because Kendo reminded him
of his younger brother, who had been shot by American
soldiers along with his sister, when their car failed to stop
at a roadblock. They had been following an Afghan army
truck, as instructed, that was supposed to escort the car
through. But the Afghan army driver had been high on
hashish, and he forgot what he was doing.

Mohamed had difficulty trusting van Praag's
tendency to keep details to himself. It would be nice to
know more about the operation, because it would reassure
him van Praag was dealing adequately with whatever
threat they faced. Their biggest threat was detection,
which would spoil the entire operation. Mohamed,
however, understood the principal of information
dissemination on a need-to-know basis. The fewer facts
known by each member of their operation, the less
damage if one of the members is caught.

Mohamed decided to keep his concerns to himself. It
was too late in the game to change anything, anyway.
There was nothing Mohamed could do about it. Winter
was coming and the camp had to be closed as planned
before snow made deconstruction difficult. The attack
could not take place as scheduled in the spring if the
camp is still in place to be found by the authorities. There

was no time for Mohamed to undertake a side mission to eliminate every threat himself.

"I have decided not to remove the sea containers," van Praag said, breaking a long silence. "They are not safe, now that they have been infected. I want you to burn them, and leave the remnants in place."

"How do I burn metal?"

"I had the interior lined with aluminum. Aluminum will ignite before steel, and it will burn hot enough to melt the steel exterior."

"How do I ignite the aluminum?"

"Use propane from the main tank. The sea containers are air tight, and I had them fitted with a propane gas inlet valve. Tonight, I will show you how to attach a gas line from the camp's main tank and fill the isolation chambers with propane. As the pressure increases to about six times regular air pressure, the propane will stay in liquid form. You can put in as much as you like as long as the main supply tank does not fall below 50% full. I will also give you a radio-frequency igniter to place inside one of the two sea containers before you seal the isolation chamber. Then you can detonate from a safe distance."

"Reminds me of my bomb-making days." Mohamed's confidence was somewhat restored. Clearly, van Praag had explosive demolition in mind from the beginning. Van Praag was a very meticulous planner, even if his ability to execute those plans was somewhat suspect.

"For safety, make sure you disconnect the propane gas hose before you detonate. The isolation chambers are far enough away from the main propane tank that it will not become involved in a fire in the chambers – unless the hose carries the fire toward it." Van Praag put his hand on Mohamed's shoulder to reinforce his next point. "And remember, at no time can you allow the main tank to fall below 50% full."

"Of course," said Mohamed. "But why? We have used only 8% of the tank since the spring. Why did you install such a large tank, and why must it never fall below half full?"

Van Praag looked at Mohamed for a few seconds, then returned his gaze to the roadway ahead. "I believe you have earned the right to a full explanation."

"Why do you tell me now?"

"You now need to know this information. The previous holder of this information, Dejeu, is incapable of using it because he is dead. You will now have additional responsibilities. I am making you responsible for the emergency destruction plan for the camp. You will be responsible, on my order, for carrying out procedures to destroy the camp in the event it is discovered and raided by the authorities."

Mohamed got the feeling that he was about to learn something he was not going to enjoy. He suppressed his urge to comment, and kept his eyes on the road.

"The main propane tank has been rigged to explode. There is a short-range radio-frequency detonator hidden inside. It can be activated within a one-mile radius of the camp. If authorities take over the camp, I would have sent Dejeu or Paxson to detonate the tank, killing whoever might be in the immediate area."

Mohamed immediately understood the reason he had not been told of this capability. He took a deep breath, trying to control his temper.

"As you know, three things are required for combustion: fuel, heat, and oxygen. The propane tank," van Praag said, "contains a large amount of pure liquid oxygen held within a separate, sealed bladder. As propane exits the tank, the bladder containing the oxygen expands. If the propane reaches the half-full point, and if pressure is lost in the tank, the oxygen bladder will rupture and the two liquids will mix freely. If a small ignition source is then applied...."

"So our fuel supply is also a huge bomb," Mohamed interrupted, eyes widening. He looked at van Praag, who ignored him. "And the reason you did not tell me is because you wanted the option to destroy the camp with me present?"

There was a long moment of silence.

"I was not certain of your reliability and determination, in the beginning," van Praag said finally. "I hope you understand."

Mohamed suddenly felt relief. For the past several weeks, Mohamed had a growing doubt that he might be killed-off after he was no longer useful to the operation. Now he realized he was trusted, valuable, and safe.

Van Praag noticed Mohamed's apprehension had eased. "If the authorities arrive unexpectedly, there is enough propane in that tank to level the entire camp. I sized it to hold ten times the amount of fuel you needed to operate the camp all summer."

Mohamed looked at van Praag, incredulous.

Van Praag winked at Mohamed, and then reached between his legs and pulled a cellphone-sized transmitter from the bag behind his feet. "Here is the remote detonator for the propane tank." He placed it on the dash.

"I have two more detonator-transmitter pairs in here." Van Praag pointed to his bag. "I shipped them to my hotel. I would never have been able to take them on the plane with me."

"Have you tested these devices?" asked Mohamed. "Will they work inside a metal container? Such as a sea container or a propane tank?"

Van Praag had not thought of that. The metal would completely surround the receiver and possibly shield it from receiving the detonation signal.

"We tested them in the open air, but not in within a metal enclosure. You make a good point." Van Praag thought for a moment. "There are a couple of other ways you could cause detonation. You could open a gas line valve and ignite the nozzle. If the tank was below half full, and the oxygen bladder was ruptured, liquid oxygen

would flow through the line and when it reached the
nozzle, kaboom."

"What about firing a bullet through the metal?"

"I believe you were supplied with some military
tracer ammunition, yes?"

"Yes."

"That should do the job. It might not penetrate the
propane tank, but it will certainly penetrate and ignite the
sea containers if you put propane in first."

Van Praag stretched and yawned. "Either way, when
it blows, it will create a fireball the size of a football field.
It will ignite the surrounding forest, and nothing left
behind will be recognizable."

27 – KENDO'S HARD DRIVE

Morris fumbled in the dark, trying to grab his vibrating cellphone. He squinted to try and focus on the name of the caller displayed on the small screen, which seemed brighter than sunlight in the dark hospital room. Conan was calling.

Morris pressed the talk button. "Better be good, whatever you have," Morris said into the phone.

"Wakey wakey, Schmuck," said Conan, enjoying the moment.

"Thank-you for adding to my pain." Now that he was awake, Morris could again feel the headache that had been bothering him all day.

"I need to give you a tour of what I have found so far," said Conan. "I sent you an email containing a link to my session. Click it, then we will have audio and you will see my desktop."

"OK. Give me a minute."

Morris pushed the button to adjust his bed into a sitting position, and pulled the tray holding his laptop into place above his knees. He had been expecting Conan to call and had prepared the equipment in advance. He put on his headset, adjusted the microphone, and tapped the space bar to awaken his computer.

There was a new email from the_barbarian@parkerholdings.com. Morris clicked the link it contained, and after a short pause, Conan's computer desktop appeared.

Morris could hear a rustling sound in his headset, then heard Conan's voice.

"I restored most of his system into a virtual machine here," said Conan.

Conan's mouse icon moved on the screen toward a minimized window, which then enlarged to fill the screen.

"This is what Kendo's desktop looked like."

An image of a pimped-up motorcycle appeared as the background to the desktop. It had high, chopper-style handlebars and a huge banana seat. The paintwork was bright, colorful and meticulous. The words 'Black Emperor' appeared above the image, with some Japanese characters below. Behind the motorcycle was a group of young men in colorful jumpsuits.

"*Bosozoku*," said Morris.

"*Gesundhite,*" said Conan.

"*Bosozoku* means something like *violent running motorcycle gang*. Kendo must have been a young biker back in Japan."

"You picked this up from your Japan trip last year?" asked Conan.

"Yes. *Bosozoku* gangs are known more as noisy, flashy, reckless and rebellious. They are not exactly Hell's Angels material. But that may explain how he got connected with them here in Canada."

"There is a lot of junk on his laptop – lots of documents from his classes at university. Photographs, too. There may be banking information – he has quite a few spreadsheets that I can open, and they appear to contain transactions downloaded from his bank. The bad news is there is a password on his email files."

"What sort of browsing history does he have?"

"Porn sites, biker sites, a few pages related to firearms. I found a user manual for a pistol."

"Show me where." Morris watched as the mouse icon moved through several folders until it opened one with the name MACDICK. The folder contained a file with the name *9mm_pistol_manual.pdf*.

"He got the gun from MacDick," Morris said. "I'm glad MacDick didn't bother to read that manual himself. What else is in this folder?"

"A spreadsheet showing some income." Conan moved the mouse pointer over a file having the name *delivery_fees.xls* and a new window opened.

Columns of dollar amounts appeared. Under a column headed 'Earnings,' the spreadsheet showed several amounts of $2,000 dollars with a different date beside each amount. The dates ranged from June to September of the current year. Under the next column to the right, headed 'Payments,' even multiples of $2,000 appeared. The totals at the bottoms of each column were not equal: $20,000 in 'Earnings' and $16,020 in 'Payments.'

"Change the date column format – see if you can reveal the day of the week," said Morris.

Conan changed the properties of the date column, and suddenly the weekday name appeared beside each date. Most of the dates fell on a Thursday.

Date	Delivery	Earnings	Payments
Thursday, June 18	L.B.	$ 2,000	
Thursday, July 02	T.R.	$ 2,000	
Saturday, July 04			$ 4,000
Thursday, July 09	J.K.	$ 2,000	
Sunday, July 12			$ 2,000
Thursday, July 23	J.W.	$ 2,000	
Friday, July 24			$ 2,000
Thursday, July 30	A.G.	$ 2,000	
Thursday, August 06	S.V.	$ 2,000	
Tuesday, August 11			$ 4,000
Thursday, August 20	T.L.	$ 2,000	
Thursday, August 27	J.P.	$ 2,000	$ 4,020
Thursday, September 17		$ 2,000	
Thursday, September 24		$ 2,000	
		$ 20,000	$ 16,020

"Does this mean anything to you, boss?" asked Conan.

"Looks like he was earning $2,000 for each delivery. The first column was the date of the delivery. Looks like delivery day was always Thursday. The last column shows when he received payment. Payday varied, but he always received payment a few days after the delivery. His payment sometimes covered two deliveries. He sometimes received payment on a non-workday."

Morris analyzed the numbers for a moment. "The payments were probably cash, and they were not made by a normal company within regular business hours. Look – one payment is for $4020. He was overpaid by accident – he possibly was paid in cash in $20 bills."

"What do you suppose these letters mean?" Conan moved the mouse pointer over the 'Delivery' column, which contained a pair of capital letters for each delivery.

"Looks like some kind of code or abbreviation describing the item delivered."

"They look like initials," said Conan.

"Could be. Whatever it is, it's probably illegal. Cash payments were occurring on weekends. Can you think of anything that this kid could earn $2,000 per delivery if it was anything legal?"

"Nope."

"What else is in this folder?" asked Morris.

"Only this one file." Conan closed he spreadsheet window and pointed to a file called *14.jpg*. Conan double-clicked the mouse to open the file. It was a slightly blurry photograph that had been taken at night.

The photo was a head and shoulder shot of two people cheek-to-cheek. On the left, sporting a grin, was Kendo in a golf shirt. He seemed to be holding the camera, pointing it at the couple. On the right was a very attractive woman in a rain jacket. She was wearing a lot of makeup. She looked quite a bit older than Kendo's 19 years. She could

have been as much as 30 years old. The amount of
makeup she wore made it hard to tell.

The woman's smile was not warm – it looked as if she
was reluctant to be in the photo.

"Kendo had a girlfriend," said Morris. "Sort of."

"What do you mean?" asked Conan.

"Dad liked gambling and hookers, when he came to
Canada. Like father, like son. This woman is probably a
stripper. From her looks, she is expensive. See how the
window behind them is shuttered? No light passes
through there. Kendo took this photo with his cellphone
in warm weather, probably not in the rain. She is likely
wearing next to nothing underneath that rain jacket. They
stepped out of the strip club together – she probably
needed a smoke break. No cameras allowed inside.
Kendo wanted a picture to show his friends how sexy his
girlfriend is. That's where I'll bet he's spending all the
cash he makes from his deliveries."

"You want us to try to find this woman?" asked
Conan.

"Yes. Give this photo to Ed. Tell him I want him to
canvass the strip joints. I need a name. I don't care if it's
her real name or her stage name."

"Stage name?"

"Have you ever spoken with a dancer at a strip joint?
They go by fake names. They don't want customers to
figure out where they live." Morris adjusted the pillow
under his back. "Show me one of the banking transaction
files."

Conan opened a spreadsheet window.

Morris glanced down the list of transactions, looking
for ATM cash withdrawals.

"Look at these. Kendo made two withdrawals of $200
followed by $100 on the same date. That probably took
him to his limit of $500. This ATM is probably at a strip
joint."

"How do you figure that?"

"Kendo's girlfriend is a pro. She gets him horny and keeps him there. *Baby, for another hundred I'll let you touch my kitten.* Kendo tries to limit himself by withdrawing only $200 at a time. But he repeatedly gives in to his temptations, and keeps going back to the ATM."

"How do you know so much about strip joints?" asked Conan.

"Sometimes you have to take the visiting business client out for a good time. He's out of town, away from his wife," said Morris. "I'm going to examine the rest of this stuff for a while. I want you to try and figure out the location of that ATM. You may have to visit the strip clubs around Ottawa and draw money out of each club's ATM. The ATM location sometimes shows up on our bank statement. Each club has an ATM. Take Ed with you, and use company credit cards."

"Tough job, but I guess we can do it," said Conan.

"Yeah, real tough. I can hear you grinning from here. What time is it?"

"1:10 AM, Schmuck. Look at the little clock in the right hand corner of the screen."

"I have a concussion." Morris blinked and saw the clock on the screen. "1:10 AM. OK, you might as well get started right now. It's prime time for strippers. Give Ed a call. I'll let Jacques sleep and tell him what you guys are up to in the morning."

Morris thought for a moment. "Wait, phone Jacques and tell him he's in charge of organizing this. If I leave him out, he'll kill me – especially on a mission like this. All expenses paid at a peeler joint. What was I thinking?! I can't leave him out."

"Can I go now?"

"Each of you should go to as many places as you can before closing time. Start with the Ottawa joints. The Quebec side stays open later. Use the cash to tip the girls, not buy beer."

"I think I can remember that, Dad."

"Remember to take the photo with you."

"Duh, should I?"

"And don't tell anyone where it came from."

"I shouldn't say I lifted it from an unsecured computer network in a dead guy's apartment?"

"Actually, crop the dead guy, just show the girl. Thanks for understanding and not adding to my pain."

28 – THE TWO MINDS OF TRAGAR

"We walk a bit from here." Mohamed turned off the headlights and stopped the engine. He had parked the SUV in a small clearing just out of sight from the road.

The moon was half and the sky was clear. It took a few moments for van Praag's eyes to adjust to the available light. He looked up at the stars. There were millions of them.

"There are no major urban areas near here. No light pollution. You can see a lot more stars."

Van Praag nodded. "It reminds me of home. But the constellations are different in South Africa."

"Also in the desert." Mohamed began to walk toward some bushes. "Follow me."

Van Praag followed him into the foliage, stumbling a bit on the uneven ground.

"I try to let the bushes here grow over the trail, to keep hikers out." Mohamed took a small flashlight out of his pocket and began to peer through the forest. Light reflected back from a metallic object. "Over this way."

They made their way through the trees toward the object. Van Praag realized it was a four-wheel ATV.

"We ride from here," said Mohamed. "You sit on the back, behind me. Kendo called it the *bitch seat*."

Van Praag looked at Mohamed with a blank stare.

"You can face backwards. Just hang on tight."

The two men mounted the vehicle, van Praag facing rearward. As he climbed aboard, van Praag struck his ankle and winced.

"Mind the hitch," said Mohamed.

Van Praag noticed a four-wheel cart with fenced sides parked under the trees. It looked like a rolling animal pen.

"We tow that cart into the camp full of pigs, once every couple of weeks." Mohamed turned the ignition key and pressed the starter.

The engine started noisily, ending the late night calm. The headlight stabbed into the darkness. Mohamed gunned the engine and put the vehicle in gear, and it began to move. Bouncing along, the riders made their way down the narrow path, stopping after about a minute.

Mohamed killed the engine and switched off the headlight. As the two men climbed off the vehicle, he pulled out his flashlight and began a slow pan from left to right.

"That's the ice cream truck, and there are the isolation chambers." Mohamed pointed the flashlight at a tall narrow building, "Behind that building – that's the furnace hut – is the pig barn. You can't quite see it from here. Just in front of us is the electric generator and next to that is the propane supply tank. To the right are the living quarters. And this building here close to us is the lab."

"Where are the toilets?"

Mohamed looked at van Praag.

"I drank too much coffee on the road."

"Just step away from the trail a bit and use the bushes."

"The coffee had a different effect on me." Van Praag looked a bit uncomfortable.

"Follow me."

Mohamed led van Praag across the camp to a small outhouse, stopping a short distance away. He pointed his flashlight at the foundation. The outhouse was positioned over a large rectangular trench dug in the ground. The base of the outhouse was square, and not big enough to cover the entire trench.

"See that hole beside the building? If you fall in it, I leave you there," Mohamed laughed. "It's full of poo."

Van Praag looked at Mohamed with an expression of distaste.

"The back hoe we rented to dig the hole hit a lot of rock. We ended up ripping out a bigger trench than we wanted, and we didn't have enough lumber to cover the hole. It stinks in the heat, when the wind blows the wrong way."

"Have you tried lime?" asked van Praag with a sniff. "Throw in a few scoops."

"I threw in germicide," said Mohamed.

"That kills the good bugs – the ones that break down the solid waste by eating it."

"How do you know that?"

"I'm in the biotech industry." And I practice good hygiene, unlike you, thought van Praag.

Mohamed sensed he was being judged. He pointed his flashlight back toward the center of the camp. "Meet me back in the lab when you're done."

Mohamed gave van Praag the flashlight.

Van Praag made his way into the small outhouse and closed the creaking door, realizing he should have provided a chemical toilet.

After he was done, van Praag found his way to the lab. As he opened the door, a dim red light spilled out. He entered the room and shut the door behind him. The room suddenly flooded with white light, making him blink as his eyes adjusted.

"We use light discipline to avoid being detected. Red light is not seen as easily from a distance," said Mohamed.

"You rigged this?" Van Praag was impressed. "It was not part of my original spec."

"Yes. I have developed my skills as a handyman."

"Women love that in a husband," said van Praag.

"When I return home as a hero, I shall have my pick of the women. I shall take many wives." Mohamed laughed. "They will have no say in choosing the qualities of their mate – they will have to put up with me."

Van Praag pointed to a large cabinet at one end of the room. "Show me the lab results."

Mohamed raised an eyebrow. "You presume that I understand the work of the great Dr. Tragar."

"I know that he talks a lot. I know that his insufferable ego compels him to seek constant acknowledgement of his greatness by lecturing to anyone around him who will listen. I know you are a very good listener." Van Praag shrugged. "I also instructed you to keep a close eye on him. I have no doubt you figured out how he is performing his job, and whether his efforts will result in a product capable of meeting our requirements or not."

"In the early days, when I could stand talking with him, yes, I learned how he does his job," Mohamed nodded. "When I accepted that assignment, had I known how much of an insufferable ass he is, I would have charged you ten times my fee for pain and suffering."

"You must put up with him for a bit longer," said van Praag. "But perhaps it will help if you understand him the way I have figured him out. Allow me to explain. Dr. Tragar expects the world to lay itself at his feet." Van Praag began to speak as if he were giving a lecture. "He thinks he has the unpublished solution to prevent AIDS, he thinks his potions can cure cancer, and he thinks he is not only a brilliant scientist, he thinks he is a fantastic businessman."

"He is tiresome and irritating to deal with," said Mohamed.

"I have also put up with the antics of the great Dr. Tragar – he has the negotiating ability of a spoiled child. But he does have certain useful abilities. He has devised not only a method for producing our new virus, he has discovered a faster and better way to mass-produce the doses of vaccine needed to fight it. But his most useful ability is his ability to delude himself. He thinks his work with us is a world-changing discovery that will benefit mankind and bring him honor and glory."

Mohamed grinned. "You have deceived him. You have concealed our intentions well."

"I have not concealed them at all." Van Praag picked up a notebook from the doctor's desk and began leafing through the pages. "It is certain he has figured out what you and I are up to."

Mohamed looked at van Praag, puzzled.

"The doctor has two personalities, I have realized." Van Praag smiled as he put down the notebook. "There is a very large 'outer-ego' personality, and a very insecure confused 'inner-ego' personality. The outer-ego filters all information before it reaches the insecure inner-ego. His insecure self needs to be protected against learning of the doctor's failings. For example, it wants to believe he is a great business leader, but I have seen that he is unable to comprehend or make simple spending and cost management decisions. He doesn't understand what a bookkeeper does. So his egotistical self explains to his insecure self that such menial understandings do not require his comprehension and it is better not to clutter the brilliant mind with trivia."

"That makes sense," Mohamed nodded. "From childhood, the doctor has been told he is a genius above all his peers. But he cannot process certain types of information as well as those peers. Things you and I find simple are beyond him. So his large ego dismisses that information in order to protect the small insecure one."

"Exactly. He thinks he is a great communicator and a great leader, surrounded by a vast network of senior contacts. He is proud of his ability to speak five languages – and quite intelligent for being able to do that – but the truth is he produces gibberish in all of them. The senior people he meets dismiss him behind his back because they cannot understand him."

Mohamed began to pace across the floor, frustration building. "Yes, he jumbles his words and produces a stream of notions that only relate vaguely to each other. He interrupts me constantly. He has no patience of his own, but demands infinite patience in those dealing with him."

Both men realized each man hated Tragar as much as the other.

"It will be fun," said Mohamed through gritted teeth, "*to kill him.*"

"After you have secured his final results, of course." Van Praag said sharply. Then his eyes became slits. "But when you do, do it slowly. Make sure he suffers, and tell me about it afterwards. I have had the displeasure of working with Tragar for four years. The first two years were a complete waste. He took it in his head to renege on every commitment he made to work on the project he was hired for. We held back his salary, yet he continued to stall until we lost the opportunity to a competitor. It cost us millions. He never explained his reasons why. I think it was because we had assigned him a business unit manager who was instructed not to implement any foolish decisions from the doctor. Tragar repeatedly tried to have him fired, but I would not allow it."

"I am curious how you motivated the doctor to turn to the bad side of health science," said Mohamed.

"I hired a flunky that he could order around to implement his small, useless decisions. He finally needed money so desperately he agreed to take on this project. His egotistical outer self filtered-out the fact that this work is beyond unethical, beyond immoral and is in fact criminal. He convinced himself that creating this disease is for the greater good."

"Now I understand what he means when he constantly says a particular quality of viruses is that they can be tailored by directed evolution."

"How so?" asked van Praag.

"His statement applies to his method of producing the new disease, but also, through his convoluted reasoning, he believes he will strengthen humanity by infecting the population with a new and dangerous virus." Mohamed had struggled to understand Tragar's motivations, and the sudden clarity excited him. "His virus will kill billions, leaving the strongest in charge. Only the few fittest will survive to produce a new generation! He thinks we are shaping human evolution!"

"Hold on! Don't kill all my customers! This virus is supposed to sicken the herd so I can sell the vaccine!" Van Praag had a shocked expression.

Mohamed suddenly realized he had said a little too much. He was fearful van Praag would figure out he had his own plan for the virus. "Of course, of course. I am merely repeating the doctor's rantings. You have made me understand the doctor. I did not mean to say billions. I was thinking millions. The disease is not that deadly – only a relatively small number of people will die. It is being tailored to spread quickly through moist air. It is not desirable to make it deadly, otherwise the subjects die before it can spread. The transmission rate and fatality rate correlate inversely." Mohamed looked at van Praag, hoping he believed that. "The transmission rate is 30%, but the death rate is only 2%. By his projections, which I have seen, there will be no more than a quarter-million deaths worldwide."

Van Praag paused, thinking. He smiled. "Don't kill all my customers," he smiled, feeling reassured. He simply wanted the massive profit that would result from his company having the only available vaccine against a new disease pandemic. "So show me the results so far."

Mohamed led his visitor across the lab floor and showed a sealed cabinet filled with neatly labeled test tube vials of blood. There were seven vials in each small stand, with about twenty stands total. Six of each group of seven bore a number beneath the label SWINE. The

seventh vial bore a number beneath the label HUMAN.
Two empty stands stood at the end of the series of stands.

Mohamed pointed to the empty stands at the end of
the shelf. "The results require six more pigs and one more
human subject to be complete, and one final human
subject after that to be confirmed."

"By the way," said Mohamed, "you said the doctor
couldn't fail to figure out how people like you and me
intend to use the virus. We intend to commit mass-murder
for profit. How does he rationalize that?"

Van Praag smiled. "The doctor has convinced himself
that the victims of the disease will be the same as our
human subjects – human derelicts. Drug abusers,
prostitutes and glue-sniffers. Thinning them from the herd
would be a good thing, according to the doctor's outer-
ego."

"But there will be no correlation like that! This virus
will kill without discrimination!"

"True. The doctor is making a simple, and convenient,
bookkeeping error."

29 – SWEET WILD ROSE

Morris rubbed his eyes and scowled at the computer screen. He had been suffering a dull headache ever since Conan's telephone call woke him up two hours ago.

Morris had specifically instructed Conan to call him when Kendo's computer disk image had been fully recovered. Conan had done as he was asked, taking more than a bit of pleasure in waking his boss in the middle of the night.

Now Conan was out on the town. Presumably, Ed and Jacques were too. They were sleuthing strip joints, no doubt enjoying their assignment. Meanwhile, Morris was sleepless in his hospital bed, trying to be productive by analyzing the copy of Kendo's computer Conan had created on the virtual computer server at PHL. This large and powerful machine served up virtual computers, and was capable of running several of them simultaneously. Morris was logged in and could view the desktop of the Kendo virtual computer as if it were running on the laptop in his hospital room.

Conan had painstakingly re-created a working copy of Kendo's computer from the disk image he had managed to acquire from Kendo's apartment. Conan had not been able to make every program Kendo had installed work like the original, but most of the computer was functioning properly – enough to get valuable information.

Morris had been working steadily since his last communication with Conan. Morris had spent the first hour browsing without finding anything valuable. There were a lot of university documents, .mp3 songs, photos of motorcycles and an extensive collection of porn videos. Kendo was a typical horny young man, Morris concluded.

The only unusual thing about Kendo's computer was the type of printer that had been installed. The software to drive a Datacard SP75 Color Card printer had been installed. Morris did a search on the Internet and was surprised to find the cost of this type of printer was over five thousand dollars. What would Kendo need with such a printer, Morris wondered.

Morris still had a mild headache, and he was about to give up for the night when he found a folder named *camping* buried deep within folders related to university courses. Morris found it interesting because the rest of the disk had been well organized by topic, but this folder contained two folders: *ID* and *flights*.

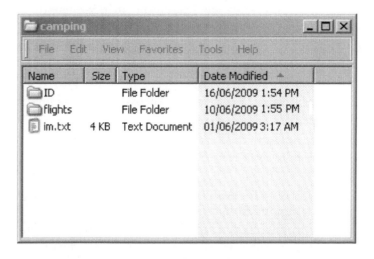

There was also a single file named *im.txt*, containing the text from an online chat Kendo had saved. Morris opened it and began to read:

Sweet Wild Rose: hello sweetie
Kamikaze Kendo: what a nice surprise
Sweet Wild Rose: i saw you come online
Kamikaze Kendo: u saw me cum yesterday lol
Sweet Wild Rose: it was fun to help you do that lol

Morris blinked and thought: *lol – laughing out loud.*
Morris checked the date stamp on the *im.txt* file and
compared it to the date stamps on the folders within the
camping folder. It was 06/1/2009 03:17 AM, before either
of the folders *ID*, or *flights* had been created. The
conversation Morris was reading had taken place before
the contents of the folders had been placed there.

Morris minimized the window containing *im.txt* and
looked at the financial files Conan had found. He found
two $200 withdrawals from the same ATM: the first
occurred at about 10 PM, and the second occurred at
about midnight on May 30, a Saturday night. Kendo may
have used the money to pay for sex with Sweet Wild
Rose. The online chat session had been saved on the disk
late the next night.

He resumed reading.

Kamikaze Kendo: i'm very excited that you will be
                                coming to visit the camp
Sweet Wild Rose: i have a job there
Kamikaze Kendo: what kind of job?
Sweet Wild Rose: you don't want to know – the usual
Kamikaze Kendo: not helping construction like me, i
                                guess, but what?
Sweet Wild Rose: you're so cute when you're curious
Kamikaze Kendo: i will keep asking until you tell me
                                what the job is. what? what?
Sweet Wild Rose: why do you need to know?
Kamikaze Kendo: i don't want to be noisy. we just
                                met a week ago. i just want to
                                make sure you're ok
Kamikaze Kendo: *nosey
Sweet Wild Rose: you're sweet
Kamikaze Kendo: tell me please
Sweet Wild Rose: brb

Morris thought: *brb – be right back*. Morris executed
a search on Kendo's files for all the videos. When a long
list of files appeared, he clicked to sort by the timestamps
on the files. Morris looked at the date on the newest file
and realized it was several weeks before the date on the
file *im.txt*. It looked to Morris like Kendo lost interest in
adding to his porn collection after he met Sweet Wild
Rose.

Sweet Wild Rose: i have to date a trucker. i'm
supposed to keep him occupied in
the back seat while somebody else
drives his truck. he's not supposed
to know where the campsite is. me
neither

Kamikaze Kendo: oh, i see

Sweet Wild Rose: the trucker has already seen my
picture and wants to date me

Kamikaze Kendo: will you be safe?

Sweet Wild Rose: yes i will be keeping the trucker
busy in his sleeper cab

Kamikaze Kendo: ok

Sweet Wild Rose: really? you're ok with it?

Kamikaze Kendo: yeah, i'm just jealous

Sweet Wild Rose: you're so cute

Kamikaze Kendo: nobody is supposed to know what's
going on at that camp. i don't know
what's going to take place there
when we're done. there is weird
stuff going in

Sweet Wild Rose: like what?

Kamikaze Kendo: a furnace! a great big furnace that
can get to 5000 degrees

Sweet Wild Rose: no way! a furnace out in the
woods, i can believe. but not one
that hot

Kamikaze Kendo: why not?

Sweet Wild Rose: the melting point of steel is around
2500 degrees Fahrenheit
Kamikaze Kendo: oh. i guess i got the temperature
limit wrong. anyway, it can get
really, really hot – just like you
make me feel lol
Sweet Wild Rose: you're so cute
Kamikaze Kendo: hey – how did you know the
melting point of steel?
Sweet Wild Rose: i went to engineering school. i
graduated in architecture, but i can
earn more money doing this job
instead
Kamikaze Kendo: wow, i like you a lot
Sweet Wild Rose: i like you too. i'll be working next
wednesday will you come and see
me at the club? i'll give you a
special dance half price! and if you
want DATY
Kamikaze Kendo: i can't. i'm going back to the camp
to finish construction
Sweet Wild Rose: i hope to see you there. my flight to
the peg is next thurs. got to go
now. bye. xox
Kamikaze Kendo: bye! XOX

This girl must be the girl in the photo, Morris thought.
She works at what had to be a strip club and takes out-of-
town jobs as a hooker. The Peg meant Winnipeg. There
was some kind of secret camp near Winnipeg, Manitoba.
But what the hell is DATY? Morris did a google
search for DATY. Up came:

**Dining at the "Y," cunnilingus. Eating a female out.
With her legs spread – she is in the shape of a Y.**

Morris shook his head. That was a new one for him.
He smiled and wondered if Terri knew that one.

Morris opened the *flights* folder and saw nine files.

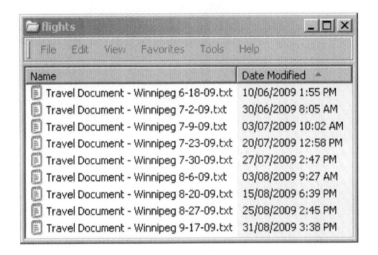

Wow, he thought, and quickly checked the dates in
comparison to the dates in Kendo's *delivery_fee.xls*. Sure
enough, the dates matched. Each flight date coincided
with a $2000 delivery fee.

Morris opened the first travel document file. The
document contained flight details delivered from an
online reservation system. It was electronic ticketing
information for an Air Canada early morning direct flight
from Ottawa to Winnipeg on June 18th. There were two
travelers: Mr. Kenneth R. Wang and Mr. Lawrence
Banks. Lawrence Banks, initials L.B., matched the item
column entry. Conan had been right about the column
showing people's initials.

Morris examined the flight on July 2nd. It was also a
direct flight, later in the day than the previous flight had
been. It was for two people: Mr. Thomas Chan and Miss
Tara Robinson.

Morris looked through the rest of the travel
documents. Each trip was a Thursday flight to Winnipeg,

but not at the exact same time of day. A few flights were
on WestJet. Every booking was for two people. The first
passenger was always an Asian name, and the second
passenger had the same initials as the item column in
delivery_fee.xls for that date. The Asian name had to be
an alias for Kendo, Morris concluded.

Morris realized the variable flight times and airlines
meant somebody did not want the Asian flyer to be
recognized. A frequent flying passenger would become
familiar to an aircrew that flew the same flight regularly.

Morris eagerly looked into the *ID* folder. By now he
knew what to expect, and found exactly what had
suspected would be there. Kendo had been making false
identity documents.

There was a folder called *Kendo,* and a folder for each
of the passengers *Lawrence Banks, Tara Robinson,* and
so on. Morris knew that rules for air travel in Canada
required passengers to present identification on boarding
the aircraft.

In the *Kendo* folder, Morris found eight different false
Ontario birth certificates for the eight different Asian
names. The age was shown as between 25 and 30 years.
Kendo had been nineteen, but could easily have passed
for older. None of the birth certificates had photos, and
Morris realized the slightly older age was important
because it meant older-style certificates would be
expected at the airport. Older certificates were easier to
fake than newer ones, which had advanced security
features built into the plastic.

Morris checked the Government of Canada website
and read that either one photo ID such as driver's license,
or two government ID's including birth certificate and
provincial health card were acceptable forms of
identification to board an aircraft.

Morris now understood why Kendo had a laminating
card printer driver installed.

Each folder for the second passenger included fake ID documents that met those requirements. Some had photos, others did not. Kendo had been accompanying people on one-way flights to Winnipeg. There was a secret camp near Winnipeg, Manitoba, and both Kendo and Sweet Wild Rose had been there.

Something big, well-funded, and highly secret was going on there. So secret, somebody had been willing to kill Morris and his whole family. Sweet Wild Rose, whoever she was, knew something.

30 – VAN PRAAG INSPECTS THE RESULTS

"In order to minimize his visits here, and avoid contact with him as much as possible, I learned as many of the doctor's duties and techniques as possible. We started with H1N1 2009, the current strain of swine flu," said Mohamed, pointing to the first stand of seven blood samples. "We infected six pigs, each of a different breed."

"Yes," van Praag replied, as the two men stood talking in the lab. "I had many long, painful discussions with Dr. Tragar during the planning stages."

"My sympathies. "

"There are about one hundred different pig breeds, and Tragar wanted to discuss all of them." Van Praag had a look of exasperation on his face. "He initially insisted on using some strange breeds that were difficult to obtain in North America. We had to limit ourselves to mainly Canadian domestic breeds. He wanted a Belarus Black Pied that I told him we could not obtain by smuggling. It's not easy to import a farm animal. He persisted, and I finally told him if he could find a pig that was a Canadian Citizen, I would gladly fly the pig first class. Otherwise, no."

Mohamed laughed, and pointed to the blood samples in the cabinet. "Each stand holds samples from the six pigs that were infected by the previous human subject in the series," he explained. "Dr. Tragar monitors the progress of the disease in the six infected pigs carefully before selecting the sample to use to infect the next human subject in the chain. We keep a computer trace of each pig's vital signs to choose the pig where the disease progress is closest to our ideal profile."

"How many spoiled results did you have?" asked van Praag.

"Only one pig managed to foul its biomedical sensor harness. Each individual stall in the pig half of the isolation chamber was small enough to keep most of the pigs from turning. A very small Berkshire somehow turned itself and strangled on the sensor cord." Mohamed made a hand motion as if choking himself. "Fortunately, that pig was not going to be selected to pass on the infection anyway, so our disease development was not affected. The symptoms it had been suffering to that point were too mild. Tragar was meticulous about selecting the pig where the symptoms were severe enough, with high probability of airborne transmission and infectivity on a microscopic dose. He shaped the disease nicely, managing the handoff from swine to human and back to swine with major improvements in all the factors we needed. We are nearing the end of 20 cycles, with virus mutation on each cycle. We now have a unique virus that will have an extreme infectivity rate with low lethality. Based on our computer models and the tailored infection growth rate of 30% per week, after one full year in the general population, 1.1 billion people will have been infected by our virus."

Van Praag nodded, impressed. "My requirement was for one billion, plus or minus 10%."

"That's at normal transmission rates if the initial infection is a general urban location with normal land traffic. Because our primary target, Boston, has a high percentage of air travelers, the effect will be much greater, much quicker."

"And what is the death rate?"

"Based on our outcomes here at the camp, we have had one disease death so far. The subject was a weak, old alcoholic, drug-addicted glue-sniffer with other health problems. He died from complications. Tragar has made a projection based on similar deaths occurring by factoring

the health of the general population. The death rate of our
final strain is 2%. Two out of every one hundred infected
individuals will die."

"Can you show me your computer models?" asked
van Praag.

"Certainly." Mohamed stepped up to a lab desk and
moved the mouse on a sleeping computer workstation.
The display lit up. It showed a map of North America. "I
was running a simulation to check the safety of our open
air release test."

Mohamed manipulated the display and the map
zoomed in to Northern Ontario, to a spot about 30 miles
north of Kenora. The map showed the campsite and
immediate surrounding area next to the lake. There was a
small stick man icon on the screen.

"This icon represents our final subject. We will tie the
actual person in an open field about a quarter mile from
here. He will be like a goat tied to a stake. I have seen
film of goats used as test victims during early tests of
nerve agents."

"Our approach is more effective than a nerve agent,"
said van Praag. "The nerve agent kills its victim
immediately. Our germ lets its victim move around and
infect other victims."

"Precisely." Mohamed agreed. "The software
parameters have been set to model human-to-human
transmission rates based on the final version of our
mutated virus. That virus has a profile of infectivity
factors, tailored to our design. Those factors include a 24-
hour highly contagious period where no symptoms are
observed. Our virus is diabolical. For our purposes, it is
ideal. It will spread very quickly in a moist, warming
springtime and summer climate, in densely populated
urban areas. People will be most contagious when they
have the least idea that they have been infected."

"You mean there are no symptoms at all during the
initial contagious period?" Van Praag was impressed.

"The victim will actually feel healthy and energetic. Just a bit warm, perhaps, and may perspire a bit." Mohamed smiled. "These symptoms are perfect for our intended target population at the event we have in mind."

"What is the risk of the disease getting out into the general population when you do your open-air infectivity test?"

"Almost zero. Watch this." Mohamed clicked a button on the screen labeled START SIMULATION. The stick man turned from white to pink.

"Here we simulate the final subject becoming infected. Pink means infected, with no visible symptoms, but not yet contagious. We will actually hit him with aerosols of increasing virus density until he becomes infected. That way we will learn the optimal concentration of the airborne germ we will need for our weaponized version of the virus."

The stick man turned from pink to red, and Mohamed pointed to a time counter on the screen. "After four hours, the subject becomes red, meaning contagious but not yet sick. He will remain contagious for about seven days. The icon turns yellow after 24 hours, when he shows symptoms."

Van Praag nodded. "This simulation should show no spread of the disease, right?"

"Right," Mohamed nodded. "No spread, because there is nobody around to infect. No pigs are running loose in the forest, and my team and I will be the only humans nearby, and we will be in our HAZMAT suits. We will remain in the suits until this victim, I mean subject, is no longer contagious."

The time counter reached 29 hours. The stick man turned from red to yellow.

"Yellow means sick and still contagious. In this scenario, the subject will most likely be in quarantine. Our stick man is now sick. He is very, very sick. There is a one-in-fifty chance he will die." Mohamed looked up

from the screen to see van Praag's reaction. "Many
children and adolescents will get sick. Many parents will
sleep in intensive care, watching their previously young
and healthy children teeter on the verge of death."

Van Praag nodded silently.

Mohamed went on. "Even a small number of deaths
in a large population will receive instant publicity. Fear of
a pandemic will generate a run on your vaccine."

Van Praag smiled. "It's a good time to buy shares in
Concourse Pharmaceuticals, my friend."

"My reward will not be entirely financial. Population
productivity loss in the Western world will be huge.
There will be an immediate crash on the stock markets.
Western economy will suffer a huge body blow. Troops
will have to be withdrawn from my country to help out
back here. The Taliban will win the war in Afghanistan. I
will return a conquering hero. Now watch this."

Mohamed moved the mouse to the yellow stick man.
He clicked the right mouse button on the small yellow
figure and a small menu popped up beside it. It had two
choices: *cure* and *kill*. Mohamed clicked *kill*. The stick
man immediately turned black. "Goodbye, Doctor
Tragar."

"Ha," said van Praag. "How fitting."

"Now we simply dispose of this little black corpse in
the usual manner," said Mohamed, in a matter-of-fact
voice. "But I have more interesting scenarios for you. Let
me prove the open air release test is a valid simulation.
Let's say we didn't have HAZMAT suits on. I'll reset and
run another simulation."

Mohamed manipulated the software and clicked on
the screen several times, adding a few stick men around
the original victim. Then he zoomed out of the local area
to include a one hundred mile radius. At this
magnification, Kenora was near the center of the screen,
and Winnipeg appeared on the left edge.

"Given that we are in a remote area, we have assumed only a single human-to-human transmission within the 24-hour no-symptom contagious period." Mohamed pointed to a small pink spot on the map at the location of the campsite. "Watch what happens if that infected person goes into the closest urban area, however."

The clock counter showed twenty hours, and suddenly a pink patch began to grow quickly in the city of Kenora. Then part of it started to turn yellow.

"If the initial infection started on a quiet day, like Sunday morning at 1:00 AM, there is a good chance the infection will not get out to the highways. There is only one major highway running through Kenora. In this scenario, the authorities would have time to detect the disease and quarantine the city. The virus stops in Kenora. Winnipeg is not affected."

"How many sick? How many die?" asked van Praag.

"In this model, on the first day, the initial infector will cause 100 cases.

"These people will be hospitalized immediately and the medical authorities will declare an emergency," Mohamed continued. "At the end of the first week, there will be between two and five deaths. Because they have no warning about the disease, and no vaccine, virtually the entire population of Kenora will get sick to varying degrees. The city will be quarantined and mostly left to fend for itself. Most people will recover on their own after about seven days. We predict the disease will finish it's run in twenty weeks total, with approximately 1,500 deaths in the population of 75,000. These people will die from complications of the disease that overwhelm the local medical system."

"What about spread beyond the city by means other than the highway?"

"There is sea traffic, but it is too slow. The ship's crew would be quarantined on arrival and the disease would not spread. A single airline called Bearskin

Airlines serves the airport, and they fly small planes with less than twenty passengers. If a single infected passenger boarded in Kenora, it would be guaranteed that twenty would be infected upon arrival at destination even on a one-hour flight. The moist, closed-air environment is perfect for virus transmission. It will pass by breath from passenger to passenger. Pilot and co-pilot will also be infected because they breathe the same air as the passengers."

Mohamed beamed with pride. "Our disease was bred for airborne transmission in this environment. A small plane has almost the exact same air volume and airflow circulation as our isolation-fitted sea containers. But in this simulation, the virus doesn't get out. There are too few flights to catch one of the early cases. In this scenario, even without your vaccine, the disease cannot spread fast enough to meet your infection target of one billion people worldwide. The health authorities are able to contain it within the city of Kenora."

"So the disease will fail?" asked van Praag, a bit confused.

"If we release it with a single infector in Kenora, it would fail. But we will have four initial infectors, and we will release them in Boston. Also, the virus serum will infect these infectors directly. Their injection will contain other drugs that increase their metabolism and make them hyper-infective. They will infect many more individuals during the first 24 hours than the subsequent infection rate, the 30% rate. Each of these infectors will, of course, die because of the crash that occurs after his 24-hour increased metabolism ends. The crash leaves him unable to fight the disease at all. Infection by injection is suicide."

"Are your men aware of this side effect? Death?"

"The men I have been provided are prepared to make the sacrifice of a suicide bomber." Mohamed glared at van Praag. "That was a requirement from the beginning. I

told you I would find and motivate men capable of
performing in the suicide-infector role. You need not
concern yourself with how I accomplish that task."

"I recall you had a man die by his own hand after an
accident in the isolation chamber," said van Praag.

Mohamed froze. "Yes, due to my inadequate training
and supervision of HAZMAT procedures. His martyrdom
training was clearly a success." Mohamed looked at van
Praag. "This event was not orchestrated just to convince
you of the willingness of our men to become martyrs."

Without waiting for a response, Mohamed turned and
manipulated the screen again. A dialog box appeared:
Choose Scenario. Mohamed double-clicked on a scenario
called *Patriots' Day Boston – Four Hyper-Infectors*.

"In this scenario, we hit our target city with four
infectors. Four of my men will circulate aggressively at
the target event, infecting as many people as possible.
They will be ten times more effective at this event than
anywhere else, because of the nature of the activity and
the fact that thousands of participants will return by
airline to major urban centers within twenty-four hours.
Watch the virus spread. I will need to zoom out."

Mohamed zoomed out to view all of North America.
There was a small pink dot on Boston, Massachusetts.

"There are over three million people living in the
greater Boston area. In this model, our four suicide-
infectors contaminate one thousand people each on the
first day. Here is the effect."

Mohamed clicked the clock display and advanced it to
24 hours. Most of the metropolitan Boston area went
from pink to bright red.

Then Mohamed advanced the clock counter until it
reached 48 hours. Every population center in North
America developed a pink spot which grew quickly and
changed to bright red. Most of Massachusetts around the
area of Boston was now yellow.

"Let me jump forward several days," said Mohamed, clicking the clock to make it advance.

"Here it is paused at seven days." Mohamed turned to examine van Praag's reaction.

Van Praag's mouth was open, eyes wide. The metropolitan centers of North America were covered with large red and pink blotches. Most had yellow centers. Boston was bright yellow.

"We now have nearly ten thousand cases," said Mohamed. "Now I will run it forward ten weeks."

A tabular display appeared, containing columns containing counts by week for new infections, accumulated infections, and deaths. There were now pinks, reds and yellows everywhere. Every city, town and village had some color.

Mohamed read from a tabular display. "After ten weeks, we have 170 thousand cases and over 3,400 deaths."

"It's too dangerous!" van Praag exclaimed.

"Not if you have the vaccine in place," said Mohamed. "Remember, this scenario runs without any vaccine. As it is introduced in large population centers, it will be effective immediately. Overnight, your vaccine will save large cities. All other population centers will clamor for it. There will be none of the usual controversy over the risk of being vaccinated. There will be a bidding war."

"What if the infection rate out of the Boston area is greater than 30%?"

"It will be 30% plus or minus 2%. We have been tuning the virus toward that number. Your isolation chambers here have worked perfectly – as designed. The disease alone could have been created with far less sophisticated equipment and methods. We concentrated on using the two additional isolation chambers and computer models and clean environment provided to develop techniques to manage the spread. We got exactly the one strain we wanted, the one that your vaccine will defeat. And we have been making sure it is not too deadly."

Van Praag remained silent, looking at the map, stunned.

"Your equipment works very, very well." Mohamed zoomed the map view out and panned across the Atlantic Ocean toward Europe and the Middle East.

"As you can see, Europe will also be infected at an identical rate. The Boston event draws an international gathering. Most of the participants return home the next day. Look what happens in Australia."

The continent of Australia showed red and yellow in all the populated areas.

"It will be autumn for them, but the air is moist, and even though it is the beginning of flu season, they will be completely unprepared for our new strain."

"Except for my vaccine."

"Except for your vaccine," Mohamed nodded. "I have one question for you."

"Ask it."

"How will you explain to the authorities how you just happened to have a huge stockpile of vaccine on hand to combat a totally new and deadly strain?"

"They would only suspect me of having advance knowledge, if I had such a stockpile."

"You have no stockpile?"

"My advantage is not in having a stockpile, it is in having the exclusive worldwide patents to a new process capable of producing massive doses of any vaccine in a very short time. None of my competitors have this technology. Not only will my facilities be used to prepare the vaccine, my competitors will also be contracted by governments everywhere, desperate to produce the vaccine, and they will need my process and they will pay me royalties."

Finally, Mohamed understood everything he needed
to know about van Praag's plan, and he was satisfied.
Satisfied that it would not interfere with his own plan.

Mohamed zoomed out to show all the major
continents. "The only unaffected areas are the Arctic,
Antarctic and Desert areas. Because the air is dry."

Mohamed thought about his own ambitions. Van
Praag must not learn his true intentions before it is too
late. Mohamed smiled to himself.

Unknown to van Praag or Dr. Tragar, Mohamed had
secretly maintained his own separate strain of the virus
throughout the experimental development period.

The development period consisted of twenty infection
cycles. Each cycle involved infecting six pigs, followed
by a choice of optimum pig for transmitting the virus to a
human subject. Plasma from the human subject was then
used to infect the next six pigs, and the pig selection was
made again.

At each cycle, Tragar chose the optimum pig subject
based on desired transmission factors while maintaining a
safe, survivable disease. Tragar was cautious in selecting
the optimum strain, and he would never choose the
sickest animal. Tragar did not want to propagate a strain
to the next cycle if the symptoms were too severe, or if
the strain actually killed the animal or human subject.
Mohamed, however, began using the sickest animal to
propagate his own strain, the Ziad strain.

At the Cycle Twelve, Mohamed had chosen the pig
with the most severe symptoms, and he had passed it to a
human subject Mohamed had secretly placed in one of
two spare chambers that Tragar had not needed at the
time. At this point, Mohamed had effectively branched
off his own strain.

Mohamed then cleverly continued with his own
cycles, infecting what always became the sickest pig
followed by an unfortunate individual who had survived a
previous cycle of the Tragar strain. Tragar was not aware

that the sickest pig was carrying a different strain. When Mohamed infected each human subject with his strain, the Ziad strain, they got sick a second time. Despite having developed some immunity to the Tragar strain, the human subject had no immunity against the Ziad strain. The Ziad strain quickly became deadly.

Mohamed's most important job at the camp was to murder and dispose of test subjects who had survived the effects of the Tragar virus strain. They had to be silenced permanently to prevent them from going to the authorities. After the first few cycles, Mohamed no longer had to murder any more subjects. The Ziad strain took care of the job for him.

Mohamed smiled as he showed van Praag the computer projections based on the Tragar strain. Mohamed had run projections on the Ziad strain. Billions of people would die. There would be global population devastation – everywhere but in his country. His country's medical system would develop a vaccine, and his countrymen would remain healthy and be in a position to dominate the ruined economies of the Western World. They would simply move in and take over assets at bargain basement prices. The West would be in no condition to resist. Mohamed's people would become the new owners of the West.

Mohamed was preparing to unleash the most deadly biological and economic attack of all time.

Mohamed thought about all the sophisticated weaponry that had been used against his Afghan countrymen. He considered the futility of all the technology and firepower and effort and expense that had been directed against them, trying to force the ways of the West upon them: arrogant, bullying ways. Attempts to change their culture at the point of a bayonet. The West would have done so much better to spend their money on health care instead of war machines. Now Mohamed had the ultimate weapon of mass destruction, overlooked by the all-mighty West because of it's simplicity.

If cockpit doors had been locked at the time of 9/11, attack by suicidal hijackers armed with only knives and boxcutters would not have succeeded. Unlocked cockpit doors had been a simple oversight.

It was amusing to Mohamed that so many Americans had eagerly followed an aggressive, single-minded president into two recent wars in the Middle East. And the US was followed willingly by other Western nations. Now, how ironic, the US has an articulate, multi-faceted, intelligent president interested in peace. Yet the most powerful nation on earth cannot reach consensus on how to improve its own health care.

And that is where Mohamed will counter-attack.

31 – ONLINE

From his hospital bed, Morris had searched Kendo's data files for just over an hour, trying to find more information about Sweet Wild Rose, but found nothing.

It was now 4:33 AM. Morris' headache had finally subsided, but he was tired. It was time to try for some sleep.

Morris was satisfied with the results of his analysis of Kendo's computer data so far. Kendo's pattern of flights to Winnipeg was a great lead. Future flights seem to be planned for Thursday September 17th and September 24th, according to Kendo's payments file. Kendo, being dead, would not be making it for those flights. But perhaps the flights would occur as scheduled using a replacement escort.

While examining the ID folders, Morris realized there were two identities that had not been listed in the travel documents. These identities might be for the people who were to be escorted on those two flights.

When he realized that fact, Morris had sent an email to Jacques instructing him to form a team and set up surveillance in Winnipeg for the next planned flight, September 17th. The team would watch incoming flights that could have originated from Ottawa that day, looking for either of the two faces in the ID photos, and follow them.

Morris was hopeful the guys had some luck identifying the stripper this night. Sweet Wild Rose was most likely the girl in the photo with Kendo. As Morris was about to close his laptop and try to get some sleep, he decided to try one final thing.

Using Kendo's virtual computer, Morris had tried to sign on to Yahoo messenger to examine Kendo's contact list. But he was unable to guess the password. He started up the application and faced the login screen once again. He filled in the username as "Kamikaze Kendo."

He stared at the blank password field briefly, then Morris typed "sweetwildrose."

The password screen disappeared and the sign-in message appeared briefly: "Signing in as Kamikaze Kendo," then Kendo's contact list was displayed. Morris had guessed the right password.

Morris looked at a short list of contacts. He began clicking on names, looking for additional information. This guy didn't have too many friends, thought Morris. There were no phone numbers in the list. He probably kept them in his cellphone. The only information for each name was an email address.

Near the end of the list, which was in alphabetical order, was an entry for Sweet Wild Rose. Just as Morris was about to click on it, he observed there was a small orange ball beside the name. All the other names had a grey ball in that position. Morris realized the orange ball meant Sweet Wild Rose was currently online. Morris quickly checked Kendo's name at the top of the application window. There was an orange ball there, too. That meant Kendo's account would appear to be online to everyone who had Kendo on his or her contact list.

Than a message appeared.

Sweet Wild Rose: hey there sexy, long time no see!
                 how you feeling, honey?
Sweet Wild Rose: *horny?

It's Sweet Wild Rose, thought Morris, and she thinks I'm Kendo. How should I reply? *I'm dead, how are you?*

Morris decided to play along. What was there to lose? He typed "i missed you. glad to see you."

There was a long pause. Then a response appeared.

Sweet Wild Rose: you seem a bit stiff. did i do
                    something wrong?

Oh oh. He thought for a moment, then typed: "you
always make me stiff. LOL"
The next message came back quickly.

Sweet Wild Rose: that's more like it! i was afraid that
                    since we haven't seen each other in
                    a few weeks, you would think i
                    forgot about you. i was out of town
                    in motreal
Sweet Wild Rose: *montreal

OK, it's working. Now, how can I get this woman to
tell me about the camp? Morris typed "how was it? good
trip?"

Sweet Wild Rose: montreal was fun. i worked for a
                    week then took two weeks off with
                    my friend

Kendo traveled to Winnipeg a lot – for business. Let's
whine a bit, Morris thought. Morris typed "i wish i had
time for a vacation trip"

Sweet Wild Rose: you get lots of trips to kenora!

Bingo. Kenora. The camp must be close to Kenora,
Ontario – east of Winnipeg, Manitoba. Morris racked his
brain, trying to think of a way to get on the topic of the
camp without being obvious. Kendo would obviously
know a lot about the camp already, so it would be
difficult to ask much about it. *What did you think of the
camp?* That would be lame. *Do you know what's going
on at the camp?* Too obvious, she'll suspect I'm not
Kendo. Morris typed: "yeah, right."

After a pause, another message appeared.

Sweet Wild Rose: have you seen candi? you
                 remember her from our doubles
                 session?

Morris thought: doubles? Not tennis, I'll bet. I guess I
better keep the conversation going. Morris typed "not
lately."

Sweet Wild Rose: i'm worried about her. i haven't
                 heard from her since she went to
                 Vancouver

Morris remembered one of the identities in Kendo's
ID folder. A young female named Candice Walker.
Morris quickly found the fake ID card for that identity. It
had a photo of a pretty, 20-something girl with cover-girl
complexion and neat, straight, black hair that flowed
beyond the picture frame. It looked like it could go all the
way down her back. She had a beautiful, attractive smile
and dark, innocent eyes. She had flown to Winnipeg on
Thursday, July 23rd with Kendo.
Morris typed "when did you last see her?"

Sweet Wild Rose: near the end of july. she flew out
                 on a thursday

Morris was tempted to ask if Candi had straight, black
back-length hair. Instead, he typed "thursday the 23rd?"

Sweet Wild Rose: yeah, it must have been then. she
                 left a note saying she was going to
                 connect if she could find a
                 computer at a public library. she
                 was out of drugs and broke and
                 was hoping for some provincial

> money when she got there. she's
> been gone over a month. i miss her

Morris was certain Candice Walker, or whatever her real name was, had not flown to Vancouver as she had told Sweet Wild Rose. Her final destination was either Winnipeg, or the camp near Kenora. Morris wished he had more information before continuing with this conversation. There was more stuff to analyze on the disk. There was Kendo's password-protected email.

Perhaps it was time to make an excuse and sign-off before I blow it, Morris thought. There was hope to re-establish contact at a later date, as long as Sweet Wild Rose didn't read any week-old Ottawa newspapers to learn that Kamikaze Kendo was *kaput*.

> Sweet Wild Rose: want a date? i'll be working at the
>   club all this week until saturday.
>   you can see me any night. i feel
>   like DATY. are you hungry? lol

Morris quickly typed "i'm starving"

> Sweet Wild Rose: come early, come often
> Sweet Wild Rose: *cum lol

"i can hardly wait," Morris typed. Then, feeling bold, he added "taste you soon."

> Sweet Wild Rose: you're so cute! cu xox

He typed "XOX," then Morris quickly changed Kendo's online availability to offline. Whew.

Morris closed his laptop and rubbed his eyes. Morning light was starting to creep through the window blinds.

Now all Morris needed was to find which of the numerous Ottawa-Gatineau strip clubs was hers. He reached toward the bedside table and picked up his blackberry to check the time. It was almost 5:00 AM. If he was lucky, Morris could get about thirty minutes of sleep before a nurse woke him to administer his morning medication.

Morris noticed the Blackberry's message light was flashing. He had received an email a few moments ago from Conan. Morris opened it.

"Schmuck, her name is Valentina and she works at Club Chaton. Love, Conan."

Morris smiled and selected the reply function. Using two thumbs, he slowly typed "I just finished chatting with her. She's scheduled to work all this week, and she wants to dine with me. I'll bet you don't know what DATY is, schmuck."

"Ha," said Morris, then he yawned widely. Morris slipped his Blackberry into the holster by his bedside and the small display went black.

32 – VAN PRAAG COMPLETES HIS INSPECTION

By 5:00 AM, Mohamed Ziad and Joris van Praag had completed their discussions about taking down the camp, ensuring all evidence of what had gone on there would be eliminated. They were standing in the furnace hut, looking at the furnace door. It was closed and the furnace was at room temperature. Mohamed had last used it two days ago.

Mohamed pointed to a rake leaning against one wall. "I had to attach a metal shaft to that garden rake because the original wooden shaft burned up. I usually burn a variety of things during a single firing, so I'm raking junk around inside while it's hot."

"You burn everything that comes in contact with any of the virus, right?" asked van Praag.

"Yes, for safety, and so we can prevent contamination from one cycle of the strain with the next cycle. The furnace is so hot there is hardly any ash to clean up. I dump regular ash with the rest of the camp's solid waste. I dump the human and animal remains at random spots out in the lake."

"What do you mean *remains*? Aren't the remains ash?"

"The only thing left after incinerating a corpse at 1500 degrees," said Mohamed, "are a few of the larger bones. There is no ash. People think of cremated remains as being ash, but they're actually ground-up bone fragments. The body liquids boil away. This industrial furnace is not an actual cremation machine, and it took me a while to figure out how to prevent leaks. Body fat burns off. All the tissues and organs burn off as gasses."

"Is the lake big enough to prevent someone from finding human bone fragments?"

"Yes, it's quite deep. The bone fragments are usually no bigger than a few inches, and even if a diver was able to recover something, the DNA has been totally denatured by the heat. The individual could never be identified."

Van Praag nodded, satisfied. "As you know, two more subjects are scheduled to come from Ottawa."

Mohamed nodded.

"I'm afraid I have some bad news." Van Praag looked at Mohamed. "Your friend Kendo will not be delivering them. He was killed in a shootout two weeks ago."

"Killed! How? By who?"

"Kendo and his partner MacDick were protecting two of my men while they conducted an unauthorized robbery of a poker game in a bar. Some ex-soldiers were in the bar and intercepted them. One of them shot Kendo in the heart."

Mohamed scowled. "I would like to know the name of this ex-soldier."

"He is an Ottawa businessman by the name of Morris Parker. I put out a contract on him." Van Praag paused to see Mohamed's reaction. "He is becoming a threat to this operation, and I am having him eliminated."

"Having him eliminated? Becoming a threat? What does that mean? A businessman should be easy to kill."

"I have an inside man on the Ottawa Police. You will meet him when he escorts Kendo's subjects here. My policeman set up Parker to take the fall for the shootout, but Parker has been more resourceful than we anticipated in getting himself out of it. My policeman was going to be in trouble for tampering with evidence."

"Why should you care if your policeman gets caught?"

"Because he could turn against us. Also, Parker now has photographs of our operatives. Dejeu was identified thanks to him."

"You said Dejeu was killed."

"They identified his body. Dejeu was killed at Parker's cottage."

"So, two men are lost and others are compromised." Mohamed was not impressed. "I enforce strict security here at the camp. It seems things are not so strict at your end."

"Parker will not survive our next attack."

"How can you be sure?"

"I will be sending six men with machineguns."

"Overkill." Mohamed's eyes narrowed. "Allow me the pleasure of executing this contract on Mr. Parker."

Van Praag shook his head. "I cannot spare you from your responsibilities here. You must clean up the camp first. We will kill him within the next week. If for some reason we cannot, I will send you after him after you are done here. You will have time to spare while we pause our operation, as planned, until spring."

Mohamed gritted his teeth. "I will wait. Kendo was a good friend. He was eager to learn, and he asked many questions about my home and family. He was sympathetic and respectful. I will have vengeance."

"He will be avenged," van Praag nodded. "You know, Kendo had been scheduled for elimination after our operation." Van Praag paused cautiously. "You knew that before you became his friend, so…."

Mohamed glared at van Praag, cutting him off. "Kendo would not have turned against us, even if he had known the purpose of our operation. He thought this camp was going to be a secret drug factory, because that's what I told him we were doing." Mohamed had decided not to kill Kendo soon after they met. "Kendo enjoyed his role in the Hell's Angels drug trade, and he enjoyed the women it brought to him. He was much like me when I was that age."

Van Praag had not intended to offend Mohamed. "What did Kendo think was happening to the subjects he brought here?"

"I told him it was not his concern. He accepted that as a professional. He was very intelligent – smart enough to know when not to ask questions."

Van Praag was satisfied to see Mohamed sticking up for his dead comrade. It validated van Praag's choice of team members. "Accept my sympathies on the loss of your friend. May Allah make your reward great and ease your pain."

Mohamed was surprised. He realized van Praag had done his homework in offering the proper condolence to a Muslim concerning the death of a non-Muslim friend. "Thank you." Mohamed found van Praag a little less dislikable now.

Van Praag nodded, and looked at his watch. "On other business, the final two virus test subjects will be delivered in two trips by Kendo's replacement. After the second visit, we will have no more need of this person. After the second delivery, you must dispose of him so he cannot later reveal the camp location or anything else he may know."

"Who is his replacement?" asked Mohamed.

"You do not need to know his name. It would be best if he does not know yours. He will be instructed that someone will meet him at the Winnipeg airport. Send one of your men instead of you." Van Praag looked at Mohamed to ensure he understood.

"Kill him at the camp. Then dispose of the body in the usual manner."

"Yes, sir." Mohamed smiled. "That would mean I must prepare the body in the usual manner."

Van Praag raised an eyebrow at Mohamed. "What exactly do you have to do to prepare a body?"

"I have a body that has been partially prepared. If you have the stomach for it, I can show you."

Van Praag looked at his watch again. "I'm not afraid of dead bodies. I have enough time for one more thing

before you take me back to Kenora. Show me what you
do."

Mohamed opened the door to the furnace hut and
motioned for van Praag to leave. The two men walked
several steps toward the ice cream truck.

"If you noticed, the furnace is not large enough to
contain a human corpse laid flat in the prone position."

"I see it will not fit – do you place it in a sitting
position?"

"Have you ever tried to place a frozen corpse into a
sitting position?" asked Mohamed.

The men were silent as they made there way to the
ice-cream truck.

"It is safe to handle the corpse ONLY if it is frozen
solid, using insulated gloves." Mohamed opened the
passenger door and took out what resembled a pair of
thickly-padded oven mitts covered in rubber.

"Put this on," said Mohamed, offering van Praag a
white face mask. He placed a mask on his own nose and
mouth. "These are just in case of airborne germs. The saw
blade generates heat, and will thaw the frozen flesh a bit.
There is a supply of germicide applied to the blade as it
circulates, but if the blade were to run dry…."

Mohamed opened the door to the truck and the two
men entered the freezing cold interior, closing the door
behind them.

Mohamed switched on an electric light switch and the
two men blinked in the white glow of four bright
overhead fluorescent lights. Mohamed motioned to the
electric bandsaw in one corner of the cube-shaped freezer
space. "I picked that up on eBay."

Van Praag suddenly felt sick to his stomach.

"I was working on a corpse the other day." Mohamed
pointed to two short body bags.

"Pigs?" asked van Praag.

"No," said Mohamed with a smile and a laugh. "Not
pigs."

Mohamed opened one of the bags. "Oops, wrong bag. Look at these...."

Mohamed pulled out what looked like the arm of a manikin. There were remnants of red nail polish on the fingernails. It was a woman's arm. Then Mohamed pulled out a frozen leg. On the foot there was more nail polish of exactly the same red. But at the other end of the leg, it became clear to van Praag that this was not the leg of a manikin. Van Praag was horrified as he observed bone and flesh neatly cut, like a hunk of frozen ham: bone in the middle, meat all around.

Mohamed casually dropped the frozen limbs back in the bag, with a hollow, heavy clatter. Mohamed opened the second small body bag.

Mohamed treated the contents of the second bag with much greater care. He stood the bag up on one end. It balanced, because the downward end was obviously flat.

Then Mohamed carefully removed the top of the bag, sliding it downward to reveal the long, beautiful black hair of a woman.

The corpse was just a torso. Her face was turned away from van Praag, so all he could see was her back.

Mohamed pushed the bag all the way to the floor, revealing the top of her bare buttocks. Her skin, although frozen and slightly purple, was of smooth complexion and her waist was narrow, giving what was left of her body a curved and feminine shape.

Mohamed removed one mitt and gently straightened her hair, teasing it with his fingers until it fell perfectly into place.

It looked to van Praag as if Mohamed was playing with a large armless and legless Barbie doll.

"She must have been no more than twenty," Mohamed said, voicing his words with regret. "I could not work on her as long as I was able to see her face."

Mohamed turned the torso completely around toward van Praag, revealing the front of the woman. The female form was exquisite, like the armless, beautiful, ancient Greek sculpture, Venus de Milo. Her young breasts were smooth and shaped perfectly.

Mohamed had covered her face completely with many short strips of black electrical tape, shaping it to fit from between her cheeks, from chin to forehead. No part of her face was visible.

Van Praag gasped in shock.

Mohamed decided to have some fun at van Praag's expense. He turned his head sharply toward van Praag, eyes suddenly wide, peering over his mask. It's time for a little payback, he thought, for van Praag keeping him in the dark about the propane tank detonation plan.

Mohamed laughed. "She wasn't quite solid when I removed her arms and legs," he said. "She had only been in here about an hour. A bit of unfrozen fluid leaked out when I tried to cut through the thicker parts. Very dangerous, infected fluid."

Mohamed jumped to his feet and took three quick steps over to the electric butchers bandsaw. "But she should be ready to go through now!" Mohamed pushed the green start button and the electric motor started up. The bandsaw blade began to turn.

Van Praag felt his knees go weak. He realized he wanted desperately not to witness what was about to happen. He felt a shudder go through his spine. He tried to turn toward the door, but his legs would not respond – he could not make himself walk. Horrified, he tried to speak. "Please…." he tried to say, but his voice was absent. His vocal chords could produce no more than a feeble whisper.

Mohamed carried the torso to the saw table surface. Taking care, he positioned her black hair over the back of the table, out of the way. Mohamed held the woman's neck in front of the moving teeth of the circulating saw blade. The upper back of the torso was on the table surface. The faceless black mask looked upward, as if pleading to the heavens for salvation.

Mohamed had both hands on the hips of the torso. He held the limbless, naked body as if he was making love to it.

Van Praag attempted to raise his arms to cover his view of the horrific scene, but he was completely immobilized.

Mohamed, satisfied with the blade and flesh alignment, turned his head to observe van Praag.

Van Praag stood eyes wide, without the strength to beg Mohamed to stop.

The saw blade screamed as Mohamed, laughing like a maniac behind his mask, cut off the woman's head.

33 – AROUND THE BOARDROOM TABLE

Waiting patiently, Jacques sat at the head of the boardroom table, in charge of the meeting. He checked his watch. It was 1300 hours, time to connect with Morris at the hospital. He turned to observe Conan's progress.

Sitting next to Zia, Conan was busy on his laptop, trying to establish a connection with Morris.

"Is he loggin' in to us, or are we loggin' in to him?" Zia asked Conan.

"He has to initiate the connection to us. We have the fixed IP address, not him."

Zia leaned over to look at Conan's laptop screen, watching him work.

"What's that for?" Zia asked, pointing to an icon on Conan's screen.

"It's a packet sniffer."

"Oh. How long does your battery last?"

Conan looked up at Zia, not smiling. "I'm trying to work here. I've been awake all night."

"You should get more sleep."

"I had an assignment from the boss."

"Me too. My wife wanted me to…"

"I mean from Morris, the head schmuck."

"What did he have you doing?"

Conan look up at the ceiling, and sighed. "Really, I have to think about this, OK?" Conan pointed to his screen.

"OK, sorry," Zia said apologetically. "I think I had too much caffeine this morning."

Watching the exchange between the two technical experts, Ed shook his head with amusement. Liam the Lawyer was also present at the table, waiting patiently.

"OK, he's in," said Conan. "Turn on the projector, Zia."

"Can everyone hear me?" asked Morris over the speakers.

"Yes, boss," replied Jacques. "Troops are assembled as ordered. Liam, Ed, Zia, Conan and me."

"Fabulous. Thanks for coming on short notice, guys. I know most of you have not had much sleep."

"I haven't had lunch, either," said Conan.

"Jacques…" Morris began.

"Already taken care of, boss. I asked Jill to order in some sandwiches."

"Excellent. I was up most of the night myself and I have found several things that need to be discussed, so I want to press on. The purpose of this meeting is to discuss our findings so far, then decide how to proceed. To start, I'd like everyone to report his activities since our last meeting a week ago.

"I'll start. I got shot, concussed, went into a coma, and was hospitalized for five days. In other words, I took some time off. I started looking at the Kendo hard drive information early this morning and have some findings to report after I hear everyone else.

"Jacques, I'd like you to go next, and take the discussion around the table."

"Right," said Jacques. "The most important thing everyone needs to know is that we cannot trust the Ottawa police to conduct an honest investigation. After we gave our previous findings to Detective Clark, Morris and his family were attacked. At our meeting, I told Clark Morris would be at the cottage. After our meeting, Clark was logged accessing a police report with the cottage address on it. We are pretty sure he is in on something that he doesn't want us to find out about. He must have ordered the attack, or gave the information to the person who ordered it.

"The next most important item is the disk information Conan was able to retrieve from the unsecured network in Kendo's apartment. Before we hear Conan's report, I have a question for Liam. Is it legal for us to use that information?"

"From what I understand," said Liam, "Conan gained unauthorized access to private information by hacking in. The short answer is he can be charged for that, as well as anyone who assisted him or ordered him to do it. The information itself, however, could be used in a court of law. If the police had taken it without a search warrant, then it would not be admissible. The police could not use it in a criminal trial, but we can probably use it, even if we stole it. We can and should use anything that will help clear Morris of his criminal charges. We should also be able to use this information in the civil suit the Kanise family has launched against us. Even if it was stolen, the information is relevant.

"It would be better, however, if we try to corroborate whatever we find or completely replace it from another source. The disk can lead us to other sources which would be even more useful in court."

"Thanks," said Jacques. "Conan, what have you found on the disk?"

"I was able to restore everything and make it readable except for the email files. They are password protected."

"What format are they?"

"Microsoft Outlook .pst files."

"I can help you with that," said Zia. "I have several cracking programs." Zia held up a small thumb drive.

Conan and Zia turned to look at Liam.

"Gentlemen, I cannot advise you to break the law," said Liam. "But I can say you are both protected by solicitor-client privilege."

Zia tossed the thumb drive to Conan. "Look in the mail cracking folder."

Conan inserted the thumb drive into his laptop's USB drive and began to fiddle with his mouse. "Morris and I looked at the drive contents last night. Morris knows what the stuff means better than me."

"I'll get to that after you finish your first go-round," said Morris over the speaker.

"OK," said Jacques. "Liam, can you report any progress on getting the charges against Morris dropped?"

"The Crown Attorney's office is stalling on providing any recordings of the 9-1-1 call. We will get it eventually, but they are not making it easy at the moment. I have collected affidavits from several witnesses that state Morris did not fire the first shot. I would say our chances of winning at trial are very good."

"Trial will be months away. Meanwhile, they have my passport and are keeping me under a cloud," said Morris.

"The Crown Attorney is not cooperating much. I've asked for the analysis report of the bullet in the beam. I'm thinking that it could be from a different ammunition lot and I could raise some reasonable doubt that the evidence was tampered with. But they say the report isn't ready. They are not in a hurry to get one. Clark is claiming the scene was guarded all night, anyway, and there is no chance of evidence tampering.

"I would love to make a motion for dismissal, but we would need some pretty compelling piece of hard physical evidence for it to succeed. We would have to pretty much destroy the believability of the pistol bullet in the ceiling beam."

"I found something interesting, speaking of pistols," said Zia. "I'm not sure what it means, but I think everyone should see it."

"Go ahead, Zia," said Jacques.

"After we found the images on the back door camera showing the getaway car, I double-checked the two images sources for other differences. The DVR in The

Arms was not recording images from that camera, but my monitor station was. The back door camera channel wasn't configured to make local recordings. I wanted to see if the DVR at the pub missed any other images. During the one-hour period leading up to the shootout, the pub's DVR and my monitor station both had the exact same count of video image clips: 27 each. From the time of the first shot until two hours later, the pub's DVR contained 84 clips but my system had 85."

Zia manipulated the mouse on his laptop and pulled up a clip. He turned his laptop so everyone in the boardroom could see his screen. "This is the missing clip. It was on my DVR, but it had been deleted from the pub's DVR."

"I can't see what you're doing, Zia," said Morris.

"I'll describe it for you. This is the view from the overhead camera disguised as a sprinkler head in the back hallway. That's Detective Clark, examining a pistol. It appears to be empty. He looks around, maybe to see if anyone is watching him. Now he puts the gun in his jacket pocket. Then he takes out his own gun from his shoulder thingy."

"Holster," said Ed.

"He empties the bullets out of his magazine, then he replaces the magazine and cocks the empty pistol. Now it looks just like the other one. Now he puts the first pistol in his holster and walks away."

"Holy shit," said Ed. "He swapped the pistols. Angela told me that prick Clark took the pub's DVR out of the building for a few days!"

"He must have erased the clip from the DVR, thinking it was the only copy," said Jacques.

"Liam, did you say Clark is claiming the scene was guarded all night?" asked Morris.

"It's in his report."

"That's the report we don't officially have," Morris said.

"Clark is lying in that report," said Ed. "He's a dirty cop, and we have the proof with this clip. He obviously used the Morris gun later that night to plant the bullet in the beam. And he must have switched the gun back the next day."

"It looks like I could make a motion based on this video clip," said Liam.

"Good work, Zia," said Morris.

Conan raised his hand toward Jacques.

"Conan has something to say," said Jacques.

"Good work, Zia," said Conan. "Your cracker works. I have opened the Kendo email file."

"I see that," said Morris, watching Conan's screen from his hospital room.

Conan reached over to the projector and turned it on. "This is my laptop screen, and Morris is logged in and he can see it also."

"Japanese characters," said Ed.

"There's a bunch of English emails too." Conan scrolled through the message headings.

"Let's get the Japanese stuff translated," said Morris. "I'll go through the English messages myself."

"Where can we get a translator?" asked Jacques.

"Jill will get it done for you," said Morris. "Let's move on."

"Now might be a good time to report our activities last night," said Jacques. "Ed, you go first."

"I had a great time," said Ed, relishing the memory. "Had a few beers, I saw some great tits, and I didn't find out a thing."

At that moment, Jill quietly entered the room with a tray of sandwiches.

"Free food! Thanks," said Zia, taking a sandwich from the tray.

Seeing Jill, Ed was suddenly subdued. "Uh, none of the girls I bought dances from recognized the photo."

Zia was about to bite into his sandwich, but stopped himself. "Dances? What kind of mission were you guys on last night?"

"Surveillance," said Conan, keeping an eye on Jill.

"Can I see you a moment?" Jacques said to Jill.

Jill nodded, put down the sandwich tray, and walked over to Jacques. Jacques quietly told her about the Japanese translation task and they conversed in a whisper while the meeting continued.

Ed leaned over and spoke quietly to Zia, trying not to be heard by Jill. "Boob watching. Muff reconnaissance. Peeler surveillance."

Zia looked confused.

"We went to strip joints," said Ed.

Zia put down his sandwich, forgetting that he was hungry. "How do I get that kind of mission?"

"Do you drink beer?" asked Conan.

"Not allowed."

"Ever been to a peeler joint?" asked Ed.

"No."

"Are you married?" asked Conan.

"Yes."

"Three strikes," said Ed.

"But you're married," Zia said to Ed. "So is Jacques. You guys got to go."

Morris felt frustrated because he could not see anyone and could just barely hear what was going on. "I'll bring you with me next time, now will you stop whining?" He went on impatiently. "I've been looking forward to this report. OK, who saw the biggest boobs? The best ass? Let's have details, gentlemen."

Jill spoke up immediately. "Should I be leaving the room?"

"Jill," said Morris, surprised and embarrassed. "I didn't know you were there."

"I just brought in the sandwiches," she said.

"Good sandwiches!" said Conan enthusiastically.

The group began complimenting the sandwiches: "Excellent." "Delicious." "Man, was I hungry!"

Then the room was silent. Jill looked around slowly. None of the men wanted to make eye contact.

"Well, I can see a lot of testosterone here. Since there's no sports channel and no beer here in the boardroom, I guess you fellas are doing the best you can. I'll let you boys get back to your discussion. Enjoy your lunch."

"Thanks, Jill." "Thank-you." "Much appreciated." "You're the greatest."

Jill left the room.

Jacques smiled at her as she passed, and closed the door behind her.

"She's gone," said Jacques.

"Was she pissed?" asked Morris.

"She gave me a wink on the way out," said Jacques. "I think she enjoyed that. My fault. I should have let you know when she came in the room."

"Apology not accepted. I sometimes act like an ass all on my own. Fortunately, Jill is a classy lady."

The sound of loud female laughter could be heard outside the boardroom door.

"She also keeps me humble," Morris added.

"I don't feel like talking about naked girls any more," said Ed.

"OK, but we still have some facts to consider," said Jacques. "Our approach was to ask for a private dance, and when we were alone with the girl, show her the picture. Our cover was to say we were trying to find our sister. We found the photo in her apartment, and assumed it showed a friend of hers. None of the girls Ed and I saw recognized the picture. The only one who got anything was Conan. He got her stage name at the Club Chaton."

"It's Valentina," said Conan.

"I got into an online chat with her, using the name Sweet Wild Rose, on Yahoo Messenger last night," said

Morris. "She's not just a stripper, she's also a hooker. I found a June chat file where she describes a trick with a trucker at a secret campsite. She's working at the Club Chaton all week. She should be easy to find. She thought I was Kendo, and she expects to meet with him."

"You killed the guy," said Conan. "She might not want to meet with you."

"I called Boyd MacDougall this morning about her," said Ed. "Boyd used her at some of his poker games. He offered his rich, losing gamblers hookers as consolation prizes. She's a real pro, he said, and always made his players happy. She's clean, smart, professional, reliable and discreet. He stopped using her after a while because she got too expensive. He said she was way more dependable than any of the other girls he uses, though."

"I think I have an approach I can use," said Morris. "She texted me that she's looking for a missing friend by the name of Candi. I found a bunch of ID photos on Kendo's disk. He was making false IDs for people, including one for a dark-haired girl with the identity Candice Walker. I can show her the photo."

"Do you plan to ask if that's the girl she's looking for?" asked Liam.

"Why not? I think I can earn her trust. She's obviously a pro, and hopefully Kendo was just a customer, not a lover."

"Can she be trusted? What if she's with the bad guys?" asked Liam.

"That's the part I don't know. I can play it safe and not reveal my identity."

"You're a pretty well-known face around Ottawa," said Liam.

"She didn't know that Kendo was dead. Maybe she doesn't read the papers. I'll have to take a bit of a chance if I want information. I can try to convince Valentina I'm on her side, and together we can get to the bottom of the secret camp thing. Kendo took a lot of people to

Winnipeg on Thursday flights. I think he duped her friend
Candi.

"On Kendo's computer, I found flight schedules and
payment information showing several Thursday flights to
Winnipeg. He was being paid $2000 for each trip. He
flew under a different identity each time, and the flight
time and airline varied to keep him from being recognized
as a regular on that route. He always traveled with a
different person using one of the fake IDs. He was taking
people to Winnipeg, and from there, probably to the
secret camp, which Valentina revealed is near Kenora. I
have no idea what these people are being taken there for."

"Kendo was earning good money for those trips," said
Ed.

"I got your email about watching arrivals in Winnipeg
next Thursday," said Jacques. "You want us to watch for
the two people in the ID photos you found on Kendo's
drive."

"Right," said Morris. "There are two photo identities
that are not named on the electronic tickets. They may be
future travelers."

"Who do you want to send?" asked Liam.

"Ed and I will go," said Jacques. "That's what we
signed up for."

"What if you are recognized?" asked Liam. "You two
are known to the other side."

"Good point," said Morris.

"Bring me," said Liam.

"And me," said Zia.

Liam went on. "You can use our help at the airport.
We are fresh faces. Plus, the airport security people will
get nervous if the two of you hang around all day
watching every flight. With four of us, it will be harder
for them to figure out what's going on."

"Good idea," said Morris.

"I'll plan for a four-man team," said Jacques.

"Consider these facts," said Morris. "Candi went to Winnipeg. Wrong. *She was escorted* to Winnipeg. Actually, she probably ended up at a camp near Kenora. She told Valentina she was going to Vancouver – because that's where she thought she was going, or that's what she was told to say. Then she lost contact. And my guess is Candi is a young prostitute. She had a session of *doubles* with Valentina and Kendo. *Doubles* is sex-worker speak for a threesome with two girls and a client."

"It sounds like you should meet Valentina," said Liam, "and confirm that photo is Candi. But you will have to be very careful. Valentina could tip off the bad guys that you are after them. They would be able to figure out where you got the photo."

"What do you think we should do with the Clark video?" asked Morris.

"If we hand in the video clip we have on Clark," said Liam, "we are bound to get a reaction. There could be other people with him, inside the Ottawa Police."

"If we turn the Clark video in, will that be the end of it?" asked Ed. "Maybe that's all the attack at the cottage was about. Clark was trying to hide the video. When Jacques and Liam turned over the other evidence, we tipped him off that we had a second set of videos."

"Don't forget Clark somehow had the motivation to fabricate evidence in the first place," said Liam. "He may have been trying to spring MacDick by setting up Morris."

Morris sounded confident. "Right. The bad guys have more resources than a single rogue cop would have. He is a part of something bigger. Somehow, I'll bet he sprung Beavis and Butthead from hospital. They must have been needed outside for something. I was set up for the same reason."

"There are risks in pushing this investigation," said Liam. "You can't trust the authorities."

"There are risks in not pushing this investigation," said Jacques.

"Let's try and find some authorities we can trust," said Morris. "Liam, let's say we take this outside the Ottawa Police. We give the video to the RCMP or the OPP."

"That might be the right way to go." Liam thought for a moment. "We can see what kind of a reaction we get, and I may not have to make a motion for dismissal of the charges against you. In light of the video, they may just be dropped."

"Send the clip to the OPP." Morris sounded satisfied. "Let's see what happens."

"What the hell," said Conan quietly, looking intently at his laptop screen.

During the discussion, Conan had been fiddling with Kendo's email. Nobody had been paying attention to what he was doing, because he had quietly turned off the projector.

"I see it," said Morris, looking at Conan's screen from his hospital bed.

Zia leaned over and turned on the projector. The group could now see an error message on the screen.

Unable to add encrypted task to database. Missing public key.

"What does that mean?" asked Ed.

"This is one of the error messages I wrote for our TaskMan product. It means the email I just opened contains an attachment that originated in a TaskMan system somewhere."

"Like I said, what does that mean?" Ed repeated.

"Lots of big businesses use our TaskMan product. Kendo received an email from one of them. It means we can figure out who's behind this whole scheme, if they

registered the software serial number with us," said
Morris. "What email message triggered the error?"

Conan clicked the OK button and the error message
disappeared to reveal an open email message. It was from
Big Mac to *Kamikaze Kendo*. The subject was RE: TASK
REMINDER – TMID34532 FLIGHT TO WINNIPEG.

"Are you saying Big Mac or the Hell's Angels are a
customer of your software?" asked Ed.

"No," said Morris. "TaskMan is mostly used by larger
companies with a hundred or more knowledge workers in
multiple departments. I don't think Hell's Angels has a
suitable corporate structure. But whoever hired Hell's
Angels originated that email. The email was forwarded
out of their TaskMan system to Big Mac and he
forwarded it to Kendo."

"I'm using my own mail reader to examine Kendo's
.pst file," said Conan. "When I tried to open this message,
my mail reader found it contains content from TaskMan.
It tried to catalog it in our database, but we don't have a
decryption key for the user that originated the task. All
we can see is the task number that was generated on the
originating system. See the number in the subject heading
– TMID34532?"

"Yeah, sure," said Ed. "What the hell is a decryption
key?"

"Each customer corporation that installs TaskMan
generates its own secret key for encrypting and
decrypting TaskMan emails," said Morris. "We don't
have the key for the system where this task originated."

"The message also has a hidden header that my mail
reader analyzed automatically," Conan said excitedly.
"Our TaskMan software embeds a line of data in there.
That data includes information about the originating
TaskMan system, including the serial number we
assigned to the copy of TaskMan that was installed by the
customer."

"You must keep a record of serial numbers, right?" asked Ed.

"Yes," said Morris. "When the software is installed, the installer is forced to connect to our license server and register the software to activate it."

"I'm looking up the serial number now," said Conan.

There was a pause while Conan manipulated his mouse, then typed at his keyboard, then moved the mouse again. Windows appeared and disappeared on the screen as he logged-in to the license control database.

Meanwhile, Morris explained. "TaskMan reminders sometimes contain attachments so the user can read task details offline – while on an airplane, for example. TaskMan will encrypt the attachment. TaskMan users sometimes make the mistake of forwarding a TaskMan notification email containing attached, encrypted task information."

"The user is supposed to use his web browser to log in and update the task data on the database," said Conan, "not use his email program to reply to or forward the reminder like a dumbass."

"Of course," said Ed, winking at Zia. "Everybody knows that."

"That's the serial number," said Conan as he pasted a long line of digits into a query field on the application screen. He clicked a button labeled EXECUTE QUERY.

"Software registered to *A. Company*," Morris read from the screen. "And there is no address information. The installer filled in a fake company name and left most of the registration page blank."

"I can tell you one thing, at least," said Conan, as he examined the screen display. "This company is a pretty good size. There are 300 licenses issued."

"Where do you get that?" asked Ed.

"The software reports its level of usage to our central server," said Morris. "But from my recollection, that doesn't narrow things down much."

"Right," said Conan as he executed another query. "We have 458 customers licensed at that level."

The room was silent for a moment.

"Conan, check if there are any other TaskMan emails in that .pst," Morris said. "And examine the header of that message to see if you can figure out anything from the routing. And email me when you're done."

"Will do," said Conan.

"Jacques, have you been taking notes? Ready for a recap?" asked Morris.

"Yes, sir. I have eight items. Item One: Detective Clark is a dirty cop, as seen from the video clip of him tampering with evidence. Item Two: the Kendo disk information is usable in court but it would be best to re-acquire evidence from a direct source. Item Three: our video clip proof of item one will hopefully get Morris off his manslaughter charge. Action for that item is Liam's responsibility."

"I will send it to the OPP and we'll see if the charges are dropped, otherwise we consider if I should make a motion," said Liam.

"Right." Jacques continued. "Item Four: we now have Kendo's email. I will arrange for Japanese translation with Jill, and Morris will examine the other messages.

"Item Five: we should act more like gentlemen when talking about our activities, just in case a lady enters the room."

"A most important action item," said Morris.

"Item Six: Morris got a lot of valuable information from Kendo's disk, and I will now plan a trip to Winnipeg with Liam, Zia and Ed. Our mission is to find and follow subjects in the Kendo ID photos to see if they lead us to a camp somewhere around Kenora.

"Item Seven: Morris will meet with Valentina to try and get her cooperation in searching for Candi.

"Item Eight: Morris will work with Conan to try and identify the company that originated the TaskMan email."

"Good summary," said Morris. "Unless somebody has anything to add, I think we're done. We can meet in the boardroom at this time again tomorrow. I get out of hospital this afternoon. Thanks everybody.

"Oh, I should add Item Nine: based on my analysis of the Kendo hard drive information, we are facing a well-financed, serious criminal organization. We don't know what they're up to, but they will try to stop us by killing if necessary."

"In my country, we call that our government," said Zia.

"We are going to have to rely on each other," said Morris.

"All for one, and one for all," said Ed.

34 – A TASKMAN REMINDER

Morris was waiting impatiently in his hospital bed, clicking to check for new mail every few minutes. In between checks, he browsed for some online trivia to share with Conan.

Finally a message arrived from the_barbarian@parkerholdings.com.

"Ready to Talk," said the subject line. It contained no additional text.

Morris had already established the necessary computer connection. He clicked OK to accept Conan in a screen-sharing conversation. He adjusted his headset microphone. After a bit of static, Conan's voice came through.

"Testing one, two. Any schmucks out there?"

"Schmuck is a surname, did you know that? It's from German, meaning jewel or jewelry. Von Schmuck."

"No shit. I thought it meant *jerk*."

"The Schmucks wouldn't want to think so. According to Wikipedia, Catherina Schmuck was the mother of Gottfried Leibniz, who discovered the binary numeral system."

"It must be pretty boring, getting all that rest. What do you do all day, google shit like that?"

"Pretty much. Google, drool, and wait for my next tray of bland hospital food. So, what have you got?"

"The only TaskMan email in Kendo's .pst was this one." Conan moved his mouse pointer and selected the subject line RE: TASK REMINDER – TMID34532 FLIGHT TO WINNIPEG. "It was an automatic reminder that came out of our system on June 10th."

"That's the timestamp on the first electronic ticketing document," said Morris. "TaskMan reminded somebody to book that flight."

"Yup. This reminder came out of TaskMan, then was forwarded twice. I should be able to see at least three email addresses in the routing history. But when I check the message header, it's weird. I can't get all the IP addresses, reply-to, or originator email addresses in the chain. All I get is the final hop of routing."

"What does that mean?"

"OK, this message started its life when TaskMan created it on the server where TaskMan was installed. IP addresses and reply-to junk would have been embedded in the header when it was transmitted. It gets embedded by the email program that receives the message."

"So?"

"Look at the first line of routing." Conan revealed the message header. "You have to read the routing information from the bottom up, starting here. This is the first hop. But the IP address is showing up as 127.0.0.1. That's non-routable. And the *from:* and *reply-to:* strings are set to *none@none.com.*"

"Like I said, what does all that mean?" asked Morris, lost.

"The routing information was purged by one or more of the email-reading programs that handled the message."

"So the Cripps are using some special privacy-assured email software?"

"I would guess the big company is using it, and maybe somebody on the outside who they gave the email reader to. Somehow this message got forwarded to Big Mac, who was not using privacy assurance – he was using a hotmail address. Big Mac forwarded it to Kendo, who was also using a hotmail address. That's the only part of the routing we can read. The people before that can't be identified."

Jim E.M. Miles

Morris thought for a moment. "Whoever originated this task has given out software to an outside party he communicates with. But because that software isn't aware that TaskMan adds license info into the header, it slipped through."

"Right. The originator has a hole in his security that he is not aware of."

"How can we exploit that hole?"

"Well, we have the ID for the task and we have the subject line: TASK REMINDER – TMID34532 FLIGHT TO WINNIPEG. We do not know which copy of our software out there generated it, but I have an idea how we can find out. I can put a small utility program in our regular product updates. When our customers' computers connect to check our server for software updates, they will pick up the program. The program will run on every machine out there, and mostly do nothing. But on the machine where there is a task with ID 34532 that has subject heading FLIGHT TO WINNIPEG, the program will identify the server for us."

"Cool! It will find lots of machines with a task ID 34532, because each installation uses its own counter to generate new ID's. But it is highly unlikely that two ID's will have the exact same subject heading."

"Like it?" Conan was enthusiastic.

"How will the program contact us?"

"We could have it send an email."

"True. Our TaskMan installation requirements mean the computer be configured to send email. But what if the installation is behind a firewall and it can generate only internal email? Or what if their server has been configured to monitor any and all data connections – we could get caught. They would see a destination email address that they could trace."

"Oh, yeah, right."

"What if I could get you in to their machine room?" asked Morris.

"If I could get my hands on the actual machine, I could do a lot."

"OK, try this. Make your utility program break something. Put out an error message for the system manager to call tech support. When they call, we offer a no-charge, on-site repair. In you go."

"Not bad, for a schmuck." Conan thought for a moment. "We might have to wait until their machine calls in for an update, though. They may not have set it to check for automatic updates."

"About 95% of our users take the updates on at least a monthly basis. We may have to wait a bit, but there's a pretty good chance we will get a nibble."

"What am I now, bait?"

"If you were, we would be fishing for shark. Nothing smaller than a Great White Shark would be interested in you."

35 – CLUB CHATON

Morris paid the $10.00 cover charge, passed through the metal detector, and entered the dimly lit main room of the Club Chaton. The sound system was blasting *American Woman* performed by Lenny Kravitz. The slow, grinding bass drum beat and his distorted, sweeping guitar licks set the scene.

Morris had not told Terri where he was going. It was Wednesday night, so he let her assume he was going to The Cumberland Arms as usual. Morris felt a tinge of guilt at not being forthcoming with that information.

Because he had gone to the cottage with the family, Morris had missed the previous Wednesday pub night. Terri would have preferred him to skip this Wednesday as well, but Morris never missed two Wednesday nights in a row unless he was out of town. So she let him go.

Morris had been released from the hospital Tuesday, yesterday, and had spent the night at home with the family. It was their first night together since the attack at the cottage. They didn't talk much about it – they just spent the night watching TV, glad to be together. They watched a few episodes of *Friends* on DVD, and the movie *Monsters, Inc.*

Morris looked around the room. It was better than he had imagined it would be.

The doorman and several other male staff members wore black tuxedos. The floor and tables were clean and the air was smoke-free. There were several large high-definition television monitors showing various sports channels mounted high on the walls. There were a couple of well-endowed waitresses in micro-miniskirts with fishnet stockings serving drinks from small silver trays. It was a classy place. Morris thought the job he was going

to do might not be so unpleasant after all, and so he
decided to leave his guilt at the door. He had $1,000 in
ten, twenty and fifty-dollar bills in the breast pocket of his
jacket.

The well-lit main stage had a single golden stripper
pole running from stage floor upwards to a very high
ceiling. There was a second floor, Morris realized. A
couple of men sat behind a railing, looking down onto the
stage. This second-floor railing surrounded the stage on
three sides. At the back of the stage, a large staircase led
down from the second floor, spreading its railings wide to
allow the incoming dancer to make a grand entrance.

Morris looked at the large percentage of empty seats.
It was early in the evening. Perhaps Wednesday never
was very busy. He needed to choose a place to sit. There
were seats at the stage, there were tables on the main and
second floors, and there were stools open at the bar.

A security man smiled and nodded hello. Morris saw
that he had an earpiece, like he was on the protection
party for the Prime Minister. The man asked Morris
where he would like to sit. Morris chose the bar, and
tipped $10 to be shown his seat. The man smiled and
thanked Morris.

The place seemed pretty safe. Considering the action
he had encountered two weeks before, Morris thought, it
was probably safer than The Arms had been that night.
Do they serve wings? Sadly, high safety marks would not
be sufficient justification to convince the guys, who
would have to convince their wives, to change the regular
Wednesday venue to Club Chaton.

The bartender nodded, and stepped up to serve
Morris.

Over the intense rock guitar, Morris had to lip read
the bartender's "What'll it be?"

"Scotch," said Morris.

"What kind," said the barman, gesturing to a row of
bottles.

"Jameson, neat."

The barman nodded and poured the drink. "That'll be twelve dollars."

"Keep the change." Morris gave him a twenty.

The barman straightened and offered a warm handshake. "Welcome. We appreciate a man like you here. I'm Jake."

Morris nodded. "Nice place, Jake. I'm Morris. When do the girls start?"

"On stage? Next one will be in about 15 minutes. But take a look behind you."

Morris turned to his right and his vision filled with the sight of a tall, beautiful redhead in a sensual burgundy evening gown heading straight toward him. He made eye contact, feeling an immediate surge of adrenaline.

"Hello," she said confidently. "My name is Jenna."

She extended her hand. Morris accepted it, and shook her hand gently. Her hand was soft, smooth and cool.

"My name is Morris."

"Oh, your hand is warm," she said as she placed her other hand on his. "May I join you?"

Morris considered whether he should simply say he was waiting for Valentina, or whether he should speak with Jenna for a bit. This place was not his usual environment. He was not a predator here – he was the prey. He decided to start a conversation.

Morris smiled at her, hoping he appeared confident and comfortable, although he felt neither. "It would be a pleasure."

She hoisted her gown a bit and positioned herself on the stool beside him. The gown had a slit on one side, and it fell away as she crossed her legs. The stage lights added to their curve appeal, making those legs appear tanned and perfectly shaped. The heels on her platform shoes must have been six inches or more.

"May I buy you a drink?" Morris said, immediately wishing he could withdraw the offer. What if Valentina

came in – it wouldn't be gentlemanly to simply shoo
Jenna away if she had not finished the drink. Morris had
come in thinking he had a prepared plan. He now realized
he was winging it.

"Yes, please. White wine."

Morris signaled Jake the bartender. As he came over,
Morris checked his drink. To his surprise, it was already
empty. Then he recognized the slight burning sensation in
his chest. He must have thrown back the Jameson without
noticing, while his senses were on overload as he met the
girl. What a schmuck.

"White wine and another Jameson. On the rocks, this
time."

"Where are you from?" asked Jenna.

"From Orleans." Morris tried to think of a joke.
Orleans was only about a thirty-minute drive to the club.
"I just flew in."

"How was your flight?"

She didn't get the joke. What joke, anyway, Morris
asked himself. Then he realized she had a slight accent.
She probably didn't know the area very well.

"Orleans is a suburb of Ottawa. I was trying to be
funny."

"Oh."

Jake brought the drinks, giving Morris something to
do with his hands, rather than just fumble around
aimlessly. He paid $20 and tipped with an extra $10.

Morris asked her about her accent. She was from the
Ukraine. Morris asked why she left. No jobs in her field.
She was qualified there as a dental hygienist. She was
unable to afford the training in Canada to re-qualify, so
she ended up in the sex trade.

It was difficult to converse, Morris noted, because the
music was too loud.

Her wine was about half-finished. "Would you like a
private dance?" she asked.

Morris had finished his second scotch. He became aware he was drinking quite quickly. But there was a benefit. He was much more at ease now. He realized the nature of the activity here at Club Chaton. Commerce. She wanted to close a deal. If not with Morris, she would move on and close with someone else. Her main, if not only, interest in Morris was his money.

Morris felt his mating instinct begin to wane, and his business instincts kicked in. Let's explore this deal, he thought.

"What does a private dance involve?" he asked.

"We go over to the open side room, and I dance for you."

"You get naked?"

"Certainly."

"How much?"

"Twenty per song."

Morris looked at the open side room. There we booths along the wall that would give a small sense of privacy to the customer by separating him from his neighbor. But it was far from a private area. And there were additional loudspeakers in there. Conversation would be no better over there.

"What if I want to touch you?"

"Not allowed over there, but there is a Champagne room upstairs."

"What's that like?"

"It's nice, private, quiet and lots and lots of fun – especially if you go with me. I'm really, really friendly."

"How much?"

"The champagne goes for $300 for a half an hour."

"They sell me champagne by the half-hour? That makes no sense."

"Well, you get the room for half an hour for each bottle you buy."

"Does that include the girl?"

She paused and looked at him.

Morris pulled out a fifty-dollar bill and gave it to her. She was surprised.

"I'm not trying to haggle. I just like to understand the deal. Please explain to me exactly how this place works."

She smiled. "I have never had a customer pay in advance just for a clear explanation."

"I'm not here to be entertained."

"Are you sure? When you tipped the security man, he signaled me right away. I'm very entertaining, honey."

"Look, you're very nice and I'm sure in the right circumstances – it's difficult to talk here, isn't it? What I really want is information."

Jenna tucked the fifty into an elastic band on her ankle. "I can do information." She straightened and adjusted her chair closer so she could speak comfortably in his ear.

Then Morris got a whiff of her scent, and wished he could be entertained.

"They make it loud to drive the customers into the Champagne Lounge," said Jenna. "The price is ambiguous so we get the customer in the elevator thinking he can have everything he wants for $300. When he gets up there, just before the waitress opens the bottle, the girl tells him her time costs extra. The customer almost never backs out, because it's private, he's drunk, and there's a hot, horny female right on top of him – it's usually overwhelming."

"What's the average sale up there?"

"My average is about six hundred. I'm not as good at taking advantage as some of the others. My deals are lower than the average girl."

"I guess they take plastic."

"They sure do. On the credit card statement this place shows up as *Brasserie Jo-anne*. The waitress takes the guy's debit or credit card when she delivers the bottle. Depending on the look of the guy, how drunk and how horny, the waitress will pre-approve a thousand or more

for the girl. If he wants the waitress, she joins in too.
You've seen how they look."

Morris looked around the room. It was starting to fill
up. There were now big-breasted beauties in tight tank
tops giving back massages to men seated in their chairs.
Cash was starting to flow.

"Thank you, Jenna."

Jenna took another sip from her wine and stood up.
She left the glass on the bar, about one-quarter full.

"You're welcome. Thanks for the tip. I hope you have
a pleasant evening. If I can do anything else for you, just
let me know."

"To be honest, I'm looking for a girl named
Valentina."

"You won't have long to wait. She's up next." Jenna
motioned toward the stage. "Drop one of these calling
cards at the end of her performance," she pointed to the
fifty on her ankle, "and she'll come out and look for you."

Thankful for the information, Morris watched Jenna
walk away. She quickly found another prospect, reeling
him in the same way she had worked Morris. She joined
him at his table, sitting facing Morris. Even though
Morris was in Jenna's field of view, she avoided eye
contact. After about three minutes, she popped the
question and they stood and headed for the elevator.
Morris wanted to give Jenna a knowing smile, to
congratulate her on her next deal. But she avoided his
gaze. It was as if Morris was no longer in the room.

Morris didn't think he was going to spend $50 just to
get Valentina's attention. He planned to use a $20.

The sound system was now blasting the ending chords
for Led Zepplin's Whole Lotta Love. "Gentlemen," the
DJ said, as the final chord faded. "Your wait is over. The
time has arrived. Give it up, because she's gonna give
you all her love – put your hands together for: Va-len-
teeeeen-a!"

Morris looked up as drum beats sounded, followed by a synthesizer chord, for an unfamiliar rock song. A male vocalist began:

How can I reach you, Valentina?
Each time we meet I want you, more and more.
And how can I read you, sweet, wild rose?
Those men, it's you, they come in for, men you come on for.

"She does only the one song," barman Jake said to Morris. "All the other girls have to do three. She reels in all the business she needs for the whole night with just this one appearance, one song. It was written for her. None of the other girls are allowed to use it. She keeps the only copy."

The song started slow. The lyrics told the story of a guy who was falling for a stripper. The dilemma for him was: he did not know if her feelings for him were real. He cautioned Valentina about taking on too many men, and faking feelings for too many men, because she would lose her ability to feel anything if she played the game too long.

Valentina was in command of the room, which Morris realized, was now crowded. She was the opening act. She only did the one song. Then she made all kinds of money. She was a marketing genius. Morris liked her already.

The song lasted six minutes. There was an extended drum, bongo and marimba solo that began as she removed her final piece of clothing. During the solo, she showed exactly what she could do, and the room became a jungle riot. By the end of the solo, the audience was ecstatic: half the guys went primitive, the other half were simply mesmerized. Drinks were no longer being served. All the girls in the room watched Valentina as she had her way with the audience.

Valentina had mastered the art of eye contact from the stage. She moved like a lioness, hunting in the dark. She

connected with the male libido. She posed and touched
herself in ways calculated to stimulate the male mating
instinct until it overwhelmed all capability for rational
thought.

As the song ended, money showered down from the
second floor. A table of US tourists had brought
American one-dollar bills.

Morris looked at the men all around the stage as they
yelled and screamed and applauded. He quickly pulled
two $50 bills from his pocket, fanned and folded them
into his fist. Now it looked like he held four bills in his
hand. He held it out before him, intending to make an
offering. No, that won't work, he thought, he wanted to
appear to be the opposite of tight-fisted.

Morris searched the bar. Seeing a pen, he reached
over and grabbed it. He picked up a cocktail napkin and
wrote on it quickly. Then he patted his pants pockets, and
pulled out a thumb drive. It had a short keychain with a
ring on it. It was a new, blank drive Morris had asked for
while he was in the hospital. He had not used it. It was
stamped CONFIDENTIAL PROPERTY OF PARKER
HOLDINGS. He forced the two fifties into the keychain
ring together with the napkin note and headed toward the
stage.

Valentina was disappearing up the stairway, naked.
Two of the tuxedo-wearing staff members were collecting
her money in a silver champagne bucket.

"Does she get that right away?" Morris asked one of
them.

"I bring it straight to the dressing room," he answered.

Morris tossed the money, napkin and thumb drive in
the bucket.

Then Morris walked back to the bar and waited.

36 – THE CHAMPAGNE LOUNGE

Morris was watching a particularly athletic girl on the stripper pole. She was all the way up at the second floor level, hanging upside down. Her thighs were wrapped around the pole, and they gave her enough grip to let her wave her arms freely. She writhed sensuously, brushing her long, dark hair from side to side. She touched her breasts and caressed herself, looking down at a couple of slack-jawed men staring up at her.

Suddenly, she plunged down the two-storey pole toward the stage. She stopped herself just in time by squeezing her thighs, which squealed like brakes.

Morris flinched. He had a sudden flashback. As a young second lieutenant, Morris had investigated a soldier who fell from a three-storey rappelling training tower. The soldier failed to attach his snap-link properly during a rappelling session and broke his neck. The army released him as a quadriplegic. He was not entitled to a medical pension, because the accident happened late at night and was not official training. The soldier and his buddies, who were drunk, had decided to play in the dark.

Morris felt a touch on his arm. He turned. It was Valentina.

"At bar, need info, will pay," she said, holding the napkin Morris had sent. "I presume this came from you?"

"Yes."

There were six other guys sitting at the bar.

"How did you know that came from me?"

"You stick out like a sore thumb."

"Really? I'm not dressed differently." Morris looked around the room. "I may be a bit older than the average, but there are a few other older guys here alone."

"You look around the room like you're interested in learning something, not like you're just curious about the sex. You seem confident, relaxed, and in charge."

"It's probably the scotch."

"And you're too fit for your age. You also tip generously, and not just to buy attention from the girls."

"How do you know how well I tip?"

"The $10 you tipped Jake is still on the bar behind you. He leaves it there to try and attract more from other customers. Most of our customers are not so generous to the regular staff."

"They work hard."

"How much are you paying, and what kind of info do you need?" asked Valentina.

"I need half an hour in the champagne lounge." Morris decided to be completely honest with Valentina. "I want to talk about Kendo."

"Now I know who you are." You're the guy who was online pretending to be Kendo, she thought. Valentina looked at Morris' shoes. "Show me your soles."

Morris crossed his right leg over his left and twisted his ankle a bit to show a scuffed surface. The shoes were well broken-in, but not showing excessive wear.

"You're probably not a cop. The shoes are too expensive. A vice detective doesn't get a lot to spend on clothing. And those shoes look like they spend their days in an office, not out on the pavement. The leather has never been wet."

"I should have worn my running shoes."

"You probably have $300 running shoes."

"Actually, you're right. I'm training for a marathon." A very bright lady, Morris thought. "I'm a businessman, not a cop."

"Come with me. I also want to talk about Kendo."

Valentina led Morris to the elevator. She was wearing a classy, strapless white gown. As she walked, Morris could see she had on a dark thong beneath. There was a

source of black light in the room, making her gown glow
slightly purple. It made her skin dark and desirable. To
Morris, she had poise – and a mysterious, confident,
sexual presence that stood out from the other girls
working the room.

There was a man at the elevator. He opened it and the
three of them stepped in. The door closed, and it was
suddenly quiet. Morris felt relief. It was getting much
easier to communicate.

"Jenna said you were looking for me. If you were a
real customer, right now I would be all over you, getting
you ready for the upstairs up-sell."

The elevator door opened, Morris tipped the man $10,
and stepped into a harem. The décor was Arabian. The
music was soft. There was a faint scent of perfume, and
the lighting was low-level and intimate. There were thick
tapestries on the walls, which deadened the acoustics. A
soft ballad was playing at low volume.

The downstairs room had been designed to be man-
heaven: booze, sports, and naked babes. The harem was a
step above man-heaven. But this place was not intended
as a reward for living a God-fearing life. Its purpose was
to lead man to temptation, not deliver him from evil.

Valentina took his hand and led him into the harem,
leaving the elevator man behind.

The harem was divided into several private rooms.
Each was curtained-off. As they walked past one of the
rooms, a female voice moaned in pleasure. They both
heard the sound of furniture creaking quietly with the
regular rhythm of a man and a woman enjoying the
mating process.

Morris felt himself getting aroused.

Valentina stopped and turned toward Morris, smiling
at him. She leaned toward him. Morris caught Valentina's
scent. It was exquisite.

"Jenna's earning average up here must be improving,"
she whispered in his ear.

"How do you know that's Jenna?"

"The guy she's with came in for me, but I put him on to her, so I could be with you."

Valentina's hair was close enough now for Morris to smell it too. He felt the sudden urge to stroke it.

Valentina turned and headed deeper into the harem. They arrived at the last room in line. She held the drape to one side, beckoning Morris to enter. They stepped in to a space just large enough to hold two sofas at right angles, with a square table in between.

"Let's take this sofa. We can get nice and close." She gestured to one of the sofas.

That sure seemed like a good idea to Morris. The room temperature was a bit cool. The air conditioning had been set to ensure couples were able to appreciate bodily warmth and closeness.

Morris had mentally prepared for this moment. In his single, youthful days, Morris did not have the amount of money he was now able to spend on leisure and recreation. Had he been wealthy back then, he would certainly have elected to spend a lot of money in a place like this. He would have eagerly accepted all the pleasure that now seemed available to him. He could now buy all the sexual gratification he wanted, buying beautiful girls in pairs if he pleased.

Morris had already made up his mind what he was going to do when this moment arrived. He knew he would be tempted, and he was already aroused more than he had expected. Clearly, experts in sexual marketing had designed everything about the Club Chaton to gain the biggest sale possible. Morris was a normal human male, and he was a perfect fit for their marketing profile.

Morris had worked everything out in his head. The purpose of his mission was to gain the trust of Valentina. To do that, it was necessary to tell her his true identity. He could not lie to her or pretend he was single. If he did, she could find out he was actually married. If he had sex with Valentina, he would be cheating on his wife. How could Valentina trust a cheater?

Still, Morris wanted to bone Valentina in the worst way possible.

Morris thought about his sister, Christine. He filled his mind with the image he had planned to use tonight. Christine was divorced. Her husband had cheated on her, and the night he announced he planned to leave her, he revealed the details of his affair, then he immediately walked out.

Morris had gone over to see Christine that night. She had been devastated. Morris filled his mind with the image of his sister in tears, saying the words: "It hurts."

Then Morris though of Terri. He could never cause her that kind of pain. Morris felt all his sexual desires vanish instantly.

"It would be great if we could sit close, but my wife would not like it." said Morris. "Why don't we sit in that corner, each on our own sofa?"

Morris watched a smile develop on Valentina's face. They sat on separate sofas as Morris had suggested.

As they were getting settled, a waitress entered the room. She was wearing a harem outfit with a see-through top.

"We don't need a bottle yet, honey," said Valentina, before the waitress could speak. "We're still negotiating. I'll come and get you."

The waitress nodded and left.

"That'll save you $300," she said.

"Thanks. My name is Morris Parker and I killed your friend Kendo."

Valentina's expression did not change. "My name is Valentina, and Kendo was a customer, not a friend."

"He was shooting at me. It was self-defence."

"I know. I read the papers."

"When?"

"Yesterday. I searched online. I was out of town when it happened."

Morris thought for a moment. "That was me online with you the other night. I posed as Kendo. I'm looking for information. My family is in danger. Somebody wants me dead to stop me nosing around, so I'm nosing around harder."

"I knew it wasn't Kendo. You didn't react like he would have reacted when I mentioned Kenora."

"How would he have reacted?"

"I was expecting him to deny it. I am not supposed to know that location. I'm still not certain that it's Kenora – I was guessing. I was hired to help keep the location a secret. Kendo's friends flew me to Winnipeg to entertain some trucker who had to make a delivery there. Some guy drove for him while I kept him busy in the sleeping compartment of his cab."

Morris nodded. "I know."

"How?"

"Before I tell you that, I need to know I can trust you."

"I'm the one who has to trust you!" she exclaimed.

"I need to know you won't take back whatever I have to the other side. At my cottage last week, two men tried to kill me, my wife, and my daughters. They almost succeeded. They were trying to cover up something big, acting on orders, as part of a well-financed secret operation. My daughter killed one of them. The other guy got away."

"You have a tough family."

"We were lucky our dog saw them before they got us. They killed our dog."

"I'm sorry." Her concern appeared to be genuine. It looked to Morris like she wanted to trust him. "How can I verify your story?"

"This story has not been picked up by the papers. But I know the name of the guy we killed. He was one of two unidentified men at The Arms. My friends and I put them both in hospital, but they escaped – probably with help from a dirty cop on the Ottawa Police force."

"I know who they are. Kendo worked with them setting up the camp, and he also did something for them here in Ottawa."

"The guy we killed at the cottage was named Daniel Dejeu." Morris pronounced the name with a proper French accent. It sounded like *de-je.*

Valentina frowned. "Kendo spoke about three guys. One of them is a member of the Ledbury Banff Cripps."

"That's Big Mac. A guy by the name of Innes MacDick."

She nodded. "That stuff was in the papers."

"The other two guys were Hell's Angels."

She nodded again. Morris could tell she wanted to believe him.

She narrowed her eyes at him. "When we came into this room, I was testing you to see if you were going to cheat on your wife. I looked you up on the Internet yesterday, trying to guess who had been online. It's a good thing you admitted it was you I was chatting with. Let me show you why."

Valentina reached behind the sofa and pulled out a gun. She pointed it at the ceiling, not at Morris.

"How did you get that past the metal detectors?"

"I own a third of this place. I have my own key. I was going to make whoever showed up tell me what I want to know, otherwise I was going to take him down the back stairway, out into the alley, make him get in the dumpster and shoot him in the head." Her expression was dead serious.

"My friends know I'm here. They know I'm trying to make contact with you."

Valentina's expression softened. "I don't want to shoot you."

"You look desperate," said Morris. "You can trust me.
I think we're in the same boat."

A thought struck Valentina like a thunderbolt. She
suddenly brightened. "The Jew! Big Mac called them *Pax*
and *'da Jew*. I only heard him talk about them with
Kendo once, when he thought I was asleep."

"An Anglo mispronunciation. His name is *Dejeu*.
He's the guy I shot in the leg at The Arms. My daughter
Susan ran him over at the cottage. He's dead."

Valentina put her gun down on the sofa.

"You can trust me. We can put our information
together. You're looking for Candi. I think Kendo took
her to Winnipeg."

"How do you know?"

Morris paused, then decided to play his most
important card. "You better not be on the wrong side. I
found her picture on Kendo's apartment computer. It was
with some false ID. The name was Candice Walker."

"Her name is Wilkinson, Candi Wilkinson. Show me
the picture."

Morris took the photo out of his pocket and put it on
the table between them, face down.

Valentina reached for it cautiously. She picked it up
slowly, without turning it over. She held the photo to her
breast, looking at Morris. "I don't want this to be her."

She looked at the photo and tears formed in her eyes.
She looked at Morris again. "It's Candi." Her expression
turned to anger. "That son of a bitch Kendo did
something to her."

Morris reached for the photo, and took her hand in
both his hands. "Try not to worry. I'll help you look for
her."

It was as if Valentina had suddenly become a little
girl. She melted. Two tears ran down her cheeks.

"I trust you. My name is Brenda Wilkinson. Candi is
my little sister."

37 – WINNIPEG STAKEOUT

As he entered the domestic arrivals area of the Winnipeg Airport, Zia avoided looking up at the security camera. He knew his baseball cap would make it very difficult to identify his face from above, but it was his third shift of the day. He was starting to get uncomfortable, thinking the authorities might grab him and begin an interrogation of what he was up to, why he was spending so much time checking arriving flights.

Zia had mentally rehearsed his cover story many times. It went that he was expecting to meet his wife, but he was not sure on which flight she was due to arrive. He was supposed to meet her in Winnipeg for a short vacation. He had arrived a day ahead of her because at the last minute she couldn't get off work and so they paid to reschedule her ticket but not his. But what if they checked out his ticket? They would see he had a return flight for tomorrow. How could they believe he and his wife would go to Winnipeg for a one-day vacation?

The previous night, as a precaution, Zia had checked the local attractions and tried to find a convincing reason.

He found Winnipeg had an art gallery, a planetarium, a railway museum, a firefighters museum, an electrical museum, the St. Boniface Museum, and the Association of Manitoba Museums.

The only thing that really interested him was the Manitoba Museum, because there was a presentation called *To The Moon: Featuring Ace Burpee*. Ace was a Winnipeg Radio Jock, and was featured as narrator. Zia found the idea of learning about the Apollo moon missions quite appealing. He was also very curious to understand how a person with such an unusual name could end up as a professional announcer. As a child,

would not classmates have ridiculed Ace mercilessly for
his name? How could a man with a name like that be
taken seriously? How was he chosen to fly to the moon?
Did he know Buzz Aldrin? Why did he choose radio
announcing as a follow-on career?

Zia was sharing a hotel room with his brother, Habib.
Zia had suggested to Jacques that Habib be added to the
team, and Jacques agreed to use him as his assistant.
Habib would ride with Jacques, acting as his navigator
and all-purpose gadget man. At present, Habib was sitting
with Jacques outside the terminal. Jacques was driving
and using his cellphone to coordinate activities, and
Habib was using a laptop to send text messages.

The group, consisting of Jacques, Ed, Liam, Zia and
Habib, had arrived from Ottawa on an early morning
flight yesterday, one day before today's stakeout. They
had rented two midsize cars and two SUVs. Each vehicle
was equipped with a navigation system. Everyone had a
Blackberry cellphone with Bluetooth headset, and they
had practiced driving in the vicinity to familiarize
themselves with Winnipeg and the surrounding area.

Jacques had given everyone maps of the arrivals
terminal, airport area, the City of Winnipeg, Eastern
Manitoba and Western Ontario. Together, they had
studied the likely routes to depart the airport and head
east toward the town of Kenora. Just in case the actual
destination was not Kenora, they had also studied all
major routes within five hundred mile radius of
Winnipeg. They had driven segments of those routes,
following Winnipeg drivers for practice. They had
rehearsed handing-off a target suspect vehicle between
each other. They did not want the real suspects to realize
they were being followed.

By the end of the day, the group was familiar with the
area, and fairly confident in their abilities to follow
someone without being noticed. They had spent most of
Wednesday evening in meetings. They had memorized

the faces and identities of all the photos from Kendo's computer.

Jacques had assigned who would cover each incoming flight. To avoid suspicion by airport security staff, he had decided to rotate everyone between four observation posts. Two surveillance team members would be waiting in their cars, while the other two watched the arrivals gate and baggage area.

After a very long day, Zia had finally fallen asleep with thoughts of being interrogated. He tossed and turned, spending almost two hours worrying up his cover story. It didn't help that Habib was working with his laptop most of the night, trying to program a device he thought would help the team.

Zia glanced at the security guard responsible to watch the arrivals door. The same guy had been there all day. Zia took a deep breath, and tried to avoid his gaze.

Zia assumed his position in anticipation of the arrival of Westjet 573 direct from Ottawa, scheduled to arrive at 3:58 PM. Jacques considered this flight as high probability. He had analyzed the previous flights and considered that, since a new escort would be used, a direct flight was more likely to be used than and indirect one. Kendo had taken indirect routes in order to vary his travel pattern and avoid being recognized by aircrew as a regular. Whoever might be escort for today would have no need to do that, because it would be his or her first trip.

Zia checked the arrival information display. Westjet 573 was on time. Zia yawned and stretched slowly, trying to appear casual.

Zia thought about why Jacques had given everyone an early wakeup call at 5:30 AM, half an hour earlier than planned. He had information for them from Morris regarding his meeting with Valentina. The first flight from Ottawa was scheduled to arrive at 8:18 AM, and

Jacques had wanted to meet beforehand to discuss the information.

Valentina's real name was Brenda Wilkinson, and she wanted to find her younger sister Candice. Candice was a 22-year old heroin addict.

Brenda, age 27, had been caring for Candice for seven years, ever since their family had broken up for unspecified reasons. Brenda supported Candice on her earnings as a stripper and prostitute. With Brenda's constant support, Candice had made it through high school, but flunked out after a half-hearted attempt at college.

Candice had worked as a part-time cashier, parking lot attendant, and in other low-paying jobs, getting fired from each one. Finally she had turned to stripping like her sister, against Brenda's wishes. When she started to earn significant money, she quickly turned to heroin. At 19, she started with snorting and quickly became addicted to the needle. After two years of addiction, Brenda had convinced Candice to try a treatment program. That was about a year ago. Candice attended the program knowing she had a problem, but didn't care. She started up the heroin again a week after completing the program.

Candice had the usual addict's daily pattern, according to Brenda: hustle, score, shoot-up. Candice would shoot up in the afternoon, every afternoon. After many months of trying to stop her, Brenda finally began to help her shoot up. Not because Brenda approved, but because Candice had overdosed twice. After the second overdose, Brenda supervised her to make sure the dose was OK, the needle was clean, and the least harm possible was being done to her little sister. And she kept trying to convince Candice to take another program.

Zia thought about his younger brother, Habib. During this Ramadan, which ended next week, the brothers had decided to give up chocolate. Just before leaving for Winnipeg, Zia had caught Habib stuffing himself with chocolate chip cookies. He had taunted him: *what next, heroin?*

Zia felt sorry for Brenda and her sister. It had been clear from Jacques' background information that Morris was concerned about Brenda and Candice. Their mission now had an additional objective: the team was expected to help them if possible.

Zia felt his Blackberry vibrate in his holster. He touched his Bluetooth earpiece to answer the incoming call.

"This is Zia."

"Touchdown," said Jacques.

Flight 573 had just landed. Jacques was in one of the cars outside, in a position where he could see the runway.

"Roger," said Zia.

"Roger," said Ed, who was also on the line.

Jacques had set up a three-way call. Now the two inside men, Ed and Zia, could speak with each other as well as Jacques. Jacques would coordinate the chase, should one commence. Liam was not on the call, but Jacques would send him a text message on his Blackberry if the chase was on.

"Ten minutes until gate time," said Jacques.

Jacques had cautioned the team to do as little speaking as possible. So for the next ten minutes, all Zia heard was background noise. Nobody had anything to say, but the line had to stay open.

"Here they come," said Ed, who was able to observe the door through which passengers exited the secure part of the airport.

Zia was keeping an eye on the baggage carousel.

"Shit! It's him." Ed did not sound happy. "I can't let him see me. I'm moving off my post."

Zia and Jacques wondered what the hell was going on, but they both remained silent until Ed was ready to report.

"It's Detective Clark," said Ed. "He's with a male
subject I can't recognize. The subject is not somebody
from Kendo's computer. Zia, I can't let Clark see me. He
doesn't know you. You'll have to cover my post."

"I don't know what Clark looks like," said Zia.

"They're headed for the exit door in a hurry."

Zia started to walk quickly toward the nearest street
exit. He was not in a position to see passengers passing
through the inner security exit. He hoped he could spot
them on the sidewalk. He burst through the door and
turned left, walking quickly toward another street exit
further up the sidewalk. They should be coming out there.

"What are they wearing?" Zia asked, urgency in his
voice. There were two pairs of men on the sidewalk
waiting for pickup.

"Short sleeve golf shirts."

"All I can see are long sleeve shirts." Zia felt his
Blackberry vibrate.

"Zia, Habib just sent you a photo of Clark," said
Jacques on the cellphone.

A large, black SUV with two people in the back
whizzed past Zia. He got a glimpse of the passenger's
faces. One was wearing long sleeves.

Zia looked at his Blackberry. An email from Habib
had arrived. It was taking several seconds for the photo to
download.

"Come on, come on," he said.

The image appeared. It resembled the passenger with
the long sleeves.

Zia looked up to see the SUV disappear around the
curving, circular airport road. "They're in a black SUV
with Ontario plates." Clark must have put on a
windbreaker, he thought.

A few moments passed as the SUV made its way
along the circular airport road, while Jacques waited
calmly. There was only one road leading away from the
terminal building.

"Got them," said Jacques. Jacques had been waiting near the exit driveway of the rental car lot. He pulled out into traffic on the airport road several car lengths behind the SUV.

Jacques quietly kicked himself for not passing out photos of Detective Clark. Everyone had met him except Zia. Zia had found the video clip of the pistol swap, but Clark's face was not visible in the overhead camera shot.

Back at the sidewalk, Zia was tense, hoping he had identified the correct car. He decided to double-check the area to make sure. As he was looking around, Ed joined him. A moment later, Liam pulled up. Ed and Zia jumped in.

Liam's task was to drive Ed and Zia to their cars. They had parked as close to the airport as possible. The trip would take about three minutes.

"Liam picked us up, Jacques. We're just passing the sign *Welcome to Winnipeg, Manitoba*," said Zia, reading from the sign.

"They went straight at King Edward," said Jacques over the phone.

"They were supposed to turn right," said Ed.

"What?" asked Liam. "You want me to turn right?"

"NO!" said Ed and Zia in unison.

"Take it easy," said Liam. "I can't hear what you guys can hear. These phones can only do a three-way call. I'm left out."

"Give me your phone, Ed," said Zia.

"They turned left on Century," said Jacques. "They're picking up speed."

"They turned left on Century," Ed said into his headset as he passed his phone to Zia. "They're heading north, not south. They're going the wrong way."

"Tell Jacques we're about a minute behind him," said Liam.

"We're a minute behind you," said Ed. "We'll be in our cars in two minutes."

It was 4:23 PM. Rush hour traffic was starting to build.

"They're signaling a right on Dublin, heading for downtown," said Jacques.

"We can see our parking lot," said Ed. "But traffic is moving slowly. We have a little over two blocks to go."

Zia was fiddling with Ed's cellphone and the car's sound system. "I just figured out how to get hands-free working. This car has built-in Bluetooth. I just paired it with your phone."

"They're in the right turn lane, stopped at a red light." Jacques' voice was now coming through the car speakers. "They just started moving again."

As Liam approached an intersection, the light turned against them.

"We just caught a red light at King Edward," said Ed.

Zia looked at the traffic. To his right, traffic had an advance green. There was a single car turning left in front of them. "I can run across before the cross-traffic starts," he said.

"Go for it!" ordered Ed.

Zia jumped out of the car and dashed to the center median. He quickly looked both ways, then crossed the rest of the way and began to run along the sidewalk.

"The subject just jumped out onto the sidewalk and Clark is going after him!" Jacques exclaimed. "They're arguing. Clark wants the guy to get back in the car. The guy is shaking his head and backing away."

"Our light is still red, but Zia is on foot, running for his car."

"I have a green light. I can't stop here. I'm too close. Clark will be able to see me. I'll have to drive past them. I need backup."

"Liam, boot it!" Ed ordered. "Go through the light! Jacques is going to lose them!"

"It's against the law!" Liam protested.

"So what! You practice in Ontario! Come on!" Ed urged.

Liam checked cross traffic and found a small gap. He hit the gas and the tires squealed. The car shot through the intersection against the light. Horns blared and cross-traffic braked quickly.

"I'm going to turn right and head past them," said Jacques on the speaker. "I'll stop a bit farther down and try to watch them through my mirrors. I'm right beside them now."

"We have one block to go," said Ed.

"The driver just got out! The two of them are trying to… SHIT!"

The sound of screeching tires came through the car speaker.

"The subject made a run for it, right in front of me. Clark is right behind him. Now he caught him. They're struggling. He's hauling him back to the SUV!"

A loud whack came through the car speaker.

"Clark just threw the guy down on my hood. The driver has a syringe! He just stuck the subject in the neck with a needle and he immediately stopped struggling. They're getting him back into the car…. I'm moving again. That was close."

"Did Clark see you?" asked Ed.

"No, he was busy with the subject. But the driver got a good look at my face. I've made my right turn now, and I'm pulling over to watch them in my mirror. The driver is looking at me. I think… he just pulled a U-turn. I'm losing him. He's heading back south down King Edward. He's headed back your way."

"Pull a U-turn and let me out on the other side of the street," Ed said to Liam. "You can pick them up back at King Edward."

"I haven't seen their vehicle, Ed," said Liam. "There's a lot of traffic now. I might not be able to pick them out."

"It's a black SUV, for fuck's sake."

"Look there – see that black SUV? There's another! Shall I follow grandma?"

"OK, I'll stay with you. You can dump me after we re-acquire them."

Liam pulled a quick U-turn, cutting in front of an oncoming car. The driver, an old lady, sounded her horn and gave Liam the finger. They passed Zia again – he was running in the opposite direction on the other side of the street. Then a police siren sounded loudly. A police cruiser was right behind them, lights flashing.

"Fuck." Liam pulled over to the curb and stopped the car.

"We just got stopped by the cops," said Ed. "I'm going to run for my car."

"Wait here," said Liam. "There's two of them. If you run, they'll chase you down. We're fucked."

"I'll be in my car in 30 seconds," said Zia over the speaker, out of breath.

"Hello, officer," said Liam.

They made Liam get out of the car. I looked like he was going to give him a street sobriety test.

"I got turned around and I'm heading south on King Edward," said Jacques over the speaker. "I can't see them – they're too far ahead."

"I see them," said Ed. "They're crossing in front of us now. We're in luck! They're pulling over. They're stopping for gas."

"I can't get too close," said Jacques. "I've been made. I can't let them see me again. I'm going to pull over before I catch up to them."

"These cops are in no hurry," said Ed. "Those guys will be done with their gas quicker than the cops will be done with us. We're going to lose them."

Zia arrived at his car, gasping for air. He fumbled for his keys, scratching the paint as he tried to insert one into the door lock. Then he remembered to press the unlock button on his key fob. His heart was pounding and adrenaline was surging. He jumped in the car and started the engine. He backed out of his parking spot and headed for the street exit. He accelerated into the street without checking for traffic.

WHAM!

A delivery truck slammed into Zia's left front fender, driving his midsize car to the right. Zia's car stopped dead, and the engine stalled. Bracing just in time, Zia felt the impact as his head struck and cracked the driver's door window. His Bluetooth earpiece went flying.

"Ouch!" said Ed. "Zia just got hit by a delivery truck!"

Stunned, Zia looked around, confused. Then he realized what had happened. His forehead was bleeding into his eyes. He fumbled for his cellphone, putting it to his ear. "I just got into an accident. Hello?" Audio was still going to his headset, so he couldn't hear anything. He disengaged the Bluetooth connection. "I just got into an accident. I'm out of the chase."

Meanwhile, Jacques sat helplessly as his plan fell apart. He could not see anything from his current position, so he pulled out into traffic. Habib sat beside him, observing the situation calmly.

"I have a Plan B," said Habib.

Jacques hit his mute button so his conversation would not go over his phone. "I hope it's good."

"I have a tracking device." Habib held up a black box the size of a deck of cards. "I brought it with me just in case. I was able to program it last night to work in this situation."

Jacques looked at the device. He looked back at the road ahead. They were quickly approaching the gas station.

"We decided against trying a tracking device," said Jacques. "Your brother said we can only get real-time data while the device is in range of a cellphone service area. We figure this secret camp will be out of range."

"Yes, but this device will record its location and report everywhere it has been the moment it comes back in range. It's a modified camera phone. If I mount it on the back hatch, it will also send photos. There's only one problem. I have to mount it where it can be seen easily. When they notice it they will know they have been tracked."

Jacques thought for a moment. "Is there any way for them to figure out who put it there?"

"Not unless they get access to the cellphone company's billing data. This phone is registered to a private number. They will not be able to trace back to PHL."

"Are you willing to risk them tracing it back to you?"

"Yes, because I will close the account as soon as the battery dies – it will last about seven days."

Jacques took a closer look at the device. "Why the Ford logo?"

"To help disguise it. I have to mount it in plain sight."

"How did you know our target vehicle would be a Ford?"

"I didn't." Habib showed Jacques a box full of small vehicle logos he had compiled from key fobs he had collected.

"You obviously thought this through." Jacques was impressed. "Alright. Let's give it a shot. We've run out of options, they're right in front of us. I'm going to turn right just before we reach the gas station. Get ready. And good luck."

Jacques turned right and stopped long enough for Habib to quickly step out.

Habib quickly looked both ways, and then crossed the street to the gas station. He saw the driver had finished gassing up and was heading inside to pay.

One of the passengers in the back seat was looking down the street where the delivery truck had clobbered

Zia. Habib saw the cop car with Liam and Ed. One of the cops was walking over to Zia.

A white compact car driven by an older lady pulled in for gas behind the black SUV just as Habib arrived at the station.

Acting confidently, Habib picked up a window-washing squeegee. He began to clean the window of the white compact, smiling at the old lady. She was surprised. Habib nodded at her. She smiled and let him continue.

Habib saw that the SUV driver was in a line-up at the cash. Habib quickly finished the windshield and approached the old lady. She lowered her window.

"May I check your oil, Ma'am?"

"You certainly may," she replied. She fumbled for the hood control.

"It should be on the left, Ma'am." Habib pointed toward the floor.

The old woman looked down. "I can't find it."

"May I?" Habib put his hand on her door handle.

The old woman nodded and Habib opened her door. He reached in and pulled the hood release, then he closed her door gently.

As he walked to the front of the car, Habib looked at the cashier and saw the driver was paying. Habib hoped he had enough time to attach the device.

Working quickly, Habib raised the hood and bent over, pretending to work on the engine. He pulled the tracking device from his pants pocket.

The device had a sticky-tape mount on the back. Habib peeled the paper coating, then checked to see if the SUV passengers were watching him. Both of them were now facing forward, oblivious to his presence behind the SUV. One man was asleep. Habib checked inside. The driver was still busy with the clerk.

Habib placed the device on the hatchback of the SUV, midway between the plate and the left turn indicator. He pressed down firmly to secure the sticky tape to the paint finish.

Habib turned back to the open hood and pulled out the dipstick, pretending to examine it. Out of the corner of his eye, Habib watched the driver re-enter the SUV. He heard the engine start, and the SUV drove off.

The SUV headed into traffic, southbound on King Edward. The device was clearly visible, proudly displaying the *Ford* logo. It was hidden in plain sight.

PART FOUR – MOVING TO THE OFFENSIVE

38 – LUNCH AT BRENDA'S

"It's a good thing you took out the extra insurance on the car rental contracts, Jacques," said Morris as Jacques climbed into the front passenger seat. "I usually take the risk and don't pay for the *zero deductible even if I get in a accident that's my fault* option." Morris pulled away from the curb.

"I asked Jill to add it this time, just in case," said Jacques as he fastened his seat belt.

It was noon on Friday. Jacques and the stakeout team had returned from Winnipeg on the first available flight today. Jacques had spent most of the morning putting information together to discuss with Morris. He had expected to meet Morris in his office, but at the last minute Morris told him he was going to take him out for lunch.

"Thanks for the lunch invitation," said Jacques. "I hope we can go some place private. I have confidential stuff to discuss with you."

"It'll be private. We're not going to a restaurant."

Jacques looked curious.

"We've been invited to Brenda Wilkinson's place."

"Oh."

"She has information for us. As you know, she visited the camp. I want her to see what you have. I'm hoping if we combine her stuff with ours, we can figure out the next step."

"Why at her place?"

"She didn't want to be seen at PHL."

Jacques wondered for a moment what she had in mind. "Do you trust her?"

"I don't think she's on their side. Are you thinking this could be an ambush?"

"It's my job to protect you and the company."

"While you were working this morning, I spoke with
Ed. I gave him her address. He went to check her place
out and it seems OK. He's going to be on stakeout while
we're there in case anything happens."

"I would have preferred that you let me know your
plan as soon as you decided to go for lunch," said
Jacques. "I would have coordinated with Ed for you."

Morris nodded, embarrassed. "You're absolutely
right. I'm not following the chain of command. It won't
happen again."

"You'll get used to it," said Jacques.

"So, do you have anything for me you would like to
cover before we get there?"

"Yeah, I have a few things." Jacques opened his
briefcase and pulled out a file folder. "I have a note from
Liam. He submitted the Clark pistol switch video clip to
the OPP. They say they now have Clark under
surveillance. They don't want him to submit a motion or
do anything unusual that might tip him off."

"So how does that help me?"

"Liam got them to change your bail conditions –
you're free to go anywhere and they gave Liam your
passport back. Clark will not be aware of this change."

"OK, that's better than nothing. Have they figured out
what Clark's up to?"

"If they did, they won't be reporting any progress to
us. But after we saw Clark in Winnipeg, I asked Liam to
find out if the OPP were aware of it. He called the
detective handling the case. That guy was away on
training for two days. His stand-in told Liam they had
Clark under surveillance. Liam asked if he were sure, and
if so where was he? The guy waffled, so Liam told him
we spotted Clark in Winnipeg."

"It doesn't sound like they're on the ball."

"Unfortunately not."

"So we can't trust the Ottawa Police, and the Ontario
Provincial Police don't seem to be putting much of a

priority on this problem. Or they just don't have the resources. What about the RCMP?"

"Liam is looking into it, but he thinks they won't get involved unless requested by the OPP."

"Bureaucracy."

"Pretty much."

"So how did the Winnipeg cops treat you?"

"They ticketed Liam for running a red light. They saw him boot it through the intersection against the red, and then do a U-turn ending up with a cruiser right behind him. He was in the middle of getting a lecture when a FedEx truck slammed into Zia a half-block away. They came very close to charging Zia for careless driving, but it turned out the FedEx driver had a high count of speeding violations, so they gave him the benefit of the doubt."

"What's your assessment of the mission?"

"We needed more practice as a surveillance team. The real cops get training and we didn't have any. We didn't have enough training time, but that couldn't be helped."

"Better an imperfect plan executed in a timely fashion, rather than a perfect plan never executed."

"Exactly. I consider our mission a success, in the end, thanks to individual initiative. Habib's GPS device saved the day. He and his brother had started working on it as soon as we made the decision to go to Winnipeg. They realized it might be useful. They were not sure they could make it work in time, which is why the didn't mention it beforehand."

"So what have we got from it so far?"

"We got photos and spot coordinates right up until about 1800 hours. That's when the device went out of cellular service range north of Kenora. We have the route up to that point. The bad guys basically headed due east on the Trans-Canada at over 90 m.p.h. until they forked onto the Kenora Bypass. It would have been difficult for us to follow them undetected at that speed – they have good SOP's to avoid being followed. They turned north on Highway 658 and went out of range. The device sent photos, but all we got were highway shots facing to the rear of the SUV."

"I understand that we have a chance of getting more coordinates if the GPS device comes back in range."

"If it comes back in range before the battery dies. The battery life is about a week, Habib says."

Morris slowed the car. "We're here. We can talk more later. I assume your recommendation before the next mission, whatever it might be, would be to do more training in advance."

"Whatever training we have time for. The more the better."

Morris had been taking directions from his on-board navigation system. He turned into a long driveway. A large, attractive, grey brick home stood at the end of the drive. It had a three-car garage and a BMW convertible parked in the driveway, with the plate 'PAY4PLAY.'

"Obviously, this is the right address," said Morris.

"I like her style," said Jacques.

"That plate works on a couple of different levels, considering the business she's in."

"How?"

"You pay for the foreplay, and I'm sure she goes all the way. They call it *full service*."

"Pay at the pump?"

"Ha. Good one."

Morris and Jacques stepped out of the car and walked to the front entrance. The property was fully landscaped and extremely well kept. The front walkway was a nice interlock without a trace of weed growth.

"It's hard to keep the weeds out of these cracks," said Morris.

"It sure is," said a female voice behind them.

Jacques and Morris turned to see Brenda, wearing
gardening clothes. Her hair was tied up and she had no
makeup.

"Sorry guys, today you get Brenda, not Valentina."
She shrugged.

"Jacques, I would like to present Brenda Wilkinson.
Brenda, this is my good friend Jacques."

"*Enchanté*, mademoiselle," said Jacques.

"Nice to meet you," she offered her hand.

"Nice place you have here," said Morris, as they
shook hands.

"It's paid for," said Brenda. "I had it built, five years
ago. I paid cash. Well, cash and other favors."

"How do you find the time to keep it looking so
good?" asked Morris, tactfully avoiding the question of
what kind of favors.

"I have a regular landscaper. He cuts the lawn and
does the heavy lifting. There's not much handyman work
since the house is quite new."

"Do you maintain everything yourself?" asked
Morris.

"That sounds like a way of asking if I live here
alone," she said. "At the moment I do. After you help me
find my sister, there will be two of us again. Follow me."

Morris and Jacques followed her, passing through an
expensive wrought iron gate into the back yard. There
was a large, kidney-shaped swimming pool surrounded
by interlock.

"More interlock. Still no weed. What's your secret?"

"Magic Sand," she said, pointing to a bag. "I keep the
cracks filled with the stuff. It inhibits weed growth."

There was a gazebo with a table and chairs on a large
patio. The table had been set for lunch.

"It's a beautiful day, so I thought we should eat out
here." Brenda gestured for her guests to sit. "I'll be right
back." She smiled and went into the house.

"I'm bloody impressed," said Jacques, after she disappeared from view.

"Me too."

"You said in your email she comes from a broken home?"

"Yes, but she was shy on details." Morris paused, thinking. "There seems to be pain there she doesn't want to share."

"She seems to be coping – putting together a great home like this."

Jacques took some documents from his briefcase. While they waited for Brenda, Morris read them, asking questions. After about ten minutes, Brenda re-appeared from the house with a tray of food and a pitcher of ice tea. She had switched from gardening clothes to slacks and a blouse. Morris was struck by the contrast between how she looked now and how she had appeared on stage at Club Chaton.

Being properly trained military gentlemen, Morris and Jacques rose to acknowledge a lady entering their presence.

Brenda was inwardly pleased, but did not want to show it. "I hope you like smoked salmon." She placed a bowl of salad on the table, followed by a tray of smoked salmon sandwiches done with bagels, croissants, and rye bread. "If not, I can do peanut butter and jam." She smiled.

As everyone sat down, Jacques and Morris looked at the food with anticipation.

"If Jacques goes for the peanut butter and jam option, I'll be happy to eat his share of the salmon."

"I'll do my part," said Jacques. "I don't want to put Brenda to any trouble. I'll just suffer with this."

"Dig in, gentlemen," said Brenda.

The group lunched together, making small talk until the sandwiches and salad were gone. Morris watched

Brenda's body language. She seemed to be getting more comfortable as the meal progressed.

"That was wonderful," said Morris. "Thank-you for inviting us."

"My pleasure," she replied.

"The reason I asked to meet was to give you the results from our team's trip to Winnipeg, and to try to figure out what to do next."

Brenda leaned back and took a sip of ice tea.

"Jacques prepared this map." Morris placed a maps.google.com printout on the table. "It shows the route the bad guys took to the Kenora area. We planted a GPS tracking device on their vehicle. Our trace ends on Highway 658 when it went out of range. We hope to pick up additional data points when the vehicle comes back in range. If we're lucky, we'll get the exact location of their camp."

Brenda examined the map. "I was picked up in Winnipeg and the ride took almost four hours total. I could tell from the angle of the sun that we were headed east for about two hours. Then we turned north. It took us about an hour and a half to get to the camp from there."

"You saw the camp, right?"

"They let me out of the truck to use the ladies room. Ha. They had a small outhouse set up. I had to cross the camp to get to it. The camp was still under construction at the time. I saw a foundation about the size of a two-car garage. There were a couple of ATCO trailers set up, and they had a generator in the middle of the campsite. There was an industrial furnace set up in a separate hut. I don't think I was supposed to see that."

"Could you tell what was the purpose of the camp?"

"I've been trying to figure that out ever since you told me they may have taken Candi there. I've no idea. It wasn't complete. I came in with a truck delivering two sea containers."

"Sea containers full of what, I wonder," said Morris.

"No idea. They needed the driver to back them into position. He had some difficulty because the ground was rough and the site was pretty tight on space, but he managed. We left the whole trailer there with the sea containers on it."

"Who was in the truck?"

"There were three of us. I don't know the name of the guy doing the driving. He was about five-ten or five-eleven, Arab features, late twenties or early thirties I would say, medium build. Short dark hair, moustache. He didn't say much to me. At the camp, he seemed to be in charge."

"Who hired you for the job?" asked Morris.

"MacDick."

Morris and Jacques were making notes as Brenda spoke.

"If your sister ended up at that camp, the question is why," said Morris after a short pause.

"When did you see her last?" asked Jacques.

"Wednesday, July 23rd. According to what Morris told me, she took a flight to Winnipeg the next day. I had not been expecting her to leave. She left a note saying she would be gone for a month, and she would get in touch with me in about a week to tell me what was going on. She didn't get in touch with me at all."

"Did you report her missing?"

"Yes, but the cops didn't do anything until after she'd been gone five weeks. They finally put her in the missing persons database two weeks ago. That's all they've done so far."

Morris finished writing and looked at Brenda.

"They know she's an addict, and they know I'm a hooker." She gestured toward her home. "I pay property taxes like everyone else, but…."

"These days, I'm not getting my tax money's worth, either," said Morris.

"I don't mind paying my fair share of taxes, but I get pretty pissed when government wastes my money."

"Don't we all?"

"Did you know the billions of our tax dollars going to the war in Afghanistan is actually increasing heroin production there?"

"How so?" asked Jacques.

"The instability of war has driven Afghan people to the Taliban in the south, the prime growing region. Corruption and poverty make it so all parties – government, Taliban and criminals – benefit from Opium production."

"Our military are trying to clean up the situation, though," said Jacques.

"No. Their mission is either anti-terrorism or women's rights – whatever you want to believe. They are turning a blind eye to the opium economy. Opium from Afghanistan kills 100,000 people around the world every year, and makes up 87 percent of the world's supply. We should be spending war dollars here in Canada to fight drug trafficking."

The group was silent for a moment.

"In Winnipeg, I saw our subject attacked with a needle," said Jacques, changing the topic.

Morris nodded. "The subject they brought in from Ottawa yesterday put up a struggle. He tried to escape from their vehicle. They drugged and dragged him back."

"We reported the incident to the Winnipeg police, but I believe all they've done so far is put it in a report," said Jacques. "The guy who did it matched the description of the Arab you just gave us."

"You should also know the other guy involved – the escort – is an Ottawa Police Detective by the name of Clark," said Morris. "Here is a photo of him. I would also like you to see these other photos from Kendo's hard drive. We have not given them to the cops."

"I've never trusted the cops," said Brenda, as she looked at the photos.

"We're having the same problem," said Morris. "It's becoming difficult to know what to tell them. We seem to be better off on our own. My family is in hiding because the cops can't protect them. I have to get to the bottom of this situation. We can't hide forever."

"You got these off Kendo's computer," said Brenda. "How did you get his computer?"

"I have a guy who's good at that sort of stuff," said Morris.

"Candi has a computer. Would you be able to find out stuff about her from it?"

"Possibly. Where is it?"

"It's at my place downtown. I also have an apartment. I meet clients there. I never meet anyone here."

"I'd be happy to have a look."

"I don't know anyone in these photos." Brenda handed them back to Morris.

"Let's go check it out," said Morris.

"OK. I'll take my car. I'd like you to ride with me," Brenda said to Morris. "I have some things I'd like to tell you."

39 – PARKWAY CHASE

Morris awkwardly inserted himself into the passenger seat of Brenda's small, 2-seat red BMW M3 Convertible. Thankfully, she had put the top down, making it much easier for him. Morris fastened his seatbelt, impressed with the black leather interior and the instrument layout.

"It has a 3.2 Liter inline-6 with 6-speed manual transmission. Three hundred thirty three horsepower." Brenda smiled at Morris. "I'm a car chick."

"You're full of surprises," said Morris. "I like your plate, PAY for PLAY."

"The neighbors don't seem to care for it," she laughed. "You'd think they'd *thank* me for not making them guess *how* I make a living without a *man* around the house." With another laugh, she turned the key in the ignition, put the small roadster in reverse gear and began to back down the long driveway.

The car had a color display mounted in the center of the dash. Brenda touched a button and the display showed her the car's rearward view. A camera mounted on the back made it look on the screen as if the car was moving forward.

Morris tried to correlate the screen picture with the rear view mirror and confused himself.

Brenda accelerated, steering by watching the screen. "Once you get used to it, it's pretty easy." She had noticed the peculiar look on Morris' face.

"This baby was a gift from a good customer. He was in Ottawa for a political thing, liked me, and took me home to Europe for a week. This was my retainer."

"You have an interesting fee structure."

"Yes. I'm a pretty good negotiator. But I'm thinking of getting out of the business." She said as she expertly backed into the street, turned 90-degrees and stopped.

"You seem to be tremendously successful. Why?"

"I want to quit while I'm ahead. I'm not into the partying anymore. The problem with this job – it's impossible to have a 'significant other.' The alpha male I'm attracted to wants to keep me to himself. This job doesn't let me do that. I haven't had a decent boyfriend since high school." Brenda glanced at Morris. "It's lonely. I have enough money now. I want to do something normal."

She shifted into first gear, gave it some gas, and the powerful little car shot forward down the country road.

Morris felt the acceleration as the overpowered car pushed him firmly into his seat. "This baby really wants to move."

"She sure does." Brenda touched a display button and a map display appeared. A little red arrow showed their current position. "I'll try and stay calm so your buddy Jacques can keep up."

"Good idea, since he doesn't know where we're headed."

Autumn leaves were starting to appear in the neighborhood. The houses were large, on estate-sized lots dense with trees, giving plenty of privacy.

Morris looked back along the winding roadway to see if Jacques was following. The road straightened a bit, and Jacques appeared from around a bend.

As Morris watched behind, a large, grey Hummer sped into view from a side road. The passenger suddenly fired a long burst of machine-gun fire at Jacques. Jacques swerved and ducked, just as the Hummer slammed into his left front fender. Jacques skidded into the ditch and his car rolled onto its roof. The Hummer passenger fired a second long burst at the overturned car, and then disappeared from view behind a curve in the road.

"Fuck!" said Morris, stunned. "Step on it!"

Brenda accelerated immediately. A few moments later, the road straightened and Morris saw the Hummer come back into view. It was accelerating, chasing them.

"There's somebody blocking the road ahead!" Brenda slammed on the brakes.

Ahead, two men with shotguns stood, one on each side of the road, beside a green Jeep that was blocking the roadway.

"We're caught!" Morris exclaimed, looking side to side for an escape route. "What's that?" Morris pointed to a small paved path intersecting the roadway ahead.

"Golf cart path."

"Take it!"

Brenda hit the gas and the small car fishtailed around the corner to the right. They were headed on a downward slope, curving left and right in the dense trees. They burst into a clearing.

Two shocked golfers were preparing to tee-off. "Playing through!" she shouted. Brenda followed the cart path to the right, swerving to avoid a parked golf cart. The engine roared, tires biting into the turf, as she took her little red car off the path and accelerated onto the fairway.

Morris looked rearward, hoping the cart path had been too narrow to fit the Jeep or the Hummer.

"They're on the right!" Brenda exclaimed.

Morris looked forward to see the Hummer burst through small trees on the right. The two vehicles were approaching each other at a right angle. If they maintained course, they would collide in the wide open middle of the fairway.

"Keep us on the driver's side!" Morris shouted, seeing the Hummer passenger bouncing up and down, struggling to get in position to fire his machine gun.

Brenda boldly swerved to the right, into the direction of the approaching Hummer. The distance closed too

quickly for the Hummer driver to react. As the cars
passed, the Hummer passenger raised the machine gun
over the Hummer roof and fired a long burst, one-handed.
The shooter could not control the machine gun. The
weapon recoiled upwards, and he over-compensated,
striking it against the roof of the Hummer. Badly aimed
bullets blasted the turf wide of the speeding BMW.

Turf flew from all four wheels, as the Hummer
braked, then accelerated, then swerved left, trying to get
the passenger side aligned for some clear shooting.
Brenda steered the BMW left, cutting across the
Hummer's tire marks, keeping the BMW on the
Hummer's driver side.

Circling, the two vehicles chewed up the fairway as
they maneuvered like fighter planes trying to gain the
advantage.

Brenda searched for a way out. There was a deep
ditch bisecting the fairway, between the BMW and the
green. Ahead on the right, she saw a large golf cart
speeding away from them. It was the drink cart, about to
cross the only bridge over the ditch. The bridge was a flat,
one lane affair with no rails. The panicky cart girl was
trying to get away from the shooting.

BLAM! BLAM! Pellets struck the rear end of the
BMW.

"The driver has a shotgun!" Morris shouted. "We
have to get out of here!"

Brenda spun the wheel left, fishtailing away from the
Hummer, aiming the BMW toward the bridge. She
accelerated swiftly.

"I hope it's wide enough!" Morris exclaimed.

The Hummer turned toward the BMW, finally able to
line up on it. At last able to aim, the Hummer driver and
passenger began to blast shotgun and machinegun fire at
the escaping red roadster.

Brenda hit the BMW horn, swerving around the drink
cart, passing it on the right side. The BMW beat the cart

to the bridge, cutting off the terrified cart girl before she could cross it. The cart girl swerved left and braked hard, losing control of the cart, toppling it and flinging her over the cart into the ditch. She tumbled down the steep slope into the water. The cart now blocked the bridge.

Driver and passenger firing wildly, the Hummer crashed into the drink cart, driving it half way across the bridge. The cooler burst open, and ice cubes and beer cans flew.

The bridge was wide enough for the small BMW, but too narrow for the Hummer. On his approach, the Hummer driver had aligned the vehicle's left side with the left side of the bridge. As a result, when reaching the bridge, the right wheels had nothing beneath them as they departed the fairway. Sparks flew as both axles dropped and ground against the right edge of the metal bridge, bringing the Hummer to a quick halt. Both wheels on the right side spun uselessly.

The little red BMW raced on, quickly zooming out of shooting range.

"Try not to spoil the green," Morris said to Brenda as they approached the flag.

Brenda steered left, back onto the cart path, avoiding the immaculate, manicured surface.

"The Greens Keeper thanks you," said Morris.

"How do we get out of here?" asked Brenda.

Morris looked at the map display. The little red arrow showed their current location. "Let's take the Parkway. Stay on the cart path, we're coming up to the clubhouse parking lot."

At that moment, the BMW crested a small hill. The parking lot was straight ahead. The green Jeep, however, blocked the street exit, and a black Trans Am had joined it. Armed men were in the process of dismounting from the vehicles. Before the men had time to react, Brenda accelerated and changed to a higher gear heading away down another narrow path.

Jim E.M. Miles

"Let's play another hole," she said.

Morris looked at the map display. "We're about to leave the golf course. I think this is a bike path."

The pathway was similar to a cart path, but it had a dividing line painted down the middle. A few moments of high speed driving later, Morris saw they were running parallel to the Ottawa River. He looked back to check for pursuers.

"The green Jeep is following us."

"I can outrun it," Brenda said confidently.

"This bike path crosses the Parkway up ahead. It's our only way out."

The BMW raced along the bike path and the green Jeep quickly fell behind. A surprised roller-blader heading toward them jumped off the path to avoid being hit, taking a tumble into the grass. Coming up from behind, Brenda forced two cyclists to depart the path in a hurry after scaring them witless with a blast of her horn.

"Watch out for a green Jeep!" she shouted to the cyclists in passing.

"There was a black Trans Am," said Morris. "If they went on ahead, we could be screwed."

"Don't be so negative!"

"We'll know in a moment."

The path curved left ahead, departing the river and heading up the slope toward the parkway.

Brenda slowed down to navigate the curve. As she completed the corner, a barrage of machine gun bullets struck all around them, coming from straight ahead.

"Stop! Back up! It's the black Trans Am!" Morris yelled.

"I'm right here," Brenda said calmly, braking hard. "I can hear you fine." She snapped the car into reverse and squealed the tires as she backed up quickly. Instead of backing down the way they had just come, she steered the opposite way and braked hard. The BMW was now facing the oncoming green Jeep. She put the car into first gear and hit the gas.

"Sorry about that." Morris, looking at the oncoming Jeep, forced himself to be calm. "What exactly do you have in mind?"

The distance between the two vehicles was closing fast.

"I'm not quite sure," Brenda replied. "Chicken?"

"Bold. But stop. I have a better idea."

Brenda slammed on the brakes and the car screeched to a halt. Sirens could be heard in the distance.

"Do these seats go flat?"

Brenda reached across and manipulated Morris' power seat control. "I thought you'd never ask, but now is no time for sex, honey."

Morris felt his seat start to recline.

"No, sorry," said Morris. "We only have about thirty seconds, and I'm not quite that quick." Morris took over his control. "Get down nice and low. Drive backwards as fast as you can. Make a run for it!"

Brenda started to get the idea. She changed the map display back to rearward facing video view. She put the car into reverse gear. She accelerated, and simultaneously reclined her seat.

The green Jeep moved faster in forward gear than the BMW could go in reverse gear. It was catching up quickly, and now almost within shooting range. The passenger had his machine gun aimed at the BMW.

"We have to try to get past the Trans Am. We'll have some protection from the car body."

"If you say so." Brenda expertly navigated the curve and the BMW began to climb the slope toward the Trans Am.

Surprised to see an open convertible with no visible driver, the Trans Am passenger did not immediately open fire.

"So far so good," said Brenda.

A blast of bullets suddenly struck the BMW from two
directions. Gunmen from both cars were firing
simultaneously.

Each shooter suddenly realized the other was in the
line of fire, and they stopped.

The Trans Am was parked in the middle of the bike
path, right where the path intersected the parkway. The
Trans Am faced the oncoming BMW squarely.

Through the video display, Brenda saw the shooter
was using the long, low open passenger door as a gun
rest. On the other side of the vehicle, the driver was
standing beside the driver's door holding a pistol. Brenda
decided to go for the driver's side. She pushed the
accelerator all the way to the floor and steered directly for
it. The driver raised his pistol to fire, but seeing the
approaching BMW, engine screaming at redline, he lost
his nerve and scrambled to get behind the Trans Am.

The passenger started firing his machine gun. Bullets
slammed into the back of the BMW and ricocheted off
the trunk lid and the bumper. A few embedded
themselves in the trunk, losing momentum as they
fragmented and made their way toward their human
targets. Shards of metal, pieces of shredded upholstery,
and fragments of hot lead splattered into the passenger
compartment of the BMW.

The machine gun shooter beside the Trans Am
smiled. His target was about to reach point blank range.
He prepared to fire a lethal burst.

Brenda took the BMW slightly off the path, bouncing
the small vehicle hard on the uneven ground. It dipped
low for an instant.

The shooter fired. His burst missed, high, as the car
dipped below the bullet stream. Keeping the BMW in his
sights, the shooter fired a second burst at point blank
range – just as the BMW disappeared from view behind
his own vehicle. He shot his burst into the right front
fender of the Trans Am. Fragments of headlight glass,

chrome, and shiny black body material flew in all directions.

A moment later, the green Jeep zoomed past the Trans Am, hot on the trail of the BMW.

Both vehicles were now on the Parkway. The BMW was going as fast as it could go in reverse gear.

"Look, there's not a scratch on your windshield." Morris raised his head and looked through the windshield at the green Jeep in pursuit.

Morris immediately flopped back down into his seat.

The Jeep passenger fired a blast from his shotgun.

Pellets smashed through the windshield, covering Morris and Brenda with glass fragments.

"They're catching up," he said.

"I can tell that's not rain, Mr. Obvious." She started to weave the bullet-damaged little red car from lane to lane. "Should I try to turn around?"

"Can you do it without stopping?"

"This is Ottawa, not Hollywood."

"I suggest you continue to weave, then."

The green Jeep was getting closer. The passenger leaned out his open window, getting in position for what he expected would be an easy shot. The Jeep was higher off the ground than the BMW, and the shooter was able to aim downwards into the passenger compartment.

Weaving frantically, Brenda kept her eyes on the screen, trying to maintain control and not run off the roadway. Morris could see the shotgun from moment to moment as the driver tried to position the Jeep for his passenger to get off a well-aimed blast.

"If he runs out of ammo, we'll have a chance to change direction," said Morris.

"Let's hope he's a lousy shot!"

Another shotgun blast ripped into the BMW.

Brenda gasped.

"You're hit!" Morris exclaimed.

A blood patch formed on Brenda's right breast. She grimaced and struggled to maintain control of the car. "Fuck," she cried.

Morris was out of ideas. The Parkway ahead was long and straight. They could not outrun the Jeep, even if they left the paved roadway. If they stopped and tried to change direction, they would be blasted for sure.

Desperate, Morris opened the glove compartment, searching for anything that might help. He found a small glass container of nail polish.

Better to go down fighting, he thought. Maybe I can hit the shooter in the eye with this.

Morris braced himself, then sat up as quickly as he could. He threw the bottle at the Jeep with all his strength.

The bottle shattered on the Jeep windshield, covering a small portion with red. Surprised, the driver slammed on his brakes.

WHAM! With an enormous crash, the Jeep's rear end suddenly deflected to one side. The vehicle lost all stability and it flipped and tumbled violently. Glass shattered, and vehicle fragments broke loose as various parts of the Jeep impacted the roadway. The passenger was ejected and spiraled into the air, losing his grip on his machine gun. He landed hard on the roadway and was immediately run over by Ed and Jacques.

Unseen behind the Jeep, Ed had rammed his Ford Ranger Super Cab up against the smaller, lighter Jeep, knocking it into instability.

As he came up from behind, Ed had aligned his right front quarter with the left rear quarter of the Jeep. With perfect timing, he had collided with the Jeep, imparting force toward the right, just as the Jeep driver decided to steer to the left. To his detriment, the Jeep driver had also touched his brake pedal at the worst possible moment. The resulting perfect storm of momentum and dynamics vectors caused the Jeep to suddenly become a rolling, self-destructing death-machine for its unbelted occupants.

"Stop! Stop! It's Ed – and Jacques is with him!"
Morris exclaimed.

Brenda braked the BMW to a full stop, stalling the
engine. She didn't have the strength to push the clutch.
She let out a low, painful moan.

Morris immediately checked her chest area. Her
blouse was already soaked in blood. He reached over and
ripped it open to inspect the wound. Her right breast was
half gone and the open wound was bleeding profusely.
Brenda coughed, and blood sprayed from her mouth.

"It hurts – I can't breathe…."

"Raise your right arm," Morris said calmly.

Morris lifted Brenda's right arm. She groaned in pain.
Her right chest just below her bra strap was bubbling
blood where a shotgun pellet had made its exit. Morris
immediately placed his left palm over the wound,
pressing firmly to seal the hole.

"Take a deep breath," Morris instructed.

Brenda coughed again. She managed a short, weak
gasp. She gritted her teeth in pain. Those beautiful white
teeth were now red with blood. She looked up at Morris,
and fear entered her eyes. She could not take a deep
breath. She could manage only short, rapid shallow pants.
Her nostrils flared and closed with each pant. She was on
the verge of panic.

Morris saw her lips were starting to turn blue.

Morris placed his right hand firmly under her neck
and lifted gently. Her head tilted back, and her mouth fell
open. She kept her eyes on his – pleading, desperate,
tearful eyes.

Morris took a deep breath. He leaned over and sealed
her mouth with his lips, feeling warm blood run down his
chin. He exhaled and felt her tense in pain, then released.
He exhaled a second time, harder, and released pressure
from his left palm. He heard the sound of air escaping, as
if from a leaky tire.

Bubbles formed around his left palm as Morris filled Brenda's one good lung. That lung inflated fully, raised her chest, and forced air out of her pleural space where it had leaked in through the pellet hole.

Brenda felt the rush of Morris' warm, welcome breath fill her chest. She had been starting to experience tunnel vision from hyperventilation. Her vision cleared quickly and she no longer feared suffocation. Her panic subsided.

"Breathe normally." Morris restored hand-pressure on her exit wound. He raised and turned his head to watch her chest fall. He felt her warm breath against his ear, listening to her breathing.

Brenda grasped Morris by the back of the neck, turned his head, and pressed his lips against hers.

Breathing normally now, through her nose, Brenda held Morris for a long, grateful kiss that Morris did not resist. They breathed in unison, hearing distant sirens and faint, muffled voices, hearts pounding from the adrenaline of the chase, until she finally released him.

Morris looked up to see Ed, Jacques and a policewoman looking at him.

"She has a sucking chest wound," Morris said.

"I have a field dressing in the truck," said Ed, and he immediately ran to get it.

"Bring a knife," Morris said to Ed.

"Paramedics are on the way," said the policewoman. "They should be here in less than five minutes."

Morris looked at the scene. The green Jeep was on its side, and only the underbody was visible from where Morris was holding Brenda. "What happened to the Trans Am?"

"You should see what a Ford Ranger Super Cab does to a Pontiac Trans Am in the T-Bone position," said Jacques.

Ed came back with a shell dressing and a large, curved, lethal-looking Rambo hunting knife.

"Open the dressing," said Morris as he reached for the knife, keeping his other hand against Brenda's wound.

Working carefully, Morris cut the front of Brenda's bra between her breasts. Her unhurt breast fell loose. Morris gently peeled the bloody fabric back from her other breast, which was blood-soaked and half gone. The nipple was not visible.

"Oh my god," said the policewoman.

Brenda looked at Morris. "Tell it like it is, Doc."

"There is a single exit wound," said Morris. "I'm keeping it sealed so you can breathe. You will survive, with a few scratches. The guy who shot you is flat as a pancake."

Ed had shaken out the dressing from the plastic packaging. He held both out for Morris. Morris took the packaging first.

"You're going to be fine," said Morris, "and with an exciting story to tell the great grandkids."

Brenda nodded, blinking back tears, trying to smile for Morris.

Morris prepared to place the plastic wrapper over the wound he had been covering with his hand. "Do I do this when the casualty exhales, or inhales?" he asked Jacques and Ed.

Both men answered simultaneously: "Exhales."

Morris nodded. "Take a deep breath, beautiful," he instructed Brenda.

She complied. As she exhaled, Morris quickly removed his hand and centered the thick plastic wrap over the wound. It made a good seal.

Ed had also brought tape, and was busy ripping it into strips. The policewoman accepted the strips and assisted Morris to tape the wrapper in place. Morris double-checked for a good seal.

"Your husband is doing a great job," she said as encouragement.

"He's a great husband," Brenda smiled. "I wish he was mine."

Ed offered Morris the large field-dressing bandage. He took it with care, avoiding touching the thick absorbent pad that would come in contact with the wound. He positioned it gently over her damaged breast. Working with the policewoman, they wrapped the long bandage around Brenda's left shoulder and under her right side.

"I should see if I can help the driver," said Morris to the policewoman as they finished. "Please keep an eye on her."

The policewoman nodded.

Morris, Ed and Jacques strode over the Jeep, walking around it and out of sight of the policewoman. The driver was crumpled in a heap. His arm protruded from the wreck, crushed between the frame and the pavement. It was broken and twisted in an un-natural direction. His seat belt was still in place, and the only reason he was still alive.

"Where's the passenger?" Morris asked Jacques.

"He's road kill," said Jacques. "He was ejected right in front of us. He went under our wheels."

"Seat belts save lives," said Morris.

"Well, well," said Morris, recognizing the driver.

"I think we know this lucky fellah," said Ed.

Morris handed Ed the Rambo knife. Jacques cupped his hands and boosted Morris up onto the Jeep. Morris reached down and opened the rear door of the 4-door vehicle, then looked down inside.

The driver, conscious, and in apparent agony, looked up a Morris. He had been propelled to the passenger side through his shoulder harness, which now entangled his legs, holding him upside down.

His forearm was through the open passenger window, caught between the Jeep frame and the pavement, with his body weight resting largely on his neck. The driver could not move, and what he saw made him want to look the other way. His eyes bulged.

Morris crouched, preparing to enter the Jeep. Morris was ready for things to get primitive, as if he had a fresh kill. Ed handed Morris the Rambo knife. With a grimace and a low, guttural growl, Morris bit down on the dull side of the knife blade. Looking like a bloody-lipped pirate, he lowered himself into the Jeep.

Outside the Jeep, the policewoman called out. "If he needs any bandages, I have a first aid kit in the cruiser."

"We'll take good care of him," said Jacques.

Inside the Jeep, there was a heavy gasoline smell.

"Hello, Mr. MacDick," said Morris. "I'm sure you remember my friends."

"Hi there, Grabbypants," Ed waved.

"Now, you are going to tell me the name of the person who you are working for, and what you're up to or…" Morris held the Rambo knife in front of MacDick, "you'll never have kids, or sex, or a pain-free piss again for as long as you live."

Innes MacDick tried to put on a brave face. "Bullshit. You're bluffing."

MacDick, suddenly, felt cold steel against his waist. Morris slid the sharp Rambo blade into MacDick's pants, stopping when the point reached the groin.

Morris pried the blade against the fabric, pressing the point of the knife against MacDick's package.

MacDick gasped.

"Have I pricked your prick, or one of your little fellas?"

"Fuck," MacDick cursed, in agony.

"I won't even have to explain how my knife marks ended up on your tiny, little Mac DICK, because after I finish this surgery, while you're screaming, I'm going climb out of here, ask Ed for a match, and then light that pool of gas I see forming in the back…."

"OK! OK! Joris! I only know him only as Joris! He needed people to build a secret camp. It's somewhere around Kenora!"

"What are all the people for – the people you round up for the camp?"

MacDick's expression showed surprise.

"I don't know."

Morris increased the leverage on MacDicks groin. MacDick yelped in pain.

Outside the vehicle, the policewoman heard MacDick's yelp and looked at the Jeep, concerned.

Jacques waved at her, smiling. "He stepped on his finger. Oops. Heh heh."

The policewoman nodded, returning her attention to Brenda.

Inside the Jeep, MacDick was panicking. "Honest, Jesus, I don't know! We told them they were going to a treatment center! A heroin treatment centre, drug addition center – they would get free drugs as part of the treatment!"

"Who was your latest victim? Who did you just send to the camp?"

A sharp rap on the windshield interrupted MacDick's reply.

Morris peered through the cracked windshield, seeing a police constable with a nightstick rapping on the glass. "You – what are you doing?" demanded the cop.

Ed was busy trying to explain the situation. "This guy was chasing my buddy with guns blazing!"

The cop was ignoring him.

Ed went on. "This is the guy who was arrested at The Arms shootings two weeks ago!"

"You – come out of the Jeep!" the cop ordered.

"This guy tried to kill me!" Morris was angry. "He has other victims! I need one minute! One minute and I'll have information that will save somebody's life!"

"Look the other way!" Ed told the cop. "Look the other way!"

The cop was confused, hesitant.

"Look – the – other – way!" said Morris.

The cop made up his mind. "Step back, sir!" the cop ordered Ed. The cop turned to Morris. "Get out of the vehicle!" He put his hand on his gun.

Morris looked down at MacDick. MacDick was grinning, triumphant.

Morris released the pressure of the knife blade on MacDick's groin, and slid the knife out without cutting any flesh.

"You're still going to jail, asshole. And tell your employer, Joris, I have some unfinished business I expect to be discussing with him soon."

40 – DECISION TIME

Ed sat in the driver seat of his Ford Ranger Super Cab. Morris sat beside him, and Jacques sat in the back seat. It was dusk on the Ottawa River Parkway. The Ottawa Police had sealed the scene, and it was crowded with emergency vehicles, lights flashing. Press trucks and TV reporters were in the area. The scene was crowded with cops, detectives, forensics investigators and miscellaneous other official-looking people rushing around importantly.

The shooting had ended over six hours ago. The three-ring circus had taken over shortly thereafter. Rain was falling.

"I didn't say a damn thing except for exactly what I did today," said Ed. "I said I just happened to be driving along the Parkway and decided to intervene."

"What about my car? It's in the ditch at Brenda's place." said Morris.

"I called Liam and he's taken care of it," said Jacques. "He had it towed. There were no cops on the scene. The residents in that area had not been home. Nobody called it in. We got things cleaned up quick."

"Good. The only thing that seems to happen on a scene like that is the press goes wild. The cops learn nothing new, but the bad guys get to see the damage they did on TV. How about you? You don't look any worse for the wear," Morris said to Jacques.

"I had my seatbelt on. The car has several bullet holes, though. A bullet hit under the driver's seat just between my legs. That's the second time this month I've almost had my nuts shot off."

"Maybe you should wear a Kevlar cup," said Ed.

"That would require a lot of Kevlar," said Jacques.

"Ha. Good one," said Ed.

"Each one of these attacks," said Morris, "gets more determined."

"I don't see how they found you," said Ed. "I was watching her place while you guys had lunch. There were no suspicious vehicles trailing you when you arrived."

"They must have followed you, Ed," said Jacques. "They must have figured out you often travel with Morris. They followed you on spec."

"These guys are fuckin' serious bad news," said Ed.

"If they keep trying to kill me, they will eventually succeed," said Morris.

The three friends sat silent for a moment, listening to the rain hitting the roof.

"Just who the hell is in charge on the good guy's side," asked Ed.

Morris and Jacques looked at him.

"We know the bad guys have a mastermind named Joris who works his organization on a need-to-know basis. He plans and executes operations using plenty of firepower, seemingly any time he wants. He hasn't achieved his objective yet, but he's able to influence the situation. He has the fuckin' initiative."

"What's your point?" asked Morris.

"We have nobody in charge on our side," said Ed. "I see a problem."

"It's time to fight back," said Jacques. "It's time to take the initiative. It's time to kill or be killed."

There was another long moment of silence, while the three friends pondered the situation.

"We'll need weapons," said Jacques.

"Look guys," said Morris. "Nothing in your terms of employment leads me to expect you to break the law...."

"At this point, it's survival for all of us. We're all in the same boat," said Ed.

"I agree with Ed. The only way to end this thing is to tackle these guys head on," said Jacques. "The cops are useless. They offer no real protection, and their bureaucratic investigation process is not moving fast enough."

"Yeah," said Ed. "What happens if we get the location of the secret camp from the GPS device? If we give it to the cops, they'll take forever to figure out what to do with it. Look at this circus. If we told them they had to raid an armed camp they would spend weeks getting ready."

Jacques spoke up. "Meanwhile, the bad guys will find the device and figure out we put it there. Maybe they found it already, and this attack was the result."

"They'll bug out of the location, or they'll launch an even stronger attack, or both," said Ed. "The moment we get location coordinates, we should go in – just the three of us. Armed and ready."

"We figure out what's going on," said Jacques. "We photograph their operation, get to the bottom of this thing. We find out whatever it is we're not supposed to find out. Then we report to the cops, CSIS, or whoever. Then they can raid the place or whatever other places are part of the scheme. Then, the pressure will come off us. Then, we'll be safe."

"We could be caught out there," said Morris. "We'll have no medevac. No re-supply. No fire support. We're on our own."

"We'll shoot our way out," said Jacques.

"I'd rather be watching them with a weapon in my hand, than be watched while I'm unarmed," said Ed.

"We're obviously sitting ducks here in the city. It's time to take the battle to them." said Jacques.

Morris thought for a moment.

"OK. Let's go in with supplies for up to ten days." Morris said to Jacques, and then he turned to Ed. "You have the Special Forces experience, Ed, I think you should be in command."

Ed and Jacques nodded.

"Commander, I have a very difficult question," said Jacques. "What do we tell our wives?"

"That's a pretty tough first question," said Ed. "Can we come back to that?"

"We need a good cover story for the cops. We'll need an alibi if we get into any shooting," said Jacques.

"Las Vegas," said Morris. "We'll go to Las Vegas."

"Sounds fun," said Ed. "But that's in the wrong direction."

"Exactly," said Morris. "We check in to a Vegas hotel, and then leave on a private jet back to Winnipeg. No, we land on the US side. We don't want a customs arrival record at the Canadian border. We want to look as if we were in Vegas the whole ten days."

"We leave an empty hotel room for ten days?" asked Ed.

"No, we fill it with three guys who spend money using our credit cards. They create a paper trail of activity at big events where they won't be remembered. That puts us in Vegas for ten days."

"Who do you have in mind?" asked Jacques.

"Conan, Zia, and his brother Habib."

"Three of the least-likely party animals ever," said Ed.

"I'm sure they'll pull it off," said Morris.

"How do we sneak back into Canada?" asked Jacques.

"By parachute," said Morris. "We pick a parachute club near the US Canada border. We pay for a private drop. We get the pilot to deviate a bit, crossing the border, and we come down in a farmer's field on the Canadian side."

"With weapons?" asked Ed.

"No. We have them pre-positioned in Canada, near the farmer's field. We pack a truck full of weapons, ammo and supplies and park it somewhere south of Winnipeg. Then we drive to the objective north of Kenora."

"How do we get back? We have to get back into the US," said Ed.

"We can just re-enter at any land crossing, using our regular passports. There will be a customs arrival record in the US system, but no departure record in the Canadian system. The Canadian authorities will have no reason to check the US system. We can cross at a land port, then fly back to Vegas and jump on a return flight to Ottawa."

"And it looks on paper like we spent the whole time in Vegas," said Ed.

"OK, that's workable except for one thing," said Jacques. "Suzette would never let me go to Vegas for two weeks with you guys. I have enough trouble just with our Wednesday night thing. Do we make up another alibi for the wives?"

"I'd rather go down in a hail of bullets rather than caught lying to Debbie," said Ed.

"You want to tell her you're pretending to go to Vegas, but not really," said Morris. "It's not really Vegas, Deb. You don't have to worry, 'cause me and Morris and Jacques, what we're really gonna do is quietly re-invade Canada with a three-man patrol against an unknown, heavily armed enemy somewhere in Northern Ontario."

"Suzette would like that story better," said Jacques. "She has a pretty bad impression of Las Vegas. It's a place she would not let me go unsupervised. She doesn't subscribe to the philosophy *what happens in Vegas stays in Vegas.*"

"Me too. What happens in Vegas, I'm accountable for," said Ed.

The three men sat thinking for the next few moments, listening to the rain, until there was a knock on the side of the truck. It was Liam.

Jacques opened the door and Liam climbed in the back seat.

"It's raining like hell," said Liam.

"It's not all sunshine and pink clouds in here," said Morris. "We've decided to get some illegal weapons, smuggle ourselves across the border, and find that fuckin' camp. If necessary, we'll murder the bastards that keep trying to kill us. What's your legal opinion?"

"It's about time," said Liam, "how can I help?"

"First figure out what we should tell our wives," said Ed.

Liam grinned. "Tell them the truth, the whole truth and nothing else. Tell them you're going on a mission, but you can't give the details because you don't want them implicated. Tell them I know this plan and I will tell them what they need to know if the time comes."

"Meaning if we don't make it back alive," said Ed.

"That makes sense," said Morris.

"By the way, you can't tell me that you plan to commit a murder," said Liam. "I would be compelled to report it to the authorities. But if you kill in self-defense, should the need arise...."

"I get it," Morris said to Liam. "All right, we'll need you to pre-position a supply truck at a location Ed will figure out. He's going to be the patrol commander. We have an alibi, Liam. Everyone except a few trusted PHL employees must think we are in Las Vegas. If something happens at the camp, we can prove to the police that we were not there."

Morris turned to Ed and Jacques. "I need you guys to know a couple of things. First, I think we're doing the right thing. There's something bad going on at that camp. Not only is it a threat to us personally right now, I have a feeling it's something big and nasty and the sort of thing we joined the army to fight against. We're not in the army anymore, but somebody has to do this job. Somebody has to do it now. We need to identify the threat, and steer the proper police or national security resources to deal with it."

Ed and Jacques nodded silently.

"The other thing – I'm going to have PHL take out large life insurance policies on you both, with your wives as beneficiaries. And guys, use Liam here for one more thing. If you don't already have one, make sure you draw up a will."

41 – VIVA LAS VEGAS

"This trip is gonna pay off. We got the camp coordinates," said Morris, hanging up his cellphone. "That was Conan. He just touched down at Chicago O'Hare with Zia and Habib."

Morris had gambled by pre-positioning himself, Ed and Jacques in Las Vegas before they had received the most important information they needed: where the camp was located. There was an extreme sense of urgency. There was one additional flight scheduled on Kendo's computer, and the group wanted to be in position to observe who arrived next Thursday.

It was Tuesday, and the three men sat in a suite at the MGM Grand Hotel. The decision in the back of Ed's Ford Ranger Super Cab, to launch the mission, had occurred four days ago. A lot of activity had occurred since then.

The group had arrived that morning, dressed for a vacation. They made their presence known during check-in, causing a bit of a scene. They had to be cautioned for rowdy behavior by hotel security. Morris left them a huge tip. Morris figured – even though the hotel has a check-in counter with twenty clerks working simultaneously – they would be remembered.

Morris had booked average size hotel rooms in order to blend in and be forgettable by the cleaning staff.

"Roger, Conan, Zia and Habib in O'Hare, that's good," said Ed. "Did Conan give you the coordinates to Kenora as planned?"

"Yes. He did that before he called me. The weather in Kenora is good and our photoreconnaissance flight will take off within the hour. The pilot will make one pass over the campsite with a high-resolution camera. We'll have pictures in a few hours."

Jim E.M. Miles

"Excellent," said Jacques. "Meanwhile, now we know where to focus our attention, we can take a closer look at the satellite photos we already have."

"We'll also be getting some bonus photos from Zia and Habib," said Morris. "The camera on the GPS tracker got some good stuff, Conan said."

"Excellent. The more photos, the better," said Jacques.

"Gentlemen, orders," said Ed, taking charge of the group. "Jacques, I asked you to prepare the intelligence briefing. Go ahead."

"Enemy: unknown strength," Jacques said with enthusiasm. "Location: we have the exact coordinates." Jacques grinned.

"We have also confirmed MacDick's information about how victims were lured away from Ottawa," Jacques said. "Yesterday, Conan examined the computer Candice Wilkinson was using. The browser history showed she had visited a site with the address www.vancouveraddictioncenter.com. It was a fake site. It emulated a genuine site that has the address www.vancouveraddictioncentre.com. On the fake site, *center* is spelt the American way, ending with *E-R*. The fake site mirrored the real one on most pages, except the fake site described a fictitious treatment program offering free heroin to addicts for as long as they wanted. The program was supposed to wean them off the drug as slowly as they wished. Conan also found that same fake site on Kendo's computer. It looks like Kendo created the site.

"Liam contacted the real Vancouver Addiction Centre. They were not aware of the website. They tried to browse the fake site, but it would not come up. Conan did some more investigation and found Candice's computer was the only one able to hit the site. The fake website seems to respond to computers only if they are using a narrow band of dynamic IP addresses, the range used by her Internet Service Provider. It's possible the other specific computers could hit the site. Kendo must have set up access for Candice by figuring out who her ISP was in advance."

"That's a pretty thorough deception plan," said Morris.

"If this program is in Vancouver, how did they get the victims on a flight to Winnipeg?" asked Ed.

"Conan found a fake flight itinerary in her email. Kendo sent her an edited version of the travel document we found on Kendo's computer. Kendo added a fake additional flight – to Vancouver. He explained in the email it was necessary to stop in Winnipeg to get a medical evaluation for admission to the Vancouver program."

"Any information about what happens to these victims?" asked Morris.

"No. It's possible that Kendo did not even know. His job was just to get them there. My guess would be these people are being used in some kind of medical experiments," said Jacques.

"What kind of medical experiments?" asked Morris.

"I'm speculating here, but one theory is they are making some new illegal drug."

"That fits," said Ed. "Heavy drug users would make ideal test subjects."

"Not only that, these people represent a segment of society that would not be missed," said Jacques. "If they overdosed on the drug, they could be disposed of and nobody would go looking for them. They would just be another missing-person statistic. They could even be released if they don't know who was running the camp – no trace-back. Even if they did have valuable information, who would listen to them?"

"So do we expect to find a commune full of happy, hippie drug users at this camp?" asked Ed.

"It's possible," said Jacques. "If so, I'm sure the cops will be happy to bust it. Any other questions about the enemy?"

Morris and Ed both shook their heads.

"Next is friendly forces," Jacques said. "Liam departed with the equipment truck two days ago. He'll be in the Winnipeg area late tonight. We'll be able to rendezvous with him by dawn tomorrow. After we link up with Liam, he will be staying in Winnipeg until our operation is over. We have a private jet on standby at Las Vegas McCarran to take us back to the Canadian border. Near the border we have a pilot ready to take us over so we can parachute and link up with Liam on the Canadian side.

"Morris, the one other resource we have is your buddy Alex James. Can you fill us in on the phone conversation you had with him this morning?"

"I called him to indicate we were on an operation," said Morris. "The conversation was – how should I describe it? It was a *very careful* conversation. Both of us know that, as a government agent, Alex would have to report any serious threats that our operation might present. In other words, even though we're friends, he would have to turn me in if I revealed I was up to something severe enough to come up on the CSIS national security radar. So I didn't give him all the details. I could tell he didn't want all the details.

"What Alex knows is this: we are on a mission to find out how deep this thing goes. I said we hope to have something to report within ten days. I told him roughly where we would be operating. He told me, as far as he can tell, there are no intelligence-gathering investigations going on at present, other than routine missing persons. The RCMP only has twenty members to cover about 200,000 square miles of northwestern Ontario. They have a gangs unit responsible for intelligence gathering and investigations. Our information to them so far has not put anything on their to-do list. There is nothing going on at CSIS, either."

"What about the OPP?" asked Ed.

"Other than keeping some kind of weak surveillance on Detective Clark, they don't seem to be doing anything. They have not opened up channels to the RCMP or CSIS."

"Nobody's on to this situation," said Ed, "except us."

"OK, we've discussed enemy and friendly forces," said Jacques. "As far as weather effects on the operation, we have great flying weather and the next ten days are expected to be above seasonal temperatures. Early fall weather. We shouldn't be too uncomfortable. There will be a full moon tonight. Night visibility on the ground should be good."

Jacques put down his notes and looked at Ed.

"That brings us to our mission," Ed picked up his own notes. "I wrote it this way: to observe the camp and deduce the purpose without making contact with the enemy."

Morris and Jacques looked at each other.

"What if we observe but can't deduce?" asked Jacques.

"He's right. We may not be able to accomplish the mission if we have to avoid contact," said Morris.

"Well, there's only one way to make this more aggressive. We only have three men, hardly enough for a serious attack. We might be able to do some sniping, and maybe we could ambush a small isolated party if we get the chance. But it would have to be limited to what contributes to the mission: observe and deduce."

"What wording would you suggest?" asked Morris.

"To observe the camp and deduce the purpose, fighting for information if necessary."

"*Hooah!* I like 'dat one," said Jacques. "I don't want to go back there a second time."

"OK, so be it: to observe activity and deduce the apparent purpose of the camp, and to fight for information if necessary," Morris repeated.

Nods and handshakes followed.

For the next two hours, the three men consulted maps to pick key locations and plan routes.

They discussed numerous details that had arisen during the day and night rehearsals they had conducted on the previous weekend. For two days, Ed had drilled his team hard. They had practiced patrolling drills in daylight and darkness, moving with their weapons and other fighting equipment. They had spent several daylight and darkness hours firing their new weapons in a remote location in the Gatineau hills of Western Quebec, setting the sights and refreshing their weapon-handling drills.

Most importantly, they had practiced infantry hand-signals and movement drills so they could move silently, with vigilance, without words, day or night.

The team had practiced with their new weapons and equipment as long as possible, finally packing everything carefully on the truck at the last minute. They couldn't keep Liam waiting any longer to start the long trip from Ottawa to Winnipeg, about 1500 miles via two-lane Northern Ontario highways. That was yesterday.

The men had slept no more than three hours each night for five days in a row. There was not enough time to do everything that needed to be done. Procuring the weapons and ammunition had not been easy, or cheap. Liam had used a law school buddy, now a criminal lawyer, to identify and contact a source of military weapons. He managed to acquire exactly what Ed had requested. Ammunition had not been difficult to come by. Ed's JTF2 friends liberated some fine night vision equipment – on loan, for a good cause, the QM had said.

Regular supplies had been easy to acquire, but were numerous and therefore time-consuming. Jill had spent two full days shopping for can openers, pocket knives, heat tabs, mosquito repellent, sunscreen, first aid kit, mosquito netting, lighters, matches, dehydrated food, camp stove, fuel, cooking gear, toilet paper, foot powder, groundsheets, flashlights, batteries, sleeping bags, scissors, tape, instant coffee, granola and chocolate bars.

Morris had acquired a power inverter to run laptop computers from vehicle power, two pairs of binoculars, a digital camera with telephoto lens, three hand-held GPS devices, camouflage clothing, camouflage net, camouflage face paint, Kevlar vests, three parachutes (which had to be shipped out in advance), two satellite phones with computer ports, three secure two-way radios with headsets and throat mikes, plus one spare, and plenty of field dressings.

The final challenge had been morphine – they had been unable to get any in time.

Morris looked at his watch as the meeting broke up. Everyone was free to head back to his room for an hour of rest before heading for the airport to greet Conan and friends.

After Ed and Jacques left the room, Morris stretched out on his bed and thought about the past few hectic days. His head buzzed with details. He did not want to forget anything. His thoughts turned to Brenda.

Her surgery had gone well. The paramedics and surgeon told Morris that his quick first aid had saved her life. Morris took no solace in that fact, however. He blamed himself for agreeing to meet at her place when it would have been much safer at PHL offices. He had apologized when he visited her after her surgery, but it didn't help his guilt.

During a long talk, she told Morris she wanted to get out of the sex worker business anyway. Her wound had firmly decided the matter. Even after cosmetic surgery, her breast would never be the same, the surgeon had said. There would be a noticeable deformity.

During his visit, they had spent time talking about
Candice. Brenda had tried to stop Candi becoming a
stripper, she told Morris, but to no avail. Candi was
turning slowly to prostitution, taking money from Kendo
for a start. There was no stopping her, Brenda had said.

It seemed important to Brenda that Morris understand
her own work in prostitution. She had a very short client
list, she said, and was very selective.

Morris did not know what to expect at the camp, but
he was hoping he would find Candi alive and well. He
was hoping he could somehow rescue her. Morris dozed
off with those thoughts.

An hour later, Ed and Jacques knocked on his door.
Morris awoke and took a moment to figure out where he
was. Adrenaline surged as he remembered what they were
about to do. He quickly got onto his feet, grabbed his
backpack, and headed out.

The cab ride to the airport took about ten minutes.
After waiting at the arrivals terminal for a few minutes,
then they saw Conan, Zia and Habib exit the security
door. Morris approached the slightly bewildered trio, who
were looking at the slot machines.

"Welcome to Sin City, boys," said Morris.

"Slot machines in the airport? How cool is that!"
exclaimed Zia.

"How old is your brother?" said Ed looking at Habib.

"Nineteen," said Zia.

"I picked out a nice girl for you, buddy!" Ed said to
Habib. "We owe you one after that GPS gadget you set
up. She's pre-paid. She'll be at your room in an hour."

Habib's eyes got big.

"You each have a bottle of champagne icing down,"
said Jacques.

"We each have our own room!" exclaimed Habib.

"You also get one or two of these," said Morris, as he
handed Conan two credit cards. "These two are in my
name. Use this one to pay for the group events, like

shows, meals, helicopter ride, limos, and souvenirs. It's got a 50K limit. That's US dollars. Try to stay within that budget. This other card has a 10K limit. Use that one for any individual expenses. And gambling. Try to keep your losses to $100 a day."

Ed and Jacques handed over one credit card each to Zia and Habib.

"Ed and Jacques' cards also have a 10K limit. Remember the mission: spend like we would spend. Our PIN codes are listed here on this business card. Everybody get a room key?" Morris handed his key to Conan.

Stunned, the three amigos accepted room keys and credit cards in silence.

"There's a high-speed internet connection in each room to maintain contact with us. You can reach our satellite phone by email and SMS. We may need to get intelligence-gathering support from time to time. Try not to all get drunk at the same time. Except for tonight. You won't be on call before noon tomorrow. Any questions?"

"What's the Internet?" asked Conan, staring at the credit cards and room key in his hand.

"Never mind," Morris laughed. "It's all written down in my room."

Jacques grinned at Zia. "It's your duty to party." He gave Zia a slap on the back.

"Have a good time, guys," said Morris.

"Wait," said Zia. "I have something for you." He rummaged in his backpack, pulling out several card-deck size gadgets.

"What the heck are these?" asked Morris.

"Motion activated, low light, self-recording video cameras," said Zia. "They're waterproof. You can mount them outside, point them at a surveillance target, and collect them up several days later. You'll see a video clip for each motion that occurred while they were active.

This red button is the power switch. After you set one up, don't forget to turn it on."

"You can use this tape to mount them," said Habib, pulling three rolls of waterproof tape from his bag.

"Camouflage colors," said Ed. "I'm very impressed. When we get back, we're gonna get you two girls, Habib."

"Hey, he just brought the tape," said Zia.

"You're married, I thought," said Ed.

"What happens in Vegas…." said Jacques.

"…could be sexually transmitted to your spouse." Ed interrupted.

"We also have photos," said Zia, handing a thumb drive to Morris. "These came from the GPS tracker mounted on the back of the black SUV. The position and direction of each photo is annotated on the image."

"Good, we'll look at these on the plane." Morris checked his watch. "We have to get moving."

There were handshakes all around. Morris, Ed and Jacques headed for the main doors. Just before passing through, Morris and Ed looked back to see the three amigos starting to get their bearings, talking excitedly. They were headed in the wrong direction, walking away from the baggage claim area.

"Those guys are geeks in babe world," said Ed. "They'll never figure this place out."

42 – EASTBOUND

"Good evening, Gentlemen, this is the captain. We have reached our cruising altitude of 35,000 feet. Distance to our destination, Grand Forks International Airport, is 1069 nautical miles. Flying time from Las Vegas will be two hours, twelve minutes at the cruising speed of our LearJet 40XR, Mach point seven-five. Arrival time is estimated to be 1833 hours, local time."

Morris was hunched over uncomfortably, making his way back to his seat. He had to crunch down his six-foot-four frame to navigate the four-foot-ten cabin height. Ed and Jacques sat relaxed facing each other over a table. On the table were maps, satellite photos, pizza and two cans of Coors Light.

Morris took his seat on the opposite side of the narrow aisle. His laptop was on the table in front of him. An email from Liam had just arrived. Subject: Air Photos. Morris opened it.

Two high-resolution photos were attached. The text indicated Liam had arranged for the photos to be printed in Grand Forks and delivered to their plane on arrival.

Morris opened a viewer to inspect the first photo and turned his laptop screen for Ed and Jacques to see.

"This photo is our objective about an hour ago," said Morris. "I count three large structures and two smaller ones. What the hell's this round thing?"

"Water tank," said Ed.

"This looks like a vehicle park." Morris pointed to a small clearing at the end of a narrow vehicle track. "I see a large truck and this bit here could be the corner of another vehicle under the trees."

"Nothing is camouflaged," said Jacques.

368

"It would look pretty suspicious if they tried to put it all under camo nets," said Morris.

"There's something painted green in the center of the camp," said Ed. "Disruptive paint pattern, but you can tell a bit from the shadow. It's long and narrow, like a cigar tube."

"My guess would be a chemical tank – maybe a fuel tank," said Jacques.

"They're using a lot of fuel for something, then. It's huge," said Ed.

"Other than a large fuel tank, this place could be a fishing camp," said Morris.

"That's what they want it to look like," said Ed. "Our job will be to figure out the purpose of each structure. We'll have to find spots where we can see without being seen. How many of those video recorder gadgets did Zia give us?"

"Five," said Morris.

"We'll put a couple on their in and out route, for a start," said Ed, looking at his watch. "We'll make that our first task. After two days, we collect them and see what they show us. We should do that before first light tomorrow. I picked a couple of likely spots for us to park and hide the truck." Ed picked up a map. "Here – roughly a mile from the objective. That will be our base camp. We'll launch our patrols from there."

Looking at his notes, Ed went on. "By my time appreciation, to be at the objective by first light, which is 0508 hrs tomorrow, we have to depart our base camp by 0330 hrs. We have a full moon, so moving in should be quick and easy. If we jump just before last light tonight, 1932 hrs, we can take up to eight hours to drive about 130 km over logging roads and dirt tracks. That's plenty of time, because it should take three hours, say four hours max. We should have enough time to link up with Liam, make the trip, select a vehicle hide, and get some rest before we start our first patrol."

"We arrive in Grand Forks at 1833 hrs, according to the pilot," said Jacques. "That only gives us 45 minutes to complete the drop before we lose all the light."

"That's cutting it pretty close," said Ed. "We want to be able to see the ground when we jump. Jacques, talk to the pilot and see if he can get any more speed out of this bucket."

"Will do." Jacques got up and headed for the cockpit.

"You made arrangements for the parachute drop," Ed said to Morris. "Will the pilot be able get us to the drop zone before dark?"

"I'll give him a call."

A few minutes later, Jacques returned to his seat, just as Morris finished his telephone call.

"The pilot put us up to Mach .81," said Jacques. "He said the jet stream is helping us with a stronger than expected tailwind. We'll save at least 15 minutes. I also told him we want to change to another airplane quickly. He said he has to taxi to the terminal at Grand Forks before he can let us out, that will take five or ten minutes. But he suggested we try another airport where we can jump out on a taxiway and change planes right there. He recommended Thief River Falls. Look here." Jacques picked up a map. "It's closer to the drop zone. We should change planes there. We'll save another 15 minutes."

"My guy suggested the same thing," said Morris.

"OK, let's do it that way," said Ed. He looked carefully at the map.

"Our jump plane is a Twin Otter," said Morris. "Flight time to the drop zone will be twenty-five minutes. We should be able to reach the drop zone at least 30 minutes before last light."

"Perfect," said Ed, as he examined the drop zone.

The drop zone was west of the Northwest Angle, a peculiar extension of the United States that went north of the 49th Parallel.

The Angle, as the locals call it, located north of Lake of the Woods, juts into Canadian territory about 30 miles, creating a nice north-south running stretch of border in a remote area. Morris had convinced the jump plane pilot to look the other way while flying over that stretch into Canadian airspace. His three passengers would leave the plane at a spot of their choosing, not his responsibility. The pilot charged an extra $2,000 to look the other way.

The recommended minimum opening altitude for a licensed skydiver is 2000 feet. None of the three men was a licensed skydiver. They had chosen to jump at 1500 feet. Reason: they did not want to be observed from the ground. That was the same reason for timing the jump to coincide with last light. Should they be observed in the air, they wanted to use darkness to escape capture and identification by Canadian authorities. The low drop height left almost no room for error. Should a main parachute fail to deploy, there was not much time to think about deploying the reserve. Only the rest of your life, Ed had said.

"Can I see the GPS photos?" asked Ed.

Morris nodded and opened a folder on his laptop. "Each image has coordinates shown in the lower left. I'm starting with the most northerly images first." He started to preview images in sequence. "These shots were taken as the vehicle departed their vehicle hide at the objective yesterday afternoon. The black SUV had been backed-in to the bush. That's why they didn't spot the GPS devices – they never used the back hatch.

"There is a new photo every fifteen seconds whenever the vehicle is moving. These first several show a beautiful sequence of exactly what we would see – in reverse order – if we walked into the camp along the vehicle track." Morris was advancing through the scenes as he spoke. "Notice there are a couple of identical shots in sequence. The vehicle stopped for about thirty seconds. Then it started moving again, and look at this."

"An armed sentry," said Ed.

"Right. We can't just walk up this trail," said Morris.

"He doesn't look too alert. He's just sitting on a chair, looking bored," said Jacques. "He's not dug in or protected at all. No vest. It looks like these guys have let their guard down."

"I wouldn't underestimate them yet," said Ed. "Look at that." Ed pointed to a small black cylindrical object with four legs by the side of the road near the sentry's foot. "Can you zoom in?"

Morris magnified the image. "That looks like a small antenna sticking out the top."

"UGS – Unattended Ground Sensor," said Ed. "It can transmit up to 300 meters if it has clear line-of-sight."

Morris and Jacques looked at each other.

Ed went on. "I see you are concerned. As long as we're quiet, even if our motion is picked up, they won't know it's a human contact. They probably get false alarms all the time. They would react if they hear a vehicle or a voice, but not if they think it's an animal."

"Now that we know where it is, we could disable it," said Morris.

"Nope," said Ed. "That would alert them. We just avoid it. We know exactly where it is – the coordinates are on the image. So let's put it on our map. Got any other good images?"

"We have quite a few. I suggest we take turns studying them. But I do want to show you these." Morris opened two more images. "These were taken on the day you guys tracked the vehicle in Winnipeg. The vehicle is turning and backing up. Look at this guy."

In the first image, Morris pointed to the side view of an Arab male, late twenties, medium build, with short dark hair. "This could be the guy Brenda saw. He might even be the leader."

In the second image, the Arab was leading a man wearing a blindfold.

"Here's a victim," said Morris.

"That's the guy who got the needle," said Jacques.

"As soon as we land, I'll send the first image to Brenda to confirm that the Arab is the guy she rode with in the spring."

Morris decided not to send Brenda the other image. It looked bad for Candice. Morris was starting to lose hope that he would find her alive.

43 – THE JUMP

Touchdown at Thief River Falls Regional Airport occurred at 1818 hrs. The LearJet pilot had coordinated with the Twin Otter Pilot, and the passengers were to change planes on the tarmac. Morris, Ed and Jacques stepped out of the LearJet wearing black skydiver jumpsuits. They had changed out of their tourist clothes in the tiny cabin of the LearJet.

The whine of the LearJet engine diminished and the throaty propeller sound of the Twin Otter increased as the team made their way toward it. Morris felt his Blackberry vibrate as he approached the airplane. It was a text message from Brenda in response to the photo of the Arab he had sent her after touchdown, moments ago. She was responding in the affirmative: the Arab was the same man who drove the truck. He seemed to be the man in charge.

"The Arab is their leader," Morris told Jacques and Ed.

The engines on the Twin Otter were running. The co-pilot greeted them each with a handshake. Ed began to speak with the co-pilot, but Morris could not hear the conversation. He looked at the double width, wide-open doorway. Inside against the walls were two rows of bench seats with a few seatbelts. This will be a very easy airplane to jump from, Morris noted with satisfaction.

Morris had completed the basic para course in the army, and he had done a couple of sport parachute jumps a few years after his release. There had been discussion of making a refresher jump as a group before leaving Ottawa, but lack of time and high winds had prevented it. They had spent a couple of hours checking over the equipment before shipping it, talked about aircraft exit

and landing procedures, and that's all they could do. Ed
was a freefall expert and Jacques had numerous
operational jumps under his belt. Morris had decided he
could rely on them to get him through.

The co-pilot gave Morris an envelope. "This is for
Morris Parker," he said, trying to make himself heard
over the engine.

"That's me." Morris opened the envelope. It
contained two large color prints of the
photoreconnaissance images he had already seen on his
laptop. Good old Liam, thought Morris, arranged for
printing and delivery of these items while on the road
somewhere south of Winnipeg. Conan, Zia and Habib
must have been in the air on the way to Vegas at the time.
Each part of the plan required coordination, and Morris
was very happy with the way his team was working
together.

Morris realized he needed to pack the envelope
somewhere, so he folded and stuffed it in his shirt just as
Ed came forward with a parachute bearing a tape labeled
Parker. Morris saw that Jacques was already wearing his
parachute and was adjusting his helmet. Ed helped Morris
strap on his parachute and equipment, which included a
small pack containing a GPS, radio communications
equipment, and survival gear, including food and water. It
was easy to become separated on the jump – each man
needed to be able to operate independently until they
could link up.

Ed checked Morris over, giving thumbs up. Ed and
Jacques then checked each other, ending with thumbs up.
The three men then climbed into the Twin Otter.

The co-pilot climbed aboard, slid the door shut, and
signaled for passengers to fasten seatbelts. He took his
seat at the controls of the plane. The pilots taxied the
airplane to the end of the ramp, and waited.

The sun was now below the horizon. Morris checked
his watch. It had taken fifteen minutes to change planes

and don parachutes. Still the plane waited. They were running out of time. Come on baby, Morris thought, come on, what's the holdup?

Finally the airplane moved forward. It turned slowly into takeoff position at the end of the runway, and powered up for takeoff. The sound level in the passenger cabin increased. A three-person conversation was now impossible. Each man could talk to, at most, one other person at a time.

As the airplane increased speed, Morris began to mentally rehearse his jump procedures. If his main chute failed to open, he would have to cutaway and quickly deploy his reserve. One thousand, two thousand, three thousand, four thousand, CHECK CANOPY. He pictured himself steering the parachute and thought about how to deal with a hazardous landing situation. He pictured himself hitting the ground, legs bent, allowing himself to fall to one side or the other to avoid injury.

Now they were airborne. They turned on a northerly heading, gaining altitude fast. Once they leveled off, Ed disconnected his seatbelt and made his way over to the exit door. He began to search for something, checking the floor, ceiling and walls on both sides of the door. The airplane was not rigged the way he had expected.

The plan was for each man to jump using a static line. A static line attaches the jumper's parachute to the airplane. As each jumper exits the airplane, he quickly reaches the end of the 15-foot line, and it pulls tight, opening the parachute automatically. Ed wanted all three jumpers to exit within one second of each other, otherwise they would be spread out on landing, making linkup on the ground more time-consuming. Ed found a single, small attach point on the floor. The airplane had been rigged for one-at-a-time static line jumps.

As a paratrooper, Ed had always used an anchor line cable that ran from airplane front to back at head level. Working in a queue, each paratrooper clips his static line

to this cable, and is followed by each other paratrooper in
single file. The static line hook slides along the anchor
line cable until the paratrooper reaches the door. This
configuration of airplane, equipment and men is optimal
for paratroopers to exit the door within one second of
each other, minimizing separation.

As Morris watched, Ed signaled for Jacques to join
him. The two men worked on the attach point, which
consisted of a small metal ring attached to the floor. They
were trying to see if there was a way to fit all three static
lines to the small ring, but they could not make both of
their clips fit in the ring at the same time.

Morris looked around the cabin. Light was starting to
fade. The interior lights had been left off so they could
allow their eyes to adjust to the dark. Morris spotted a
small mesh bag mounted in the back against a bulkhead.
He walked over and saw – with relief – it contained
several metal D-shaped carabiner snap links. He pulled
one out of the bag and took it to Ed.

Ed accepted it with a grin and a nod. He snapped it to
the attach point, then attached his static line. He motioned
for Jacques to attach his line, and then for Morris to
attach his line. All three static lines clips fit with room to
spare. Ed stood up and pulled on his line to test the
strength of the attach point. It held nicely.

Ed pointed at Jacques, and then pointed to the bench
seat next to the door. Jacques sat where Ed pointed. Ed
motioned for Morris to sit next to Jacques, and Morris
complied. Then Ed sat in the third position on the bench.
Then Ed pointed to Jacques and raised his index finger,
mouthing a count: "ONE." Jacques nodded. Ed pointed at
Morris and showed a count of "TWO." Morris nodded.
Ed pointed at himself, mouthing "THREE." Ed then
motioned for the others to check their equipment and to
ensure the static lines on the floor would not entangle
each other.

For the next few minutes, the three men rode side by side, each with his private thoughts.

Morris again thought about his jump drills. He remembered the old song telling the story of an unfortunate paratrooper whose chute entangled and failed to open. It went to the tune of *Glory, Glory Hallelujah*, which Morris began to hum:

There was blood upon the risers, there were brains upon the 'chute
Intestines were a-dangling from his paratrooper suit
He was a mess, they picked him up and poured him from his boots
And he ain't gonna jump no more

Gory, gory, what a hell of way to die
Gory, gory, what a hell of way to die
Gory, gory, what a hell of way to die
He ain't gonna jump no more

Macabre humor. A perfect way to deal with frayed nerves, Morris thought.

Ed left his seat and went forward to speak with the co-pilot. After about five minutes, he returned. The co-pilot followed. It was time to open the door.

The pilot wore headgear with earphones and microphone fitted with a long, black, coiled intercom cord hanging from one side. He carried a small flashlight. The passenger cabin was now almost completely dark. The co-pilot approached the door and shone his light above it to the right. He plugged his intercom cord into a jack mounted there, said something, then nodded. He was able to speak with the pilot.

The co-pilot then fumbled for the door handle. Finding it, he released the door and slid it toward to the rear of the plane, moving with it to a position on the left side of the open doorway. The blast of outside air rushing past the open doorframe increased the noise level.

Morris felt a surge of adrenaline. After stepping through the door, he would experience sudden acceleration aft followed by the shock of his chute opening. Morris was looking forward to the silence that would follow, and the gentle ride down to a hopefully peaceful, uneventful landing.

Ed stood up and motioned for the others to do the same. Jacques and Morris got up. Ed motioned for Morris to check Jacques. Morris checked Jacques one last time, front then back. He gave Jacques the thumbs up. Ed then checked Morris, followed by thumbs up. Morris then checked Ed, giving thumbs up. Ed then gave thumbs-up to the co-pilot. Everyone was ready.

Following the planned route, the airplane was executing a slow, wide left turn that would "accidentally" clip the Canadian Border and encroach briefly into Canadian airspace over the Reed River Indian Reserve. Liam had positioned the truck to make a pickup on a small road not far from an open area they had designated as the drop zone. The low altitude of the drop meant it would be easy to hit this target and not the trees surrounding it.

The co-pilot was nodding and talking to the pilot.

Jacques looked out toward the large, dark lake below. They were headed north west now, crossing Lake of the Woods, heading toward land.

Morris noticed Jacques cross himself.

Ed kept his eye on the co-pilot, waiting for the signal that they were at the correct altitude and in position to exit the airplane.

Finally, it came. The pilot gave Ed a nod, and slapped Jacques on the shoulder.

Jacques stepped forward quickly and immediately tripped on his way out the door. The co-pilot's intercom cord, unseen in the dark, had been dangling inches from the floor.

The co-pilots head was jerked violently forward. He braced himself, and pulled backwards sharply to avoid being pulled toward the doorway.

Morris saw the intercom cord snapping upwards and raised his right leg to step over it. Trying to follow Jacques without undue delay, Morris looked down at his left leg as he lifted it over so it too would clear the cord. With big clumsy steps, Morris leaned out the open doorway and fell into the rushing airflow. It was not a graceful exit, but Morris figured it would have to do.

Morris entered a blast of cool rushing air upside-down, and a sudden, intense pain stabbed in his left calf. The sound of the engines was deafening, and the airflow roared in his ears. The blast of air from the propeller on this side of the airplane was supposed to be momentary, but it continued. Morris expected to feel his body jerk upright as his parachute opened, but he did not. Morris remained upside down, buffeted by the prop blast.

Morris had entangled his left leg in Jacques' static line. He dangled about ten feet below and aft of the aircraft exit doorway, like a yo-yo on a string.

"…three thousand, four thousand, CHECK CANOPY," Morris counted, unheard by human ears, even his own. Morris arched his back, trying to get oriented. The wind was so intense he had to force his eyes shut. Up was down. Nothing made sense. He raised his arms, trying to feel for parachute straps. Instead of finding comfort in sensing a properly deployed parachute, Morris felt himself start to spin. One arm had deflected the airflow, and he started to corkscrew at the end of the static line. Morris immediately dragged his arms back to his chest, but it required an effort to fight the wind. So much wind, it was hard to breathe. I NEED AIR! I'M DROWNING! WHAT THE HELL IS HAPPENNING TO ME?

In the plane, Ed was trying to size up the situation. It did not look good. The co-pilot was trying to find and reconnect his intercom cable. He was clueless that Morris was in trouble.

Leaning out the door, Ed could make out Morris
spinning and flailing, somehow caught in two static lines.
Down on one knee, Ed reached out, giving one of the
lines a pull. It was tight. He pulled the other one. It
moved slightly. He braced himself, preparing to give it a
stronger pull. Perhaps, with the co-pilot's help, they could
haul Morris in. He abruptly stopped himself, suddenly
realizing what might have happened.

Ed looked at the static line in his hand. He quickly
followed it back to the attach point. This static line
belonged to Morris, not Jacques. Morris was hung on
Jacques' line. If Ed pulled the line in his hand, it would
deploy Morris' parachute. If the chute deployed, it would
rip Morris apart.

Ed looked out the doorway. It was too dark to see
Morris clearly. The co-pilot had his flashlight in hand and
was inspecting the damaged jack on his intercom cord. Ed
grabbed the flashlight and shone it down on Morris,
trying to see how he was entangled. Ed saw Morris was
caught by one ankle. His arms and his free leg were
flailing in the airflow – he was like a rag doll in a
tornado.

He's fucked, thought Ed. He doesn't even look
conscious. Ed looked below. The airplane was now over
water. I can't cut him loose – he'll drown, even if he *is*
conscious.

Below, Morris was in full panic. His heart rate was
maxed, adrenaline was maxed, and he was on sensory
overload. Slowly though, one particular feeling began to
rise above all other inputs: pain in his left ankle.
Increasing, unrelenting, anger-inducing *pain*. Morris
realized another thing about his left leg. All other limbs
were free, but not that leg. Slowly, rational thoughts
began to emerge, crystallizing around that one clear
message: FUCK, THAT HURTS!

I'm being dragged behind the fuckin' airplane, Morris
realized. He got angry. Where is my knife? Enough of

this shit. I'll cut myself loose. Morris forced his eyes open. He looked at the ground – it was shiny. It was the goddam lake. Better not cut loose here.

Each time Morris made a move, he spun and bounced in the airflow. A flashlight glare from the plane caught his attention. Ed! Ed is still in the plane. Ed will help. Got to get a grip. Got to show Ed I'm OK.

Morris pulled his free knee toward his chest and hugged it with both arms. Fetal position, except for his caught leg, turned out to be fairly stable. He held his knee firmly, and the spinning and flailing stopped.

Ed looked down at Morris again, shining the light down the static line. Morris was no longer flailing. He had a grip on his free knee with both arms. Unbelievable, Ed thought. Morris was showing thumbs up.

The co-pilot finally clued-in. "Your guy's hooked up!" he yelled at Ed.

No shit. Hooked up. Ed suddenly remembered a military acronym. HUPRA. Hooked Up Parachutist's Release Assembly. He had seen a video of a paratrooper caught in an impossible tangle. There was no way the airplane could land with a trooper hanging – he would be killed. The only way out was to cut the trooper loose. But this trooper was in such a tangle that his chute had no chance of opening. The HUPRA includes an emergency parachute to be connected to the end of the static line of a hung up trooper. That connection is made from within the airplane. The static line is then cut and the chute is pulled out, inflating as the trooper falls. The end result – chute, 15-foot static line, and trooper in a knot – looked like hell in the sky, but it worked.

Ed came up with a plan. He grabbed the co-pilot by his headset intercom cord and led him back to the cockpit.

Morris, meanwhile, had recovered enough situational awareness to realize he now had several ways to die, not all within his control. His first idea had been to deploy his reserve and hope he could pull away. But he decided

against it. Landing without a leg in open water was not
attractive. Option two – stay put – and be killed on
landing. Option three – try to cut himself loose over land.
That, he decided, would be good. Then he realized he did
not have the strength to reach far enough to cut the static
line. Option four – I'm fucked. Let Ed figure out
something.

Morris detected an increase in engine noise. The
airplane was turning. It was also climbing. Good, get
some altitude. Get away from the water. Get me the hell
out of here.

The minutes seemed like hours. The moon was full,
and near the horizon. The earth below was no longer a
part of his world, Morris thought. He knew people in that
world. His wife. He had daughters there. And Brenda was
there. Would he see this world again?

It was getting colder. Morris felt his hands growing
numb. His arms were aching with fatigue. He could not
hold on much longer. The flailing would start again. Was
it time to say goodbye? Was it time to get religion?

Suddenly my leg is no longer being pulled, thought
Morris. I feel myself tumbling, in freefall. The engine
noise has faded. The airflow noise has diminished. Wait, I
feel the pull on my leg again, but it is gentle this time.
Just enough to upend me and stabilize my tumble. What's
that above? Silhouetted against the stars, I see Jesus on
the cross. Arms spread wide, Jesus is going to take me to
heaven.

Bullshit. This Jesus is opening a parachute.

Pressure on his ankle increased, and Morris felt the
deceleration of opening shock. Airflow in his ears ceased,
replaced by bloodflow to his head. Morris felt his
eyeballs popping out. "How do I get off this fuckin'
ride?" he demanded to the sky.

"We have two options," said Ed.

Normal conversation is now possible, Morris realized.
"Ed! I thought you were Jesus."

"Praise be to me. Listen up. Option one, we land together. The disadvantage is, since there are two of us on a chute designed for one, we are falling twice as fast as normal."

"Not to mention, I will land on my head, Jesus."

"Option two, I cut you loose. Can you open your reserve chute?"

Morris patted his equipment. "Everything seems normal except for my left foot. Cut me loose."

"So be it. After I do that, you must fly in a specific direction. I'm headed that way now. Look at the lights on the ground."

Morris twisted his head to look in the direction they were flying. On the ground he saw they were headed for burning lights in the shape of a 'T.'

"Are you shitting me?" Morris was incredulous. "We have pathfinders?"

"Jacques contacted us by radio. He had flares. That's were he wants us to land. I hereby say onto you, follow the path, my son."

Morris began to laugh. "Amen to that."

"The leg of the T is pointing in the direction of the wind. Fly your last leg upwind, and try to land at the base of the T. I better cut you loose before we get too low."

"One question, Ed."

"Yes boss?"

"In case my chute doesn't open, I cannot die not knowing how you managed to attach me to your rig."

"I'll explain on the ground. For now, you just need to know I have a static line looped through my groin straps."

"Ouch!" Morris laughed. "I'm motivated. Cut me loose!"

Morris no sooner placed his hands on his reserve chute than he felt a sudden drop. He immediately pulled the reserve chute ripcord. It opened normally.

Feeling relief to the point of euphoria, Morris laughed continuously to himself for the balance of the descent, interrupted only by the occasional instruction from above, to which he would answer 'Yes Lord,' or 'Thy Will be Done.'

Ed guided Morris to make four 90-degree turns, the final one bringing him into perfect alignment with the base of the T. Morris managed to flare his chute perfectly at the exact moment, producing a feather landing and remaining on his feet.

"What took you so long?" Jacques called from the edge of the clearing.

Morris looked in the direction of the voice. A light flashed twice. Morris detached his parachute and bundled it quickly, then made his way over to the light. He limped a bit, favoring his ankle, which dragged a tangled length of static line complete with carabiner snap links.

Ed landed in the clearing not far away. Within two minutes, Jacques, Ed and Morris were crouched in the trees together.

"What the hell did I trip over?" asked Jacques.

"That bonehead co-pilot managed to make a tripwire out of his intercom cord," said Ed. "His cord fouled your static line, holding it at the perfect angle for Morris to catch his ankle in it."

"How did you get me loose?" asked Morris, working to cut the static line from his ankle.

"I had the pilot take us up 8,000 feet to give us some drop height, and re-align to the DZ for another attempt. I left my static line clipped in the D-ring at the attachment point. I re-tied the chute end of the line to my groin straps, then had the co-pilot unscrew the attach point with a power driver. I sat in the doorway until it flew loose, and I let the static line pull me out."

"You exited a perfectly good airplane – yanked out by your groin?" asked Jacques, incredulous.

"No big deal. He'd have done the same for me," Ed shrugged.

44 – SENTRY DUTY

Morris awoke with a start. In a sweat, he blinked his eyes and tried to figure out where he was. It came back to him.

It was day four of the reconnaissance mission at the secret camp. Morris was not actually dangling from a Twin Otter somewhere over Lake of the Woods. Death was not imminent. Tension eased a bit, it was just a bad dream. Not that Morris felt entirely safe, because if the enemy discovered them, there would be a firefight for sure.

"Morris, it's your shift," Jacques' voice said in his earpiece.

"Yes. My shift. Right." Morris pulled himself out of his sleeping bag and looked at his watch. It was 1355. He would be on sentry duty for the next two hours, 1400 to 1600, while Jacques and Ed slept at base camp. Morris pressed to transmit: "Roger."

Base camp consisted of their well-camouflaged vehicle, a cooking area, three individual hootchies made of groundsheets for sleeping, and a place to take a crap. The hootchies were laid out in a triangle surrounding the cooking area, and the crapper was located well out of smelling distance.

So far, the group had been operating at night and sleeping during the day. Each man slept with his weapon and kept his two-way radio headset on, so whoever was on sentry duty could alert the others without leaving the sentry post.

The sentry post was about a hundred meters away, next to the roadway. Jacques was there now. Morris went for a piss and then to the vehicle to get some food. He grabbed a couple of granola bars and made sure his

canteen was full. Then he checked his weapon,
ammunition and radio battery. He made sure he had a
spare battery in his pocket, and headed to the sentry post.

Morris crawled up beside Jacques. "Any activity?" he
asked.

"Two guys passed by on a road run heading south
about 90 minutes ago. I managed only to get photos from
behind. You should be able to get face shots when they
get back."

"Have we seen these guys before?"

"The tall one, yes – we've been calling him Beanpole.
We haven't got a photo of the other guy yet."

Jacques handed Morris a digital SLR camera with a
long telephoto lens. Morris activated the LCD monitor
and viewed the images Jacques had shot: two men in
shorts and running shoes headed away from the camera,
one tall, one short.

"How many more do you figure before we have a
complete collection?" asked Morris.

"Other than the Arab, I think our rogue's gallery will
be complete when you get the short guy. We'll have a
total of six."

Morris nodded. The Arab had been difficult to
photograph. All the others did regular sentry duty at the
one post Ed had identified. They also went out on daily
road runs, making it easy to get good face shots.

"See you later," said Jacques as he left. "It's
dinnertime."

Morris settled in to the spot Jacques had vacated.
Well-concealed in the bushes, it was a good spot to
observe the road. Morris lined up the camera and took a
practice shot to check the exposure.

The day was warm and sunny. This spot was quite
pleasant, Morris thought. The mission was going well.

The first night had been difficult. The parachute drop
had been a near-disaster, and the move-in during darkness

had been stressful. As planned, they had pulled their vehicle into the trees a mile short of the objective.

The team had been ahead of schedule, but everyone was too keyed-up to rest as planned. They decided to start their first patrol early, about 0100 hrs. It had taken four hours to approach the objective on foot through the woods. The night vision equipment had worked well, but the group was on edge and highly cautious. They used the extra time to move slowly and securely. Subsequent night trips on the same path were much quicker, taking less than an hour.

The next day had also been difficult, and fruitless. That day was Thursday. The date was September 24th. It was the day of Kendo's second scheduled flight. The previous flight had produced the surprise visit of Detective Clark. They were hoping he would put in another appearance. No such luck. The team had watched the roadway for the entire day, and was rewarded with nothing.

The next period of time was much more productive. For two nights now, the team had been active during the entire period of darkness. They had confirmed the locations of every structure, access point, and sentry post at the objective. Tonight's task was to identify concealed positions from which manned, daytime observation of the objective would be possible. It was also time to visit five remote video cameras that had been placed two nights ago. It would be a full night of work.

Morris chewed on his granola bar as he thought about life. Long, slow periods with extensive sleep loss had been his least favorite activity while in the army. The best times had been when there was a mission to accomplish, and he had been on a motivated, determined team. If every mission in the army had been like this one, Morris thought, he might have stayed in.

The sound of running footsteps disturbed his thoughts. The two runners were returning from the south, sprinting for the finish line. Morris switched on the digital camera and lined up a shot. The two men came into view, running straight toward the camera. Morris shot six shots in rapid succession, and then ducked his head down into the bushes to avoid being seen.

Out of breath, the two men were laughing. The shorter man had won the race. Morris was impressed that these two had been running for the better part of two hours, and still had a strong finishing kick. They were strong runners.

"*In-akah tes-tahech raqm fee asi-baq!*" the taller man gasped. "*In-akah tes-tahech raqm fee asi-baq.*" He slapped the shorter man on the back.

Grinning, they began their walk back to camp together.

It sounded like Arabic. Morris pronounced the phrase to himself twice, then recorded it quietly with his Blackberry. Perhaps there would be intelligence value. It probably had no significant meaning.

Morris reviewed the images he had just captured. "I dub thee – Dopey," he whispered as he looked at a shot of the shorter runner. "Now we have five dwarfs: Sleepy, Bashful, Grumpy, Sneezy and Dopey. But no Snow White, just *the Arab*."

Having nothing else to do, Morris repeated the Arabic he had just heard to himself a few times.

45 – CLARK ARRIVES

It was first light, and Morris and Ed were well hidden in the forest about 200 meters south of the objective, about 50 meters from the road. Jacques was in a firing position keeping an eye on the road while Ed and Morris reviewed clips collected from the remote video cameras.

Morris loaded the memory stick from the fifth and final camera into the laptop. Speaking softly, Morris and Ed discussed what they had seen.

Camera one showed several clips of the Arab visiting one of the two sea containers. On one occasion, he brought food and spent an hour inside before leaving with an empty plate. On two other visits, he brought food but did not stay. On a fourth visit, he brought no food, stayed two hours, and walked away combing his hair. Morris and Ed agreed someone was living in the sea container.

Camera two had been located on a trail running north from the objective. It showed several trips made by Grumpy and Sneezy on an All Terrain Vehicle hauling a small trailer containing several long planks of lumber. They must have been constructing something up the trail somewhere, Morris and Ed agreed.

Cameras three and four showed movement of items into what looked to Morris like a storage building. Morris and his group were not aware it was the pig barn. Because Mohamed's team had completed the germ development phase, pigs were no longer needed at the camp, so none were present in the barn. Mohamed had given orders to move furniture and equipment that was no longer needed into the barn, which he planned to burn down shortly.

"I see lumber, a couple of gas cans, garbage bags…" said Morris as he examined thumbnail images for several clips. "What the hell is this?" He zoomed in on a yellow container that resembled a kitchen waste container.

"I recognize the symbol for medical waste," said Ed. "That looks like a syringe disposal container."

"And look what else this guy's carrying," said Morris. "Looks like a body bag."

"Here's another one," whispered Ed, pointing. "Only smaller."

"A body bag for a child!" Morris was shocked. "What the fuck!"

The two men looked at each other. In spite of the low light and dark camouflage face paint, each man could tell the other was smoldering with anger. There was the sound of a vehicle on the roadway.

"Guys, the black SUV just passed my position heading south," said Jacques over the radio. "It looked like Bashful was driving."

"It's Sunday morning," Ed replied. "There's nothing open in town yet."

"Something new is happening," said Morris. "Let's hang around."

Ed nodded. "Jacques, RV at our location."

A few moments later, Jacques joined them.

"Morris and I looked at the images, Jacques. They're preparing to do something interesting. Instead of going back to base camp for a rest, we want to return and observe the objective."

"Count me in," Jacques nodded.

"We move in ten minutes," said Ed. "Piss break. If you have something to eat, do it now. We'll be in close, and we may be stuck until nightfall." Ed showed Jacques the images on the laptop.

The team had already been active at the objective all night long. Undaunted, after exactly ten minutes, they headed back to the objective.

Ed put the group in an all-around defensive position, located where Ed could observe the vehicle hide. Being three men, each was responsible for one-third of the 360 degree circle. They kept close enough to kick each other, waiting for the SUV to return. They took turns maintaining watch, with two men at a time dozing in their firing positions. At 1000 hrs, the black SUV returned to the vehicle hide with two additional people inside.

Ed kicked to make sure Morris and Jacques were awake, and they both responded alertly.

The SUV stopped in the middle of the clearing. From the front, out stepped Detective Clark. Mohamed stepped out of the trees to greet him.

"How have you been, David?" Mohamed greeted the detective with a handshake.

"I drove all night. It was nicer coming here by plane." He stretched and yawned.

"Any problems with your passenger, this time?" asked Mohamed.

"None. He slept most of the way. I gave him a bottle of vodka."

"Good." Mohamed turned to speak with Grumpy and Sneezy. "This is subject number twenty. He is the open field test case. He is to be treated immediately." By 'treated,' Grumpy and Sneezy understood Mohamed meant 'infected' – Subject Twenty is to be *infected* immediately.

"I'm sorry about the mess with Subject Nineteen," said Clark.

"It is a good thing I was prepared with a sedative." Mohamed said to Clark. "It would have been good if you had been better prepared with a convincing cover story."

"I was filling in for Kendo, who managed to get himself killed." Clark was tired and in no mood to be challenged by Mohamed.

"Well, things don't always go as planned." Mohamed waved Grumpy and Sneezy forward to take Subject Twenty, who was too drunk to resist. They extracted him quickly from the back seat, tied his hands behind his back, and threw a sack over his head.

Mohamed watched as the driver backed the SUV into the hide position. Suddenly he raised his arm to stop the driver.

Mohamed strode to the back of the SUV and yanked off the tracking device from where Habib had mounted it ten days ago. "What the hell is this!" he exclaimed. He turned to the driver and slapped him hard. "You fucking idiot! Was this car in your sight the whole time?"

Hesam cringed and held his reddening cheek. "No, sir."

"The three of us had breakfast," said Detective Clark, "at the restaurant where you arranged for us meet. Both our cars were unattended for about an hour."

"This is a tracking device!" exclaimed Mohamed.

The two men who were escorting subject twenty had stopped. Mohamed turned to them.

"Tell Qamar the camp is now on alert! Everyone is to carry his weapon at all times! I want double surveillance on our perimeter. Tell Qamar to come and see me right away!"

The men nodded and hustled away.

Mohamed turned to Clark and drew his pistol, pointing it at him. "I was not impressed with your ability to execute your mission at our last meeting, David, now I am even less so."

Clark raised his hands, surprised and fearful.

"You have been followed from Ottawa." Mohamed took two quick steps toward Clark. "Get on your knees."

Clark was slow to comply. With a sharp stabbing motion, Mohamed struck him in the gut. Clark reacted as if he had been shot, falling to his knees with a groan. Mohamed put the pistol to Clark's forehead.

"Tell me why I should not kill you," he said coldly.

"I slipped my tail!" Clark gasped. "They've been watching me for a week, but I've been aware of it! I ditched the car that was following me before I left Ottawa."

"Did you tell Joris you were under surveillance?"

"No."

"Why am I the only one concerned about not being discovered!" Mohamed backhanded Clark on the side of the head with the pistol, knocking him to the ground. Mohamed then removed Clark's pistol from its holster. "If you wish to live, tell me what you think is going on here!"

Clark began to babble. "I don't know – I don't care – something to do with drugs – making a new drug and testing it on the human trash we send you – as long as I get paid, I'm not curious. Nobody knows about my participation, not even my wife. All we care about is the money."

"I am surrounded by idiots. You are pathetic. Get up." Mohamed stepped back, keeping his pistol pointed at Clark as he got up. "I know you are a terrible liar under pressure. You demonstrated that when Subject Nineteen became so concerned in Winnipeg that he fled the car because he did not believe you. I'll let you live for now. Later, you will tell me more about your relationship with Joris, and then I will let you go free. You can wait in isolation, where the pigs died."

Mohamed watched to see if Clark reacted to that statement. Clark had no reaction. If he had been alarmed, Mohamed would have concluded that Clark knew about the virus development. Clark did not seem fearful of becoming infected, so Mohamed concluded van Praag had not told Clark any details about the camp. Mohamed planned to lock Clark in Isolation 1A, the pig chamber. Mohamed had cleaned it thoroughly after the latest group of pigs had been put through because Dr. Tragar had neglected to tell him there were no new pigs expected.

Ed, Morris and Jacques watched from concealment as Mohamed marched Clark down the trail, and then the driver finished backing the SUV into the hide position.

"All clear," Ed whispered.

"People are dying," Morris said to Ed and Jacques. "The Arab refers to them as pigs."

"He said *isolation* – that might mean the sea containers. Let's find out where he puts Clark," said Jacques.

"OK." Ed pulled out his sketch of the objective. "We'll use our west approach and occupy OP 3. We can observe the sea containers from there, and also see the ATV path they use on their trips north."

Moving slowly and cautiously, the men made their way through the woods and got into position. OP 3 was in dense brush, where they could not lay on the ground without losing visibility on the sea containers. For about five hours, they had to use a kneeling position in order to see through the brush. During that period, the group observed two interesting events.

Using binoculars, Morris observed the dead body of Subject Nineteen as it was removed from Isolation Chamber 1B. Morris could not discern the identity of the corpse, because it was contained within a body bag. He could not tell who was removing it, because that person – Mohamed – was wearing a HAZMAT suit. Morris saw Mohamed wheel the corpse to the Ice Cream Truck, which he could tell was refrigerated. Vapor appeared around the door crack when Mohamed opened it, clearly visible to Morris through his binoculars. Jacques used the telephoto lens to capture all these images.

The second event occurred at 1500 hours. Ed saw two men with rifles in HAZMAT suits drive past riding an ATV hauling a trailer with Subject Twenty tied up in it. Morris watched through his binoculars as the two men placed him in one of the two sea containers. Morris observed the double-door system and realized it was an airlock.

At 1530 hours, Ed gave hand signals to withdraw. He led the team back to the spot Ed had previously designated as their objective rendezvous – located 200 meters south, a safe distance from the objective – so they could talk without being heard.

"These people are not inventing a new drug," said Morris.

"No shit," said Ed.

"They seem to be doing some kind of bio-weapon. The test subjects are guinea pigs," said Jacques.

"It's time to call the fuckin' cavalry," said Ed.

"I agree," said Morris. "The cops need to bust this place ASAP."

"The Arab knows his camp has been discovered," said Jacques. "His guys are all armed and on alert. The cops will need a major force."

"They'll need a fifty guys to surround this place," said Ed.

"That will take them some time to organize," said Jacques. "It'll take them until dawn to get in position without daytime recce. There's not enough time before dark. It'll be last light in a couple of hours."

"You can guide them," said Morris. "You're our LO," meaning Liaison Officer.

"What about our cover story? If we report now, they will know we are not in Las Vegas." said Ed.

"This thing is too big to worry about that," said Morris. "Liam will have to keep us out of legal hot water for what we've done. We can't let these terrorists get away. Agreed?"

Ed and Jacques nodded.

"What do you want us to do, boss?" asked Ed.

"You two should go back to our base camp and send an email to Liam and Alex James. Give them everything we have, including the images we just got. Then follow up with a phone call. Jacques, you should take the truck back to Kenora and link up with the cops there. Ed, you come back and join me here.

"Where are you going to be?" asked Ed.

"I'll be at OP 3, keeping an eye on them."

"All you have is your walkie-talkie gear," said Jacques. "The base camp will be out of range."

"I know." Morris turned to Ed. "Get back as soon as you finish reporting. Bring some food, a satellite phone, and all the ammo you can carry."

46 – DEAD MEN WALKING

It was midnight, and Morris was about to try to get some rest while Ed maintained watch. Morris had been watching activity at the camp from concealment in OP 3 for about nine hours.

He heard a floatplane arrive on the lake at sunset and then depart, but it had not been visible from OP 3. Shortly after that, Morris observed a new person, presumably from the floatplane, as he entered one of the ATCO trailers, arguing loudly with the Arab. The Arab had departed the trailer ten minutes later. Morris regretted he was unable to photograph the new arrival because Jacques had taken the camera.

At last light, the storage building was set ablaze. Morris realized the enemy was planning to depart, and was burning evidence.

Ed returned an hour after that, carrying two belts of 7.62mm caliber machine gun ammunition around his chest, and a C7 machine gun. He reported that Jacques had taken the truck, laptop, photos, sketches and maps that would be needed for the police to plan an assault on the camp.

Ed was currently using night vision goggles. The storage building had burned down to embers. There was enough moonlight to see easily, and Ed saw a figure in HAZMAT equipment emerge from a trailer.

Ed gave Morris a nudge and pointed to the figure. Morris got up and put on his goggles.

The figure crossed the clearing at a brisk pace and entered the sea container where Subject Twenty had been placed. A few moments later, the muffled sound of a man inside, screaming frantically, was followed by three shots, and then the screaming stopped. Morris felt a surge of adrenaline and his mouth went dry.

Twenty minutes later, the HAZMAT figure departed the container carrying a cylindrical object resembling a large coffee urn, taking it with him back to the trailer.

It started to piss down rain. Morris no longer felt he could fall asleep, so he took the satellite phone and moved a safe distance into the woods where he would not be heard by the enemy, and then placed a phone call to Jacques to report the situation. On his return to OP 3, he took care to avoid the extra enemy sentries that the Arab had put out.

In the lab, Mohamed was getting very tired of the discussion he was having with Dr. Tragar. "But Graciano, we must have a safety sample. What if the primary sample develops a problem during the next six months before it is needed for use?"

"I have been working since my arrival here today to ensure the plasma I have processed from Subject Nineteen is satisfactory. All unbound protein was concentrated by ultra filtration using YM9 membrane, and the concentrate was applied and eluted using a linear gradient at a flow rate of 9.52 milliliters per minute!"

"Doctor, the point is not the quality of your work. My point is that the use of only one single source for our virus does not follow the protocol ordered by van Praag. We are to obtain, purify and process two samples in total. We must produce plasma from a second subject, namely Subject Twenty. The purpose is to have a complete duplicate sample of our virus from a different individual. If one individual has an unexpected medical condition that might interfere with the virus, we have a second unrelated individual that we can rely on!"

"I can assure you I incubated correctly."

"That is not the point, Doctor. The point is you agreed to produce two separately-sourced, one-liter virus samples as your final deliverables for this project."

"But I can assure you the isocratic elution phase was at the optimum."

Mohamed pushed the sample container toward Tragar. "If you do not produce a complete second sample from the blood I have drained from Subject Twenty here, I can assure you that van Praag will not pay the final installment of your honorarium fee."

"I take this opportunity to inform you, that..."

With that, Mohamed decided enough was enough. He sucker-punched Tragar, breaking several teeth and causing blood to flow immediately from his nose. Tragar turned to run but Mohamed hauled him to the floor and sat on his chest. After pinning Tragar's arms to prevent the doctor from fending off blows, Mohamed beat Tragar's face with his fists until it was a bloody, swollen pulp.

Subject Nineteen had been infected with the Tragar strain, and the doctor had properly prepared one liter of concentrated virus plasma and placed it in a double-sealed cylindrical container made of stainless steel. But it was vital for Mohamed's plan that Tragar processed the blood from Subject Twenty as well, because Mohamed had infected Subject Twenty with the Ziad strain of the virus. Mohamed needed a one-liter container of his own strain, for his own purposes.

Mohamed stopped the beating. Not because his rage had subsided, but because his arms were tired. He realized Tragar was losing consciousness. He stood and fetched a glass of water, then threw it in Tragar's face. Tragar gasped and coughed, spitting blood and two teeth.

"Now will you process Subject Twenty?"

Tragar nodded silently.

Mohamed helped Tragar to his feet and guided him to the lab bench.

For the next three hours, Mohamed watched Tragar work, making him explain each step to ensure he was doing it properly. When the doctor was finished, Mohamed tied him securely to a chair.

"Now, I am going to show you something, you fool." Mohamed turned on the computer monitor.

For the next fifteen minutes, Mohamed explained to Tragar how the Ziad strain had been developed. Tragar was, at first, incredulous. As Mohamed went on, demonstrating his own quantitative results. The results established the kill rate of the Ziad strain using Tragar's own methods, and Tragar gradually became a believer. Mohamed finished with a run-through of the Ziad Scenario on the computer simulation.

"So, as you can see, the Ziad strain has the exact same infectivity ratio as the Tragar strain, but with an 80% fatality rate. Fantastic, no? Shall we publish a paper together? Please, you may list your name first."

Mohamed could tell from Tragar's reaction that the doctor had been convinced. And Mohamed was reassured that his strain would be successful. Up until that moment, Mohamed had not been absolutely certain that the Ziad virus would work at the 80% rate when he released it.

"What's wrong, doctor?" Mohamed began laughing. "At a loss for words? Does the great Graciano Tragar-Mierda, Ph.D., CEO and Chairman of Nothing have no speech prepared for this moment? No need to answer, Doctor, you have no audience."

Tragar hung his head.

"No, wait – I see your audience, doctor." Mohamed pointed to the number at the bottom of the screen. "At the end of week fifty of my scenario, your audience will be five billion, three-hundred eleven million, two-hundred thirty four thousand, three hundred seventy eight dead people, killed by our virus. Congratulations, doctor, on your world-changing discovery."

Using a felt marker, Mohamed wrote a 'T' on Tragar container and 'Z' on the Ziad container. "I better not mix them up," he said, laughing again.

"I have other work to do now, which will include killing you – if these samples do not test out in the morning. I will see you in a few hours and we will examine the samples together in the microscope, so I can be assured of the quality of our work."

"My work is immaculate," whispered the doctor.

"You are arrogant and self-assured to the end." Mohamed double-checked Tragar's binding ropes. "Enjoy the rest of your evening."

Mohamed switched the lab lighting from white to red. Taking the two virus containers with him, he stepped out of the lab into the darkness.

Ed noticed the flash of red light as Mohamed exited the lab. Putting on his night vision goggles, Ed watched him work. The rain had let up, and the night was still and quiet.

Mohamed ran a flexible hose from the propane tank to a connector fitted on the outside of the first sea container. He then drew his pistol, opened the airlock door, and entered. Muffled yelling emitted from the sea container, and fifteen minutes later he brought out Detective Clark, badly beaten, in leg irons. Mohamed chained him to the sea container.

Mohamed opened the tank valve feeding the propane hose. Morris and Ed heard a faint hiss as propane began to flow into the first sea container. Out of sight from OP 3, Mohamed then used a screwdriver to remove the valve handle, making it impossible to close the valve.

For the next half hour, nothing happened except for the lightening of the sky. It would soon be dawn. It was time for Morris and Ed to decide what to do next.

"That first sea container is rigged to burn," Ed whispered into Morris' ear.

"They must be planning to burn or blow up this whole place," whispered Morris.

"I also think the Arab intends to kill Clark."

Morris nodded. "Serves him right, but Clark may know what's going on here. He's worth more to us alive. If the Arab plans to shoot him out there in the clearing, I'll shoot the Arab first."

Ed nodded. "That will draw return fire. I'll move east to OP 4 and cover you from there."

"Good enough. After I take out the Arab, I'll go in and grab Clark and bring him back here. Then we use fire and movement to withdraw."

"Where is the cavalry?" asked Ed.

"I've been getting text updates from Jacques all night. They left Kenora about an hour ago with OPP SWAT and RCMP ERT. They have about 20 troops. All we have to do is keep the enemy contained here until they arrive and surround the place. We don't want to kill the enemy – we need to find out who they're working for. All we need to do is prevent them breaking out and heading north. If they go south, they'll run right into the troops."

Nodding, Ed turned and moved out. Ed headed slowly and quietly to OP 4. It took about ten minutes for him to report that he was in position. The rain had increased conveniently, hitting the leaves and nicely drowning out the sound of his movement.

Morris removed the scope from his rifle. Water on the lenses was a problem. In the rain, at this close distance, iron sights would be more effective. As he watched Clark in the compound, waiting for the next development, Morris wondered who it was Mohamed had been feeding in the second sea container.

47 – DECISIVE ENGAGEMENT

Clark was on his knees, tears in his eyes, looking down at the dirt. Mohamed had unchained him and made him walk closer to the furnace, so he would not have to drag the body very far to burn it.

Mohamed's pistol was still pointed at the ground, not at Clark. Mohamed was talking to Clark. Here it comes, thought Morris, as he saw Mohamed raise his pistol arm slightly.

"I'm taking a shot," Morris whispered in his microphone to Ed.

"Roger. I'm ready to support."

Now was the moment of truth – to kill or not to kill. The shot, thought Morris, does not get much easier. From the kneeling position, at less than 40 meters from the target, Morris could aim for any part of the Arab's anatomy and expect a hit.

He placed the foresight on the Arab's temple, and evaluated his sight picture.

This shot would be an immediate kill, thought Morris. But there is information in that brain that would be good to have.

The Arab held his pistol straight-armed, with arm raised at a 45-degree angle. Morris inhaled and moved the foresight to the Arab's bicep, exhaled a half-breath, then held his breath and squeezed off the shot.

BANG!

Morris kept track of his sight picture as the rifle recoiled upwards. The bullet spun clockwise, flying a nearly flat trajectory, breaking the sound barrier in its short flight to the target. It produced a mini sonic boom in the form of a loud crack as it passed through Mohamed's bicep, struck and broke his humerus, and then deflected slightly downwards, eventually embedding itself in a tree on the far side of the clearing.

Mohamed's arm fell because it suddenly lacked the skeletal support necessary to hold up the pistol. Mohamed dropped it and grabbed his bicep. Clark screamed and fell onto his side, thinking he had been shot.

Mohamed turned to look into the trees, searching for the source of the bullet. He reached for the pistol with his good arm. Two more shots from Morris struck the ground near the pistol, splattering Mohamed's face with mud. Mohamed left the pistol and darted between the two sea containers for cover.

From inside the living quarters, Qamar and Hesam heard the shooting. Qamar yelled in Arabic and they grabbed their weapons.

Mohamed saw Qamar as he came through the doorway. Mohamed yelled in Arabic and pointed at Clark with his good arm.

Qamar was alarmed to see Mohamed's arm and hand were soaked in blood. Qamar and Hesam raised their rifles to shoot Clark. Qamar fired a burst, hitting Clark in the thigh.

Ed opened fire on Qamar with two 5-round bursts into the wet ground in front of him. Qamar heard the crack of the bullets and saw dirt and muddy water fly up in front of him. He turned and ran behind the living quarters followed by Hesam.

Mohamed decided the authorities had arrived, and an all-out assault was underway. With his good arm, he opened the valve connecting the two sea containers, and propane from Isolation Chamber One began to flow into Isolation Chamber Two. Then he made a run for it, joining Qamar and Hesam behind the living quarters.

Seeing all clear, Morris moved forward quickly into the clearing, grabbing Clark by the collar.

"Get up!" Morris pulled Clark to his feet and helped him hobble toward the trees. As they approached the edge of the clearing, Morris heard a pounding coming from one of the sea containers. There was someone inside, he realized, being poisoned by the propane gas!

Morris dragged the detective stumbling through the brush. After several steps, Morris stopped and tripped Clark to the ground, keeping him at gunpoint.

"Ed, there's somebody locked in the sea container." Morris said into his microphone, breathing hard. "I'm going back."

"Roger. Let me move so I can cover you better. Give me thirty seconds."

Clark looked up at Morris. "It's you!"

"You're lucky I didn't let the Arab kill you," Morris said to Clark. "You happen to be more valuable alive than dead."

Coming from the camp, yells in Arabic were followed by bursts of fire.

Morris looked back at the sea containers. "I'm looking for somebody." He looked at Clark. "Stay here, or else."

"I can't move on my own," said Clark, pointing to the hole in his leg.

Morris looked at the wound. There was not much blood. The small, speedy 5.56mm caliber bullet had passed through fat and muscle, missing the bone. "Bullshit. The round from that M-16 passed through clean. It's a known problem that the bullet does not always change direction when it penetrates flesh. It doesn't always stop a determined enemy soldier."

Morris started to search Clark's pockets. He found a Blackberry cellphone, and quickly removed the battery. Morris put the phone and battery in his pocket to take it with him.

Morris looked at Clark one last time. "Ed is in the woods. If he sees you moving, he will kill you."

From his new position, Ed heard the sound of an approaching propeller airplane. He spoke into his mouthpiece. "I think their plane is coming back. I'm in position, move now."

"Roger, I'm going back in." Morris turned and ran toward the sea container.

Morris approached the door, seeing it was locked. The person inside had stopped pounding. He gave the padlock a tug, but it was secure. Turning the lock to the right, Morris jammed the muzzle of his rifle against the body of the lock, then stepped away, turning to avoid being hit by flying metal parts. "This better not light the propane," he said to Ed. He fired a single shot, hoping there were no leaks in the vicinity of his muzzle flash.

The bullet's steel penetrator tip pierced the brass body of the lock and destroyed the lock mechanism. Morris gave the lock another tug, but it would not open. Morris lined up and fired another shot. This time the shackle flew open.

Morris tossed the lock aside and pulled the lever to operate the door mechanism. The door suddenly burst open with a loud bass-drum bang, and Morris could smell the escaping propane. He looked at the dimly lit interior, and pulled out his flashlight.

Morris took a deep breath, and entered the sea container. He heard a burst of machinegun fire behind him and hoped it was Ed providing some covering fire. He shone the flashlight around the interior. There was a person lying on the floor, not moving.

From his new firing position, Ed could hear more yelling and saw some fleeting targets, which he did not bother to shoot at. The enemy were staying well clear of the sea containers, and were not showing much interest in fighting back. They were firing indiscriminately at Ed's previous firing position, at random trees, and into the air, seemingly to give themselves the courage to maneuver.

Then Ed heard the floatplane approaching the dock.

"They're gathering up to withdraw," Ed said to Morris. "There's a floatplane arriving at the dock." Ed saw Morris in the clearing. He had a woman with long dark hair over his shoulder. He was carrying her quickly out of the clearing. When Ed saw they were out of sight in the trees, he grabbed his satellite phone and speed-dialed Jacques.

"Jacques here."

"We're going to need some air support, quick," said Ed. "These guys have a floatplane at the dock. They're going to escape!"

"Roger. I hear shooting in the background."

"The Arab was about to kill Clark, so Morris shot him in the arm. I pushed the enemy back with harassing fire so Morris could pull a girl out of the sea container. She's going to need medical attention."

"Roger. We have paramedics and we're heading straight up the road now. We are 10 clicks south of your location."

"Ed!" It was Morris over the radio. "I need you here."

"Roger," Ed said into his microphone. "Gotta go, Jacques," he said into the satellite phone. Ed got up and started moving quickly through the trees.

Ed found Morris kneeling with the girl laying on the ground in front of him.

"She has a pulse," said Morris.

But she was not breathing, so Morris began mouth-to-mouth rescue breathing. He caught a faint whiff of propane gas come out of her lungs.

"Jacques and the ERT are less than 10 clicks away," said Ed. "I reported the floatplane."

The girl suddenly gasped, and then began to breathe on her own.

"I left Clark over there in the direction of OP 3," said Morris. "Go get him."

A minute later, Ed came back. "I can't find him."

Morris held the unconscious girl in his arms. "This is Candice. She needs medical attention ASAP. You'll have to take her to the roadway."

Ed took her in his arms. "What are you going to do?"

"I'm going back to see if I can turn off the propane."

"Fuck that! It's too dangerous!"

Coming from the lake, they heard the sound of the floatplane running up for takeoff.

"I think the Arab and his dwarves are departing." Morris picked up his weapon. "How big was that plane?"

"It could hold them all," said Ed.

"If I can't cut off the propane easily, I'll be right back." Morris turned and ran.

Morris paused at the edge of the clearing, and then entered it on the run, dashing over to the sea containers. Keeping his back to the metal wall, he made his way along the length of the container in the direction of the propane tank at the center of the camp. At the end corner, Morris found the hose connection leading to the main propane tank.

Here is where the propane is going in, thought Morris. There's no valve! Morris looked at the main tank. There must be a valve at that end of the hose, he thought, but could not see one.

Morris considered making a run to the tank through the clearing. The floatplane had finished takeoff. There was probably nobody left in the camp.

"Help me! *Au secours! Aiutatemi! Ayúdame!*" There was someone in the trailer.

Morris aimed his rifle at the source of the sound. The trailer door was open. Morris could see the silhouette of a man seated in a chair. It looked like his hands were tied behind his back.

Morris ran across the clearing and in through the trailer doorway. He dropped to the kneeling position and swung his weapon in a rapid arc, looking for targets. The only person in the room was the man in the chair. Morris saw that his eyes were swollen shut, and his face had numerous cuts and abrasions. He had been badly beaten.

"Who are you?" Morris demanded.

"I take this opportunity to inform you, the cull was to be less than two-hundred and fifty million people – not more than that." Dr. Tragar slurred his speech because of his missing teeth and swollen jaw. "I am Chief Scientist. My work was meticulous. It is not 80%! It was beyond my scope of responsibility to manage all the attributes and contingencies of the daily operation of this lab. My colleagues here did not adhere to the testing protocols. I have no legal or moral responsibility for the outcome projected in the scenario."

"What the hell have you been doing here?"

"Morris!" It was Jacques' voice, coming over the radio headset.

"Jacques! You're back in range. I'm in the camp, in what appears to be a lab."

"I see Ed – he's by the side of the road!"

"He's got Candice. She was overcome by propane gas. Keep your men back – this place stinks of propane. The Arab took off with his men a minute ago. I'm here with a scientist tied in a chair."

Dr. Tragar was completely confused. He could not see Morris well, and thought Morris was talking to him. He began to babble loudly while Morris tried in vain to hear Jacques.

"Shut up!" Morris ordered Tragar. "I'm trying to talk on my radio!"

Tragar continued to produce a stream of unrelated, legalistic sentences seemingly intended to fend off blame.

"Just a minute Jacques." Morris pulled out his Rambo knife and began to cut the ropes holding Tragar. "You're dominating the conversation," said Morris, exasperated. "But the words coming out of your mouth make no sense!" Morris cut the final rope and helped Tragar to his feet.

Morris grabbed Tragar by the shoulders. "Do you know how to turn off the propane?"

Tragar would not stop talking.

"Will you shut the fuck up?" Morris led him to the door, pushed him through, and slammed it behind him.

"Jacques, the Arab and his dwarves have been developing some kind of super-germ that will kill hundreds of millions of people. I just spoke with their Chief Scientist. I'm going to do a quick walk through and report what I see."

"Go ahead."

"There's a computer. The screen saver is on." Morris touched the shift key and the monitor lit up. "The display shows a continental map of the earth. There are big black blobs in all the metropolitan areas, with small spots of pink, yellow and red around. The cities in the desert areas are white and blue. The screen title is Ziad Scenario, and there is a very big number at the bottom of the screen. Write this down: five billion, three hundred eleven million, two hundred thirty four thousand, three hundred seventy eight. It also says week equals fifty. Got that?"

"Got it."

Outside the trailer, Tragar stumbled toward the propane tank, staring at the ground. His knees were stiff and weak from being tied up all night. He stumbled and fell. At that moment, the floatplane zoomed overhead.

In the plane, Mohamed had just pressed the button on one of the detonators for the umpteenth time. He had tried two devices, and neither one triggered a detonation. "Curse these devices!"

"But we must surely be in range now!" exclaimed Qamar.

"That idiot van Praag had the detonators installed inside metal containers, shielding them from the signal. The sea containers and propane tank are metal!"

"What do you want to do?" asked Qamar.

"I have tracer ammunition." Mohamed inserted a magazine and cocked his weapon. "Have the pilot fly over again."

Qamar placed his pistol against the pilot's head. "You heard him."

Back on the ground, Tragar had found Mohamed's pistol where it had fallen. Squinting through swollen eyelids, Tragar could make out the floatplane as it turned over the lake, heading for another pass. Tragar sniffed and glared at the sea containers. Propane was leaking through the air filtration systems in both containers.

Mohamed forced the floatplane door open with his foot and shoved the muzzle of his automatic weapon into the air stream. As the plane passed over the campsite, he fired a long burst, emptying the 30-round magazine. Ejecting brass casings bounced all around the aircraft cabin.

On the ground, red-hot tracer bullets struck the earth in an advancing line following the flight path, narrowly missing Tragar and the sea containers.

Angered, Tragar pointed the pistol at the rapidly departing airplane and gave the trigger a jerk. The pistol did not fire. "*Merde*," he said.

The airplane lined up for another pass as Tragar examined the pistol. Seeing another attack from the air was imminent, Tragar took shelter between the two sea containers. He wrinkled his nose at the increasing bad odor of the propane.

As the plane finished its turn, Mohamed loaded another 30-round magazine and cocked his weapon. He looked to his left and saw a line of police cars and tactical trucks speeding along the roadway toward his camp. This would be his last chance.

On the ground, fumbling with the pistol, Tragar discovered the safety catch and disengaged it. "The Great Graciano can understand anything!" He gently pinched his bloody nostrils with his free hand, and aimed the pistol at the approaching plane.

He pulled the trigger.

Illumination from the instant fireball created a second sunrise.

From the air, Qamar and the pilot saw the flash fire engulf the sea containers and Dr. Tragar. The pressure wave from the blast shook the plane and deafened the passengers as the pilot veered left to avoid the rising flames. Twin jets of flame spewed from the ends of the first sea container as the end doors blew out. Fire spread from the first container to the second through the connecting pipe that was supposed to carry infected air. The second container blew one-half second after the first, propelling its doors outward followed by flames rivaling a rocket liftoff.

From the lead police car, Jacques saw flashes reflecting off the lake and squinted to view a mushroom cloud of black smoke and brilliant orange flame form and rise quickly. He saw the floatplane just miss the rising cloud.

Ed was at the roadside. He threw his body over the girl lying on the ground to shield her.

Inside the lab, Morris had just clicked the button RUN SCENARIO AGAIN. The shock wave shattered laboratory glass and rocked the trailer on its foundation. Morris was knocked onto his ass and the computer monitor tumbled into his lap. Morris picked up the monitor and stared at the display intently. He had just missed the start of the scenario – it was already at week three. As the weeks ticked by in rapid succession, Morris looked at a spread of infection that was rapid and simultaneous in all parts of the world. The part along the US Eastern Seaboard appeared to be in the lead.

Morris dumped the monitor and as he was getting off the floor, he noticed a paper printout that fluttered next to his hand. He grabbed it and ran directly for the door.

Morris ran through the doorway into a wall of heat. Shielding his eyes, he saw flames belching from a sea container were blasting the propane tank 20 feet away.

Bacon Boxcutters

The gas hose connected to the tank was flailing wildly like a fire hose without a fireman, spewing a jet of flame in random directions. The propane tank was heating up, and it started to emit a screaming sound as the safety valves began to vent hot propane.

Unseen by anyone, the fuel gauge needle on the propane tank was at 51% and falling.

The accommodation trailer, having been in alignment with the first sea container to explode, was cracked open in the middle. Morris picked his way through the rubble as he rushed to place it between himself and the propane tank. Morris thought about diving into the lake and making a swim for it, but decided that would be too slow. Then he spotted the outhouse. Without hesitation, Morris slid quickly feet first into the exposed end of the rectangular trench and down into the ten-foot deep hole, the bottom four feet of which consisted of shit and piss.

"Once more unto the breach, dear friends," Morris said over the radio.

The propane tank was screaming louder and the pitch continued to increase. The gauge now read 50%.

"Morris!" The headset was still working as Morris stood up to his chest in human waste.

"I'm alive," Morris replied. "But I'm not sure I want to be." Morris looked at the paper in his hand, and then tucked it in his jacket. "The propane tank is screaming, and it's going to blow at any moment!"

"Get out of there!" ordered Jacques.

"I'm in shit, and for once, that's a good thing," said Morris. "I'm going to stay right here at the bottom of their *latrine facility*."

"I just told the ERT Commander to hold his men back. Ed is here with a female who is getting medical attention."

"Keep a look out for Clark. He got away. Did you get anything airborne to go after the floatplane?"

"Just a second, the ERT Commander wants to speak with you."

"Fine. I don't seem to have any other calls right now," said Morris. Morris cupped his hands over both ears, attempting to block the sound of the screaming propane tank.

"Mr. Parker? This is Captain Sylvester. I understand the sea containers were rigged for detonation. Is that what happened?"

"Yes. Captain, did you get any air assets to go after the floatplane?"

"What floatplane?"

"The one that landed on the lake here ten minutes ago! It's full of escaping terrorists!"

"Uh, we seem to have a communication problem on that one. We didn't bring the right radio…."

"Jacques has a satellite phone. Use that!"

"OK, will do. Just tell me about that propane tank."

"It's painted in disruptive pattern – quite a good match for the forest decor. What else do you need to know?"

"The sound. Is it going up in pitch, or down?"

Morris listened for a moment. "The pitch is decreasing now!"

"That's great! The safety valves are working to release excess pressure. Reduction in pitch means the temperature is going down. The fire in the sea containers must be burning out."

"I'm not reassured," said Morris. "And it stinks like shit in here!"

Unseen by anyone, the propane gas volume gauge read 49%, and the oxygen bladder ruptured. Hot liquid propane began to mix with liquid oxygen inside the tank becoming rocket fuel. Tank Pressure approached 1000 psi. After fabrication, the tank had been factory pressure-tested to 375 psi.

Flames continued to heat the tank and its contents. The mix of hot liquid propane and liquid oxygen circulating in the lower half of the tank caused the steel below the level of the liquid to heat at a different rate than the steel above. The steel below was kept relatively cool by the liquid. Because there was no liquid near the top of the tank to absorb the heat, the line between very hot steel and less-hot steel was subject to an enormous amount of shear stress, and the tank was about to rupture like a fatty sausage on the grill.

Back at the ERT command truck, Captain Sylvester was feeling confident. "Let me reassure you there, Mr. Parker. My brother is a fireman and he tells me that large tanks like the one you photographed have government-approved safety features that will absolutely prevent..."

KABOOM!

The propane tank burst like a gigantic hand grenade, sending chunks of steel the size of dinner plates and larger in all directions.

Detective Clark was speeding northbound on an ATV when the propane tank exploded, causing him to miss a sharp turn and crash into the bushes. He looked back to see the forest was ablaze. He shunted the ATV around and got it back on the road, then took off again.

Trees all around the camp were fully enflamed. Despite being very wet, the fireball had been hot enough and large enough to bend, break and/or ignite everything within a one-hundred meter radius of ground zero.

Two hundred meters from ground zero, a hunk of steel the size of the Federal Government Telephone Directory struck the ERT command truck just above Captain Sylvester's head, smashing a large hole through the wall and the squad's fantasy hockey pool standings chart on the inside of the vehicle. On the far side of the interior, the steel embedded itself into a bank of electronic communications equipment. Sparks flew as the equipment shorted out, and then flames erupted with a sharp puff of smoke.

"Morris!" Ed shouted into his microhone. There was no answer. "Come with me." Ed grabbed a paramedic and a fire extinguisher and headed toward the blaze.

The Captain could no longer communicate with Morris because his handset had gone dead. Turning to look at the truck behind him, the Captain went pale as he saw the size of the hole and its proximity to his head. "Fire! Fire!" he shouted, when he saw the flames.

A nearby constable calmly removed the vehicle's fire extinguisher and quickly put out the fire.

Jacques had just finished a conversation in French on the satellite phone, when a corporal came to speak to Captain Sylvester.

"Sir," said the corporal. "Our closest air asset is in Winnipeg, and it can't get off the ground in less than half an hour. They just found the helicopter crew at Tim Horton's."

"Is that the best we can do, dammit?" exclaimed Captain Sylvester.

"I made a call to my nephew," Jacques explained. "He's on OJT in Cold Lake, Alberta. He's the duty officer this morning, and I told him what's going on here. As a favor to me, he's going to send along some air assets. I promised him that you would put in a priority request through your chain so he doesn't end up doing extra duties for exceeding his authority."

In Cold Lake, Second-Lieutenant Nicholas Tremblay was performing his first shift as Duty Officer in the Operations Center of 409 Tactical Fighter Squadron that early Sunday morning, while senior officers from his squadron were in Winnipeg. The purpose of their visit was for a Change of Appointment Ceremony and the Battle of Britain Parade, which included a flypast of CF-18 Fighter Aircraft.

Jacques had told Nicholas that the floatplane passengers were escaping terrorists who had been preparing a super-germ capable of killing hundreds of millions of people worldwide. Second-Lieutenant Tremblay, on his own initiative, caused a flash operational message to be sent ordering the four visiting fighter planes to be scrambled on an anti-terrorist intercept mission over Kenora. That order caused two Lieutenant-Colonels (including his Commanding Officer) and two Majors to be aroused from their beds and get airborne as soon as possible. Takeoff occurred within 12 minutes after receipt of the message by the Winnipeg Operations Center. The four fighter jets proceeded at Mach 1.8, fanning out to search for their target.

The CO identified and intercepted the floatplane seven minutes later as it was crossing into US airspace. North American Aerospace Defense Command, NORAD, ordered the fighters to follow the target. They were unable to do anything more than observe, however, buzzing like angry hornets, as the floatplane landed on Lake of the Woods and discharged its passengers into the forest. Mohamed and his men waited until the jets headed back to base, and then they left the area in vehicles that had been pre-positioned for their escape.

It had taken twenty minutes before Captain Sylvester's request for air support made its way through the chain, receiving final approval two minutes after the fighters had already made their interception.

After the mission was over, Second-Lieutenant Tremblay received an *attaboy* from his CO for his prompt and decisive action based on the information received from his uncle.

The pilot of the floatplane later credited the arrival of the fighter jets with saving his life. He was certain that he would have been shot after landing, but the terrorists were spooked by the jets and convinced that they were about to be caught. They simply wanted to escape into the woods as quickly as possible.

48 – PHL CHRISTMAS PARTY

It was the annual Christmas Party, and PHL employees packed The Cumberland Arms. Morris, Ed and Jacques sat at their regular table, holding court.

Conan had just heard the story of Ed discovering Morris in the outhouse hole for about the fifth time since it happened almost three months ago. He left the table shaking his head. Each time Ed told it, it got funnier. In this version, Morris lifted a burning slab of rubble as he rose heroically from beneath the ground to the sound of quadruple sonic booms as the F-18 jets arrived over the objective traveling at Mach 2.

In searching the objective while it was still surrounded by burning trees, Ed and the ERT squad had been expecting to find only dead bodies.

The first body found consisted of not much more than a torso. It had been embedded in the electric generator mechanism where it had obviously been propelled by the blast. It could not be identified because it was too badly burned. Morris suspected it was the Chief Scientist.

The second body had been found in the wrecked refrigerator truck, still partially frozen. Ed ensured that body was immediately placed in a double-sealed body bag because he suspected it to be infected. Using DNA samples and some good basic police work, that body had later been identified as the man they had called Subject Nineteen. He was Harold Kozminski, a homeless Ottawa man. This person was the subject who had arrived with Clark in Winnipeg on stakeout day.

The third body had been Morris, still alive, but in the most gross and scary condition of all three, according to Ed. Ed was reluctant to assist Morris to get out of the hole, because he was blackened by soot and stinking with

human waste. Morris had hollered just before the jets
passed over, startling an ERT member witless. They
removed a large chunk of charred roofing to discover him
below. They lowered a rope and Morris was able to climb
out without anyone having to touch him, and then he
proceeded straight to the lake to rinse off.

Due to the heat and magnitude of the propane blast,
very little intelligence had been recovered from the camp.
But two items were proving to be valuable.

The printout showed projected infections for each
week in a fifty-week period, computed with an infection
growth rate of 30% and a death rate of 2%. At week one,
there were four thousand infections and eighty deaths. For
each week it showed 130% of the count of the previous
week's infections and deaths. At week fifty, the
projection showed 6,639,042,973 total infections with
132,780,859 deaths. Morris found it troublesome that
neither of those figures matched the number Morris had
reported to Jacques: 5,311,234,378.

The most valuable item had been the virus, recovered
from the frozen body of Mr. Kozminski. The Centers for
Disease Control and Public Health Agency of Canada
were now working up a vaccine.

Morris watched Conan move from person to person.
He was trying to recruit new players for the weekly poker
game he started hosting upon his return from Las Vegas.
Morris smiled to think how that trip had worked out.

The first night, Habib met the girl Ed had arranged.
But being a faithful Muslim, Habib would not use the
services of a prostitute. To be polite, he saw the date
through, and she taught him how blackjack was played in
the big casinos. For the next couple of days, the three
geeks spent money and did some gambling as they had
been sent to do, but they were soon looking for a
technical challenge.

They devised a scheme involving tracking what cards
had been dealt at the blackjack table in order to improve

the odds for the player. Conan wrote a utility program, Zia wired himself to transmit video images back to the hotel room, and Habib implemented a signaling system to advise Zia when to hit and when to hold. Their net winnings amounted to just over $223,000.00, which they turned over to Morris.

Morris explained that card counting was not permitted in Las Vegas, and donated the money to a charity that rehabilitated drug addicts.

"Did we terminate their operation, guys?" Morris asked Ed and Jacques. "Or was the camp already terminal, and they were moving on to the next phase?"

"It's hard to say," said Jacques.

"They're not done yet," said Ed.

"Perhaps not, but we've made things difficult for them," said Jacques. "We had good photographs of every one of the guys who escaped except for the Arab. Those images have been disseminated to every law enforcement facility in North America. Candice came up with a pretty good composite sketch of the Arab, too. If they're still in the US or Canada, they are lying pretty low."

"We still don't know who's behind it all," said Morris. "The Taskman message hasn't paid off so far."

"But that could come any day," said Jacques.

"So could a biological attack," said Ed.

"True, but they have a pretty weak delivery system, according to what I heard," said Jacques.

Morris had seen other things in the lab during his short search. He saw drawings for a homemade hand-held tube launcher that seemed designed to shoot a 2-3 pound projectile a short distance. The plans showed a 4-foot aluminum tube, open at both ends, with a pistol grip firing mechanism. Morris found a video clip on the computer desktop. It showed a projectile with rocket fins being loaded into the tube, and then fired. The test had fizzled, with the projectile going only a short distance in a wildly erratic flight before striking the ground. When he described the weapon to the police firearms experts, they expressed the opinion that it would not have been a very effective method of dispersing the germ due to its limited range and lack of accuracy.

"It may have been weak," said Morris. "But under the right circumstances, like firing into a crowd, it could be effective. Our medical experts have no idea how this virus was produced, by the way. The printout I gave them is their only clue as to the infectivity rate. They are not planning any human trials to try and verify the results, needless to say."

Jill came by to say hello. "Merry Christmas, gentlemen."

"Cheers," said Morris.

"Did you get my final report on the translation of Kendo's Japanese emails?"

"Yes," said Morris. "And I sent a copy to CSIS."

"What was the outcome?" asked Jacques.

"CSIS swallowed it," said Morris. "Like everything else we gave them, and if they burped, I didn't hear anything back."

"No, I mean what were the emails about?" Jacques asked Jill.

"Well, there was a lot of correspondence with his grandfather about his experience in the second world war," said Jill. "He was a Navy pilot, and he wrote a lot about his job training suicide pilots as the war came to a close."

"Kendo's grandfather trained kamikaze pilots?" asked Ed.

"Yes. Kendo asked a lot of questions about how those men were motivated to do what they had to do. By the dates on the emails, he got interested just after his first trip to Winnipeg."

"Merry Christmas, gentlemen," said Liam as he walked up to the table.

"Merry Christmas, Liam. How was Washington?"

"Compared to a trip to Northern Ontario with you guys, pretty boring."

"Where were you, again?" asked Jacques.

"I was at the US Department of Homeland Security National Bioforensic Analysis Center, the NBFAC. They conduct bioforensic analysis of evidence from a biocrime or terrorist attack to attain a 'biological fingerprint' to help investigators identify perpetrators and determine the origin and method of attack."

"How was it?" asked Morris.

"We were unable to determine the origin of the virus, identify the perpetrators, or their likely method of attack. Other than that, it was great. I observed a lot of spin control."

"Spin control?"

"The Americans do not like it in the least that this threat originated here in Canada and got across the border into their territory chased by our forces but not caught. Even though our forensics teams have been working the campsite along with FBI and CIA resources, they have come up with very little – not enough to prepare a definitive response. Some of their team members are in favor of letting the whole story out, others want the threat suppressed from the public. In the end, they spin the story that the RCMP raid ended the threat where it originated, because the germ-making capability has been destroyed."

"What if the germ had been completed, and it's out there ready to be released?" asked Morris.

"They have adequate counter-measures. They have assembled a large quick-reaction force who they plan to immunize, and they are working with law enforcement and first responder organizations in all the major metropolitan areas, especially along the Eastern Seaboard, to respond if there is a release."

"So they are claiming the authorities have everything under control," said Ed.

"That's what I would do," said Liam. "Otherwise you have panic."

"Not only that, if you tip off the enemy on what you know about them, they will change their plan of attack," said Ed.

"Agreed." said Liam. "It's also a natural outcome of keeping our own part of this thing quiet. The RCMP gets credit for all the reconnaissance photos and intelligence that you guys gathered because it's not in their interest or ours to let out the fact that it was a private operation – just you three – that did all the work."

"We probably shouldn't be discussing all this here," said Jacques.

"Should I leave?" asked Jill.

"You already know what went on," said Morris. "You're in the circle of trust."

"Clark disappeared, as you know," said Liam. "He left his wife without finances and she's been forced to put the house up for sale. She's been providing information on Clark's activities but she does not appear to know where the money was coming from, and she didn't care as long as there was lots of it."

"Sounds like they had quite the loving relationship," said Morris. "He's in shit with his wife, not because he's a criminal, but because he got discovered."

"As a husband, it's not that you're in shit that matters," said Jill, laughing. "It's how much shit you're in." With that, Jill left to join friends at another table.

Liam took a seat. "They recovered what they could off Clark's Blackberry. When you took it from him, why did you remove the battery, by the way?"

"The Blackberry has a remote kill command that the user can send if the device is lost or stolen. It will erase all the information on it."

"That's why they recovered it in a shielded room," said Liam. "My cellphone would not work while I was in that lab."

"Right. So what did they get off the device?" asked Morris.

"Clark had configured it to save his call history for only 24 hours, and the address book was empty. He had not made or received any calls in that timeframe, but there was one email message that had been sent to a hotmail account. The text was: 'See Jason for payment.'"

"So he was paying somebody, for something," said Morris.

"Through a guy named Jason," said Liam. "There is nobody on the Ottawa Police Force by that name."

"What else did you get from Washington?" asked Morris.

"They are extremely hopeful Conan's TaskMan update program leads somewhere. They investigated the entire PHL customer list – every single company in the world that uses a registered version of TaskMan. Nothing came up. There is nobody with the first or last name of Joris – that's what the Arab called him – on that list."

"What about witnesses in Kenora?" asked Jacques. "Those guys must have gone to town for supplies."

"Some of the faces were familiar to grocery store clerks and at a hardware store. The Arab went to several local banks, but used different identities and company names for his mostly cash transactions. They all went to a dead end."

"What about the information Candice was able to provide?"

"The Arab kept her in the dark, literally. But they discovered she has immunity to a different strain of the virus. That really puzzled the bioforensics guys."

"She had been there almost two months, from the end of July until we got her out at the end of September," said Morris. "They infected her, she recovered, and the Arab kept her around for his own pleasure because she was beautiful. She must have been subject number ten or eleven. How did the virus mutate between her case and Subject Nineteen?"

Liam shrugged. "That's the question they're trying to resolve."

Morris was looking at Jill as he listened to Liam. Suddenly it hit him. "It's how much shit you are in, the lady just said." He grabbed a napkin and started scribbling on it.

Liam, Ed and Jacques watched Morris draw a rectangle and scribble some dimensions on it, followed by some calculations.

"How much shit can one guy produce? From spring until fall, how many dumps would a guy take, and how much volume would that be?"

"Well," said Jacques. "Assume half a year, or make it 200 days for round figures. At one dump a day, 200 dumps."

"How many guys at the camp?" Morris was getting excited.

"We saw six regulars," said Ed.

"Six times 200, 1200 dumps. Plus visitors, lets say 1500 dumps. How much space does one dump take? Lets say, two cups, plus piss. Then there would be evaporation…."

"Where the hell are you going with this, boss?" asked Ed.

"Just a sec." Morris completed his calculations. "The amount of shit I was in was too much for those guys. The most that team could shit and piss in a summer would be about 750 liters. The outhouse trench was approximately two meters long, three meters deep, and one point five meters wide. I was up to my chest in shit. That's about four point five cubic meters of shit. Each cubic meter is one thousand liters. There was 4,500 liters of shit in that hole."

"Where did the extra shit come from?" asked Ed.

"Pigs." Morris grinned. "When the Arab said to put Clark where the pigs had died, he meant real pigs. They were keeping pigs there, and using them to mutate the virus. The virus is a new variant of the swine flu."

49 – BRENDA, JUNIOR ARCHITECT

Whenever he though of Brenda, Morris unconsciously increased his usual pace. He was surprised to find he had completed his ten-mile morning run two minutes faster than usual, despite the snow.

Morris was still feeling good about that result when he walked in to his office. And he was still thinking about Brenda, until an idea popped into his head. He opened his desk drawer and pulled out an image of the printout he had recovered from the lab before the camp was destroyed. He had photographed it before turning the original over to the forensic team at the camp. The printout showed a four-column table of numbers. No number anywhere on the page matched the number from the computer scenario that he had reported to Jacques: 5,311,234,378.

Morris logged-in and opened a blank spreadsheet. He labeled the first column 'Week' and ran a series of numbers from 1 to 50 down the column. In the next column, he entered the value 4,000 in the row for week 1. Then, by creating a formula, he calculated a new value for each week from 2 to 50 that increased by 30% each week. The value in week 50 was 1,532,089,917. These numbers matched the printout.

There were no column headings on the printout. Morris added the heading 'New Victims' on his spreadsheet.

To get his third column to match the printout, he had to make the number for each week show the running total of the 'New Victims' column in each week. He created a formula to calculate that value, running it down to week 50. The value at week 50 was 6,639,042,973. He gave this column the label 'Total Victims.'

To make the last column match, he needed a formula to compute exactly 2% of the 'Total Victims' column. This column, he gave the heading 'Deaths.'

The printout went to 50 weeks. Morris added two additional weeks to his spreadsheet, extrapolating the formulas to see the values that would appear at week 52. The number of deaths was 224,399,836. The Chief Scientist had said *"the cull was to be less than two-hundred and fifty million people – not more than that."* Morris realized the number of deaths on his spreadsheet met that criterion.

Then Morris recalled what else he had said: "I am Chief Scientist. My work was meticulous. It is not 80%!" He was not just bragging, Morris realized. He was trying to avoid the blame for a result of 80%. Morris changed the 2% value in his spreadsheet to 80%. The value for the death rate in week 50 became 5,311,234,378. This number matched the computer scenario Morris reported to Jacques.

The Chief Scientist had created a strain of swine flu that was supposed to kill 2% of its victims, but somebody ran a scenario of 80%.

If these were terrorists, why would they be interested in trying to get 2% death rate and consider it a screw up if they ended up with 80% instead? The higher the weapon yield, the better, if you're a terrorist.

Morris typed up an email with his observations and questions and added his theory about the amount of shit proving there were pigs present at the camp, and therefore the whole plot was about swine flu. He attached his spreadsheet and sent the email to Liam to be forwarded to the bioforensic investigators in Washington.

Morris pulled a ziplock containing the Blackberry he had carried at the camp. CSIS had tried to recover information, but the device had been soaked. Morris wrote a note asking Jill to send it out to test for traces of pig shit.

Jill had left a small stack of messages on his desk. Morris sighed and picked up the first one, read it, and placed a call to the architect's office.

"Engineering," said a female voice.

"Brenda?" Morris was surprised.

There was a pause. "It's me. Hi."

Morris smiled. "How are you doing?"

"I'm OK."

"I didn't see you at the Christmas party yesterday. Your boss said you weren't sure you could make it."

"He's been keeping me pretty busy. I'm pretty tired by the end of the day."

"You used to be a night person – uh, at your old job." Morris winced at himself.

"Yeah, and I could sleep late!" She laughed. "Now I have all kinds of stuff to do to prepare for these morning meetings. I hardly have time to put on my makeup in the mornings."

"I hear nothing but good things about your work."

"Thanks. School was a long time ago. It's nice of you to say that."

"How's Candice?"

"She's doing well. For a change, *she's* been looking after *me*. It's good to have her back. She's seeing a therapist about her nightmares – she was locked in for so long.... Anyways, the dreams are subsiding."

"We haven't spoken much since the day she went free."

"I remember when you called to offer me this job."

"I needed a good junior architect. You were looking for a career change. It worked out well."

"Hey, I sold my shares in Club Chaton. I also sold my apartment, and I want to invest the money. Do you have a project where I could participate?"

"I always have projects. I would welcome your participation. Let's meet."

There was a pause. She didn't want to meet. Morris
felt like there was an 800-pound gorilla in the situation.

"Could you just send a list?" she asked.

Morris was disappointed. He decided to confront the
gorilla.

"I haven't seen you since you were in hospital."

"We talked over the satellite phone."

"When I was 48 hours without sleep, covered in fecal
matter and soot, and my ears were still ringing from a ten-
megaton propane blast over my head."

Brenda laughed. "You mean you weren't at your
best?"

"I've been better."

"You sounded perfect to me." Her voice started to
break. "Just perfect."

There was a long pause. Morris had never seen
Brenda cry, but he suddenly pictured tears in her eyes. He
heard a sniffle to confirm that image.

"Look," she began, voice unsteady. "I was sure my
sister was dead. You called me and told me she was alive.
I was overjoyed. I was awake worrying for days in that
damn hospital. Worried about her – and about you. You
saved my life on the parkway, then you went and saved
my sister. I owe you everything. You found me this job
and it's helping me and my sister get our lives straight. I
told you something that day that I never should have said.
But I meant it."

"I couldn't respond to that."

"I still feel it."

Silence. They listened to each other breathe for a
while.

"This job is yours for as long as you want it," Morris
said carefully. "But if you decide to leave, I will
understand. It's because of you that I was able to get into
the camp and end the attacks against me and my family."

"I don't want to leave!" The pain in her voice was
evident. "You know what I want. No man has ever treated

me the way you did. You made me feel respectable, like
an equal – and like a lady, even when I was a slut."

"You're a beautiful woman. Lots of men will treat
you that way. You can have any man you want."

"I want you."

Morris ached to respond. There was another long
silence.

"The feeling will pass…"

"I don't want it to pass!"

Morris wanted to wrap his arms around her. He
wanted to comfort her. He wanted to make love to her,
and take Brenda away and be together.

After another long pause, Morris cleared his throat
and swallowed with a dry mouth. "I think we should try
to get back to work…."

"Let me say it to you, OK? You don't have to say
anything. Just let me say it."

Morris wanted to hear it. He wanted to respond to it.
"If you think it will help…."

Brenda took a deep breath. "I love you," she said,
with a tremble in her voice. Morris heard a deep, long
sigh. "I love you, dammit."

Morris felt a surge of emotion. He gritted his teeth
and looked out the window. "I can't respond to that."

"I know. I know." The sound of background
conversation came over the phone as someone entered the
room with Brenda. "Thanks for listening. Thanks for
letting me say it."

Morris felt weak. "Please tell Derrick I returned his
call."

"I will. Bye."

"Good-bye, Brenda. Bye for now. Take care."

Morris looked at the other messages on his desk. He
looked at his agenda. He couldn't remember any of the
things he had planned to do.

His concentration was shot.

PART FIVE – RUNNING BATTLES

50 – CITY BAR, BOSTON

Tomorrow would be April 19th, the 114th running of the Boston Marathon, the World's oldest marathon. Last year in the Ottawa Marathon, after several years of effort, Morris had finally qualified by running fast enough for his age group, with a time of 3:15:58.

It was the night before his big race. Morris, Ed and Jacques were in the City Bar at the Lenox Hotel in Boston's Back Bay. Ed and Jacques were officially there as the security team. But unofficially, they were there to make up for the Las Vegas trip the group never made.

The three boys were sitting at the bar. "Tell me more about Patriot's Day," Ed said to the beautiful, dark-haired bartender as she poured him an Azure-metro, a Martini drink made with Absolut Kurant, Lillet Blanc, Chambord, and lime juice. Being a Hoegaarden man, the only ingredient Ed recognized was the lime juice.

"Tomorrow is one of the most important holidays in New England," said Carolina, sounding Irish, even though she was actually from Venezuela, the boys had learned. "Patriot's Day marks the start of the American Revolution. The battle that started it all is re-enacted in Lexington starting at about 5:00 AM, tomorrow, and the day goes on all around Boston as one huge party."

"I'm a descendant of the John Parker that started that battle," said Morris, vying for Carolina's attention. "Captain Parker was in command of the militia company that formed up at Lexington on April 19th, 1775, to face the British Redcoats as they were advancing to Concord to check for an illegal arms cache."

Seeing that Carolina looked interested, Morris continued. "Parker had not intended to fight a battle. In fact, the only clear order he seems to have given, at the moment of confrontation, was for his militiamen to disperse. He had realized his troops, being formed up near the road, were being perceived as hostile. One side or the other fired the first shot – nobody knows who."

"I seem to remember a recent controversy about who fired the first shot back in Ottawa," said Ed, trying to draw Carolina's eyes back to him.

"Tell me more," she said to Morris, ignoring Ed.

"It could have even been somebody sniping from the sidelines," said Morris, looking at Ed. "Or even an accidental discharge, like what happens to Ed sometimes...." Take that, Ed, Morris thought.

Jacques grinned, seeing that Carolina got the joke at Ed's expense.

"The British officers lost control of their advancing troops, who fired a volley and charged forward." Morris was enjoying Carolina's attention. "Eight of the militia died, with no casualties to the British side. News of this one-sided result spread quickly through the countryside, and the farmers responded with multiple attacks on the Redcoats during their return march from Concord. The soldier-farmers called themselves Patriots."

"So the entire American Revolution, the foundation of my country, started with a screw-up by one of your ancestors," said Ed.

"Absolutely," Morris grinned. "Without it, there would be no Patriots' Day. I think that calls for a toast."

"To Patriot's Day," said Jacques, as the three men raised their fancy martinis.

"Patriot's Day," Morris and Ed said in unison.

Carolina went back to work, leaving Morris with a smile.

"So do we get up for the battle re-enactment?" Jacques asked Ed.

"Not me," Ed replied. "I intend to enjoy that Red Sox game, so I will prepare for a full day by sleeping as long as possible. I plan to watch the marathon leaders with a beer in my hand as they pass that famous Citgo sign."

"Apparently we can keep track of Morris through automatic email alerts when he passes certain points along the 26.2 mile route," said Jacques.

"Yeah," said Morris. "For the 25,000 registered runners with a bib number. But don't expect to see any record times from me. My objective is just to run in the race, not set a personal record."

"People run without bib numbers?" asked Jacques.

"Yes, they are called Bandits. They are a storied part of this race. They did not post a qualifying time at a qualifying race, and they pay no entry fee. But they've always been there, even in years before the race was popular. There will be about a million people along the route to cheer on the runners. Many runners write their name on themselves to get personal encouragement and Bandits get the same encouragement as the numbered runners."

A pair of young men sitting at the bar had been listening to Morris. One of them turned to the other and began to speak in a foreign language. As Morris sipped his martini, thinking that it would be wise to make it his only drink, he heard the man's remarks cut through a lull in the general background noise in the bar. Morris felt a sudden adrenaline surge. He recognized the language. He remembered hearing these strange words before.

"What did you just say?" Morris asked the man.

The man looked at him, taken aback.

"I'm sorry, I heard that phrase spoken before. It's Arabic, right? What does it mean?"

The man seemed not to like being questioned.

"It's OK, we're just Canadians, eh," said Jacques.

The man looked at Jacques and nodded. "It's sometimes difficult to be an Arab in America," said the man, more at ease. "I said *in-akah tes-tahech raqm fee asi-baq.* It means you deserve a race number."

Holy shit, thought Morris. He pulled a couple of $20 dollar bills and put them on the bar. "Follow me guys – I just figured something out!"

Ed and Jacques downed their drinks and followed Morris out into the street. Morris turned right on Boylston Street.

"Our hotel is the other way," said Ed, walking swiftly to keep up.

"We need a quiet place to talk." Morris went silent, thinking hard.

The group marched quickly past the Boston Public Library, passing the Boston Marathon's finish line, as Morris led the way along the busy sidewalk. It was 11:00 PM the night before a big holiday, and there were people everywhere moving between the bars of Boylston Street. The men passed through a crowd exiting the subway station and Morris intended to cross Dartmouth Street to the middle of the grassy area of Copley Square, but it was fenced off. The square had been set up with tents and equipment to support the marathon.

Morris stopped and turned. "The germ attack will be here – tomorrow!"

Ed and Jacques looked incredulous.

"I heard that phrase at the camp. Two of the dwarves were training for a marathon. They sprinted to the finish, and the loser told the winner he deserved a number. He was talking about this race. They were training to run as bandits.

"I recorded the Arabic phrase in my Blackberry, but I couldn't retrieve it after the mission because the thing didn't survive being dunked in pig shit. I recognized the Arabic in the bar. And last month I remembered seeing a strange poster at the camp. It had been posted inside the living quarters – green birds flying in a purple sky. I did some research online because I was curious about the Kamikaze stuff in Kendo's email. Palestinian suicide bombers use those symbols.

"The terrorists are going to use suicide infectors. They projected 4,000 as the initial infection on the printout I found. They will put the four dwarves in as bandits, and they will run slow and infect the other runners catching up on them from behind. There are so many runners in this race they run almost shoulder-to-shoulder over four-lane highways. You can stand and watch them pass for hours, packed in like sardines.

"The virus transmits through the air, from the infector to the other runners. The runners go home to various countries the next day, and pass on the germ. The simulation seemed to start on the East coast – Boston! Patriots' Day!"

"We Americans also have Patriot Day – no plural, no apostrophe – that's September 11th!" exclaimed Ed. "They are planning to make a statement."

"*Osti de tabarnac*," exclaimed Jacques.

"I agree," said Ed.

"I'm going to call Liam. He'll put out the alert."

51 – RACE DAY

Sitting in the hotel restaurant, Morris looked at his coffee cup. He had been busy all night. Sleep had been impossible. The front desk had gotten used to routing calls to his room.

The phone calls had started about midnight, after Morris spoke with Liam and emailed background information. Alex James called to review Morris' reasoning before passing it on within CSIS. A scientist from the US Department of Homeland Security National Bioforensic Analysis Center called to discuss the germ. Agents from the FBI and CIA had collected Morris from his room at about 2:00 AM, and taken him to where people could speak with him via secure telephone.

After the destruction of the secret camp, a Special Situation Team had been formed to deal specifically with the Northern Ontario Virus, as they had named it. The Team Intelligence Officer had called to grill Morris on his deductions. Someone from the White House called. At 0300 hours, the decision was made ordering the Special Situation Team to deploy to Boston, by order of the President of the United States.

Not bad for an amateur James Bond, Morris thought. They woke him in the middle of the night for this. Especially since he was not entirely certain of his own deductions. The US authorities were reacting with similar lack of certainty, because there had been no decision to cancel the race.

Morris did not know the composition or capabilities of the Special Situation Team, but he knew its members had been vaccinated against the virus recovered from Subject Nineteen.

At 5:00 AM, Morris had been returned to his room. He had lain sleepless for two hours before getting up for breakfast. The laughing child Blackberry alarm went off at 7:00 AM. He got up slowly, having decided to skip the race.

Morris was reading the paper alone at his breakfast table when Ed and Jacques showed up at the hotel restaurant.

"You decided to give this race a pass?" asked Ed.

"No sleep," said Morris. "No energy. Besides, if I'm right about the attack, it's safer here."

"Want to join us at the Red Sox game?" asked Jacques.

"I doubt we could get an extra ticket," said Morris.

"You don't have any strings you can pull?" asked Ed.

"Well, I could call the President," said Morris. "But they interrupted his sleep to consider my information. He wouldn't be in the mood to help."

"I thought you were President," said Ed.

"President of the United States. At 0300, he mobilized the Special Situation Team based on my hunch."

"No shit," said Ed, dumbfounded. "I think I'm going to hang out with you. Baseball suddenly seems kind of slow."

The group ate a leisurely breakfast without much conversation. Then they spent most of the morning walking around the Boylston Street area, watching the race leaders cross the finish line.

The boys had just settled in for a pre-lunch beer at a street-level Irish pub called Solas, when Morris' cellphone rang. It was Alex James. He told Morris he had some information to pass on by Blackberry confidential PIN.

A moment later, Morris read the message to Ed and Jacques.

"A car rental clerk came on shift this morning and recognized one of the suicide infectors," Alex had

442   Jim E.M. Miles

written. "The police passed out suspect photos after you put out the alert. A van was rented at Logan Airport yesterday. A massive ground and air search is underway. The Massachusetts National Guard has been called up in the event they are needed for crowd control. They are now deploying to cordon your location."

Wow, thought Morris, I was right. They didn't wake the President for nothing. Cordon my location? That must mean they are afraid the infectors got into the race!

"They called in ground forces," Morris said to Ed and Jacques. "I'm going to have a look outside."

Morris walked out of the bar and looked around, searching for soldiers or police. When the race leaders had crossed the finish line, there had been hundreds of police officers visible. They had lined five blocks on both sides of Boylston Street to ensure the security of the runners. Now there were very few police in sight. Looking up, Morris saw several civilian helicopters were in the air. There had been only a couple all morning; he now counted six. He realized they were news helicopters. Morris rushed back into the bar.

"WROR radio is reporting police and military roadblocks are in place all around the Back Bay," said Jacques, who was with the bartender.

"That's where the police went," said Morris. "They moved from the center area here to establish a cordon."

"There are roadblocks going up along Mass Ave," said the bartender, with a cellphone in his hand. "My waitress can't get in to work!" He listened to his cellphone, and suddenly his face went white. "She says there are soldiers wearing chemical protection suits and gas masks!"

Morris and the boys went back out to the street. Runners that had passed the finish line were still in the area, wandering around. Over the next half hour, the streets seemed to fill quickly with people. The roadblocks seemed to be preventing people from leaving the Back Bay area, but runners kept arriving.

A white truck pulled up just beyond the finish line. Four people in full HAZMAT suits got out and started handing white flu face masks to the arriving runners. The mood on the street suddenly got grim. Morris saw a squad of police arrive wearing gas mask respirators, full body armor, and carrying machine guns. They started to examine the arriving runners. They must be trying to find the infectors.

"They haven't stopped the race!" Morris said to Ed and Jacques. "They're collecting all the runners here and searching them."

"I think they must be trying to isolate the runners from each other," said Jacques. "I saw one refusing to put on his flu face mask. A cop cuffed him and made him wear it."

"There's an incubation period for the virus," said Morris. "I spoke with a CDC official this morning. After exposure, the victim incubates the virus for about four hours before he becomes contagious. They will probably try to keep all the runners contained in this downtown area for at least four hours, to see if they show symptoms."

"They'll have to keep spectators too. It's going to be chaos!" exclaimed Jacques.

People were starting to cross Boylston Street in front of the runners. The people density in the immediate area continued to increase. The group slowly made their way south toward their hotel, The Westin Copley Place, on the other side of the square.

"Look at the number of people starting to pile up in Copley Square!" exclaimed Ed. "Their medical tent has overflowed. There are people in masks sitting on the fountain, on the church steps, the library steps, everywhere. The place is crawling with people in masks!"

"Fuck this, it's too crowded heading this way," said Morris. "I know a guy in Boston with an office in that big tall shiny glass building, The Hancock Tower. He's working today. He was going to meet me after the race. Let's see if we can get inside."

As they approached the Hancock Tower, Morris felt his Blackberry vibrate. A new confidential PIN had arrived from Alex James. He read it quickly as he kept walking.

"Guys, they caught the rental van, and identified three of the dwarves! They arrested and isolated Dopey, Grumpy, and Sneezy at the halfway point before they could join the race."

"What about Bashful?" asked Ed.

"I can hardly hear you." Morris cupped his ear. Not only was there quite a bit of crowd noise, the wind had suddenly come up. Morris was wearing a baseball cap, and he had to jam it down to keep it from flying off his head.

"I said what about Bashful and Sleepy?" Ed repeated. "And what about the Arab?"

"No sign of them, I guess."

"But they think they identified the leader. They found a handwritten note in the van – a grocery list. It said 'Mohamed Z said to buy…' and listed a bunch of items. I saw 'Ziad Scenario' on the computer screen I at the camp, remember? They ran the name 'Mohamed Ziad,' and it came back positive. He's on the no-fly list."

Morris realized they had been absorbed in their discussion and had walked past the Hancock Tower.

"Hey guys, we missed it!" Morris turned quickly and before he could take a step, his cap blew off and flew away behind him. Jacques grabbed it before it got very far.

Morris was curious. The wind had been in his face as they approached the Hancock Tower. After walking past, they faced it from the other side, and the wind was still blowing towards them. Morris walked forward twenty steps closer to the building. Now there seemed to be no wind. He looked up at the skyscraper. It was as if the wind was coming down the face of the building, and splitting in two directions.

They had captured the suicide infectors, he thought. What happened to the launcher? It could work if fired into a crowd, Morris had realized. Here was a huge crowd. It would work even better if fired from a *very high building* into a huge crowd. The airflow Morris had just experienced would ensure immediate and wide dispersion of a weaponized aerosol germ.

Morris looked around. There were tall buildings everywhere.

Why was the leader not with his suicide troops? Where was the fourth infector? Could there be a second attack planned?

Suddenly he was certain there would be a second attack. There had been multiple attacks on September 11th. In New York City, *two towers had been hit by two separate planes.*

Morris realized both Jacques and Ed were looking at him standing there.

"Just before Christmas, I emailed a theory to the bioforensics guys in Washington. I did some calculations and found that, if you start with 4,000 infections, with an 80% death rate, the virus kills over five billion people in 50 weeks. It takes an 80% kill rate to match the number of deaths at week fifty that I reported to you, Jacques.

"This morning, a CDC guy said they had discounted my theory after testing the recovered virus on pigs. It would have a kill rate matching the printout – 2%, they figured."

"You told me there was a Ziad Scenario," said Jacques. "That was the name on the computer screen."

"*There are two scenarios*! The Arab was going to kill Clark, clean and efficient. He didn't treat the Chief

Scientist that way. That guy was almost beaten to death.
That partnership had a huge falling-out! That was a
hugely dysfunctional group of bad guys."

"Why two scenarios?" asked Ed.

"Because there are two different objectives! The
scientist said: *my work was meticulous. It is not 80%!* Ask
yourself why would the scientist want 2%? Vaccine sales!
The scientist wanted the profit – the Arab just wants to
kill as many people as possible. When partners want
different things, partnerships end."

"So what do you want to do?" asked Jacques.

"I think somebody should check these buildings!"
exclaimed Morris as he speed-dialed Alex James.

52 – TWO TOWERS

For about ten minutes Morris, Ed and Jacques had been waiting patiently outside the Boston Police Mobile Command Vehicle parked at Copley Square. Morris had tried to explain the situation twice to officers on their way in or out, but had been cut off each time because the officer had been too busy to listen to a member of the public trying to tell a long, complicated and uncertain story.

Finally the door opened and an overworked looking Sergeant appeared.

"Morris Parker?" he asked, looking at the three of them.

"That's me," said Morris.

"Please come in."

As Morris stepped through the doorway into the thirty-foot vehicle, the Sergeant put up his hand to stop Ed and Jacques.

"Its kinda crowded in heah, gentlemen," said the Sergeant in a heavy Boston accent.

Ed nodded and they stepped back.

"You have some high and mighty friends, sir," the Sergeant said to Morris. "What do I need to do to help you?"

Morris was suddenly not too comfortable with his latest theory. He could see the staff in the Command Post was already stretched very thin dealing with the first level of crisis. He did not want to waste anyone's time with a wild goose chase.

"I have reasons to believe there is a high likelihood of a second germ attack. The concentration of people here in Copley Square is a huge target."

"What, like I said, should we do? I have been ordered
to provide whatever resources we have not committed
yet, which is not much at the moment, I'm afraid."

"I believe you should search the tall buildings in the
vicinity for a couple of Arab men with a hand-held
launcher that looks like a bazooka."

"A bazooka?"

"It doesn't fire an explosive projectile. It was
designed to launch a germ canister, firing it a short range.
From a tall building, it could spread a germ quickly and
effectively."

"What do these Arab men look like?"

"One of them is a member of the group of photos that
your people have been using. The other is Mohamed
Ziad, and I don't know if there is photo available or not,
but my friends and I know what he looks like."

"I'll get the photos, meanwhile you can start a search.
We have two people here right now. I have one
policeman acting as our runner, and one sniper. You can
start with them and we'll send more your way as our
resources come off their other tasks."

"Fine. I'll use my friends to help. We should start
with your two tallest buildings."

"That would be John Hancock and the Pru."

"We'll need access to the buildings."

"I'll have the local security people take you through.
I'll meet you outside in two minutes." The Sergeant
pointed Morris to the exit door and turned to speak with
one of the female communications operators.

"We didn't put anyone on the roof of the Pru," Morris
heard her say as he left the Command Vehicle.

A minute later, a sniper in a black uniform came
around the corner carrying a huge rifle with an enormous
scope attached. He introduced himself as Jordan. A
moment later, a policeman arrived, and then the Sergeant
stepped out of the Command Vehicle.

"Each of these men has radio communication on our command net," said the Sergeant. "This policeman just came from the Hancock Building."

"Jacques and I can go back with him and check the Hancock Building," said Ed.

"Off you go," said the Sergeant.

Ed, Jacques, and one of the Boston police officers broke into a run, heading for the Hancock Building.

"Jaw-don, you go with Mr. Pah-kah in that car," said the Sergeant, pointing. "I'll let the Pru team know you're on your way."

Jordan nodded and slung his rifle, and ran to catch up with Morris, who was getting into the back of the police car.

The ride from Copley Square to the Prudential Center Shopping Plaza was going to be quick, thanks to the fact soldiers and police had restricted the runners to half of Boylston Street. The other half was now open to emergency vehicles only. Morris observed disappointment, frustration and anger on the faces of runners being denied the final dash to the finish. They were instead being forced to queue up to get across the finish line and receive a flu face mask.

There were not enough security forces to keep everyone off the street, unfortunately. There was a lot of pedestrian traffic, and the speeding police car had to brake hard on two occasions to avoid hitting people who were crossing the street without looking.

People were paying no attention to the police car despite the scream of its siren. Anxiety levels were high and going higher, as word spread that some kind of germ attack was happening. People did not like seeing ground forces in chemical protection suits and HAZMAT gear. The effect on people who did not yet have a mask upon seeing more and more people who did was predictable: panic was setting in. Morris saw a two-man ambulance

crew trying to hand out masks to a crowd that was
pressing in on all sides. When they ran out, what then?

"Give that back, you! HEY!" Jordan yelled out the
window on his side of the car. "I just saw a guy push
down an old lady and take her mask!"

Before Morris had a chance to respond, the car
stopped and a Boston policewoman opened the door for
Morris.

"You must be Parker. Follow me." On the double,
Morris and Jordan followed her into the shopping center.
It was packed.

People had been getting the idea that it would be safer
inside a building than out on the street. The hallways
were approaching full capacity, and Morris saw police
forces were now deploying to try and keep people out.
Morris considered the irony that a single infector in the
crowded mall would be much more dangerous than out on
the street. People had no idea how the germ was being
spread, and the shelter-seeking instinct was the worst
possible reaction for the situation.

A security man in a blazer waved them past his
security desk, and they entered a cordoned off area,
breaking free from the crowd. They had arrived at the
base of the Prudential Tower, and Morris looked at a wall
of elevators in front of him.

"Follow him." The Boston policewoman pointed to
another man in a blue blazer waiting by one of the
elevators, then she promptly headed back into the crowd.

Morris and Jordan rushed to the elevator.

"This express elevator goes to the Top of the Hub
Restaurant," said the security man.

"Did they send anyone up before us?" asked Morris,
feeling his ears pop as the high-speed elevator started the
trip to the 52nd floor.

"No," said the security man. "Crowd control is taking
every man they have."

"Is this the highest building in Boston?" asked Morris.

"No, the John Hancock tower has 60 floors. We have 52." The man smiled. "But we have the highest observation deck in Boston. The Hancock observatory was closed after 9/11, and never re-opened."

"Is that space vacant or was it refitted as office space?" Morris could only guess at the rent that a single floor represented. One-sixtieth of the building rent, obviously, and it came right off the bottom line if it remained empty.

"I don't believe so," said the security man.

Morris thought about that information as the elevator ascended. Ziad, if he intended to attack using his launcher, might favor making a statement while doing it. That would mean doing it from the tallest building in Boston. It would enhance the statement to do it from the vacant floor – not only because he could hide himself days in advance to bypass the enhanced security of the marathon, but because it was symbolic to use ground that had been won in a previous battle to launch the next attack.

The elevator door opened and Morris and Jordan stepped out, following the security man as he approached a locked door.

"This door leads to the roof," said the security man.

Morris nodded as he put on his Bluetooth headset and speed-dialed Jacques.

"Hello."

"It's Morris. Where are you guys?" he asked, watching the security man open the door.

"We're on the 55th floor and working our way down. The offices are mostly empty. There's hardly anyone here because of the Patriot's Day holiday."

"Did you check the observation deck?"

"They said there's no access," said Jacques.

"I have a hunch. I think you should check it anyway."

"Will do."

The security man swiped his proximity card and opened it, leading Morris and Jordan up a metal stairway. At the top was a large landing with a couple of lockers, some shelving and tools and a rough-looking metal door leading outside. The security man opened it and stepped out onto the roof. Jordan followed him.

Looking down, Morris noticed a small black object on the floor. He paused, curious, and bent to pick it up. He paused just before grasping it – it was an eye patch.

A blast of machinegun fire ripped into the security man and Jordan, who were several steps ahead. Both men went down instantly. Morris grabbed the door handle, pulling the door shut and stepped to one side just as a second burst of bullets punched through the metal door.

"Jacques! Somebody just shot at us from the rooftop!"

Three more bullets burst through the door. Morris looked around, searching for a weapon. He saw a long-handled snow shovel leaning in the corner. He ran and grabbed it.

Then Morris heard a key being inserted. Somebody was about to open the door! Morris quickly inverted the shovel and slid the long shaft diagonally between the panic bar and the surface of the door. The head of the shovel protruded to the right of the doorway, jammed tightly against the wall. The door could not be opened from the outside.

After a couple of heavy kicks against the door, another burst of shots came through.

"Are you OK?" asked Jacques.

"I'm fine, but Jordan and a Pru security guard are down. Somebody was watching the doorway exit to the roof. They must have the launcher up here!"

"Just a second," said Jacques.

Morris could hear Jacques speaking quickly in the background.

"The Boston police have a helicopter in the air," he said. "They're going to send it over. I just gave them your cell number. Hang up and they'll call you."

"OK." Morris ended the call.

Over at the John Hancock building, Jacques, Ed and the Boston cop had been searching floors with the help of two building security staff.

"We can't help Morris from over here," said Ed, looking at Jacques.

"Is that it for us, then?" asked one of the security staff.

"Morris said to check the observation deck," Jacques said to the Boston cop. "I think we should do that."

"Shua." The Boston cop motioned for the security man to take them up.

Back at the Pru, Morris felt his Blackberry vibrate, so he touched his headset. "Morris Parker." Morris could hear the sound of a helicopter engine.

"This is the Boston Police. We are in a helicopter observing the top of the Prudential Tower. What's going on over there?"

"Somebody on the roof may be preparing to fire a biological weapon. They tried to get to me, but I wedged the door shut."

"Good. Help is on the way. Keep that door locked."

"I said they may be preparing to fire a biological weapon. How long until I get some help?"

"Five or ten minutes."

"We don't have five minutes! If they fire that weapon, it'll infect thousands of people! There will be no way you can control all of them! Look below – there must be fifty thousand people in this area. It will start an epidemic that will be impossible to contain!"

"Wait a moment, I'm checking for orders." There was an agonizing pause. "Lethal force has been authorized by POTUS. Mister Parker, we are in the air 100 meters north above the Prudential tower. We have visibility on most of the roof, but we can't see behind every structure and there are too many antennas to land."

"Can you fire on the roof?"

"Yes, we have automatic weapons."

"Somebody shot two men. Can you see them?"

"Not from this position."

"I think I'm on the south side. Check the exit door. They're right outside this door."

There was a short pause. "We see them now."

"Can you see my door?"

"Yes."

"Do you see anyone else?"

"No."

"I'm going to exit this door and try to get the downed men. When I say fire, start firing."

"OK, we're ready for you to move."

Morris jerked the shovel out, tossed it aside, and pushed the panic bar to disengage the lock. The door opened about an inch, then he stepped back a few steps. "FIRE!"

Morris heard a flurry of shots being fired as he rushed toward the door, slamming it fully open. He dove through the doorway and landed on the roof, scrambling forward. Jordan was no longer where he had fallen – but his rifle was there. Morris picked it up, and then noticed a blood trail leading around the corner. Crawling on his belly, Morris followed it.

Jordan was alive, with his pistol drawn. He had dragged himself next to a microwave dish, leaving a blood trail.

"Police helicopter! Stop firing!" ordered Morris.

The firing stopped. Morris crawled up beside Jordan.

"Where are you hit?" asked Morris.

"Leg and shoulder," he grunted. "I think the security man is dead. He didn't answer me."

"How many men did you see?"

"Two. One has a pistol. One has an M16."

"Did you see any other equipment?"

"The guy with the pistol also had binoculars."

"Where are they?"

"They went around to the left."

"I have an idea." Morris looked at Jordan's sniper rifle. It had a huge optical scope that Morris was not familiar with. "How many rounds in your magazine?"

"It's holding five rounds of 50 caliber match grade ammunition. The chamber is empty right now. Are you a shooter?"

"Years ago. Lately, I've been more of a target." Morris cocked the weapon, and then removed the scope, placing it down gently. "We're in a little too close for this. Are these iron sights zeroed?"

Jordan nodded. "Set for 100 yards."

Morris put the rifle to his cheek to check the sight picture. "Police helicopter, are you ready for an idea?"

"Yes."

"I want you to climb and get observation on the whole rooftop from a few hundred feet straight up."

"We can do that, but we cannot provide accurate fire from there."

"Fine. Just see if you can acquire some targets."

"Will do."

The chopper engine revved and the machine rapidly climbed straight up.

"We see a target. He is on the other side of the main antenna base mount, the large red antenna."

"Can't miss it," said Morris. "Do I have authority to fire?"

"Yes. Your biological weapon threat has been confirmed."

"Can you put my voice on your loudhailer?"

"Yes. Go ahead."

"Testing, testing." Morris heard his voice coming from above. "Attention all terrorists!" Morris took aim at one of the steel antenna mounts that were scattered all

456   Jim E.M. Miles

over the rooftop. "I wish to direct your attention to the antenna with the white box on the top. I will now demonstrate something."

Morris thumbed the safety into the 'fire' position, aimed at the roof just below the base of the antenna, took a breath, exhaled half way, and squeezed off a shot.

BLAM.

The 50 caliber sniper rifle sounded like a cannon. "One," said Morris, hearing his voice come over the load hailer an instant later. Morris squeezed off two more shots in quick succession, operating the bolt action quickly and expertly, shooting at the bases of the next two antennas to the right.

BLAM. BLAM.

"Two. Three."

From his position behind the main antenna base mount, John Paxson watched as the bullets struck the bases of the antennas. Concrete fragments flew into the air as the heavy bullets tunneled in, striking mounting bolts and destroying other parts of the steel frames, sending pieces flying. Each antenna leaned and fell in succession, pulling electrical wires and shorting them in a shower of sparks.

"This is a fifty-caliber sniper rifle capable of pinpoint accuracy at over 1000 yards. I am firing a depleted uranium armor-piercing round capable of penetrating up to 48 inches of reinforced concrete." Morris paused for effect.

Jordan was grinning at him.

"Mr. Beavis, each time we meet, you end up a little worse off. Round one, you lose an eye. Round two, you break an arm.

"We tracked your team's movements by remote video surveillance devices and satellite imagery. That helicopter above you is using a sophisticated acoustic triangulation device to pinpoint the exact location of your heartbeat." Morris shrugged at Jordan. "And I am using a special x-ray gun sight that can see through the concrete and steel you're hiding behind…."

"OK! OK! We give up!" Paxson threw his rifle and Hesam's pistol to one side. "Don't shoot! We're coming out." He came out with Hesam beside him.

"It can even see your really, really small dick," Morris added, as he walked up to the two men with the rifle. "Welcome to Boston, Beavis and Bashful."

Two Boston Cops rushed onto the roof and came up behind Morris, guns drawn. A pair of paramedics came behind them and started to attend to Jordan and the downed security man.

Paxson looked at the rifle Morris was carrying. His jaw dropped. "There's no fancy gun sight on that fucking thing!"

The cops began to cuff Paxson and Hesam.

"It won't shoot through four feet of concrete, either." Morris said. "Police helicopter, you can turn off the heartbeat triangulator. My atomic dick locator did the job."

"Roger."

"Thanks for the help." Morris touched his headset to disconnect the call. "What the hell have you been up to?" Morris asked Paxson. Morris began looking around, searching for the launcher.

Paxson was silent.

Morris noticed a pair of binoculars near the edge of the building. He approached the rail, feeling his balls shrivel. Morris did not like heights. Jumping from an airplane was fine, because there was no sense of perspective. Seeing a child spread-eagle looking down through the glass floor at the top of the Toronto CN Tower was intolerable.

Morris grabbed the rail and forced himself to look over the edge. The view was outstanding. It was easy to see the police roadblocks and the size and locations of the crowd congestion they had created.

Beside the binoculars, Morris saw an odd piece of equipment. It looked like a digital voltmeter about the size of a TV remote, with a hand-held piece attached by a curly telephone cord. Morris picked up the equipment. The hand-held piece had propeller vanes in it, reminding Morris of hair dryer.

"This is a Digital Anemometer," Morris said to the cop beside him. "It's used to measure airspeed." Morris suddenly looked over at the John Hancock building. Storm clouds were rolling in, and the shiny blue windows were looked ominous as they started turning grey.

"These guys are spotting the wind for another location!"

Over at the Hancock building, Mohamed ordered Qamar to fire.

Qamar pressed the detonator button, sending a charge to the loop of det cord that had been taped to the inside of the windowpane. The blast shattered the 500-pound window on the Hancock observation deck, sending fragments flying out from the 60th floor.

Mohamed wore coveralls with the words CLEAN SWEEP on his back. He was pointing his M16 at Jacques and Ed, who were standing nose to the wall. Their Hancock security guard was also guarding them with a pistol. A Boston cop lay dead on the floor.

53 – JOHN HANCOCK'S BUILDING

Mohamed counted four news helicopters in sight. "Now we give them something really interesting to look at." He motioned to Qamar. "Throw out the cop."

Back at the roof of the Pru, Morris pointed the binoculars at the shattered Hancock Tower window. At the same time as millions of television viewers, he saw two men heave the body of a uniformed police officer through the window opening. Watching it tumble and spin to the ground, Morris was reminded of victims falling from the Twin Towers on 9/11, and felt sick to his stomach.

Morris walked quickly over to Jordan, who was now on a stretcher, and picked up the sniper scope. He re-attached it firmly to the huge rifle.

"Can you work?" Morris asked Jordan, offering the binoculars. "I need a spotter."

"My pleasure." Jordan turned to the paramedic. "Help me sit up."

Working quickly, the paramedics propped the stretcher against a wall facing the Hancock Tower.

"There is a power button on the left side," Jordan said to Morris. "Push it to turn on the scope. It's an experimental fully electronic rifle aiming system. It's basically a high power video camera lens with computerized imaging."

Morris was in a firing position watching the sight boot up. "It's asking me if I shoot right or left-handed!" he exclaimed.

"Use the blue button to make a choice," said Jordan. "And then select the Imaging Menu."

Morris pushed the blue button to make the selections. "This must be a Mac. I'm there."

"Choose laser imaging. That method works through mirrored glass."

"Done." Morris watched as the small display screen changed from real world colors to shades of green.

"The sight will auto-focus and set elevation by itself. Can you see people through the windows?"

"Range reads 618 meters, bearing 68.42 degrees Azimuth." Morris saw several ghostly human shapes moving around. It was impossible to make out any features.

"I can't see who's a good guy and who's a bad guy."

There was a light rain starting, making it possible for Jordan to judge wind speed by looking at the angle of the rain drops. "I make the wind ten to fifteen, from left to right. You have two rounds left," said Jordan.

A Boston cop moved next to Morris. "The crowd reacted to the falling body by *moving closer!*"

"Fucking rubberneckers," said Jordan.

"What are your people doing now?" Morris asked the cop.

"SWAT will be there in about five minutes."

"I can see the launcher through the broken window. It must be ready to fire." Morris spoke to the cop without looking away from the sight. "If SWAT puts in an assault, they will fire that germ over the crowd. The rain will bring it right down on them."

The cop nodded.

"Jordan, I have a target," said Morris, looking through scope. "I will need one shot for zero."

Jordan used his good arm to hold up the binoculars. "Ready."

"Going three floors down, center of the windowpane. That should be between floors – safe if there's anyone on the floor above or below."

"Seen."

"Firing…." Morris began his breathing sequence. In… half-way out… hold… squeeze….

BLAM.

"Four," said Morris, re-cocking the weapon.

Jordan watched the bullet strike the window and spider the glass left of the center of the pane. "Go right one quarter-pane exactly. Your elevation is good. Fire for effect. You have one round left."

Morris could see several of the figures moving quickly now. He aimed one quarter-pane right of his target.

Then the heavy rain hit.

"It's starting to rain!" Morris exclaimed.

"The laser image should still be good," said Jordan.

"I can see it's good, but the barometric pressure has just changed! That's what happens when rain starts to fall!" This same situation had occurred to Morris during a long-range competitive rifle shooting match. Morris had zeroed his rifle under dry conditions at the start of the match, and when the rain started, his shots started to go higher up the paper target, costing him points.

"Fuck. The sight doesn't monitor changes in pressure or relative humidity!"

"Pressure goes down, bullet goes high…."

"You'll have to eyeball it."

"I should be OK. My target shape is vertical." Morris aimed slightly lower on the cylindrical shape and began his breathing sequence. In… half-way out… hold… squeeze….

BLAM.

The bullet struck the air tank dead center, rupturing it with an ear-splitting blast. The tank flew up and sideways, venting and spinning like a misguided rocket, pulling free from the launch tube. The tube was jerked out of alignment as the tank reached the end of the pressure hose. The tank changed direction and flew through the windowpane next to the open window space, shattering it.

"The launcher is destroyed," said Jordan.

"Confirmed," said Morris, zooming in through the scope.

Through the freshly shattered window, Morris recognized Mohamed as he picked himself up from the floor, clearly enraged. Fleeting target! Morris operated the bolt in a flash, aimed quickly, and squeezed the trigger.

Click.

Morris had already fired his fifth and final round. He had lost count.

"I need more bullets!"

Back at the Hancock Tower, Mohamed was spewing a stream of Arabic. He realized where the shot had come from, and quickly stepped away from the open window spaces, dragging the launcher tube with him.

Holding an M16 rifle, Qamar was guarding Ed and Jacques as they lay face down on the floor. The Hancock security guard holstered his pistol and picked up Mohamed's M16, pointing it at Ed and Jacques.

Ed didn't like the way Mohamed was preceding, undaunted by the seeming setback. Mohamed was purposefully manipulating the launcher's loading mechanism.

"You better get ready for an assault, asshole," Ed said to Mohamed. "SWAT will be on their way. I suggest you give up."

Mohamed gave an order in Arabic and Qamar and the Hancock security guard pointed their M16s at the door.

"We will have plenty of warning," Mohamed smiled at Ed. "They will throw in a charge after they blast the door open. I need only one minute more. It would have been nice to get away as we had planned, but it is not the mission of our martyrdom cell to give up."

Mohamed pulled out the projectile, a soup-can sized cylinder with a long, thin cable coiled at one end. "This germ can be released manually. When the canister reaches the end of this cable, it will release the pressurized contents in an aerosol. From this height above that large crowd, it is almost as effective without the launcher." Mohamed smiled. "It can still kill billions of infidels."

Ed and Jacques made eye contact.

"Your sniper friends cannot see through this glass. Even infrared imaging will reveal only a black surface." Mohamed approached the outside windows, taking care not to expose himself through the smashed window openings. The windows did not go all the way to the floor. There was a wall about a foot high all around the perimeter of the floor. Mohamed went down on one knee and peeked over the low wall at the crowd below.

"Your police are finally starting to move this crowd away," Mohamed drew back his arm to throw, then grimaced. He suddenly lost strength in his throwing arm, where Morris had shot him.

He placed the canister in his other hand and decided to crawl toward the window, keeping low, out of sight below the low wall. Looking at the hovering television helicopters he said, "Perhaps I should stand up and show your people the courage of a martyr."

"Courage of a martyr?" yelled Ed. "You call your people blowing themselves up along with innocent women and children courageous? I call it deluded! Deceived and deluded!"

"You are entitled to your beliefs."

"Your beliefs are fucked!"

Mohamed shook his head. "Perhaps we can talk more after I release my virus. We will have lots of time until your SWAT team comes in and kills us all."

"Why not give up?"

"The Americans will execute us anyway! I'd rather go down fighting! Wouldn't you?"

"We already have your germ under control. We've had a vaccine since shortly after we recovered it from Subject Nineteen at your camp!"

"Interesting, then it should not matter if I do this one little thing…." Mohamed. "By the way, this virus is my own recipe. This virus was collected from Subject Twenty."

Ed and Jacques nodded to each other, and both men jumped to their feet, charging forward.

Qamar opened fire with his M16, but with no effect. If any bullets hit either Ed or Jacques, they did not stop the two charging men.

The Hancock guard had been aiming at the door, and was too slow in changing his aim. By the time he was ready to fire, Ed and Jacques were on top of Mohamed. At that moment, Qamar stopped firing for fear of hitting Mohamed.

Ed hit Mohamed with a flying tackle, bringing both of them to the floor. Jacques stayed on his feet for a couple of extra steps, then lowered his shoulder and let himself fall, driving Mohamed's head to the floor and fracturing his skull. Mohamed went limp instantly.

Qamar began cursing in Arabic. He strode across the floor purposefully, arrogantly, and ready to murder the two infidels.

As he approached the men on the floor, he noticed blood everywhere. Both Ed and Jacques had sustained bullet wounds in the torso.

"So, I did not miss either of you!" Qamar raised his rifle to aim at Ed, point blank.

There was nowhere to hide. Neither Ed nor Jacques had the strength to get up again.

"Happy Patriots' Day, American pig!"

BLAM!

Qamar's skull exploded as the 50-caliber bullet struck his right temple and passed through his brain, exiting and blasting away his left cheekbone. The pressure knocked his left eye from its socket. His body fell to the floor and began to twitch.

BLAM!

A second 50-caliber bullet struck the Hancock guard. Before entering his midsection, the bullet passed through the magazine of his M16, exploding two rounds and sending brass, lead and metal fragments in as well. After exiting, the bullet left behind a large hole and a shattered spine. The guard collapsed to the floor, still alive, but not for long.

The room was now silent except for the wind and the rain.

Ed and Jacques lay on the floor, bleeding heavily. Jacques saw Ed had a stomach wound and was in enormous pain. Slowly, Jacques dragged the shirt off Mohamed and tried to fashion a bandage for his friend. By the time he had finished, Ed was unconcious.

Jacques looked at Mohamed. He was still breathing, so Jacques crawled over beside him. Mohamed had been carrying his large, sharp, shiny knife in a sheath under his shirt. Jacques removed it and passed it across Mohamed's throat. The flesh separated easily, and blood spurted in several directions, and then quickly subsided.

Jacques started to feel weak. There was nothing more he could do. He was not exactly sure where he had been hit, or by how many bullets.

Jacques reached into the pocket of his windbreaker, fumbling for his cellphone. He looked at it, but it was difficult to focus, so he pulled out and put on his reading glasses. He got blood on his cellphone and glasses because his hands were covered in it. He managed to activate the Blackberry screen, and he fumbled through the icons until he found what he wanted.

Although he was starting to experience tunnel vision, Jacques could feel himself smile. He looked at a photo of his wife and daughter, re-activating the backlight several times, until he finally passed out.

54 – SMOKING GUNS

It was late Wednesday afternoon, and Morris Parker sat alone in his usual Wednesday night booth at the Cumberland Arms. He was shuffling papers and working on his second pitcher of Keith's. He had been there since lunch, but still had not eaten. Morris had asked Jill to cancel his meetings, intercept all his calls, and misdirect the press. She was doing a great job, because for the first time in three weeks Morris was able to be out in public without being accosted by the press or curious members of the public.

He had a page in front of him from Liam Latham. It listed several patents owned by a company named Concourse Pharmaceuticals. The day after the Boston Marathon, Morris had asked Liam to search for patents related to vaccine production processes, in particular any patents that described a significantly faster process than existed in the market today. Concourse owned a method that was three times faster than anything else. Concourse Pharmaceuticals also had an unregistered copy of the TaskMan software.

Given those facts, the FBI had seized the Concourse computer containing the relevant evidence. Within hours, Conan identified the originator of the intercepted TaskMan reminder as Joris van Praag, CEO. Mr. van Praag was promptly arrested as he was attempting to flee the country.

Morris looked at an email from Alex James informing him that the three suicide infectors had died from the 2% strain, and thirty people got sick with no deaths and no onward transmission.

Alex had not provided any information about what happened to the 80% strain, the canister for which Ed and

Jacques had paid such a high price. There was no official word that it even existed. Morris had been asked, and had agreed, to keep the existence of that strain a secret.

Because of secrecy, neither Ed nor Jacques were being recognized as the heroes of the day. Morris had been appointed to take the credit. Word had come back that the family of one of the infectors had received $3000 for their martyred son, and he was being treated as a hero in his small neighborhood in Libya.

The irony of this situation had prompted Morris to spend a sleepless night researching suicide attacks. His papers included an article containing information about the training of Japanese Kamikaze pilots at the end of the Second World War.

Morris looked at the translated text of a letter home from Hayashi Ichizo, who died February 22 1945. "I find it so hard to leave you behind. I want to be held in your arms and sleep, yet all men born in Japan are destined to die fighting for the country. You have done a splendid job raising me to become an honorable man."

It seemed to Morris the motivation is always the same. It's always about honor to family and community. The Arab suicide bomber always leaves a testament on video tape to set the example for those to follow, and the community calls him a hero, which encourages others.

On another sleepless night, Morris had re-read an old copy of *The Battle Road* by Charles H. Bradford, describing the battle of Lexington and Concord, the first battle fought in the American Revolution. In that very first engagement, the very first fight of what would become the independent United States of America, Captain Parker's militia had suffered a lopsided defeat: eight dead, nine wounded without a single casualty on the British side.

Morris took a long drink of beer, and then looked at text he had highlighted in that book, describing the actions of a militiaman who was convinced he could not

escape after seeing his friends killed and wounded. Rather
be shot dashing from the Meeting House where he had
been cornered, the militiaman had "struck his loaded
musket in the powder barrel that was stored there,
planning to blow up himself and his assailant if anyone
entered. With his eye glued to the door, he waited, but no
soldier appeared."

If a British soldier *had* appeared, the first lethal
retaliation by an American Patriot would have been a
suicide bombing, Morris surmised.

Morris emptied the pitcher into his glass. Should he
order another one? Dinnertime was approaching, and he
had not eaten all day. He could feel alcohol numbness
setting in, and his pain was diminishing.

Ed would arrive tomorrow from Boston. Morris had
seen to it that both his friends had received the best
medical care available. Jacques had returned to a hospital
in Canada a week ago, leaving Ed behind for additional
surgery. Despite being full of tubes when Morris had
visited them two days after the marathon, they had been
their usual selves, threatening to pull the plug on each
other. At that time, Ed had just been told he would never
walk again.

When Morris met Jacques and Suzette at the Ottawa
airport, it had been very difficult. The sight of Jacques
walking with a cane, looking thin and pale, knowing that
he could have prevented the damage, was almost too
much for Morris.

Morris was kicking himself. He had a clear shot at the
Arab, but no round in the chamber.

Morris looked at an architectural drawing of Ed's
house. Renovations were underway now in preparation
for his arrival. The name on the drawing was Brenda
Wilkinson. She had done a splendid job incorporating the
necessary changes to accommodate a wheelchair.

Morris looked up from his papers to see a large
woman on a ladder. She was working on a ceiling beam.

It was the same beam, Morris realized, where Clark had planted the bullet that incriminated Morris. As she stepped down from the ladder, they made eye contact. She came over to speak with Morris.

"I'm Sandy Monroe. I'm a forensic investigator with the Ottawa Police." She extended her hand.

Morris stood up and shook hands. "I remember you from the night of the shootings here. Would you care to join me?"

"Yes, please." Sandy sat down.

Suddenly Morris felt a bit embarrassed to be caught drinking alone. "Can I buy you a drink?" asked Morris, gesturing to his pitcher of beer.

"I'm pregnant, but a coke would be great."

Angela had been attending to Morris all afternoon from a distance, leaving him some space. She was there in an instant to take the order.

"I just lifted a print from that beam," said Sandy. "If it turns out to be Clark, we'll have him on evidence tampering."

"Has he showed up anywhere?"

"Unfortunately no, but if he ever does, I want that son-of-a-bitch to be taken down." She looked determined. "I'm here on my day off. It occurred to me Clark may have touched the beam to steady himself when he planted the bullet. Sure enough, I found a print in the most likely location."

Morris was impressed. "Why are you so determined?"

"I have my reasons." Sandy realized that sounded rude. "Sorry."

Morris wondered if the OPP investigation into corruption within the Ottawa Police department was still open. He started to shuffle through his papers, pulling up a list of personal notes.

"This four-digit number is an Ottawa Police internal extension. Can you tell me what extension?"

"It's the Crown Attorney's office. I use it all the time. It belongs to the administrative secretary."

Morris hoped he was on to something. "When my lawyer was in Clark's office, a call came in from this number that seemed to tip Clark off. I think there was somebody else inside helping him."

Sandy had read a lot of press about Morris lately. She decided to trust him. She pulled a printout out of her purse.

"This is a list of all the evidence we found in Clark's office after he abandoned it." She handed Morris the printout.

Morris sipped his beer as he read the list. An item caught his eye.

"*The Bourne Identity*. A very good film," he said. "I have information that Clark was dealing with a person by the name of Jason, relating to money. I find it unusual that Clark would keep a copy of a DVD in his office. I only bring a DVD to the office if there's somebody I intend to lend it to, or I have borrowed it from." Morris glanced through the rest of the list. "I don't see any cash on this list."

Morris looked up at Sandy. "A DVD case would be the right size to conceal a number of bills. Would the DVD case have been inspected for that?"

Sandy shrugged. "I didn't catalogue this stuff. My partner did. I'll ask him." Sandy pulled out her cellphone.

"I'll be right back." Morris went for a leak, and when he returned, Sandy was excited.

"He found $2000 in large bills!" She could hardly wait for Morris to sit down. "And there have been several requests from the Crown Attorney's office to access the Clark evidence, by one of the lawyers!"

"That may be your insider," said Morris.

"Damn right. Ever since the Clark pistol swap, we watch anyone who wants to examine evidence like a hawk. There's no way for this lawyer to get at that cash without being observed by one of us."

"I need to make a private phone call." Morris got up and headed outside for a conversation with Alex James. He returned a few minutes later.

"You will be receiving a visit from someone at CSIS. They will set up a sting that involves only you and nobody else from the Ottawa Police. You must not tell anyone."

Sandy's eyes got wide. "OK," she gulped, and then a big smile came across her face as she figured out how the sting would work. "I have just the chemical to catch this guy red-handed."

"I hope that helps," Morris smiled.

Sandy's smile suddenly disappeared. "I would like to tell you something."

"Go ahead. You can trust me."

"Detective Clark raped me. He gave me a drug. I had the coffee analyzed – it contained GHB. I also have his DNA. I'm pregnant with his child."

Morris nodded sympathetically. He did not know what to say.

"I decided to have the child. I'm gay. My partner wants to raise the child with me, so that part is working out." Sandy tensed up. "But at the same time, I want to get that bastard for what he did to me!"

Morris thought for a moment.

"He has fled, but he could not take all his assets. I'm sure he hid the money he was taking on the side, but he and his wife have a house. Do you have his home address?"

Sandy called her partner for that information while Morris placed a call to Jill to ask her to do a land title search. Within a few minutes, they had discovered that Clark held the house in his name alone, it was mortgage-free, and it was worth $350,000.

"I guess he's having trouble selling the house, being that he is in hiding somewhere and can't come in to sign any documents," said Morris, smiling. "I have a very good lawyer friend who will help you sue Clark for child support. You should be able to take his house. I'll have him call you tomorrow morning."

Sandy expressed enormous gratitude as she left the bar. A weight had lifted off her shoulders.

In the coming weeks and months, it would turn out the lawyer in the Crown Attorney's office was still in contact with Clark, trying to help him and his wife sell their house and gather their other ill-gotten gains to complete an escape. Sandy would be present at the arrest, shining the light to reveal the lawyer had touched the chemically-treated cash that had been set out as bait. His assets were then frozen along with Clark's.

Sandy would give birth to a beautiful baby girl. It would take a year of legal proceedings, but she would eventually win title to the Clark home as lump-sum compensation in lieu of child support. She and her partner would move in to the home together.

Clark's wife, being left with nothing, would promptly dump him.

But all that was yet to happen.

When the laughing child audio clip played, the bartender looked up and smiled at Morris.

Morris withdrew his Blackberry and cancelled the alarm he had set for himself. It was time to go home for supper. Morris realized he was in no shape to drive, so he sent a text message to Susan to come and pick him up. She agreed to rescue him, but she texted back that Mom was not going to be impressed when she found out he had been in the pub all afternoon.

Morris had time to make one more call before Susan arrived. He phoned Jill and asked her to acquire concert tickets and arrange airfare and hotel accommodation for two. Morris had decided to take Terri to New York City. Next week, the Rolling Stones were going to be in town.

Morris saw Susan arrive in the parking lot. He left cash on the table, including a generous tip for Angela. On his way out, he passed the bartender, who thanked him for the business.

Then Morris remembered the name. "See you next Wednesday, Tim."

THE END

A Note From the Author

Maurice Albert Parker, Major
Officer Commanding, D Company
The Royal Rifles of Canada

Morris Parker, the main character, was named after my grandfather, Maurice A. Parker, businessman, family man, and a pretty good boxer who, according to him, "could have done better if I hadn't kept hitting the other guy's fist with my face."

As part of the battle for Hong Kong, Major Maurice Albert Parker commanded D Company of the Royal Rifles of Canada in a counter-attack against Japanese forces on Christmas Day, 1941, at Stanley Village. It was almost a suicide attack against overwhelming forces. He was captured along with his men and spent four years as a POW.

The Battle of Hong Kong cost D Company 26 killed and 78 wounded, 82% on Christmas Day alone.

"We went in as a Company, and came out as a Company. No deserters, no stragglers, but minus our dead and wounded."

The story of the Battle of Hong Kong is told in Deadly December, by his son Ronald C. Parker.

www.battleofhongkong.com

About the Author

Jim E.M. Miles was born in Ottawa, Ontario. He graduated from University of Victoria.

In a multi-faceted career, Jim has been a military man, teacher, and businessman. He has a passion for photography, drumming, songwriting and most recently, attempting to become a novelist.

In a former life, Jim commanded an infantry platoon in CFB Gagetown.

Jim was also a competitive combat rifle shooter, and worked in Ottawa and Kingston as a Signals Officer pioneering in tactical use of command and control information systems.

Jim Miles founded Enterprise Information Systems Inc. in 1991, and continues as president today. Jim has established and led dynamic teams for business administration, technical support, consulting, information systems development, career-transition training and courseware development. Jim also owns EIS Canada Inc, which holds and operates an 8600 square foot office building in Orléans, Ontario. In addition to proven strategic planning, corporate leadership, and management skills, Jim has extensive information systems design, project management, application development and problem-solving abilities and experience.

Jim lives in Orléans, Ontario with his wife and business partner Thérèse, and their three daughters.

On Wednesday nights, Jim can usually be found at the Tartan Pub with his beer buddies Jacques, Ed and several real people.

More Bacon Boxcutters

To see additional graphics and photographs of Boston, Ottawa, and other locations that were the inspiration for this story, visit:

www.BaconBoxcutters.com

Bacon Boxcutters also has a page on Facebook. Search for "Bacon Boxcutters." Become a fan and receive updates and announcements about the book.

If you liked Bacon Boxcutters, and if you would like to see future stories, please submit a review online or by email to jim@eisamerica.com.

Made in the USA
Charleston, SC
03 February 2010